"Do it fo **ce as devoid ot** **e it. "Run the test ag****.**

"Oh, well, if it's for you, sure, I'll run it again." There was more than a touch of sarcasm in Susie's voice. "I can see why finding out that your sister vandalized the family stables might be upsetting to you. Now, if you don't mind getting out of my lab, I'll get started."

She turned her back on him, pretending that he was already gone. "I'll have someone call you with the results."

When Ryan's reflection remained exactly where it was, she asked, "Is there anything else?"

"Yes," he said after a moment. "I want to apologize for treating you so badly when I broke it off between us. But I did it for you, for your own good."

She almost swung around then, calling him an idiot and a fool—and a liar. But she didn't. What would be the point? She had moved on.

Or told herself she had.

SECOND CHANCE COLTON
& THE COLTON BODYGUARD

USA TODAY BESTSELLING AUTHOR
MARIE FERRARELLA

NEW YORK TIMES BESTSELLING AUTHOR
CARLA CASSIDY

HARLEQUIN® ROMANTIC SUSPENSE

ISBN-13: 978-1-335-08158-2

Second Chance Colton & The Colton Bodyguard

Copyright © 2019 by Harlequin Books S.A.

The publisher acknowledges the copyright holders of the individual works as follows:

Second Chance Colton
Copyright © 2015 by Harlequin Books S.A.

The Colton Bodyguard
Copyright © 2015 by Harlequin Books S.A.

Special thanks and acknowledgment are given to Marie Ferrarella and Carla Cassidy for their contributions to the Coltons of Oklahoma miniseries.

Recycling programs for this product may not exist in your area.

Printed in U.S.A.

www.Harlequin.com

CONTENTS

USA TODAY bestselling and RITA® Award–winning author **Marie Ferrarella** has written more than two hundred and fifty books for Harlequin, some under the name Marie Nicole. Her romances are beloved by fans worldwide. Visit her website, marieferrarella.com.

Books by Marie Ferrarella

Harlequin Special Edition

Forever, Texas

The Cowboy's Lesson in Love

Matchmaking Mamas

Diamond in the Ruff
Her Red-Carpet Romance
Coming Home for Christmas
Dr. Forget-Me-Not
Twice a Hero, Always Her Man
Meant to Be Mine
A Second Chance for the Single Dad
Christmastime Courtship
Engagement for Two
Adding Up to Family

The Fortunes of Texas: The Secret Fortunes

Fortune's Second-Chance Cowboy

The Fortunes of Texas: The Rulebreakers

The Fortune Most Likely To...

Visit the Author Profile page
at Harlequin.com for more titles.

SECOND CHANCE COLTON

Marie Ferrarella

To
Carly Silver,
and
Brave New Frontiers

PROLOGUE

THERE WAS A time when he loved coming up to this ranch. Loved riding through its fields, getting lost in its acreage.

Right now, that time seemed as if it were a million years ago. Back then he'd been a boy and this had been his ranch.

Well, his and his family's, Ryan Colton amended silently.

Back then, the only crimes, large or small, harmless or serious, had all been made-up, part of the make-believe games he, his brothers Jack, Eric and Brett, as well as his half brother, Daniel, and his baby sister, Greta, would play.

Playing had been serious business back then.

He wished for a moment that he could go back to that point in time. Back to when innocence had been a major player in all their lives.

But a lot of things had happened since then. Jack had gotten married, become a father and then gotten divorced before he finally got it right and found Tracy. Eric had left the ranch to become a trauma surgeon at Tulsa General Hospital, where he had met Kara, the love of his life. Daniel, along with his wife Megan, and Brett and his wife, Hannah, were still here on the ranch, along with Jack, but Daniel and Brett had ideas about managing the ranch that differed from the direction that Jack had initially wanted to take. All three were currently trying to iron things out rather than clashing over methods the way they had once done.

And Greta, well, Greta was Greta. Her gift for training horses took her away from the ranch a great deal more than it once had. These days found her in Oklahoma City more than here because of her engagement to Mark Stanton. But even when she was gone, her presence seemed to just ooze out of the very shadows, as if unconsciously reminding the others that she, too, was a Colton and every bit as much a part of this ranch as they were.

As for him, well, he had gone into the Marines in search of himself. He came back still looking, except now he did it as a homicide detective with the Tulsa police department.

And it was in that capacity, as a police detective rather than a Colton sibling, that he was here now, standing in one of the Lucky C's smaller stables, staring at a broken windowpane with blood smeared on the jagged edges.

Whose blood was it and why had they broken in? Other than defacing some of the property, he saw no reason for this. Nothing seemed to have been taken.

But it was obvious that something sinister was going on here at the Lucky C—something that seemed to call the ranch's very name into question.

This wasn't the first time he'd been called up to the ranch to investigate a sinister occurrence. In the past few months there had been a series of "mishaps," for lack of a better word, Ryan thought darkly as he methodically examined the crime scene.

There'd been the fire that'd started up for no apparent reason—no faulty wiring, no carelessly discarded matches or cigarette butts—and several wanton, sense-less acts of vandalism. And there was that break-in that had occurred just the other day, also with no particular rhyme or reason to it.

And then there had been that initial break-in at the main house, shortly after Greta's engagement party, that had been the start of it all. Someone had broken in and stolen some things—and beaten his mother in the process. Beaten her senseless. Jack had been the one to find her that day. Ryan didn't want to think about what the possible consequences of that beating could have been if he hadn't.

As it was, Abra Colton had remained in the hospital for some time, in a coma and all but lost to all of them. He'd thought his father would come completely apart during that time.

Mercifully, his mother was out of the hospital now and back home, but when he'd finally questioned her, she'd been unable to shed any real light on what had happened to provoke that attack—or, more important, the name of the person who had attacked her. Her tes-timony—when his mother was finally up to giving it—had been jumbled and vague.

And then she had just shut down, saying she didn't want to "speak of it." Afraid for her mental state, Ryan knew better than to try to push her. So he was resigned to waiting until such time as his mother was ready to "speak of it."

He sighed, moving slowly about this latest crime scene. His mother's attack—and the robbery—had been the beginning. These other senseless acts of destruc-tion had followed, but they'd left no discernible pattern.

What he was now looking at was the most recent of

several lesser acts of vandalism that had befallen the family. The Lucky C, it seemed, had found itself at the very center of some strange activity—activity that just reeked of malice.

The only thing Ryan knew with certainty was that the attack, the acts that had followed, weren't random, the way he'd initially hoped. Someone definitely had it in for his family.

The questions that were on the table now were why and who?

He knew that he was too close to this. But who had more of an incentive to solve this thing than he did? Whoever had orchestrated this had already tried—unsuccessfully, thank God—to eliminate his mother, Abra, from the family tree. He didn't want to hang back, spinning theories and coming up empty, potentially leaving the ranch and his family wide-open for another all-out assault.

Who knew, the next time it might not just be a broken window he'd find himself dealing with, but someone's broken neck.

This had to stop before then.

Ryan frowned. He needed to put the call in for the crime scene unit to get out here. They had a sharper eye for this sort of thing than he did. With luck and their combined efforts, he could put an end to this, whatever "this" was.

With luck.

The very phrase mocked him, but he was determined to get to the bottom of all this.

And soon.

He *had* to.

CHAPTER ONE

"YOU'RE WRONG."

Ryan Colton's booming, resonant voice filled every available nook and cranny within the small, albeit state-of-the-art, Tulsa PD forensic lab.

"No, I'm not."

Susie Howard, the lab's chief forensic expert, refused to be intimidated and stood her ground, even though a part of her could understand why the homicide detective before her had balked. After all, she'd just told him that the person who had broken into and apparently vandalized one of the ranch's stables—and was possibly responsible for the numerous vandalisms that had occurred prior to this latest one—was his sister, Greta.

But like it or not, Susie thought, evidence was evidence.

Doing her best to sound professional and remain removed—no easy feat in this case—Susie stated the obvious. "You asked me to put a rush on the DNA evidence, so I did. The sample from the Lucky C's crime scene went to the head of the line and that's your answer," she told him, tapping the name that had been generated by her trusty machine after the test had been completed. Greta Colton's prints and DNA were in the system because of the nature of her work.

Frowning, Susie withdrew her well-manicured finger. "I can't help it if you don't like the answer, but that's it. The machine doesn't lie—even if you think that I do," she concluded, her hazel eyes narrowing as she tossed her head. A blond tendril came loose from the tightly wound bun she wore at the back of her neck as she looked up at the six-foot-two detective.

Ryan struggled to keep his temper in check. It had grown very frayed lately. Yelling wasn't going to get him anywhere, he knew that. Especially not with Susie.

But she just couldn't be right.

She *couldn't* be.

His words were carefully measured as he spoke. "I didn't say you were lying, but there's always the possibility that there's a margin of error."

Which was what he was pinning all his hopes on now. He *knew* Greta, had watched her grow up. There was no reason he could come up with for why she would do something like this.

"Run the test again," Ryan instructed, his voice leaving no room for argument. "I don't want to tell you your job—"

"Then don't!" Susie retorted.

Ryan continued on the subject as if she hadn't said a single word. "But there was enough blood on that broken window to take several swabs. Run a second sample. And a third if you need to," he added before the forensic expert could protest.

"How many do you want me to run before you accept the results?" Susie challenged.

"Just run the test again," Ryan ordered, doing his best to remain removed from the discussion.

Fat chance of that. The woman who had just told him that the blood belonged to his sister, Greta, was the same woman he had once been seriously involved with. The same woman, after their relationship had become serious, he had deliberately cut off all ties with.

He'd been a Marine back then, home on leave, when their paths had first crossed. They had hit it off instantly—hot and heavy, and very, very serious. He spent every moment he could with her, and she with him. Neither of their families knew about their relationship because they never made time for anyone else. It was as if somehow, subconsciously, they both understood that they were on a timetable. When he received word that he was being deployed overseas again, Susie had naturally been upset, but she'd promised to wait for him no matter how long it took.

That had been the problem. The burden of having someone waiting for him, loving him and praying for his safe return, was just too much for him to carry into battle. The weight of that responsibility threatened to sap away his edge, to blur his focus, and survival depended heavily on focus.

Besides, if he didn't make it back, he knew how that could affect the rest of Susie's life—how it could *destroy* the rest of her life. He couldn't do anything about the way his family reacted to news like that, but he could do something about Susie.

There was far too much guilt attached to their relationship for him, so he chose the simple way out. He broke things off between them—doing so in a letter rather than in person.

In effect, he had chosen the coward's way out. He never found out how she felt about the breakup because Susie never wrote back. Eventually, he convinced himself that that was for the best and that this was the way things were meant to be. He was meant to be alone.

With that in mind, he struggled to move on, to move forward. After his honorable discharge, he wound up becoming a police detective. In the beginning, it all boiled down to a matter of putting one foot in front of the other. And somehow, while he wasn't looking, six years managed to pass by.

He'd assumed he would never see Susie again. It got a little easier dealing with that with each year that went by.

The sight of Susie walking down the hall at the Tulsa police department one morning four years ago had completely knocked the air right out of him. But after a few seconds, he'd recovered and managed to push on.

For the past four years, they had politely but determinedly ignored one another, pretending not to be aware of the other person's existence whenever they found themselves in the same general vicinity. His cases were such that he found he didn't need any help from the forensic department.

But now, with the vandalism at the Lucky C amped up to a dangerous degree, Ryan resigned himself to the fact that he needed her help. Needed her training and her lab to help him solve this all-too-personal case he had taken on before things went from bad to fatal.

And now the attractive blonde who still sometimes turned up in his dreams had given him an answer that had all but left him numb and speechless. Was this her way of getting even with him for breaking up with her?

No, whatever else he might feel about Susie Howard, he knew that she had a great deal of integrity. He was allowing his imagination to run away with him, something that didn't happen very often. He would be the first to admit that the situation had made him desperate.

He forced himself to remember that Susie wasn't the kind of person who would let her feelings get in the way of her work—and she certainly wasn't the type to frame an innocent person, no matter how much she might want to because she was in effect jilted by that person's older brother.

That wasn't the way Susie operated. Her sense of honor was something that he'd found admirable about her all those years ago.

Since he knew that Susie wasn't responsible for the results that were damning his sister, that left Ryan clinging to the only possible excuse he had left—that somehow, the periodically calibrated forensic equipment had malfunctioned.

Susie looked as if she was going to continue staunchly refusing to rerun the test. He had to get her to reverse that position.

"Do it for me," he requested, his voice as devoid of emotion as he could possibly render it. "Run the test again."

"Oh, well, if it's for you, sure, I'll run it again." There was more than a touch of sarcasm in Susie's voice. "And if it *wasn't* for you, I'd still run the test again, just because there seems to be some sort of doubt involved here," she went on to add icily. "I can see why finding out that your sister vandalized the family stables might be upsetting to you, so yes, I'll run the test again," she informed him coldly. "Now, if you don't mind getting out of my lab, I'll get started on that second test."

She turned her back on him, pretending that he was already gone.

She knew he wasn't because she could see his distorted reflection on the surface of her mass spectrometer. The machine was facing her. Her parting words to Ryan were "I'll have someone call you with the results once they're in."

When Ryan's reflection continued to remain exactly where it was, she asked in as disinterested a voice as she could summon, "Is there anything else?"

This had to be said. He knew that. If the air wasn't cleared between them, then she might be sorely tempted not to do her best job. He felt confident she wouldn't manufacture evidence, but he wasn't so sure that she'd bring her A game to the case.

"Yes," he said after a long moment, addressing the words to the back of Susie's head since she wasn't turning around again, "there's something else. I want to apologize for treating you so badly when I broke it off between us. But I did it for you, for your own good."

She almost swung around then, almost fired at him with both barrels, calling him an idiot and a fool—and a liar. Calling him an egotist for using that pathetic excuse when the real reason he had pulled his emotional vanishing act on her was because he'd obviously been afraid of commitment.

Any first-year psychology student would have been able to tell him that.

But she didn't swing around, didn't give Ryan a tongue-lashing and didn't tell him exactly what she thought. What would be the point? He had his lie, which he was holding on to for dear life, and she had moved on.

Or told herself she had.

So she remained facing her workbench, acting as if

Ryan hadn't said a single word to her about their past or its abrupt ending.

"I'll have someone call you the minute the second results are in," she repeated.

This time, she saw his reflection retreat and then disappear.

Heard the door to the lab close again.

Only then did she turn around on her stool. "You jerk," Susie murmured, staring at the closed door. Her voice grew louder, more heated with every word she uttered. "You big, self-centered, blind, stupid, stupid jerk."

"Two degrees, six years in college and that's the best you can come up with?" Harold Gould marveled as the tall, thin lab assistant stepped out from the computer tech area where he had been working.

His white lab coat hung like a bland curtain about his all but emaciated frame, giving the impression that it would begin flapping wildly about that same frame at the first sign of a breeze.

Startled, Susie's eyes met those of her junior assistant, who was also a lab intern. The brown eyes continued looking back at her, the assistant never flinching.

"I didn't know anyone else was here," Susie told the intern.

"Obviously. When I saw him walk in I was going to clear my throat in case something private was going to be said. But Colton started talking right away and it sounded kind of personal from the get-go." The look he gave her was sympathetic. "I didn't want to embarrass you."

"You just wanted to eavesdrop, hoping to score some juicy gossip," Susie countered.

She knew how the man operated. Harold Gould knew

more about what was going on in the precinct after being here for a little more than three months than some of the twenty-year veterans did. It wasn't only lab procedures that he absorbed faster than a sponge.

The painfully thin shoulders rose and fell quickly, indicating that Harold had no intention of even attempting to contest her take on the situation. They both knew he enjoyed being a font of information, both technical and private.

"Yeah, well, there's that, too," he agreed, and then he tried to set her mind at ease. "Don't worry, I don't have any time to talk to anyone so this isn't going into the rumor mill. And besides, I might be had for a song when it comes to certain things, but don't ever doubt my loyalty."

She liked Harold and was fairly certain that his heart was in the right place. But she'd paid the price for blind faith before and that had made her leery. Harold could just be offering her pretty words to distract her, Susie thought. "If it does hit the rumor mill, I'll know who to come after."

A small, amused smile played across all but nonexistent lips. "Should I be shaking in my shoes now—or wait until later?" he asked her.

"Later," she told him. "We have work to do now." She glanced again at the closed door. "I'm going to have *you* run the DNA test on the blood this time."

"Really run the test, or…?" He raised one eyebrow, leaving the rest of the sentence unspoken but definitely understood.

Susie wanted to make one thing perfectly clear even as she cut the intern some slack because he was, after all, still relatively new.

"We don't do 'or' here, Harold. We don't even *think* about 'or.' Just one tiny instance—or even the *hint* of that kind of impropriety—and everything we've ever done here is going to be viewed as suspect and called into question. The amount of work that would be generated by something like that would be astronomical. Have I made that clear enough for you?"

She didn't want to come off as sounding belligerent, but there should be no question about how procedures were conducted.

"Just kidding, boss lady," Harold told her, raising his hands as a sign of surrender.

"I know. But it doesn't hurt to reiterate how we do things out loud every so often so that we don't *ever* lose sight of our function here. Because it only has to happen *once* and suddenly, we'll get our walking papers and be out on the street."

"Understood," Harold assured her. "But even so, you could stand to improve your vocabulary," he told her. "I could work up a whole host of multiple-syllable expletives you could hurl at yon studly homicide detective the next time your paths cross. You don't want to be caught unarmed, do you? Or worse, tongue-tied?" he concluded, pretending to shiver at the very thought of that happening.

"You miss the salient point. I don't want our paths crossing, *period*," she said, getting to the heart of the matter.

"For that even to be a remote possibility at this police precinct, one of you is going to have to put in for a transfer. Like, to a different city." Harold's shallow complexion seemed to brighten instantly as he thought over possibilities. "Do I get a vote as to which one of you should go?"

She wasn't about to feed the intern any more straight lines. Given half a chance, the man could go on talking for hours, like a windup toy whose spring had somehow malfunctioned and while she liked him and felt he did have a great deal of potential, she definitely didn't want to encourage him, especially not when there was work to do.

"Just do the test, Harold," Susie requested.

The lab intern saluted her comically as he said, "I hear and obey, my liege."

Susie rolled her eyes as she got back to her work.

SUSIE COULDN'T BE RIGHT, Ryan stubbornly thought as he got back into his car. Starting it up, he pulled out of his parking spot, turned the sedan around and headed back to the Lucky C.

The forensic team, obviously, had come and gone. They had a reputation for being very thorough. Although he had been the one to initially call them in to see if he had missed something, he wanted to go back and go over the latest crime scene one more time to see if perhaps *they* had missed something this time around.

It was worth a shot. What did he have to lose?

Especially when he stood to gain so much more if he was right and Susie wasn't.

What he wanted to do with this latest return trip to the Lucky C was find something that would negate what Susie was claiming: that that was Greta's blood at the crime scene. That it was Greta's blood that was all over the jagged edges of the broken window.

What possible reason could Greta have for vandalizing the family ranch?

If his sister had a grievance—which would have been news to him—she would have gone to talk to whomever she had the issue with.

Talk to them, not deface their property. For heaven sakes, if anything, Greta had become even closer to the family—certainly closer to their mother—ever since she'd gotten engaged. Greta and their mother were busy planning Greta's *wedding*. She wouldn't just suddenly turn on her mother like that, despite any bizarre tales of hormonal bridezillas to the contrary.

Still, he knew how conscientious Susie was. She wouldn't have just haphazardly conducted that DNA test, or allowed it to become contaminated.

Yet how could her findings be right?

Ryan felt a surge of anger flare up within his chest, anger where his heart was supposed to be.

Try as he might, he couldn't come up with a way that both he and Susie could be right. One of them had to be wrong and he found the idea that it was him really upsetting. *Not* because he had any kind of a problem with his ego—he'd been wrong before, most notably when he'd deployed back overseas and cut Susie loose like that, as if she was some inconvenience instead of someone he had found himself caring for deeply—but because that would mean that there was something seriously bad going on with Greta.

He *knew* Greta. His sister wasn't a criminal. And she didn't harbor some dark side that none of them were aware of. That was just plain ridiculous.

Leaning over, Ryan switched on the radio. The car was instantly filled with the strains of music, instrumental music meant to promote and instill a sense of peace into what was usually a hectic day. He'd never needed it more than he did now.

If he couldn't find evidence at the crime scene that could point him in another direction—the *right* direction—he was going to have to call his sister and question her about the events that had been transpiring here at the ranch. He wasn't looking forward to that because, despite his attempts to keep to himself, he found that he was rather transparent when he was dealing with his family. And once he started questioning Greta about the strange events at the ranch and she realized what he was getting at, there would be a breach between them.

And most likely, between him and the rest of the family, as well. Greta was, after all, the baby of the family, as well as the only girl. Brothers tended to be protective of their little sisters.

Hell, he felt that way, too. But he was also a homicide detective and he had a job to do, a sworn duty to get to the bottom of things and to bring the guilty parties in as well as to protect the innocent ones.

"Damn it, Greta, I sure hope that you're innocent—for both our sakes," he murmured.

And then, because it wasn't affecting him, he turned the music up louder, hoping to be in a better, calmer frame of mind by the time he got back to the Lucky C.

Hoping, but being realistic enough to know that hope alone didn't change a damn thing no matter how much someone might want it to.

CHAPTER TWO

Ryan isn't going to like this.

The thought echoed over and over again in Susie's head as she looked down at the results from the latest DNA test. It was the third such test she'd authorized and this one she'd again done herself. She knew she was wasting her own time, not to mention the lab's precious resources, just to make doubly sure—or triply sure as the case was— that the final results were the same as what had already been concluded the first and second times the test had been run.

There was no mistaking the findings. It was Greta Colton's blood that had been found along the edges of the broken glass from the vandalized stable. It wasn't just a vague familial match, which would have meant that the blood might have belonged to a family member, like Big J or one of Greta's brothers. The match she was looking at was dead-on.

The blood belonged to Greta.

There wasn't a single trace of anyone else's blood on the jagged broken glass. No accomplice, no one else's blood on the scene.

Only Greta's.

Greta had been the one, for whatever reason, who had broken into the stables via the window instead of going in through the door, which as far as she knew, had been Greta's normal custom.

What the hell was going on here?

Why would Greta be breaking into the stables through the window? It just didn't make any sense.

Far from happy, Susie blew out a breath. Much as she really would have preferred coming up with a different conclusion, she had definitely nailed down the who. Now it was up to Ryan to find out the why.

Ryan definitely wasn't going to be happy.

"That did *not* sound like a good sigh."

Perched on a stool against the equipment-laden counter, Susie managed to swivel her stool around to face the doorway. She knew who she would be looking at before she was actually turned around. Nobody else's voice undulated under her skin the way his had.

The way it still did.

Water under the bridge, remember? Water under the bridge. You've moved on. So keep moving, Susie told herself fiercely, albeit silently. Ryan no longer figured into her life, except professionally.

Doing her best to collect herself and look every inch the forensic expert that she was, Susie replied, "It wasn't. And it definitely won't be from your point of view."

Ryan's gut tightened. He knew what was coming and he braced himself—or tried to. "The DNA—"

Susie had never been one to prolong a verdict for the sake of dramatic effect. With distasteful news, it was best to get it out as quickly as possible and move on.

"—is still Greta's," she said, completing his sentence. "I'm sorry, Ryan. I had the test run a total of three times using three different samples from three different areas on the broken glass. I ran two of the tests and had someone else run another one." To back herself up, Susie held up the three separate printouts that had resulted. "It came out the same each and every time. It's Greta's DNA. The blood found at the scene belongs to your sister."

Ryan took the printouts from her and stared at the results on the top sheet. The findings on the two sheets beneath it were identical.

He felt as if someone had driven a knife into his stomach—and was still twisting it.

"There has to be an explanation," he insisted, talking more to himself than to the woman perched on the stool.

"Ask her," Susie suggested matter-of-factly. When Ryan looked down at her with confusion in his eyes, as if he had suddenly realized that he wasn't alone in the room, she said, "If you really think that this doesn't make sense, then ask her why she broke the stable window. Maybe she didn't do it to get into the stables. Maybe there's another plausible reason why the window was broken." And why the stables were vandalized, she added silently.

"You don't believe that," he said, going by the expression on her face.

Susie shrugged away his observation. "What I believe—or don't believe—isn't the point here. I'm the forensic expert, you're the detective. It's up to you to take what I give you and arrange it into some sort of a complete picture that gives you the plausible answers you're looking for."

It almost sounded cut-and-dried—but he knew from experience nothing ever was.

He frowned, looking down at the printout Susie had given him. "This doesn't give me any answers, just more questions."

"It's a start," she told him crisply. "Use it to help you get those answers."

"So now you're telling me my job?" he asked, recalling that she had accused him of doing the same yesterday. He wasn't being defensive, he told himself, just curious to see what the woman would say if he asked. "What is this, a demonstration of 'turnabout is fair play'?"

Maybe she shouldn't have said anything to him, Susie thought. She'd run the tests, done her job and given him the results. It was now up to him to work with what he had. Her part in this was over. She had to keep telling herself that, keep reminding herself to keep her distance, even though something inside her still insisted on holding out the hope that…

That nothing, Susie upbraided herself. There was nothing between them anymore except for business. He'd seen to that.

"Just trying to make the results more palatable for you, Detective Colton," she told him.

Ryan winced. He could almost feel the frost encrusted around her words. "Ouch. That's pretty formal. But I guess I deserve that."

Yes, you do. That and a hell of a lot more, she added silently. "See, you're detecting already," she told him, doing her best to keep distancing herself from Ryan. She knew if she didn't, if she allowed just a crack to open up, no matter how small, he'd somehow seep into her system, and just like that she'd be vulnerable all over again. In danger of having her heart ripped out again. She'd been down that route once and had no desire to revisit it. "Now, if you don't mind, I've got cases other than yours all clamoring for my time…" She allowed her voice to drift off as she deliberately made a show of getting back to work.

"No. Sure. Thanks." The single-word sentences came out of his mouth in staccato fashion, as if he was firing each word one by one, pausing in between each.

She heard Ryan begin to walk toward the exit. This was where she was supposed to continue looking down at the work on her desk, the work she was already supposed to have finished but had moved aside so that she could run those additional DNA tests in hopes of finding another suspect, one that wasn't Ryan's sister.

All she had to do was hold out a total of thirty seconds. Fifty, tops, and he would be gone, Susie told herself.

There was really no need for her to say anything more to the man than she'd already said.

No need at all—except, perhaps, to satisfy her own curiosity about a man she had once believed herself to be madly in love with.

Once?

Hell, you're still in love with him, you big idiot. You think you would've learned by now, Susie upbraided herself, annoyed at her own lack of discipline, not to mention a certain dearth of self-respect.

But for her internal lectures never took, no matter how driven they were by common sense, and she found herself turning all the way around on her stool. She was just in time to see Ryan about to step over the threshold, out into the hall.

Two more seconds and she'd be home free.

One—

"So what are you going to do?" she heard herself asking Ryan.

Apparently already lost in thought, Ryan jerked his head up. He'd heard her voice, but not the words that she'd said. "What?"

"So what are you going to do?" Susie repeated, enunciating each word.

Ryan crossed back over the threshold, but only took a couple of steps toward her before he stopped. He had to admit he was surprised that she was interested enough to ask him that. "I'm going to call Greta and do just what you suggested. I'm going to ask her what she was doing in the stable and why she had to break the window in order to get in."

Susie thought for a moment. "Your sister's a horse trainer, isn't she?"

He was surprised that Susie had taken the time to find that out. It wasn't as if they ran in the same circles these days. And back when they were together, their worlds had contained only each other, to the exclusion of everyone else. That meant family members, as well.

"Best in the business," Ryan confirmed.

"Maybe she was passing by the stable at that hour for some reason, looked in and thought she saw smoke coming from the stable. Or maybe she thought she saw a horse in distress. The fastest way from point A to point B is still a straight line." She shrugged carelessly, unable to come up with any better explanations at the moment. "Maybe that was why she broke the window."

Although he appreciated her effort, he thought that Susie was definitely reaching. "And she didn't stick around to tell anyone what she did?" Ryan asked skeptically.

Susie took her theory to the next step. "She was probably too embarrassed about breaking the window for no reason so she didn't hang around, waiting for someone from the family to hear her out. Most likely, she's just working up the nerve to answer for what she did. Nobody likes to admit that they made a mistake or acted rashly," she pointed out.

They were talking about his sister, and Susie was giving him ammunition to defend Greta's actions, but he really wasn't convinced.

"I suppose that sounds plausible enough," he allowed. "But I'll believe it when I hear it from Greta's own lips. Last I heard, she's not even supposed to be in Tulsa right now."

"Well, *she* might not be, but her blood certainly is," Susie said, indicating the printouts he was holding. "I don't have to point out that you can't have one without the other."

"Unless someone's trying to frame you," Ryan said as the idea suddenly occurred to him. The only thing that wasn't occurring to him was why someone would go to the sort of trouble that actually framing his sister would require.

But even as he began to vaguely entertain the idea, he saw Susie shaking her head.

Exasperation seeped into his tone. "What?" he asked.

She had to stop him before he got carried away with the idea he seemed to be embracing. "If someone for some obscure reason actually *did* manage to have a sample of your sister's blood—and I'm talking about enough to smear on the jagged edges of the window—it would have started to coagulate in a vial. There are certain characteristics of stored blood that would have shown up in the blood workup that was done. They didn't," she informed him flatly. "This blood was fresh when it came in contact with the broken glass."

"I was afraid of that," he murmured, again more to himself than to her.

Susie's slender shoulders rose and fell, not in a show of indifference, but to signify that some things just couldn't be changed no matter how much one might want them to be different.

"So, go back to your initial plan," she told him.

"Which was?" he asked, wanting to see what Susie thought his plan had been.

"You said you were going to go question your sister and ask Greta what she was doing there at that time of night. Ask her why she thought it was necessary to break into stables that she could have just as easily accessed the proper way—through the door."

Susie was right of course. But the more he thought about it, the more this proposed conversation with Greta was *not* going to be a conversation that he was looking forward to. Added to that was the fact that Greta had been a little jumpy since their mother had been found battered and beaten.

In the past couple of months his normally cheerful little sister had become increasingly uneasy, at times acting almost paranoid, and questioning her about the acts of vandalism and the break-in at the Lucky C was definitely *not* going to help the situation *or* Greta's frame of mind, he thought.

He could feel Susie's eyes on him, as if scrutinizing his very thought process. What she said next all but confirmed his suspicions.

"Maybe you should take another family member with you when you go to question her," Susie suggested.

Susie pressed her lips together. She knew she should just keep out of this. After all, the man had all but callously torn her heart right out of her chest without so much as a warning shot. She owed him nothing.

But even so, the look on his face had her feeling for him. She knew that if she were in his place, confronting this sort of situation, she would feel awful.

Memories from the past tried to break through, memories of a time when they were each other's entire world.

But that was then, this was now, she reminded herself. She had to get a grip on her emotions. They had absolutely no place here.

"Thanks," he said, surprised that Susie would even bother to attempt to give him helpful suggestions, given their past. "But that's not a good idea. If I take one of my brothers with me, Greta will think we're ganging up on her. She's been on edge ever since our mother was attacked." He remembered being called to the scene by his frantic father and racing to his mother's side. The whole episode was vividly imprinted on his mind.

"Just before she slipped into an unconscious state, when I asked my mother who did this to her, she just stared at me and then started to cry. I couldn't get her to say anything or even indicate whether or not she had seen the attacker's face. She slipped into a coma right after that.

"When she finally came out of her coma, every time Greta was anywhere near her, my mother looked, I don't know, *spooked* I guess is the best word for it. As for Greta, she just looked uncomfortable—and hurt." He shrugged helplessly. "I don't know what to make of any of it."

For a moment Susie forgot that she wasn't supposed to

be talking to Ryan beyond uttering a few monosyllabic responses. All she saw was an all-too-human homicide detective, torn between job responsibilities and familial loyalties—a fellow human being in need of some kind of support.

That was the Ryan she was talking to.

"If not another family member, maybe you could take another female with you to be supportive of Greta as well as you," she proposed.

"You?" Ryan asked in surprise. Was she actually offering to come with him to question Greta?

Susie shrugged. She had painted herself into a corner with that one, she thought. The focus wasn't supposed to be on her but on the situation—and the crime. She'd meant the suggestion in a general way, but there was no denying that she *was* a female.

"I do qualify for the category," she was forced to admit, almost against her will.

Ryan smiled then, remembering a time prior to the breakup he had engineered. A time when everything had seemed perfect despite the claim the service had on him. Remembering a very small island of time when he had been in love, and had just allowed things to "be" without any in-depth analysis.

"If memory serves me, you more than qualify—and thanks for offering—but this is something I have to do on my own," he told her. "I think that the less people Greta sees when I arrive, the better this whole situation might work out."

Or at least that was what he hoped.

Susie didn't know if he was just being protective of his sister, or if Ryan was once again dismissing her wholesale out of his life.

In either case, she told herself, her conscience was clear. Despite the extenuating circumstances, she'd offered to do the right thing. That she had done so was not negated by his refusal of her offer. It just made her square with him.

"Suit yourself," she responded, doing what she could to sound indifferent. "You always know best."

The last part had sounded incredibly cold as well as formal and withdrawn to his ear. Whatever bridge they had crossed a moment ago was now officially uncrossed again and they were back to their initial corners. They were once again on the opposite sides of the fence, the words *opposite sides* all but ten feet tall with neon lights dancing around them.

He didn't have time for this, didn't have time to deal with any regrets, small or, in this case, large. What was done was done and he had to focus on the present. Just possibly, he had a sister to bring back to the fold. A sister that he had to take care not to alienate as he tried to subtly question her about her part—if she *had* played a part—in these bizarre, random attacks of vandalism and destruction that were occurring on the ranch.

A sister who just might never forgive him if she proved to be innocent of any wrongdoing and thought that he was accusing her of the exact opposite.

There were times when he scolded himself for not having chosen a simpler, easier path in life. But everyone had to follow their strengths, he reasoned, and his involved ferreting out the truth and taking down the bad guys.

"Thanks for all your help," he said to Susie as he started to leave again.

She looked up at him. "I'm sure you don't mean that, but you're welcome."

He was about to take exception with the way she had phrased that—it sounded as if she had stopped just short of calling him a liar—but he caught himself just in time. There was no point in attempting to contradict her point of view about the immediate matter at hand. She had a right to her opinion, even if she was dead wrong. Because he *had* meant what he'd just said.

He was deliberately wasting time. Every minute he stood here was another minute that he was delaying the inevitable because it was going to be, at best, awkward and uncomfortable. He didn't want to think about what it would be like at its worst.

Squaring his shoulders, he left the lab. He needed to get this over with. Now.

And then, he thought as he went down the corridor, he could move on to something else.

Hopefully more successfully than the last time he'd told himself he was moving on.

He sincerely doubted that he could do any worse.

CHAPTER THREE

RYAN KNEW THAT as an investigating detective with the Tulsa PD, even if he was questioning his own sister, because he was doing it in reference to a current active case he was working on, it was in everyone's best interest to keep things businesslike and official. Among other things, that meant that he should be making this call from the phone on his desk at the precinct, not from his personal cell phone while he was sitting in his car.

He supposed that he could argue that he was doing it for the quiet, because the precinct was usually almost too noisy to allow anyone to hear themselves think. But the truth of the matter was that his real reason for making the call from inside his vehicle was that he didn't want to be overheard.

It was bad enough that he had to ask his sister painful, probing questions like this without having everyone within a ten-foot radius *hearing* him asking. He was a Colton. One of *the* Coltons. The family that had, through absolutely no fault of their own, their very own serial killer in their family tree, thanks to his father's brother, Matthew.

Granted, it all had happened a long time ago and his uncle had been locked away in prison for a while now, but he was well aware of the fact that people loved to point an accusing finger and watch people of prominence come tumbling down. They loved watching their fallen-from-grace sinners every bit as much as they loved cheering on their saints and heroes.

Sometimes even more so.

He wanted no part in supplying those people with any sort of ammunition, especially if there did actually turn out to be a reasonable excuse for all this.

He supposed a tiny part of him hadn't turned cynical yet and still believed in miracles.

So he sat in his vehicle, trying not to notice how stuffy it seemed with the windows rolled up and his doors locked, and he called his sister's number.

After a short delay, he heard the cell phone start to ring. Waiting for Greta to answer her phone, Ryan counted off the number of times her cell rang. After four, her voice mail kicked in. Impatient, he was about to terminate the call and try again in a couple of minutes when he heard Greta's breathless voice as she came on the line.

"Hello?"

Rather than relax, he felt his shoulders stiffen. "Greta? It's me. Ryan."

"Hi." And then he heard her ask guardedly, "What's up?"

Was that just his imagination—or her guilty conscience stepping up? "I'm coming up to the ranch to see you."

He heard her laugh softly. "Well, you can come up to the ranch, but you won't see me."

Was he tipping her off with this call? Was she planning on taking off? He needed more to work with. "Why?" he asked.

"Why do you think?" Not waiting for him to respond,

she gave him the answer to her own question. "Because I'm not at the ranch. I'm not in Tulsa at all. I'm back in Oklahoma City."

Ryan frowned to himself. Ever since Greta had gotten engaged, she'd spent more and more of her time in Oklahoma City, where her fiancé lived. She'd even taken on horse training jobs there.

"I thought you'd stick around the ranch for a while, you know, because of Mother."

There was silence on the other end of the line and for a moment, he thought that the call had been dropped. But then Greta said, "Yes, well, I wasn't really doing her any good just hanging around the house. Especially since she kept looking at me as if she was afraid of me. As if she thought I was going to do something to her. I don't know what's with that," Greta complained, sounding as if she was at a complete loss.

"Did you ask her about it?" Ryan asked.

"Yes. But when I asked her why she was looking at me like that," Greta went on, obviously upset about the matter, "she denied it."

"So what's the problem?"

He heard Greta sigh. "I got the feeling she denied it because she was afraid if she didn't, I'd do something to her."

He couldn't believe that things between his mother and sister had actually degenerated down to this, but then Abra was prone to mood swings. "You're imagining things, Greta."

He heard Greta sigh. "I suppose that maybe I am, but just the other day she asked me if I was doing any recreational drugs. Me, who's never taken anything stronger than an aspirin. I think that beating Mother took might have been even more serious than any of us suspected."

It was Ryan's turn to sigh. No one was more frustrated about not being able to find whoever had hurt his mother than he was. But right now, he had the break-in to deal with.

The break-in with the evidence mounting against Greta. There *had* to be an explanation for all this, he thought, but he needed to talk to her in person to get at the truth.

Growing up, Greta had been a tomboy almost in self-defense. She'd been outnumbered by her brothers five to one and had learned to hold her own at a very early age. At five-nine she was tall and willowy, and at first glance, very feminine.

But she was also tough to the point that he was certain no one could easily push her around. As far as he knew, his sister didn't really have much of a temper, but then he supposed everyone could be pushed to their limit. What was Greta's limit? he couldn't help wondering.

Was there something that could push Greta over the edge?

His thought process suddenly took him in a very new direction, almost against his will. What if, for some reason, their mother had suddenly taken exception to Greta's pending marriage to Mark Stanton? Handsome and glibly charming, it was no secret that the younger brother of the president of Stanton Oil got by on his looks, not his work ethic. Maybe, despite the fact that she had been instrumental in throwing Greta and Mark an engagement party—their father always left such things to his wife—Abra had told Greta to slow down and think things through and Greta had balked. One thing could have had led to another and—

And what? Ryan silently demanded. Greta had had a complete reversal in personality and gone ballistic on their mother? That account just didn't fly for him.

None of this was making any sense to him—and he was getting one hell of a headache just reviewing all the various details over and over again in his head.

"Ryan? Are you still there?" The stress in Greta's voice broke through his thoughts.

"What?" Embarrassed, he flushed. Luckily there was no one to see him. "Yeah, I'm still here, Greta. How long have you been in Oklahoma City?" he asked her abruptly, changing direction.

He heard her hesitate. Was she thinking, or…?

"A couple of weeks or so," Greta finally answered. "Why?"

Ryan suppressed his sigh. "Which is it? A couple of weeks? Or 'so'?"

"Three weeks," she replied more specifically, irritation evident in her voice. "Just what's this all about, Ryan?"

He didn't address her question. Instead, he asked her another one of his own. "So you weren't there—at the ranch—yesterday morning? Or the night before?"

"No, I already told you," she replied, annoyed. "I was here, working. Why are you asking me all these weird questions?" she asked. And then, as if she had a premonition about what was happening, she asked, "Ryan, what's going on?"

He gave her the unvarnished details. "Someone broke into the stables early yesterday morning."

"That's awful," she cried, upset. And then realization entered her voice, as did abject horror. "Wait, why would you think that it was me?"

Maybe he should have refrained from telling her this until later, but Greta *was* his sister and he had to give her every benefit of the doubt. "Because one of the windows had been deliberately broken and there was blood on the jagged edges."

Even as she said the words, she couldn't really get herself to believe it. It was there in her voice as she asked in stunned disbelief, "My blood?"

He had never hated sharing a piece of information more than this. "Yes."

She felt as if she had slipped into some sort of parallel universe, one that was not bound by the laws of reason—or reality for that matter.

Stunned, she protested, "That's not possible," because she couldn't see how it could be. "What reason would I have to break into the stable, going through a window for heaven's sake?" she demanded.

"I don't know, Greta. That's what I'm trying to find out," he told her wearily. "The DNA test that came back from the lab was conclusive."

"Then you need better equipment—or better people doing the test—because the results they came up with are *wrong*. I wasn't there," Greta insisted heatedly one more time. "I was here, in Oklahoma City, working with the horses."

Ryan paused for a moment, hating what he had to ask. But this was protocol, not something personal—even though he knew that Greta would take it that way. And in her place, he would have felt the same way. "Can anyone vouch for you?"

"The horses aren't talking," she snapped at him in exasperation.

"I didn't think so," he replied, hoping to inject a tiny trace of humor into the extremely awkward exchange. "How about the rancher who hired you?"

"Sorry, no help in that quarter," she informed her brother coldly. "He's away on business. Apparently *he* trusts me because I've got free access to his ranch while he's away so I can come and go at will."

Ryan took no offense at the attitude that had slipped into his sister's voice. If someone had been listening to their exchange, it would sound as if he was trying to break Greta down.

"How about Mark?" he asked hopefully. Personally, he didn't care for his sister's intended, but maybe the man could prove good for something. Maybe he could provide the alibi that Greta needed. "Is he—"

Greta cut him off. "Mark's just away. I don't know where he is."

What she didn't say was that her fiancé had been rather flaky of late, not showing up when he said he would, being secretive whenever he did show up. She had a very uneasy feeling that the second she had agreed to marry him, Mark had decided he no longer had to be on his best behavior.

But none of this was something she wanted to share with her family, especially since someone had almost killed her mother, and apparently her police detective brother thought that she might be the one who was responsible for that.

Ryan jumped on the last thing she'd said like a hungry dog on his first bone after suffering a week of deprivation. "What do you mean you don't know where he is?"

Greta's tone became entirely defensive. It was obvious that she was tired of having to defend herself. "Just what I said. He's my fiancé, Ryan, not my pet. I don't keep track of him when he's 'off leash,'" she informed her brother heatedly.

Ryan felt he would have had to have been deaf to have missed her hostility. Not that he could blame her. Again, he supposed he'd feel the same way in her place if she'd all but accused him of hurting their mother and then began questioning him about vandalizing the family ranch.

The Lucky C was their father's pride and joy. Big J treated the ranch as if it was actually an entity unto itself, as human as the rest of them—at times, maybe even more so.

Much as he hated to admit it, he had lost control of this conversation. All he'd wanted to do was arrange to get together with Greta to have this discussion face-to-face and it had veered completely off track. He had no idea how to smooth things over, only that he had to do it in order to get something to work with.

Pausing, he searched for words. But before they could come to him, his cell buzzed, announcing a second call was attempting to come in.

The phrase "saved by the bell" suddenly occurred to him.

"Hold on a minute, Greta, I've got another call coming in."

He could almost hear her sign of relief. "Take your call, Ryan. I've got to go," she told him a beat before the line went dead.

Frustrated, Ryan blew out a breath. He'd just been

about to tell her to remain on the line but she had hung up before he had the chance.

He tried not to read anything incriminating into Greta's quick and abrupt withdrawal. If need be, he'd get Susie's rather annoying intern to pinpoint Greta's exact location to make doubly sure that his sister was actually where she said she was. Armed with that information, he could determine just where she was staying so he could drive to Oklahoma City and bring his sister back if he needed to.

He hated this.

What he hated even more was that he had a very strong hunch that "needed to" was going to turn out to be a reality, and soon.

Very soon.

"Colton," he announced as he took the incoming call.

"You better get out here, boy," a shaken voice instructed him.

For one isolated moment, Ryan didn't recognize the voice. But he could be forgiven for that since he had never heard his father sounding this way. Stunned. Numb. And battling complete disbelief—as well as sounding just the tiniest bit fearful.

"Dad?" Ryan asked, still only half-certain that he was right.

"Yeah, it's me." His father's voice, usually so bombastic and full of life, sounded incredibly old. "Get out here as quick as you can, Ryan. And come *alone*," his father added, emphasizing the last word.

"More vandalism?" Ryan asked wearily. He'd had just about enough drama to last for a while.

"No," his father snapped, dismissing the question as inconsequential. "It's bad."

Okay, Ryan thought. This sounded serious. And personal. He could only think of one thing that would prompt his father to evaluate the situation this way. "Is it Mother?" he asked, even as he prayed—something he hadn't done in more years than he could remember—that it wasn't.

"No. No, it's not Abra," his father was quick to say. "But you have to get out here."

The urgency in his father's voice was unnerving. There was a time when their father had them all intimidated. John Colton was a big man who cast a large shadow and had a voice like gravel.

"Then what is it?" Ryan asked. Now that he thought about it, his father almost sounded spooked. If this didn't involve his mother, why did his father sound like he was frightened?

"Damn it, Ryan, I can't talk about this over the phone. What good is it having a police detective in the family if I have to argue with you every time I need you to handle something for me? Just get out here, Ryan," his father ordered. *"Now."*

He knew better than to think that his father was playing games. Something else had happened on the ranch and rather than wasting time trying to get his father to tell him what was going on, he needed to see this for himself.

"Where's 'here,' Dad?" he asked.

"The ranch, of course," Big J retorted. "You suddenly gone dumb on me?"

Ryan didn't bother answering that. "It's big ranch, Dad. *Where* on the ranch? The main house, the Cabin, what?"

The main house was where his parents lived, along

with Brett, his wife and Greta when she was in Tulsa. Jack, his wife and his son lived in what had once been the main house until the new one had been built, while Daniel and Megan lived in what everyone just referred to as "the Cabin." That, too, was located on the ranch.

"Come to the bunkhouse," his father instructed in a voice that was almost eerily still.

After terminating the call, Ryan tossed his cell phone onto the passenger seat and started up his vehicle.

Given the situation, the logical thing would have been to bring backup with him, especially since his father had sounded so shaken up, an unusual state of affairs when it came to Big J.

But since his father had also been adamant no one else come to the ranch to see this—whatever "this" was— except for him, Ryan felt as if he had to go with his father's instincts.

Besides, *his* instincts told him to play this very close to his vest—at least until he knew what the hell was going on.

Ryan paused only long enough to reach into his glove compartment to take out his vehicle's emergency-light attachment. Switching it on, he placed the whirling red and yellow lights onto his roof, securing it. Once he had, he hit the gas and took off.

Ryan did between eighty and ninety all the way to the ranch, something he would have loved to have done as a teenager. He would have enjoyed it a lot more then than now.

Once he reached the ranch, he took the long way around to the bunkhouse, passing all the other buildings just in case his father had been addled when he'd told him where to go. Ryan assumed that if that was the case, he would see his father standing in front of whatever structure he'd actually meant to direct him toward.

But Big J was not out in front of the main house.

Or the old main house.

Or the Cabin.

The process of elimination told him that his father had really meant to direct him to the bunkhouse.

Why was his father being so melodramatic? Was this actually just another break-in, complete with its own acts of vandalism?

This was definitely getting old, Ryan thought as he headed toward the bunkhouse.

His father was waiting for him out front.

Ryan could make out the lines etched in his father's face. They were evident even at this distance.

After pulling up in front of the bunkhouse, Ryan got out of his vehicle. Maybe this wouldn't be as bad as his father was making it sound.

"Okay, what's the big emergency?" Ryan asked his father as he approached.

"This way," was all his father said as he gestured for Ryan to follow him into the bunkhouse.

"What the hell is all this mystery about?" Ryan asked impatiently.

"You'll see," Big J told him grimly.

Walking behind his father as they entered the building, Ryan thought that he was pretty much prepared for anything.

But he was wrong.

CHAPTER FOUR

THERE WAS A dead man lying on his back in the center of the bunkhouse floor, a drying pool of blood beneath him, a surprised look frozen on his young face.

Whatever he had expected to find when his father had summoned him, deliberately refraining from giving him any details, it definitely hadn't been this.

Ryan felt as if he was moving in slow motion as he circled the prone body of the young cowboy with the conspicuous hole in his chest. He was careful not to step into or otherwise disturb the wide pool of blood that had had at least several hours to seep out of the man's body.

Only after he had completely circumvented the ranch hand's—Kurt Rodgers's—earthly remains did Ryan squat down beside him.

Rodgers's complexion was already beginning to take on a grayish pallor. That, and the condition of the blood on the floor, indicated that the cowboy had been dead for a while.

Even so, Ryan pulled out the handkerchief he had tucked into the back pocket of his jeans and gingerly felt along the cowboy's throat and neck for any sign of a pulse.

There was none.

He hadn't really expected one, but there was always that wild, outside chance that the man might have somehow still been clinging to life. Ryan felt he couldn't rule that possibility out until he'd made absolutely sure.

Ryan caught himself thinking that the victim—a fairly recent hire who had an affinity for horses and had helped Greta and Daniel train the ranch's horses—looked awfully young.

Just yesterday, Kurt's whole life had been ahead of him. And now, it wasn't.

Ryan was aware that his father had crept closer during the cursory exam and now hovered around him, peering over his shoulder. "That's Kurt Rodgers," Big J said.

Ryan didn't bother looking his way. "I know who it is, Dad."

Big J shrugged in response. "It's just that lately, unless you're investigating something going on at the Lucky C, you're never here."

Rising, Ryan pocketed his handkerchief. Irritation filled his voice. "I said I know who it is. Sorry," he apologized the next moment.

He wasn't annoyed with his father but with this latest, far more serious turn of events. Was this just a random murder or one that involved his family?

"It's just that checking out a dead body in my family's bunkhouse isn't exactly something I ever expected to be doing." Taking a breath, he looked around the otherwise empty bunkhouse. "Who found him?"

"Brett," his father answered. At twenty-eight, Brett was the youngest of the Colton brothers. "Near as I can figure, he was coming in from one of his late-night work sessions," Big J explained. "Boy was all white when he came and got me—I couldn't sleep and was in the study," his father added as an afterthought. "Brett looked like he'd seen a ghost or something."

"Or something," Ryan repeated, stifling a frustrated sigh. "Was anyone else with him at the time?" Ryan asked.

Big J guessed at what his son was really asking him. "You mean was Hannah with him? If she was, she took off before anyone else saw her. As far as I know, he was alone when he saw Rodgers lying there like that." He shook his head sadly as he looked down at his murdered employee.

Ryan absently nodded, jotting down key points from his father's statement. "Where's Brett now?"

"At the house, most likely trying to steady his nerves." A vague shrug accompanied his father's words, as if he wasn't a hundred percent certain that his youngest son was still where he just said he was. "I gave him my best Kentucky bourbon."

Ryan rolled his eyes. "Great, just what I need. An intoxicated witness to question."

"He's not a witness," Big J countered defensively, as if the term was somehow tainted, or would taint anyone it came in contact with. "He's your brother."

Ryan didn't see why that fact should create a discrepancy in the description. "Who was also the first one who found the body, that makes him a witness—of the scene, since he wasn't here for the commission of the crime." Ryan assumed that his father would have said as much if Brett had seen who had killed the ranch hand. "Was there anyone else here at the time?" he asked, rephrasing his previous question.

"Like I said, not that I saw," Big J answered. "I called you the minute I saw Rodgers lying there like that."

Ryan pressed his lips together, far from happy about this turn of events—or the predicament it would most likely put him in. What if, for some reason, another one of his siblings was behind this, or at least somehow connected to this?

It hadn't been a great week for family relations, he couldn't help thinking.

Reaching into his other back pocket, Ryan pulled out his cell phone. As he did so, he waved his father back. "You can't be here right now."

Full, bushy eyebrows drew together over Big J's patrician nose. "Why not?" the big man demanded, for the moment sounding every bit like his former, larger-than-life self. "This is my bunkhouse, boy."

"Nobody's disputing that, Dad," Ryan replied. "But right now it's my crime scene, and until it's processed, that tops your claim to it."

"Possession's nine-tenths of the law and I've got the deed, boy." Although he was proud of his sons, Big J was not about to be easily usurped. He was the head of the family. "Okay, okay," Big J said, raising his hands defensively when Ryan looked at him darkly, giving no sign of backing down. "I'll get on out."

John Colton began to do just that when he stopped suddenly to take a closer look at his son's face, as if he was trying to gauge the gravity of what was transpiring on his property.

"Should I be calling Preston?" he asked, referring to David Preston, the fifty-year-old lawyer who he kept on retainer to handle any legal matters involving either him or his family.

"Not yet, Dad. But it wouldn't hurt to let him know what's going on," Ryan told him.

His father began to say something in response to that, but Ryan raised his hand, stopping him. The phone on the other end of the call he was making had stopped ringing and had been picked up.

A melodic, albeit preoccupied female voice announced, "Crime lab."

Susie.

Because his father was standing not that far off, despite his instructions to the contrary, Ryan addressed the woman he had called—the woman he had once made love to with abandon—formally.

"This is Detective Ryan Colton. I need the CSI unit to come out to the Lucky C."

The impatient exhale echoed in his ear as he heard Susie say, "Look, I understand how you feel, Colton, but we just don't have time to run a fourth DNA test on that broken window," she told him in a voice that declared that there would be no further discussions on the matter.

"This isn't about the broken window," Ryan said sharply, cutting in before she had the opportunity to continue.

There was a long pause on the other end, as if the forensic expert was debating whether or not she believed him. "Then what?" she finally asked.

"We've got a body at the bunkhouse," he answered grimly.

"Do you know who it is?" she asked him.

Ryan thought he heard rustling on the other end of the line, like she was getting her evidence case together to bring to the crime scene. "Yeah, it's one of the ranch hands, a relatively new hire named Kurt Rodgers."

"Are there signs of a struggle?" Susie asked.

Ryan turned around to look at the area around the cowboy's body. The only thing that appeared out of place was Rodgers's body itself—and the pool of blood beneath it, that went without saying. Nothing else seemed to be disturbed.

"From all indications, he didn't see whatever it was coming," Ryan answered. "Send your people out here."

"Right away," she promised, snapping the locks on her case.

Ryan thought that was the end of their conversation and was about to terminate the call when he heard Susie's voice.

"Ryan?"

He put the phone back up to his ear. "Yeah?" He saw his father looking at him, as if Big J was trying to ascertain what was going on.

Her voice softened just a touch as she told him, "I'm sorry."

Ryan didn't have to ask about what. He knew. Susie was telling him that she was sorry he was going through this. It was hard enough investigating a murder, but when the murder took place on his own family's ranch, that added an extra dimension to the case. A dimension that made it almost too delicate to work on, at least for him.

"Thanks," he told her, adding, "Me, too."

With that, Ryan ended the call and tucked his cell phone back into his pocket. He knew he was going to have to call his boss, Boyd Benson, who was the Tulsa chief of police, and tell him what was going on. The man wouldn't be happy about this. But then, in all fairness, he had no idea what *did* make the police chief happy. Benson's regular expression was a dour one. Ryan couldn't recall ever seeing the man smile, not even at one of the Christmas parties.

Now that he thought about it, he'd never seen the man

actually attend a Christmas party. The chief was fair and honest, but not exactly a pleasure to get along with.

Ryan put off calling Benson for a few minutes, giving himself time to nail down exactly what he would tell his boss when he called him. Benson preferred having the maximum amount of information delivered to him using the minimum number of words.

"'You, too' what?" Big J asked the moment he saw his son putting his phone away.

Caught off guard, Ryan could only eye his father quizzically. "What?"

"That person you called, the one you told to send that crime scene unit of yours out here, you said 'me, too' when he or she said something to you," Big J said. "I'm just asking what you were talking about."

He supposed it would do no harm to fill his father in on something that was innocuous. "The forensic expert said she was sorry you were going through this." Okay, so he had reworded it, but he thought it might make the situation a bit more palatable for his father if Big J thought the head of the crime lab sympathized. "And just so you understand, it isn't *my* crime scene unit. It's the police department's crime scene unit."

"But you're part of the police department, aren't you?" his father pressed doggedly.

Ryan could see where this was going. Nonetheless, he played along. "You know I am."

"Then it's *your* crime scene unit," Big J concluded triumphantly.

Ryan paused. It wasn't very hard to read between the lines. "Dad, this isn't a matter of you and I being on opposite sides of this investigation."

Big J became defensive. "Yeah, I know. I was the one

who called you and told you to come here in the first place, remember?"

"Yes, Dad," Ryan replied, doing his best to remain patient, or at least to sound as if he was being patient. "I remember." There were times when he wished he'd never left the Marines. He had a feeling that this would soon be one of those times. "I'm going to tape off the crime scene and then talk to Brett," he told his father, knowing that the man wanted to be kept abreast of everything that was going on.

Though it was far from standard procedure, he was trying his best to keep Big J informed, hoping that would be enough to keep his father in the background rather than hovering front and center.

"But this is the bunkhouse," Big J protested. "You can't go 'taping' it off. I've got people sleeping here at night."

He really felt as if they were butting heads at every turn. And the man wasn't dumb. He knew better, yet he kept challenging him.

"You're going to have to make other arrangements for them for the time being, Dad. I'll try to get this processed as soon as possible, but until that happens, your ranch hands are going to have to sleep somewhere else."

He saw that the information left his father slightly confused for a moment. He hated seeing that because that was a sign of the creeping dementia that was slowly laying siege to and overtaking his father's mind.

It was hard for either one of them to become reconciled to that hard fact. Big J had always been a vital presence and the thought of his father being any less vital, of being diminished in any way, was difficult for Ryan to accept.

It had to be twice as hard for his father.

Nonetheless, Ryan had become aware that sometimes the most logical of thought processes could escape his father for a moment, if not longer.

Life was nothing if not cruel, he couldn't help thinking.

"How about having them stay at the old house?" Ryan suggested patiently.

If his father noticed the shift in tone, he wasn't letting on. Instead, Big J commented on his suggestion. "Jack's not going to like that."

The old main house, as Ryan thought of it, was where his oldest brother, John Jr.; Tracy, his wife; and Ryan's nephew, five-year-old Seth, currently called home. The boy was the proverbial apple of everyone's eye and the one continuing bright spot as all these mishaps kept on occurring.

"Maybe," Ryan agreed. "But Seth's going to be thrilled. He'll get all these new 'playmates,'" he pointed out to his father.

It was no secret that the ranch hands all doted on the boy. They took turns teaching him various things that would come in handy for him as he grew older and took a bigger part in working on the ranch alongside his father, uncles and aunt.

Right now, the boy was half kid, half mascot, Ryan mused.

And all energy, he silently added, wishing, not for the first time, that he could find a way to tap into that energy, at least for a little while.

Going to his car, Ryan took out the yellow crime scene tape. So armed, he wrapped the tape around the entire exterior of the bunkhouse, making sure that the front door would be accessible to Susie and her team when they arrived.

He was beginning to really hate the color yellow, he thought, putting what was left of the roll back into his vehicle.

"Okay, take me to Brett," he told his father. "I need to question him.

For a moment, his father remained exactly where he was. "You sure about this, son?" he questioned. "Brett's been through a lot already. It's his first dead body," Big J reminded him.

Ryan gently but firmly herded his father toward his car. "Yeah, I'm sure. I need to find out if he saw something and just what the crime scene was like when he got there. Nothing looks like it was moved, but..." His voice trailed off.

"You want to be sure," Big J guessed.

"I want to be sure," Ryan reiterated. "And as for Brett, with any luck at all, he'll never see another dead body again."

"Amen to that, boy," his father said as he got into the passenger seat of the sedan.

Ryan wished he could say the same thing for himself, but the job he had signed on for didn't just require him to handle the pristine cases. He dealt with them all. The only thing that gave him a measure of comfort was the fact that if he were the law in some tiny town where the biggest excitement involved getting a treed cat back down on solid ground, he'd most likely go insane from the acute boredom within a month.

However, that didn't negate the fact that every once in a while he would really like things to go smoothly and peacefully for more than a couple of days at a time.

REACHING THE MAIN HOUSE, Ryan left his vehicle parked out front. Even though he was as familiar with the layout of the house as his father was, he allowed Big J to lead the way.

"There he is," Big J announced, standing just short of the threshold leading into the formal dining room.

Brett was sitting at the table, one hand still firmly wrapped around the bourbon bottle his father had given him. His face was flat against the tabletop and he looked, for all intents and purposes, to be dead to the world. With work, a wife and a new baby on the way, he had to be down for the count.

At least temporarily.

Ryan walked up to his younger brother and gave waking him up one try. He shook Brett's shoulder.

Brett made no response, other than to snore loudly for a total of thirty seconds. After that, as Ryan backed away, his brother's breathing returned to a steadier, softer cadence.

"I'm not getting anything out of him for at least a few hours," Ryan concluded.

If then, he added silently. With that, he left the main house and went back to the bunkhouse to wait for the crime scene unit.

CHAPTER FIVE

SUSIE FELT TORN.

Torn between hiding behind the safety of her position at the crime lab—thus allowing her to keep as much distance between herself and the man who had skewered her heart ten years ago—and going out to the crime scene with her team and personally working it. If she did the latter, she would most likely all but trip over Ryan Colton.

There had been a time, ten years ago, when she would have eagerly welcomed the second scenario. But ten years ago, she had been starry-eyed and incredibly naive. She had been desperately, *desperately* in love with the six-foot-two, muscular, green-eyed, dark-haired Marine from the very first moment she had laid eyes on him. And, from the way he had acted, she had been certain that the feeling was mutual. Certain that they would love one another forever—or for as long as their forever lasted. At the time, she'd thought that would be the next fifty, sixty years, which just showed how very naive she'd been back then because in their case, "forever" had an incredibly short life span.

When Ryan had told her the news that he was being deployed overseas again, she'd been upset—who wouldn't be?—but she promised that she would wait for him no matter how long it took. Love to her meant taking the bad times with the good. It meant staying home and praying for his safe return while her Marine went off to fight. It meant patience and waiting.

However, it apparently meant none of those things to Ryan. For him, the key phrase was "out of sight, out of mind" and it was applicable to love, because she had obviously faded from his mind the very moment he had left American soil.

His letter to her had said as much, if not in so many words. By any standards, what he'd written had been an exceedingly harsh breakup letter without an iota of tenderness to it.

She kept the letter, not for any sentimental reason but to remind her, should she ever be tempted to give away her heart again, *not to*. Not unless she wanted to be the less-than-proud owner of a trampled heart for a second time.

Once was more than enough for her, and although the incident had happened ten years ago it still felt like only yesterday—but never so vividly as four years ago when she saw Ryan walking down the PD hallway, headed in her direction.

Only later, after they had both recovered the use of their tongues—he, of course, faster than she—did it come to light that they were both working for the Tulsa police department, he as a homicide detective and she in the forensic lab, something that had always interested her.

Her first reaction to seeing Ryan had been thinking that she had to resign and find another police department in another city. But then she'd thought, why should she? *He* had been the one who had behaved badly. *He* had been the one to break *her* heart, not the other way around. If anyone should have resigned and gone to another city, it was him.

But it had been plain that with his family embedded just outside of Tulsa, at the Lucky C ranch, Ryan wasn't going anywhere.

Well, neither was she.

At least, not anytime in the near future. She'd built up a good reputation here, not to mention a good rapport with the members of the police force, as well as the other people in the lab. Besides, her family lived in Tulsa. If she had left at that point, she would have felt that Ryan had pushed her out.

That was when she had made up her mind. She decided to dig in because she was *not* about to go anywhere. This was her home and she was staying. Ryan couldn't chase her away.

Since then, when their paths did cross, they had been polite but distant. He asked her no questions and she didn't interact with him at all. If any of his cases needed forensic backup, there were others in her lab she could refer the work to—which was exactly what she had done.

Until this latest incident involving vandalism and who knew what else on his family's ranch.

She knew in her heart—the same organ the man had so cavalierly dragged nails over—that she should be as professionally detached from this case as she might have been with any other case that crossed her desk. But, like it or not, the look in Ryan's eyes had gotten to her. He would have been surprised to know that beneath his carefully maintained, steely exterior, she saw the concern, the worry that was in his eyes.

For him, this was not just close to home, this *was* home, and he needed someone to help him navigate through the troubled waters until the culprit—whoever that turned out to be—was caught.

"That doesn't have to be you," Harold had glibly pointed out when she'd made her decision to lead the forensic investigation known to him. In the young intern's typically uncanny manner, he'd obviously honed in on her unspoken reasons for being at the crime scene. "We're actually competent enough to report back to you with the evidence. No need for you to come with us and hover around where Mr. Terrific can see you."

Where the lab intern got his flippant references from was beyond her, but she wasn't about to hang back and be perceived as having gone into hiding. She *knew* that was the way it would look to anyone who was aware of their—hers and Ryan's—history. Since Harold knew about them, she had little doubt that slowly but surely— or maybe even quickly—everyone else would know, as well.

It had become evident to her in lightning fashion, after the intern had been on the job for less than a few weeks, that he was nothing if not loyal to her. But Harold clearly also loved to talk, and inevitably everything he knew rose to the surface and burst out into the air with enthusiasm, like homing pigeons that had been locked up far too long when their cage door was accidentally opened.

So she told herself that she did it to keep her reputation as the head of the forensic lab intact, even though she was well aware that it was because she felt that Ryan—whether he knew it or not—needed someone in his corner. A sympathetic someone rather than someone looking to take him down a peg. Ryan was a good detective, but he was definitely not a beloved fixture around the precinct. He had a ways to go before his people skills rose above the level of "barely acceptable."

Which was why, whether he knew it or not, Ryan needed her. She just wasn't going to say as much out loud.

RYAN WAS MORE than a little surprised to see Susie getting out of the crime scene investigations SUV ahead of her forensic team. He'd put the call in to her, but he'd just assumed that, given their history, she would send her people without venturing out herself.

He was well aware that she was busy enough at the lab. This case had become a top priority to him, but it couldn't be the same for her. Her lab processed *all* the evidence that was taken in from the cases that were being handled by the department. That meant, as far as he could see, that one case for her was pretty much like another.

He didn't realize how happy he'd be to see her here until he was actually *looking* at her exit the SUV, carrying her forensic case in her hand.

He also had no idea that his mouth had dropped open as he watched her get out of the vehicle.

"If you don't close your mouth, if it starts raining like they said it might, you're liable to drown," Susie told him glibly as she walked right past him.

Confused, for a second he didn't know what Susie was talking about. And then, almost as an afterthought, he shut his mouth.

At least for a second.

And then he said, "I just didn't expect to see you here."

"Why? That was you on the phone, wasn't it?" she

asked as if she wasn't acutely aware of the sound of his voice, a voice that for the first year after they broke up had haunted her every dream, her every thought. "Asking me to come out to the bunkhouse on the Lucky C," she said by way of a reminder.

Ryan shrugged, as if his call to her had been a mere formality. "Yes, but I was asking for your team to come out. I didn't think you'd come with them."

Susie paused and gave him a look he couldn't read. "Surprise," she declared flippantly. "Now, why don't you take me to the crime scene so the team and I can get down to work?" she suggested, deliberately sounding professional and removed.

It pleased her to see that just for a fraction of a moment, Ryan appeared the tiniest bit rattled by her presence.

"Sure," he said the next moment, pulling himself together. "Right in here." With that, he proceeded to lead the way to the bunkhouse.

His stride was longer and she had to lengthen hers, almost beginning to trot in order to keep up. She did rather than asking him to slow down.

"What can you tell me about the victim?" she asked.

Ryan didn't answer her immediately. They had reached the bunkhouse and he held the door open for her, letting her walk inside first.

Susie could see the dead man. The victim was lying on his back, staring unseeingly at the ceiling, a darkened pool of blood beneath him.

"He's twenty-four and was a relatively new hire on the ranch." Ryan said, answering her question.

"Twenty-four?" she repeated. A note of sorrow had entered her voice. "He's just a baby."

Ryan slanted a glance in her direction. "Said the old woman of thirty," he commented.

"Some of us *are* old at thirty," she pointed out with conviction. Heaven knew there were times she felt old, as if she had lived an entire lifetime already. Susie didn't bother looking in his direction to underscore her comment to him. Instead, she got down to business. "Do you know if he got into fights, had any enemies, got drunk and abusive on a regular basis?" she asked Ryan as she bent over the body for a closer look.

"All good questions," Ryan told her—she had no idea if he was being sarcastic or not—but then he answered, "No, no and no."

Well, that was no help, she thought, looking around. She tried not to move the body in any manner until the coroner arrived and had his time with the victim, taking whatever readings he needed to.

The man should have been here by now.

Turning to Ryan, she asked, "Has the coroner arrived yet?"

"Also no," Ryan told her. "But he's on his way. Or at least that was what he said when I called his office after I made the call to you."

She nodded. For now, she had to be satisfied taking photographs of the crime scene—and the victim—keeping a closer examination on ice until the coroner completed his on-site examination.

"I'm surprised Benson's letting you work this case, given your connection," Susie commented in between taking photographs of the scene from every angle.

Ryan avoided making eye contact with her. Instead, he shrugged and brazened it out. "I'm a good cop and the department's shorthanded."

"The department's always shorthanded, it's a given." And then Susie paused. Her eyes narrowed as she looked up at Ryan, scrutinizing him for a moment. "You didn't tell him about this, did you?"

For a brief second, Ryan thought about saying that of course he had. But for the most part, he relied on omissions to give the illusion that he was telling the truth. He didn't lie outright and decided that now was not the time to start. Especially since, for whatever reason, she had come out to help him.

"Not yet," he admitted. "I haven't gotten around to it."

"Uh-huh." She went back to taking photographs. Ryan didn't fool her for a moment. He hadn't called the chief, because he wanted to work the case. If Benson vetoed the idea, then he would be forced to stop. But if he didn't ask, then Benson couldn't say no. "And just when do you think you'll 'get around to it'?"

Ryan shrugged again as he followed her without realizing it. "Depends. How long before you can give me some input on time of death, cause of death—other than that the man bled out," he specified. "And any other useful, pertinent information?" he asked.

Finished with taking photographs for the time being, Susie set down her camera. "I can give you the 'any other useful, pertinent information' right now," she told him. "Go tell Benson," she instructed in a forceful, no-nonsense voice as she slipped on a pair of plastic gloves in order to conduct another phase of her examination.

But Ryan shook his head. "I'm too busy now," he told her.

She looked at him over her shoulder. "Too busy doing what?" she asked.

"Watching you and learning," Ryan replied, his face a mask of seriousness.

She had to stop what she was doing and give the man his due. "You know, you keep a straight enough face, you could almost sell that."

Ryan inclined his head. For just the smallest island of time he allowed the years to dial back, and they were just two young people, hopelessly in love, with the world at their feet and endless possibilities in the wind. Back then he had almost convinced himself that scenario could last—and then the call had come, telling him his unit had been called up and he was to head back to the frontline fighting.

Then the possibilities disappeared like soap bubbles that couldn't live beyond the moment. The breakup, in his eyes, had been inevitable.

"I'll work on it," he told her, the coolness in his voice utterly dismissing her comment. "Now, how can I help?"

Most detectives didn't phrase things that way. They made it known that she was working "their" crime scenes and she was just a visitor while they were the major players—the ones who counted.

Susie couldn't help wondering if he had just made the offer to help to get on her good side. Most likely he had. It would be in keeping with the man she had come to know, not the one she had initially fallen in love with. In all likelihood, that man hadn't existed except in the recesses of her romantic soul.

Remember what he did to you. You didn't have any warning of that breakup coming, either. Don't buy into his charm or any other part of his act. You're older and supposedly wiser now. Don't play into his hand.

The silent pep talk wasn't working.

"You can stop hovering over me like that."

Susie raised her eyes to his. Damn but she had loved his eyes. They were so green, they reminded her of the ocean, an ocean she had wanted to go wading in. To get lost in.

Now the only part of that that had been prophetic was the word *lost*.

"I don't do well with hovering," she informed him coolly.

Ryan raised his hands as if surrendering to her instructions. "Backing up now," he informed her. "No longer hovering."

"Since you're no longer hovering, you could try calling Benson and letting him know we're working a homicide that happened on your family's ranch. If the chief finds out from someone else, it's not going to be pretty—and it won't go well for you," she warned Ryan. "He doesn't like not being on top of things—or at least in the loop to start with."

Ryan knew she was right.

However, that didn't make the chore ahead of him any more palatable. The second he told his superior the location where the homicide had taken place, there was a strong chance he would be taken off the case. He could operate in so-called ignorance for only so long. If he was told to get off the case, he would have to follow orders.

What he needed to do was frame his argument for staying before he actually called the less-than-friendly chief of police with an update.

He supposed if the chief took him off the case, he could always put in for some vacation time and take on the investigation privately.

Ryan felt that his father would respond a great deal

better to having a member of the family questioning him rather than a stranger. When it came to Big J, he knew just how to phrase things in order to not get his father's back up. A great deal of time could be wasted that way, apologizing for inferring the wrong thing or saying something that his father perceived to be an insult to him or to his family—or worse, to both.

Ryan heard the phone on the other end being picked up. "Chief, it's Colton. Just hear me out on this before you make up your mind how you want to go ahead on this case."

"What case?" Benson asked gruffly, suspicion weaving itself through his words.

Definitely not friendly and open to suspending a few rules, Ryan thought. "There's a dead ranch hand at the Lucky C."

"Regular fun house, that ranch of yours," he heard Benson mutter.

The chief was being cryptic, but for the life of him, Ryan had no idea how to take the man's comment.

CHAPTER SIX

HOPING FOR THE BEST, Ryan plowed ahead, giving the chief all the details that he had available to him at the present time.

However, at least for now, he left out the fact that, according to the tests that had previously been run, forensics had placed his sister at the scene of the last act of vandalism on the ranch. Ryan placated his conscience by telling himself that for the time being, Benson didn't need that particular piece of information regarding a minor crime cluttering up the details that surrounded this latest, far more serious occurrence at the Lucky C.

When Ryan was finished relaying what he knew, he paused, waiting for his superior's input.

The chief made him wait for a while, or at least it felt that way to Ryan. When the chief did finally speak, it was to ask him another question. "That's all you've got?"

Ryan curbed his impatience. He wanted nothing more than to be done with this unproductive back-and-forth exchange.

"So far, yes. The coroner's on his way and the CSI unit just arrived a few minutes ago," he replied, measuring out each word as he waited for the chief's final verdict.

When none was volunteered, Ryan pushed the matter a little further, thinking that maybe a direct approach was necessary. "So, can I continue working the investigation?"

There was another prolonged pause before he heard the chief say, "You're right, you know."

At this point, Ryan felt as if he was in some sort of strange game of hide-and-seek—and he, apparently, was "it." What was "hiding" was the one word he was waiting to hear: *yes*.

"About?" Ryan asked, doing his best to sound as if he was relaxed instead of edgy. It was bad enough that this was happening on what was essentially his home turf. To be kept dangling on the outskirts like this was almost more than he could put up with.

"Under normal circumstances, I'd tell you to get your tail out of there pronto and hand off the case to someone else. Except that right now there *is* no someone else. But you already knew that, didn't you?"

He could almost feel Benson's dark eyes drilling into him. Ryan knew better than to feign ignorance around the chief. Chief Benson had been around the block more than once and seemed to be uncannily up on almost everything that was going on in his territory—and if he wasn't, he would be before the day was out.

So Ryan said, "Yes, sir," in a genial voice and waited for the chief's orders.

"So you already know," Benson bit off, "that you'll be working the case until Detective Mahoney comes off sick leave and we get people to fill those other two vacancies in Homicide that I suddenly, for no apparent reason, find myself staring at."

Ryan had been well aware that two detectives in his department had put in their papers, one for retirement and one for transfer to a different department. Benson wasn't everyone's cup of tea. "Just wanted to make sure, sir," Ryan responded and felt safe in magnanimously adding, "I don't like taking anything for granted."

He heard Benson make some sort of unintelligible noise that might or might not have been a grunt, or possibly a disparaging remark about the "humble" card he'd just played.

Ryan braced himself to be chewed out—the chief was an expert at it—but instead, what he heard from his superior was, "Keep me posted, Colton."

The next second, the chief abruptly hung up before another word could be exchanged.

Just as well, Ryan thought.

Ryan wasn't aware of blowing out a long, relieved breath as he closed his cell phone and pocketed it again, but Susie was.

She had edged nearer ever so slightly and had been quietly watching Ryan beneath hooded eyes as he made the call to the chief of police. She felt fairly confident that no one else noticed her observing the detective even as she went about her work, carefully documenting everything in its place before taking samples with what appeared to a layman to be an elongated version of a Q-tip that was then deposited into a long, see-through, cylindrical tube with a cap on top to keep it in place.

When Ryan turned in her direction, she could see by his expression that he was suddenly aware of the fact that she'd overheard his conversation.

She tried to make light of it. "I take it you managed to sweet-talk the chief into letting you stay on the case?"

Somewhat preoccupied, Ryan was momentarily confused by her statement. "What?"

Susie waved her words away. They certainly didn't

bear repeating. "Just kidding," she told him. "Besides, we both know that you're not physically capable of sweet talk."

At that point Ryan had replayed her words in his head. "It's not necessary to sweet-talk the chief into letting me work the case when the department's shorthanded."

"Lucky you," she replied glibly.

She meant something by that, he thought. Most likely it was some sort of hidden reference to their time to-gether—or, more specifically, to the breakup. But he didn't have time to get into that now, or to feel guilty for the way he had treated her. Definitely not his finest hour, but he'd had his reasons.

He changed the subject. "How long is it going to take you to process all this?" he asked, waving his hand around to indicate the new crime scene.

She didn't even pause to calculate a ballpark figure. "That all depends on whether you want a rush job or a thorough job."

Ryan frowned. He didn't want the former, but the latter implied a long wait. "Can't it be both?" he asked.

She knew he was going to ask something like that. Susie sighed. "We'll do our best," she told him, speak-ing for her team.

At least she was being honest—and she wasn't play-ing up her part in this or the fact that some considered forensics more important than the department's actual legwork. She was, if nothing else, a team player. He just had to get used to the idea that they were part of the same team.

Ryan inclined his head. "Can't ask for more than that."

The comment—the last word in reasonableness—

surprised her, and she looked at Ryan. "Oh, you can ask," she told him.

He knew what that meant. He could ask until he was blue in the face, but she was only going to deliver what she could. That was all right by him.

"Have someone come get me once the coroner gets here and finishes his preliminary exam," Ryan requested just before he started to walk out of the bunkhouse.

Susie snapped her fingers, as if suddenly remembering something. "Drat, I'm afraid I left all my lackeys at the lab," she told him glibly, indicating that she had no one to send to him with the message.

Ryan's mouth curved ever so slightly, a hint of a smile in his eyes. "You'll find a way," he countered confidently. "You always do."

With that, he went out to the corral. He knew from experience that the other ranch hands had gathered there to exchange information and theories—and speculate on all sorts of things that were related to the murder of the newest hire at the ranch. Back in the day, the same corral had been a favorite gathering spot for him and his siblings.

Drawing closer to the corral, Ryan smiled to himself. He was right. There were six ranch hands presently in the corral. None of them were even pretending to be doing anything remotely connected to their work. Instead, they were all over to one side, conferring. They appeared uneasy.

More so when they saw him approaching.

Ryan noticed Juan Alvarez nudging the man next to him and nodding in his direction as he came up to the gathering.

An uneasy silence wiggled its way into and through the group.

Not exactly the most comfortable of situations, Ryan thought to himself. But then, he hadn't gone into law enforcement for the comfort of the work. He'd gone into it to keep the peace and to make sure that the good people were safe by rounding up the bad ones and separating them from the general population.

"Anything any of you boys can tell me about Kurt Rodgers?" Ryan asked as he leaned against the corral and looked from one ranch hand to the next.

The ranch hands shrugged, almost in unison. After a beat, a cacophony of mumbled negative responses met his question.

"Nothing?" Ryan questioned in surprise, his piercing gaze shifting from one face to another. "C'mon, you guys must have some kind of an opinion about the man. What did he do in his down time? Did he drink too much? Gamble to excess? Get on somebody's bad side?" He looked from one face to the next as he threw out possible vices and offenses. None of the men's expressions changed or gave anything away. "Nothing?" he questioned skeptically. "What was Rodgers, a saint?"

"He kept to himself mostly," a wiry, redheaded ranch hand appropriately nicknamed "Red" said.

The others instantly bobbed their heads up and down in agreement.

"Best one to ask about Rodgers is Miss Greta," another ranch hand—Jim Walsh—volunteered.

Ryan turned his attention to Walsh. Why he cringed inwardly when his sister's name was brought up he didn't want to think about. It wasn't something he could have easily explained if Benson were here. Luckily, the man wasn't, and besides, he hadn't cringed outwardly, which was all that really mattered.

He did his best to sound casual as he asked Walsh, "Why Greta?"

"'Cause Rodgers was working with her, helping her train the horses. I heard her telling him that he had a real knack for it. Rodgers lit up like a damn Christmas tree every time she said a kind word to him," Walsh recalled. There was nothing in his voice to indicate that he was jealous of the man or the attention Rodgers had garnered from Greta.

"Well, he ain't gonna be lighting up no more," another one of the hands declared dourly.

"Somebody should go and tell her what happened," another of the ranch hands, George O'Brien, said, looking at Ryan. "She's gonna be real upset about losing him."

Walsh made a dismissive noise and Ryan looked in his direction, waiting for more. He didn't have that long to wait.

"She didn't look like she was worried about losing him yesterday. I heard her yelling something at Rodgers and he looked real upset," Walsh told the others. "And confused as hell to boot."

"Wait a second," Ryan said, interrupting Walsh before the latter could veer off topic. None of what the ranch hand said made any sense to him. "You saw my sister here yesterday?"

"Yes, sir," Walsh answered respectfully. "And she looked pretty mad, too. And Rodgers, he seemed like he was scared and confused at the same time. I just thought it was 'cause he'd done something wrong with the horses. I've never heard Miss Greta yelling like that before," he admitted. "Hell, if you don't mind my saying so, I've never heard her yelling before."

"Me, neither," Alvarez agreed.

Ryan had, but only when she was greatly provoked—and he'd never heard of her yelling at the people who worked for them. She wasn't one who liked throwing her weight around and thought little of people who did.

Setting that aside, Ryan went on questioning Walsh. He wasn't through with the ranch hand yet.

"You actually *saw* my sister here yesterday?" he asked the older ranch hand.

Ryan moved so that he was rather close to being in the man's face. He did it in order to cut Walsh off from the other men in the corral. In these sorts of situations, he'd learned that the person being questioned looked to take his cue from the friends—or at the very least, the people—standing around him.

Almost reluctantly, Walsh nodded his head. "Yes, sir, I did."

Ryan had a sinking feeling in the pit of his stomach. When he'd spoken to her, Greta had sworn she was in Oklahoma City and had been there for three weeks now. "You're absolutely sure of that," Ryan pressed.

Walsh straightened slightly, bringing his shoulders back like a soldier, not like a career ranch hand. "Yes, sir, I am," he said solemnly.

Ryan approached the statement from every side he could, never taking his eyes off the ranch hand. "You saw her here, on the Lucky C."

"If you don't want me to say that, then I won't," Walsh volunteered.

"What I want is for you to tell me the truth, never mind what I'd like to hear," Ryan told him sternly.

The cowhand bobbed his head up and down with feeling. "Then yes, sir, I saw her. Miss Greta, she was here, at the ranch." He paused for a split second, as if debating his next words. And then he said, "I thought there might have been something, well, wrong."

There *was* something wrong, Ryan thought. But what? Was there something about his sister that he wasn't aware of? Or was there someone in the vicinity that just *looked* like Greta? That would explain some of it, but not everything. It certainly didn't explain the DNA findings that Susie had documented.

"Why's that?" he asked Walsh.

Walsh was visibly uncomfortable saying this, Ryan noted. "There was this really weird look on Miss Greta's face, like, I dunno, she was listening to someone give her orders, some inner voice or something like that," he added, shrugging his shoulders.

This was beginning to sound stranger and stranger. *Was* Greta having a breakdown? Or was there some sort of other explanation? In either case, Ryan was instantly even more alert than he had been a few minutes ago.

"Go on," he ordered sternly.

Walsh shrugged helplessly, obviously looking for a way to explain what he meant. "She had this expression on her face—like she'd sucked on a bunch of lemons and she was mad at the world because of it."

Ryan nodded, then glanced at the other ranch hands again. "Anyone else see my sister here yesterday? Or hear her having words with Rodgers?" He looked from one face to another. "Anything?" he pressed, unsure if he actually *wanted* to hear anything more or not. But he was a cop—it was his job to get to the bottom of things, not just the neat and tidy cases, but *all* of them.

A disjoined gaggle of heads, all shaking at their own tempo, told Ryan that was all the confirmation—and information—regarding the murder that he was going to get from this group. If anyone else *had* witnessed Greta saying or doing something yesterday, they were keeping it to themselves.

"Thanks, that's all for now," he said to the ranch hands. "I'll get back to you."

Dismissed, the group wasted no time in quickly dispersing.

Feeling drained, Ryan turned and saw his father walking toward him slowly. Each step for the man was obviously an effort.

It almost hurt to see the once robust man in this condition. Ryan wished his father would stay put and rest more. He was no doctor, but he knew that getting tired certainly didn't help his father's condition any.

Striding toward the older man quickly, Ryan deliberately cut his father's "journey" short. He wasn't looking forward to this part, either, but he needed to confront his father on this overlooked piece of information.

"You didn't tell me that Greta was here yesterday, Dad."

Big J looked at his son as if he had caught his third born in a lie. For the sake of argument, John Colton allowed that what Ryan was alleging was actually true.

"That's 'cause I didn't know," Big J told him. "You sure about this information, boy?" his father asked. "She usually comes by the house when she's here, you know, to talk with her mama and maybe spend a little time with her—and with her old man." Big J rolled the question put to him over in his head a second time. Frowning slightly, the patriarch was forced to shake his head.

"I think someone's pulling your leg, boy. Greta wasn't here yesterday. I'd bet you a big steak dinner at the best restaurant in Tulsa that she wasn't. She ain't been here for more than three weeks, as I recall."

He paused again, thinking. Ryan didn't rush him, but waited for his father to speak again.

"She's off down in Oklahoma City," his father declared, happy that he remembered. "That's where she spends most of her time these days, being around that man she claims to be so in love with."

Ryan could tell by his father's expression that although the match was seen as a prestigious one in general, Big J didn't think that his daughter's fiancé was good enough for her.

The mantra of every father since Adam, Ryan couldn't help thinking.

His father's next words confirmed it. "You ask me, he don't deserve her, but then," he concluded with a shrug, "nobody's asking me, so I'm keeping my mouth shut."

That would be the day, Ryan thought. His father *never* kept his opinions to himself. Everyone and his brother knew if the big man was displeased or if someone or something had rubbed him the wrong way. Everyone was well aware of the fact that his father was *not* a man given to suffering in silence.

Getting back to the matter at hand, Ryan thought his father sounded very adamant about Greta not having been here at the ranch recently.

Just as convinced as Walsh had been that Greta *was* here.

They couldn't both be right.

Either his father really hadn't seen Greta—or he had, and for some reason he was being protective of her. It wasn't impossible. After all, she was the youngest and a girl to boot. His father often protected the "weakling," although Greta would probably really balk at that description. It didn't fit her. As far as he and his brothers were concerned, their baby sister was a scrapper.

Walsh's scenario was still believable—except he still couldn't come up with a reason why Greta would go off on someone she worked with that way. She just wasn't the type to throw her weight—or the fact that she was a Colton—around. It wasn't in her nature.

Actually, from everything he had ever witnessed, Greta's behavior was quite the opposite. She loved working with horses, loved being a mentor to anyone else who shared the same passion.

The more he found out about this case, the less he felt he knew.

He sincerely hoped that Susie could come up with something after she and her team gathered up all the pertinent traces they needed to analyze, because apparently forensic evidence was all he was going to be able to trust.

Even if he wasn't quite willing to admit that to Susie yet.

CHAPTER SEVEN

WALKING BACK TO the bunkhouse, Ryan was just in time to see the coroner's vehicle disappearing from view, obviously on its way back to the coroner's office.

His mood was none too cheerful when he walked into what was still an active crime scene.

Susie was just wrapping up her initial investigation and repacking her case. He lost no time in getting over to her. "You were supposed to have someone come get me when Doc got here," he reminded her, irritated over the lost opportunity.

Susie looked up and just for a moment, she found herself distracted. Maybe it was the expression on his face, or the sound of his voice, but she had to struggle to keep her mind from wandering back to another, better time. She was going to have to watch that, she silently lectured. If she slipped up, there would be questions about her competence.

Shaking off her thoughts, she braced herself for a display of temper.

"No," she corrected, "you said you wanted to talk to him when he finished his preliminary examination. But the second he was done, Doc started packing up to leave. I tried to tell him to wait because you wanted to talk to him." She paused, not for effect, but to get the wording just right. "I believe his exact words were 'If he wants to talk to me, he can come to the coroner's office. Colton knows where it is.'"

Ryan shook his head. "The man gets more cantankerous every day," he complained.

Susie went back to packing up. "Well, in Doc's defense, being a coroner isn't exactly a fun line of work."

The way he saw it, that was no excuse. "Yeah, but the man knew that when he signed up for it," Ryan pointed out.

Susie's eyes narrowed as she took a closer look at the man in front of her. Funny how she'd gotten to be so good at reading someone she kept trying to convince herself she didn't care about any longer. She supposed it was like riding a bicycle. Once you learned how, you never really lost the knack.

"Ryan, what's wrong?" she asked.

Ryan.

He felt something stir inside. She hadn't called him by his first name since before he had deployed to the Middle East all those many years ago. More than an eternity ago. When they ran into one another that first time after their breakup, she hadn't really called him anything—which he felt was a better way to go, seeing as how if she had called him something, he had a feeling it wouldn't have been anything that was repeatable in polite society.

Whenever she'd been forced to address him since then, she'd used either his last name or his rank, never his first name.

That she called him by his given name now changed the parameters a bit for him. He wasn't altogether sure what to make of it yet, or how he felt about it.

The real problem was, he didn't want to *feel* at all.

"What do you mean?" he asked, stalling.

"I mean you look like you just found out you're going to have to go on a fifty-mile forced march through the desert with a seventy-five-pound backpack strapped to your back—after having run a marathon. So talk. What's wrong?" she repeated just a tad more forcefully.

He debated whether or not to let her know, then decided that she'd undoubtedly find out, one way or another. She was dogged that way.

"One of the ranch hands said he overheard Greta arguing with our victim yesterday."

"Yesterday?" Susie echoed. Her eyebrows drew together as confusion had her narrowing her eyes. "Didn't you tell me that your sister wasn't in Tulsa yesterday?"

Just talking about it—and the idea that Greta might have lied to him   really annoyed Ryan. When he answered, he sounded almost waspish. "Yeah, that's what I told you because that's what she told me when I called and talked to her."

"The ranch hand could have been mistaken," she told Ryan, giving him a way out. "Did you ask your father about that?"

"Yes." Ryan all but bit off the single word.

Getting information out of Ryan was like pulling teeth. It just wasn't in the man's nature to be forthcoming. "What did he say?" Susie pressed.

Ryan sighed and repeated in a monotone, "That she couldn't have been here because she would have stopped by to see my mother and him the way she always does when she's back in Tulsa. Hell, she stays at the house each and every time."

It wasn't hard to read between the lines. "But you don't believe him," she concluded.

Ryan shrugged almost helplessly. "Big J would cover for Greta if he had to. And who knows, maybe she doesn't come by to see my parents each time she's in town. Maybe there was some other reason that Greta was here and she didn't want anyone else to know about it." He looked at Susie and his frown deepened measurably. "I know what you're thinking."

"You've added mind reading to your repertoire," she pretended to marvel, duly "impressed."

"That must come in handy, given your line of work," she said.

"Don't get smart with me, Howard," Ryan warned, deliberately using her last name to keep a professional distance between them no matter how much he wanted to bring this to a personal level. He told himself that he was dealing with too much at the moment to cope with that added dimension—a dimension he recalled vividly no matter what he told himself to the contrary.

The more time he spent around Susie, the more those memories from the past tried to claim him.

Susan assumed an innocent expression. "But I thought that the department liked their forensic experts to be smart."

Ryan shot her a dark look. His temper was dangerously close to the surface. It was a vain attempt to stop his feelings from getting the better of him. "You know what I mean."

"Not usually," she admitted. "But according to that comment of yours, you seem to think that you know what I mean—or at least what I'm thinking."

"You were thinking that there was no point in me going back and forth about whether or not Greta was here since you already had her DNA placing her at the last so-called crime scene. And if she was at one, why wouldn't she be at this latest one? Well, I can tell you why—because there's a big difference between breaking a window and leaving graffiti on the wall, and killing someone."

"No one's arguing that point," Susie pointed out. "Least of all me."

Finished packing, Susie closed the lid on her case and snapped the locks into place. The black valise was completely filled with vials and tiny containers, each with separate samples of possible evidence that might, with any luck, just lead them to the identity of Kurt Rodgers's killer.

Susie patted the closed case. "Well, I've got my work cut out for me, so I'm going to get my team together and go back to the lab to see what we can find out."

She was about to walk away from him when she stopped abruptly and turned around to look at Ryan again. She knew she was going to regret this. After all this time, her heart should have hardened to at least flint grade, if not downright steel.

But the look she saw in his eyes had gotten to her. There was something about Ryan Colton that *always* got to her, despite all her concerted efforts to keep her distance and notwithstanding all the internal pep talks she gave herself.

The bottom line was that she just couldn't stand to see him in pain.

"You had lunch yet?" she asked.

Ryan stared at the woman he had once cut loose for the noblest of reasons as if she had just launched into some strange, alien tongue.

But then he made sense of her words. Thinking for

a moment, he tried to remember what his morning had been like before he'd gotten the call that brought him here. He shook his head.

"No, I don't think I even had breakfast yet." At least none that he could remember. "Definitely not lunch."

"Neither have I," she told him matter-of-factly. "I work better with something in my stomach. You want to stop and grab a cup of coffee and a couple of sandwiches or something?" she suggested.

The offer to in essence go out for lunch together caught him completely off guard. "You mean to go?"

Susie shrugged, indifferent to the choice. "To go, to stay, whatever. Just something to sustain us and remind us that we're still human and not just robots engaged in endlessly processing crime scenes."

There, she thought, that put it all in vague enough terms. She figured that would make it harder for him to find a reason to pass up the suggestion.

Ryan thought her offer over for a minute. "I still have to talk to the coroner."

"Doc's on his way to the office and he's not going anywhere—unless there's another dead body to pick up," she qualified, "which I hope to God there isn't."

Ryan had to admit that she had a point. He knew from experience that he didn't do all that well running on empty and coffee always helped to jump-start his brain. Pocketing the badly worn notepad he used to collect stray data and even more stray thoughts, Ryan crossed over to Susie.

Acting on manners that had been bred into him so that his reaction was automatic, he took her case from her, intent on carrying it to the car.

The second the case changed hands, it commandeered

all of his attention. "Wow, you didn't tell me the coroner's having you transport the body in your case. This is *heavy*," he declared. Ryan looked at the five-foot-seven woman with new respect. "You carry this case yourself?"

She flashed a quick smile in his direction, reacting to the question, not the man. "Like I said, my lackeys are at the office." And then she became serious. "Of course I carry that myself."

His eyes slid over her from top to bottom. She was curvy but not particularly strong-looking. He would have expected her to struggle with this sort of weight. And yet, she had easily moved the heavy case.

The woman had to be all muscle, he couldn't help thinking. Either that, or just too damn stubborn to ask anyone for help. He had a feeling it was at least partially the latter. "You know, you're a lot stronger than you look," he said as he accompanied her to her vehicle.

Opening the truck, her eyes met his. "I have to be," she replied.

Susie banked down the urge to say something more. Instead, she got in behind the steering wheel and buckled up, waiting for Ryan to do the same in the shotgun seat. Once he did, she took off.

She didn't have to say more. The message still came across. It always did—frequently—courtesy of his guilty conscience. A conscience that never allowed him to forget for long how she must have felt when he forced himself to cut her loose, letting her know not in person, or even over the phone, but via a letter with half a world between them.

That made up his mind for him. "I guess the evidence isn't going to go anywhere if I take forty minutes for lunch."

"Good response, especially considering that you're already in my car and I'm driving," Susie said with a laugh.

He'd always loved the sound of that laugh and tried not to allow it to filter through him. "Do you have any place in particular in mind?"

"Any place they have food is fine with me," she told him. "I'm not picky."

The corners of his mouth lifted. Memories flooded his brain, even though he had made no effort to summon them. "Yeah, I remember that about you."

Susie inclined her head. "I'm flattered you remember something."

Ryan didn't know if she was being serious, or just flippant. He certainly couldn't blame her if it was the latter.

"I remember a lot," he asserted quietly.

It took a moment for her to respond. "Must come in handy when you're working a case."

Was she putting him in his place, or reminding him that they were professionals and that despite the fact that they were stopping to eat, it was just in the framework of being two coworkers and nothing more?

Regardless of her intent, it was safer for him to go with the latter scenario. But at this point in his life, did he really *want* to be all that safe?

Safe was synonymous with isolated, with cut off. With being alone. And he'd been that way—alone in the only way that it mattered—for a long, long time. Maybe what he really needed was a change.

Leopards don't change their spots.

It was a hackneyed saying at best, but he couldn't help thinking it still contained more than an element of truth in it.

Maybe he *couldn't* change, not at this stage of his life.

Susie glanced at him as she took a corner, turning down a one-way street.

"You know, it's all right to talk," she told him. "I'm taking us to get something to eat, not picking up a quart of hemlock to sneak into your drinking water. You don't have to sit there like you're facing death."

He supposed she was right. He was overthinking this and taking it far too seriously. It was lunch—food—not a commitment for life.

With a shrug, he gave her a vague excuse. "I was just thinking."

She accepted the excuse and joked, "I thought I heard wheels grinding. Did you know that the best thing for your mind is to let it relax once in a while, have a little free-form fun?"

He knew she was kidding, but in reality, there was some truth to that school of thought. Still, he felt he couldn't concede that point to her without first delivering some sort of a comeback.

"I must have missed that in my latest copy of *Health and Welfare Guide*," he quipped.

"Well then, consider it my gift to you," Susie told him.

He didn't need another gift from her. The one she had given him ten years ago—when she'd given him herself—was more than he felt worthy of, especially given his subsequent behavior. The memory of their breakup made Ryan uncomfortable again. He shouldn't be here like this with her. The most innocent of things could easily become too tempting in a blink of an eye.

"Look, maybe this wasn't such a good idea," he told her, beginning to beg off. "If you drop me back at my car, I'll just take a rain check—"

"Too late," she declared. "We're here. No need to talk about rain checks. It'll only take a few minutes. We'll get it to go," she proposed as a compromise—she would have preferred sitting at a booth in the restaurant, even if the restaurant *was* geared toward fast food.

"And then you can," she continued. "Go, I mean," she added in case she had lost him. He had a look on his face that she couldn't place. "We'll use the drive-through," Susie added as she steered her vehicle into the lane that fed past the outdoor menu and its companying speaker. "It'll be faster that way."

"Not usually," Ryan contradicted.

In his experience, unless it involved a fast-food run sometime in the dead of night, he'd found that using the drive-through window, rather than just going into the restaurant and ordering something to go, took more time. Cars would queue up behind one another, moving at what amounted to a snail's pace, especially at the window where they paid.

And inevitably, there would be one, at times two, drivers directly in front of his car who would have trouble making up their minds as to what they wanted to order.

"Trust me on this," Susie told him. They reached the order window rather quickly.

"Welcome to Burger Heaven. What can we serve you today?"

Ryan saw her smile widely in response to the server's voice. "This'll be quick," Susie promised him in a whisper before asking in an audible voice, "Rusty?"

"That you, Susie-Q?" the deep, hearty voice asked, clearly pleased to hear hers.

"One and the same," Susie answered. "I want the usual—except that I want two of them, packed in separate bags."

"You got it, Susie-Q. Two usuals. Go on through. They'll be waiting for you at window three."

Susie shifted her car into Drive and glided her vehicle around the corner of the building.

"What's a usual?" Ryan asked once they were moving again.

Rather than answering his question, Susie allowed a smile to play on her lips. "You'll see."

Driving through, Susie had her money—down to the exact penny—ready in her hand when it came her turn at the next window.

A tall, heavyset young man, who obviously enjoyed more than his share of complimentary meals at the fast-food restaurant, was waiting for them—or rather her—at the last window. He had two large bags in one hand and a sturdy cardboard tray holding two tall, covered soft drinks in the other.

As Susie snaked the CSI SUV up to the window, the uniformed attendant leaned slightly forward to reach her. Susie offered him a wide smile as she took first the bags, then the tray, handing each over to Ryan in the passenger seat.

"Always a pleasure, Susie-Q," the young man said, beaming broadly.

Susie responded with warmth. "Same here, Rusty. Take care of yourself."

The attendant winked, obviously enjoying the short,

carefree flirtation, or so it appeared from where Ryan was sitting. "I always do, Susie-Q. I always do."

"What was that all about?" Trying to balance the two bags and the tray with their soft drinks as he held them on his lap, Ryan asked the question the moment she drove away from the last window.

"Lunch." She glanced at him, amused, just before she left the parking lot and went back out onto the open road. "You sure you're really a detective?" she teased.

"Sometimes," he said, thinking back to the case waiting for him the second his lunch break was over, "I'm not all that sure."

What he was sure of was that right now he wanted to be anything *but* a detective. Especially if his sister wound up being implicated.

Or worse.

CHAPTER EIGHT

"IT'S CIRCUMSTANTIAL, but it *is* there."

Susie hated having to tell him this almost as much, judging by the expression on his face, as Ryan hated hearing it. But she had no choice.

A full day had gone by and she'd run all the tests she could think of. The results were still the same. Another damning piece of the puzzle was coming together. Another piece that pointed to Ryan's sister being behind this latest, not to mention the most serious, crime to have occurred on the grounds of the Lucky C ranch.

Working feverishly for the past day, when these results came in, she had still been debating how to break the news to Ryan when he had suddenly turned up in her lab. Dispensing with any small talk or niceties, he had gone right to the heart of his reason for being there: he asked if any headway had been made with what she and her team had collected at the bunkhouse.

Knowing that there was no getting around this, Susie took him into her cubbyhole of an office so that she could talk to him without anyone else overhearing. If nothing else, she felt she owed Ryan that much. It was only common decency.

Approaching the subject slowly, she began by referring to the prints that had been lifted from on and around the bunkhouse door. There had been myriad prints, which had turned out to be matches for all of the current hired hands who occupied the bunkhouse.

The only prints that hadn't belonged to any of the other ranch hands had belonged to Greta.

Ryan's face darkened. He was not receiving the news well. But for a moment, he said nothing.

Despite everything he had once put her through, Susie's heart went out to him.

"You realize that there's any number of reasons why Greta's prints would be on the door," Susie pointed out. "After all, your sister *did* stay at the ranch a great deal, and she *was* in charge of training the horses. Since Rodgers was her assistant, they had to have interacted, and that's all this might be." Susie shrugged, as if what she was saying to him was self-evident. "Greta could have innocently come by the bunkhouse, looking for Rodgers if he wasn't ready to work with the horses when she was."

"So now you're on her side?" Ryan demanded sharply, his voice echoing with the stress he was laboring under. This latest piece of information piled on the already damning stack of evidence against Greta was almost too much for him to deal with.

The next moment, Ryan flushed, regretting his momentary lapse. He had no right to take his frustration with the investigation out on Susie. She was just doing her job, something he would have to do even though his family was going to be dead set against his doing it.

An apology rose to his lips, but Susie didn't give him a chance to say it.

"I don't take sides, Colton," Susie retorted in the same sharp tone that he had used. "I interpret the evidence." And then her voice softened just a touch. "Look, you know your sister a lot better than I do. Be honest now, do you think that Greta is capable of actually killing someone?"

"*Everyone's* capable of killing someone if they're pushed hard enough," Ryan answered her none too happily. It was a hard fact of life, but he had seen it happen before.

Susie appeared uncomfortable with his answer. "That's really cold." Her eyes narrowed, scrutinizing Ryan. "Is that what you really believe?"

Ryan sighed. He looked almost worn to her. "I don't know what I believe anymore. But I do know that I've got enough on Greta to bring her in for questioning. Maybe even arrest her," he added quietly, hating the very sound of the words, hating being put in this position.

Susie upbraided herself for being an idiot, but she still felt sorry for him, for what he had to be going through. And she said as much.

"Oh, Ryan, I'm so sorry."

Ryan's laugh was harsh and completely devoid of even a single drop of humor. "You and me both, Susie." And then, as if he had come to some sort of an internal conclusion, Ryan squared his shoulders, as if bracing himself for what he was going to be forced to have to do. "If you find anything else with those fancy whirling machines of yours—" he waved his hand vaguely behind him at the lab equipment that was right outside her tiny office "—call me and let me know."

Not waiting for her to make any sort of a response, Ryan walked out.

Susie rose and stood in the doorway of her office, looking after Ryan for a long moment, fighting the urge to run after him, to offer to help him bear the load before it broke him.

But she knew better than that. Ryan was much too proud to accept any help. He was infuriatingly stubborn that way.

And maybe, just maybe, that had been what had made her fall in love with him in the first place.

With a deep sigh, Susie left her tiny office and went back into the lab.

She had work to do.

"Are you crazy?" Jack demanded angrily a little more than an hour later.

Ryan had come to him, looking for Greta and asking if she was there at the old main house. When his older brother had said no, of course not, Ryan had pressed the issue, wanting to know if he was hiding her because she'd asked him to.

Jack looked at him as if he had lost his mind. "Greta's not here. She's not even in Tulsa. Why would I be hiding her?" he demanded. "Why would she even *ask* me to hide her?"

It killed Ryan to even say this, but he wasn't here as one of the Colton brothers—he was here in his official capacity. "Because she killed Kurt Rodgers and needed a place to lie low for a while."

Jack stared at him as if he had just turned into a stranger right before his eyes. After a second, he shook his head.

"You *are* crazy," Jack declared, then demanded, "Do you even *hear* yourself? Greta killed Kurt Rodgers? Greta doesn't even kill *spiders*, for God sakes. She catches them and puts them outside, like some kind of patron saint of creepy-crawlies. Greta's our golden girl, not to mention that she's hip-deep in planning her wedding to that jerk, Mark. Killing Rodgers isn't on her to-do list," Jack angrily assured him. "Between the wedding and her work, Greta doesn't have time for any extracurricular activities like killing people."

Ryan struggled to keep his temper under control. "This isn't a joke, Jack."

"And I'm not joking," Jack retorted, raising his voice so that it would be heard over Ryan's. "Get this through your thick head. Greta didn't kill Rodgers, so pick up your marbles and go play somewhere else," he ordered.

Drawn by the sound of raised voices coming from the front room, Brett, Daniel and Eric came in to join in on the argument in progress. All three looked from one brother to the next.

As the next oldest, Eric spoke up first. "What's all the shouting about?"

"Nobody's shouting," Ryan bit off, all but growling the words.

The three latecomers exchanged looks. "There're some cracks in the ceiling that beg to differ with you," Brett told Ryan and Jack. "C'mon, guys, give. What's this all about?"

Ryan did *not* want to get into this with the others, but Jack spoke up.

Jerking his thumb at Ryan, he accused, "He thinks Greta's behind all the weird stuff that's been happening here at the ranch."

Eric looked stunned. "You're not talking about killing Rodgers, are you?"

"Among other things, yeah, he is," Jack confirmed angrily, glaring at Ryan.

Brett joined in, as outraged as Jack and Eric were. "You're crazy, Ryan. This is *Greta*," he stressed. "She couldn't have killed Rodgers."

"That's what I told him," Jack said.

The look Jack gave Ryan put him on notice that the line had been drawn in the sand, and Ryan was standing on one side of it with his brothers all gathered on the other.

Eric turned to look closely at Ryan. "So just what is it that you intend to do?" he asked, crossing his arms before his chest and looking, for all the world, as if he was sitting in judgment of his younger brother's actions.

Damn it, didn't they realize that he hated this as much as they did? "I'm going to bring Greta down to the precinct for questioning," Ryan informed his brothers stoically.

"Like a common criminal?" Jack accused.

"Like a suspect," Ryan answered, holding his ground and hating that it had come to this. But if his brothers were going to bandy words around, they damn well better bandy the right ones. "Look, I don't want her to be guilty any more than you do, but I've got to work with the facts and the facts point to her being at the site of the break-in at the stables, and her prints *were* found on the bunkhouse door."

"Yeah, along with everybody else's prints. Dad's fingerprints are probably all over the bunkhouse. You want to bring him in for questioning to see if he killed Rodgers?" Eric asked heatedly.

"Leave Ryan alone," Daniel told his brothers. "He's just doing his job. It's hard enough for him as it is without all of you ganging up on him and giving him guff." He glanced in Ryan's direction, reading his half brother's weary expression. He took what he felt was a safe guess at what Ryan was thinking. "He doesn't like having to bring Greta in any more than we do."

"What the hell is this now?" Jack angrily demanded. "Since when did *you* start taking Ryan's side against Greta?"

Daniel swung around to face Jack. Jack was the oldest, but that didn't automatically make him right. Daniel had already butted heads with his half brother over the way he and Greta were training the horses. Now it seemed he would have to fight yet another battle against his father's namesake.

It just went to reinforce the fact that he had always felt like the outsider when it came to the family. Though he resembled his half brothers in his general features, the fact that he was one-quarter Cherokee sometimes made him feel isolated.

"All I'm saying is cut him a little slack. Ryan did everything he could to prove me innocent when everything pointed to me being a suspect in that assault a couple of months ago. And I'm not against Greta. I'm just not against Ryan for doing what he's supposed to be doing as a police detective."

"And what's that?" Jack asked. "Breaking up the family?"

"No," Daniel maintained stubbornly, "finding who's behind all these break-ins and this murder. Now, if you really want to help Greta, why don't you try helping *him*?" Daniel suggested.

"You bucking to be a lawyer now?" Eric asked.

"I'm bucking for the truth," Daniel countered. "Now, if you're not going to help Ryan, at least don't get in his way. Otherwise, we're never going to get to the bottom of all this."

Jack still didn't look as if he had been a hundred percent convinced. "It better be the right bottom," he warned.

Ryan fervently hoped he was going to be able to do that as he left the house.

His first order of business—since he was here—was to have a word with his father to see if the man had changed his story.

THERE WAS A time when his father had a mind like a steel trap, Ryan recalled as he went to see him. These days, however, that trap showed signs of being old and somewhat rusted. Still, Big John was lucid more often than he wasn't and Ryan would work with whatever he had and hope for the best.

Finding his father in the study at the main house, Ryan lost no time in putting his questions to the man who had once given every indication that he would live forever. But he had been a lot younger then, Ryan recalled ruefully.

For his part, Big John looked pleased with having the opportunity to talk.

After he took a seat on the soft leather upholstered sofa that faced his father, Ryan got right to it. "Think back, Dad. When was the last time you saw Greta?" Ryan watched his father's face for any signs of vagueness or a wandering mind.

But his father appeared sharp and on point as he answered, "I remember seeing her at her engagement party. She was like a bright, shiny penny, laughing, having a good time. That Mark's one lucky son of a gun, having my girl fall in love with him."

Ryan decided to move the story along a little. Though it pained him to do so, he got to the ugly part. "And then Mom was found…"

Ryan deliberately let his voice trail off, waiting for his father to continue the narrative.

Big John's face darkened from the fateful memory of that awful moment when Jack had called him into the bedroom and he'd seen his wife lying on the floor, bruised and bleeding.

"Some bastard beat her. He hurt my Abra. She was like a broken little sparrow." Tears filled the big man's eyes. He wiped them away with the back of his hand, like a child might. "I find the person who did that, I'm going to break him right in two."

Ryan had no doubt that older or not, his father was still very capable of doing just that.

"No, you'll let the law handle it, Dad," Ryan told him firmly. "The last thing I want is for you to be in trouble with the law, too."

Big J looked at him sharply. "What do you mean 'too'? Who else is in trouble with the law? Is it one of your brothers?" his father demanded. "You know that they can be a little hotheaded at times, but they're all good boys—just like you, Ryan," Big J emphasized. "They've just got a little too much steam to let off sometimes. But boys will be boys, you know that."

"No, Dad, it's not about my brothers." This was really taking a toll on him, Ryan thought. "Now focus, Dad, focus. Was the engagement party the last time you remember seeing Greta here?"

Instead of answering the question, Big J's eyes narrowed, his bushy eyebrows hovering over the bridge of his nose like two furry caterpillars in conference, both vying for the same space.

"What's with all these questions about Greta? Why do you keep asking about where Greta was?" And then, abruptly, it seemed to dawn on him. This time, the two furry caterpillars drew together in obvious anger. "Boy, I don't think I like where you're headed with this. Your sister's got nothing to do with nothing, you hear me?" he demanded, his voice rising.

For a moment, nothing but the sound of Big J's heavy breathing filled the room. And when he spoke again, none of his anger abated.

"I moved heaven and earth to get that girl and I'm not going to stand around, twiddling my thumbs and whistling Dixie while you accuse your sister of doing God knows what. Greta's a good girl, you hear me, boy?" he shouted. "If she says she wasn't in Tulsa, then she wasn't in Tulsa. Don't go turning over rocks, looking for rattlesnakes that ain't there." An edge entered Big John's voice as his complexion took on a definite red hue. "And you leave your sister be, if you know what's good for you."

I only wish I could, Dad.

Out loud, he murmured a cryptic "Good talk, Dad," and walked out of the main house, far more troubled now than he had been when he had first walked onto the property yesterday.

Big J watched his son walk away, forcing himself to put their conversation out of his mind. He couldn't allow it to clutter up what little space he had there. He had to focus on what was ultimately the most important thing in his life.

His wife.

He'd never been a dumb man. Dumb men didn't build up the kind of empire that he had managed to assemble. He knew what was happening, knew that he was slowly beginning to lose bits and pieces of himself. He'd beaten back opponents time and again, but this was one opponent that he wasn't going to be able to win against. In the end, time had a way of bringing all of them to their knees, making beggars out of kings, broken old men out of former proud, undefeated warriors. In his case, it was not his health but his mind that was being stolen from him. He hung on and fought as hard and as long as he could and he intended to go on fighting until the day came when he finally forgot what it was that he was fighting for. Because he wasn't fighting just for himself, he was doing it for Abra.

After all, he was her protector, especially now, when she was so very fragile. He couldn't be her protector if he just gave up and faded into some shadowy world where memories existed in fragmented pieces with entire sections missing.

He didn't want to go there. He wanted to be here, with his lovely princess. It was his fault her spirit had been as delicate as it was. When he'd married her, it wasn't because she'd captured his heart or because he was even a little in love with her. It was because marrying her had been a good business match. Marrying Abra meant gaining her father's property which in turn meant doubling his own. That was the prize to him back then.

He'd been too young and too stupid to realize that while land was what you left as your legacy, the true prize was the love of a good woman. He'd done nothing to earn her love and slowly, though she never said anything, he knew that Abra must have realized that he didn't love her, not then, anyway.

Still, she'd stood by him, done her wifely duty and given him four sons and a daughter. And he, in turn, had added a love child to that mix. A bastard son by a woman who had temporarily won the passion that should have been Abra's.

That had broken her, he thought, affected her health and made her less than the mother to her children than she should have been. Growing up, she was hardly involved in their lives, hardly knew them. Choosing, instead, to travel and be away from them.

And that had all been his fault.

In a strange twist of fate, as the years went by, he found himself loving her more and more. So much so that when that unspeakable attack on her had happened, he thought he'd go crazy with grief and kept vigil by her hospital bed, waiting for the moment when her eyes would finally open again. He wanted to be the first person she saw.

Concerned, his sons and daughter kept encouraging him to take it easy, to go home and rest. How could he rest at home when his heart was elsewhere?

And now she was conscious and home. And bit by bit, things were coming back to her. She was his Abra again.

He just didn't know how much longer he could continue being her Big J.

But he couldn't think about that today. Today he could still remember her the day she became his bride and so could she. They were joined in that mutual memory, together then, together now.

That was all that mattered.

RYAN GAVE HIMSELF till the count of ten, then counted to ten another two times as he got into his car. That had been a frustrating interview with his father, but he finally got his temper under some sort of control. Only then did he start up his vehicle, pointing it back toward town and the precinct.

It took him a little longer before he felt calm enough—or at least relatively so—to place another call to his sister.

Part of him was angry at her for putting him in this sort of a position—the other part of him desperately wanted her to give him something to work with so that he could prove her innocent of all these misdeeds. He really wanted peace to be restored to the family, but he had a sinking feeling that it just wasn't going to happen.

"Where are you?" he asked the second he heard Greta's voice on the other end of his cell phone. He had his phone temporarily mounted on his dashboard, his hands on the steering wheel as he drove back to the precinct.

"I'm still in Oklahoma City, the same place I was the last time you called. Why?" she asked with a laugh, then teased, "You miss me, big brother?"

He didn't engage in the banter she was tendering. Instead, he went to the heart of the matter.

"Then you don't know?" He really wanted to give his sister the benefit of the doubt, but at this point Ryan just couldn't manage to keep the accusation out of his voice.

"Know what?"

He could hear the confusion in her voice. Or was that just part of the act? "That Kurt Rodgers was found shot to death in the bunkhouse yesterday morning."

Ryan heard his sister stifling a cry of horror. Like her confusion, it sounded genuine, but then Greta had been the star of her high school play. He knew that she could be very convincing when she wanted to be.

And avoiding the death penalty was quite a motivator, he couldn't help thinking.

"Do you know who did it?" she asked him in a voice that wasn't quite steady.

"Not yet. But I'm working on it," he answered in a flat tone, then added, "I want you at the precinct by five o'clock."

"Why?" she asked, clearly bewildered. "You think I can help you find who did this terrible thing? I don't know anything, Ryan. I left Tulsa right after the engagement party. I only came back when I heard that Mother was in the hospital and I left after she regained consciousness and was released."

Ryan wanted to shout at her, to tell her to stop pretending. He wanted to tell her that so far, she was the only suspect he had. But he didn't. He refrained, keeping everything all safely bottled up inside of him until he thought he'd explode from the pressure of keeping it all within.

"Just get here," he told her sternly. "And come up to my floor."

"I'm a little busy right now, Ryan, but I'll be there as soon as I can," she promised, adding, "I want to help any way I can. Kurt was a sweet man and he had tremendous potential. He was so great with the horses." Ryan thought he heard her hesitate for a moment before hanging up. "Is there anything else?" she asked.

Yes, there's something else. Bring Preston with you. You should have a lawyer present when we go over this because, heaven help me, if you did this, I can't let you get away with it.

The unspoken words burned in his throat, as did other words, other warnings Ryan wanted to shout at her.

But those were words that came to him as her brother. There was no room for that here. In this case, he wasn't her brother, he was a homicide detective, dedicated to the single cause of finding perpetrators and bringing them to justice. That was his job, his purpose. His *only* purpose. Issuing warnings to sisters wasn't part of his job description and would only get in the way of his doing the right thing.

The law-abiding thing.

Which, in the long run, he couldn't help thinking, didn't always turn out to be the *right* thing.

But that wasn't his to differentiate.

CHAPTER NINE

GRETA FOUND HERSELF feeling oddly ill at ease, considering the fact that she was waiting for Ryan, not only her brother but someone she had always had the very best relationship with. Granted they fought when they were younger, but that was to be expected in a family the size of theirs. Like all her brothers, Greta knew that she could always turn to Ryan if she had a problem.

But there had been something strange in his voice, a strained note she had never heard before. Maybe the job was getting to him.

Or maybe it was the fact that one of the ranch hands had been killed.

Part of her uneasiness stemmed from the fact that she *knew* that no matter what name might be whimsically attached to the room she was presently in, she was sitting, her hands folded, her back arrow straight, at the rectangular table of what was, quite plainly, an interrogation room.

Not an interview room, or a conference room, but an *interrogation* room.

And she wasn't a fool. She was sitting here, waiting to be *interrogated* by her brother, the homicide detective, about a murder that had occurred on the ranch.

For the life of her, Greta had no idea why.

Until just a few hours ago, she had been vaguely

aware that some really strange things had been going on at her beloved ranch, the ranch where she had spent her childhood. But she hadn't been on the ranch for a good part of the time that these things had been happening. She'd been busy with preparing for her wedding.

Under any circumstances, since she had worked with Kurt, she would have assumed that Ryan would want to question her about the ranch hand—she still couldn't get herself to believe that Kurt was really dead. But why Ryan had insisted that he wanted her here rather than just talking to her over the phone was something that continued to eat away at her. It just didn't make any sense.

And, she had to admit, she found it somewhat disturbing.

For the most part, Greta knew that her big brother wasn't a completely by-the-book police detective, but maybe the powers that be were cracking down at the precinct. Maybe *that* was why she was here, but she wished he had told her as much instead of letting her stew like this. The Ryan she had grown up with would have given her a heads-up about all this.

This made her more aware than ever that, sadly, she and her brothers were no longer really that up on each others' lives, the way they had been when they were all kids.

Fidgeting, Greta glanced at her watch. This was cutting into her time, but she'd gone along with Ryan's request because she felt she owed it to poor Kurt. If the ranch hand had actually been murdered, then she wanted justice for him. He deserved nothing less than that if she had anything to say about it.

Greta focused on that aspect of her being here and not on what, if she allowed it, could really get under her skin and bother her: the fact that Mark hadn't offered to come with her when she'd called him about this. She'd told her fiancé about Kurt's murder and that she was going to Tulsa to talk to Ryan.

To her surprise, the man she was going to be exchanging vows with had opted to let her come here alone—apparently never once thinking that she might need a little emotional support. Or at least not saying anything to that effect—or even asking about that possibility.

Greta frowned to herself. She was beginning to have some grave doubts about her pending nuptials and she didn't know if it was just a pronounced case of cold feet or if her gut instinct was trying to warn her of something far more serious.

Tyler, Mark's older brother, the man she had initially come to work for in Oklahoma City, training his horses, was beginning to strike her as a far more compassionate, caring person than Mark was. This despite the fact that if the two were compared, Tyler, who was the president of Stanton Oil, was far busier, with a great many more responsibilities to occupy his time and his mind than Mark. Even so, *Tyler* had time to offer her a shoulder to lean on when she needed it.

Shifting impatiently, wishing Ryan was here already so they could get on with this, Greta unconsciously chewed on her lower lip as she thought back to the other night when she had done a little more than just lean on Tyler's shoulder. She'd opened up too much and said some things that she'd immediately taken back. But she had a feeling it was too late. Tyler had seen the unhappiness in her eyes. She knew he had by the way he had looked at her just before he left.

It made her wonder if she was making a mistake in

marrying Mark. What she found herself feeling for his brother was…complicated.

Really complicated, Greta thought with a really deep sigh.

She had a lot of soul-searching ahead of her before the wedding, Greta told herself. Shirking that chore would be nothing short of dishonest, not to mention that she just might be sentencing herself to a lifetime of frustration and an eternity of feeling really unfulfilled.

Greta pressed her lips together in the silent, sealed-off room.

Maybe she needed to postpone the ceremony until she worked all this out in her own mind. But the very thought of postponing the wedding and all the repercussions that action would have sent a very cold shiver up and down her spine.

Her poor mother, who was still recovering from that nasty beating, would have absolute *heart failure* if she even suspected that the wedding might be called off or put on temporary hold.

This was the closest she and her mother had been in a while—possibly ever—and part of her felt that her mother was looking forward to the wedding more than even *she* was. To suddenly pull the rug out from under the woman by announcing that the wedding was being postponed would just be too cruel to do, Greta thought.

Damned if she did and damned if she didn't.

Maybe it *was* just cold feet.

Or maybe—

The door opened just then and Greta's head jerked up, turning toward the sound. She saw Ryan come walking into the room.

A very grave-looking Ryan.

Had he actually aged prematurely for some reason in the past month, or was it just the somber expression on his face that was making him look older?

"Ryan, what's wrong?" Greta asked. Her mother had been attacked and her father was clearly deteriorating. If there was something going on with Ryan as well, she didn't know if she could stand it.

Ryan dropped a file folder onto the shiny, dark gray tabletop. "You mean other than Kurt Rodgers being murdered?"

"Well, yes, of course." The words spilled awkwardly out of her mouth. She couldn't recall ever seeing her brother looking this austere, this unyielding. "What I mean is—you look as if there's something *personally* wrong."

Sitting down, Ryan pulled his chair up closer and looked at her for a long, drawn-out moment. "Maybe there is."

Was there something else going on that she wasn't aware of? She felt her stomach muscles tightening. "Ryan, you're making me feel nervous."

The expression on his face gave none of his thoughts away. "Are you, Greta? Are you nervous? Why?"

This was *not* the Ryan she had grown up with. "Ryan, you're really beginning to scare me. Please, what's going on?"

His eyes never left hers. If anyone had asked him at the beginning of the year, he would have sworn that he knew his sister inside and out, knew what she was thinking before she did. Now, he wasn't so sure.

"I was wondering that myself. Wondering that a *lot*," he told her with emphasis.

She was starting to think that this job with the police department was not only stressing her brother out, it was changing him into someone she didn't recognize. She didn't want to feel this way about Ryan.

"Maybe we should do this some other time." Greta rose to her feet, gathering up her purse. "I've really got things—"

"Sit down, Greta," Ryan ordered, his voice low, gravelly. But the authority in it was ringing out, loud and clear.

Greta sank back down, doing as she was told. Waiting.

With precise movements, Ryan opened up the folder and began spreading out the eight-by-ten color photographs that were contained inside in front of his sister. They were crime scene photos that the CSI unit had taken, documenting not just Kurt's murder but the break-in at the stable and a couple of the other crime scenes that had occurred on the ranch before that.

When he had finished putting them side by side in front of Greta, he asked pointedly, "Do any of these photos look familiar to you?"

She looked from one photo to the next. Some of them were painful to view, like those of Kurt's body and the inexcusable vandalism and graffiti that had marked the stables and some of the walls.

She took a breath and raised her eyes to his. "Those are all photographs taken at the ranch," she finally answered.

Ryan inclined his head. That wasn't what he was going for. "What else?"

Greta reviewed the photographs for a second time, feeling ever sicker, right down to the pit of her stomach.

When she raised her eyes this time, she saw that Ryan was watching her carefully. Why?

"Just what do you want me to say?" Greta finally demanded, becoming angry.

"You can say whatever you want to say," Ryan told her. He continued studying her, hating the thoughts that were going through his head. Hating the fact that he was in this position and that she had put him there.

"Okay, you want more of a description? Fine," she told him impatiently. She pushed forward two of the photographs, turning them upside down and moving them in front of Ryan. "That's poor Kurt and that looks like the stable that Daniel told me was broken into. Anything else?" she asked.

Ryan leaned back slightly in his chair, crossing his arms before his chest. "You tell me."

She suppressed an exasperated, nervous sigh. "Ryan, I don't have time for a game of cat and mouse."

"Neither do I, Greta," he told her, then decided that maybe it was time to get down to business. "Why did you do it?"

Her brow furrowed. What was he talking about? "Do what?"

And then her eyes widened, opening so far that for a second, it looked as if her very eyes might fall out. "Are you actually accusing me of killing Kurt? Really?" she demanded, verging on speechlessness.

"Did you?" Ryan asked her, never raising his voice above a whisper.

Horrified, Greta had to hold herself in check to keep from leaping to her feet. "No!" she cried.

"Okay," Ryan replied. "Convince me." It was an obvious challenge. "Where were you between the hours of 10:00 p.m. and 2:00 a.m. two days ago?"

It took effort to keep her complexion from reddening. "I was home."

"Tulsa home, or Oklahoma City home?" Ryan asked.

She didn't have to pause to think. She knew exactly where she had been. "Oklahoma City," she ground out. "Can I go now?"

He didn't answer her question. Instead, he continued asking her his questions. Continued closing in on her. On his sister. He felt absolutely sick about it, but he kept pushing because he had no choice.

"Was anyone there with you?" he asked.

She hesitated for a moment. Ordinarily, she could just cite Mark as her corroborating witness. But Mark hadn't been there that night. She had her suspicions about where her fiancé had actually been, but she didn't have any hard-and-fast proof—it had never occurred to her to get that, just as it had never occurred to her that she might need an alibi for any reason.

"No," she finally said, answering the question even though it was really hard for her to say this. "Mark was out of town."

Ryan had seen the hesitation in her eyes. It made him wonder if she was protecting Mark for some reason. "You're sure about that?"

This time she answered Ryan with unwavering conviction. "Yes, Detective Colton, I'm sure. *Now* can I go?"

He felt as if *he* was the one who had been pushed into the corner. But, it didn't matter what he felt about it. He had a responsibility to face up to.

"I'm afraid not, Greta. I've got to hold you overnight for further questioning."

She stared at Ryan, waiting for him to tell her this was all a joke. But no such confession was forthcoming. She felt something cold grip her heart.

"You're serious?" Greta cried, her voice almost breaking.

"Yeah," he told her none too happily. "I'm afraid I am."

Greta felt as if she was totally shell-shocked. It was as if the ground had just opened up beneath her feet, sending her plummeting. "Ryan, how can you possibly think it was me?" she demanded, incredibly hurt.

He tried to remain detached, even though the big brother in him wanted desperately just to protect her, to tell her that it was going to be all right.

"Well, for one thing, your prints were found in the vicinity of the dead man."

"It was the bunkhouse," she pointed out, remembering what Daniel had told her when he'd called to fill her in on the details. "*Everyone's* prints were in the vicinity," she protested.

But Ryan wasn't budging. "Right now, you're our prime person of interest. Now, if someone could vouch for your whereabouts—" It was almost a plea this time, and Ryan watched her face, hoping for a glimmer of a breakthrough.

Greta opened her mouth, as if she was going to say something, but then she closed it again.

She couldn't go that route. It would open up a Pandora's box she *knew* she wouldn't be able to close again. And besides, she really wasn't at liberty to open that box in the first place. There would be a severe penalty to pay, not to mention that Tyler Stanton had only been with her for a few hours, not the entire time in question.

Greta looked down at her folded hands. Ryan could have sworn she looked as if she was praying. "No," she finally said, "I was alone."

Ryan sighed. This was killing him. He wanted to tell her she was free and to go home, but he had rules to follow. "Have it your way. Greta Colton, I'm placing you under arrest for the murder of Kurt Rodgers. You have the right…"

His voice droned on as he said the familiar words to the one person he never thought he would be saying them to.

Ryan stopped abruptly when he thought he heard a quick rap against the one-way glass that ran the length of the interrogation room.

Greta looked at him, as if hoping for some sort of an eleventh-hour reprieve.

He did his best not to look his sister's way as he went toward the door. "Take her to the holding cell," he told the uniformed policeman standing to the side.

"Not to booking?" the man asked.

"No, not yet. We can hold off on that for today," Ryan said, still avoiding making eye contact with his sister. Maybe he was hoping for a miracle after all.

The police officer stood behind the woman he'd taken charge of. "You want me to cuff her, Detective?"

"I don't think that'll be necessary," he told the officer. "She won't try to escape."

With that, he turned a corner, going to the area that was behind the one-way glass.

He wasn't completely surprised to see that Susie was standing there. She had obviously watched the entire session. He knew she would.

"That you playing at being Woody Woodpecker?" he

asked, referring to the tapping sound that had brought him out here.

Susie didn't bother returning his cryptic banter. This was far too serious for her to engage in wordplay. Instead, she asked, "You're arresting Greta?"

Ryan scowled, immediately on the defensive. "Don't give me a hard time, Howard. You were the one who said she found DNA evidence placing Greta at the scene of the crimes."

A wave of guilt passed over Susie. She couldn't deny her part in this, but she could defend it. "Yes, but I thought you'd hold off doing anything until we found an explanation for it being there."

He looked at her intently, knowing the answer to the question he asked her even before he asked it. "Well, did you?"

Susie looked really crestfallen to have to admit this. "No."

He tried not to look at the hopeless side of the issue. "Well, neither did I."

Susie sighed as she watched through the glass as the police officer Ryan had charged with her care took Greta from the room. "Where's Mark?" she asked. "I was sure I'd see him here."

Ryan spread his hands helplessly. "You got me. Greta said he wasn't around the night in question, so it goes without saying that he can't be her alibi."

"I heard that part," Susie said, dismissing it. "But I'm asking why isn't he here now, getting her a lawyer, putting up her bail? What kind of a fiancé *is* he?" she asked.

"Don't get me started on that, Susie," Ryan growled at the very thought of the man his sister was engaged to. "The man is a worthless pile of—"

Ryan caught himself before he became too descriptive. He was supposed to be impartial here.

But the problem was, as Greta's brother, he was none too thrilled with her choice of a husband. Mark Stanton struck him as a ne'er-do-well who was only interested in money but definitely *not* interested in earning it if that required any actual labor on his part.

Thinking over Susie's question again, Ryan had to shake his head. "But you're right. It doesn't seem right to me, a man not being there for the woman he supposedly loves."

Hearing the comment, Susie slanted a glance in his direction. "There's lot of that going around," she murmured under her breath.

Ryan caught that, but he wasn't sure he'd heard her correctly. "What?"

"Nothing," Susie answered quickly. "Listen, I'm going to get back to the lab. There's got to be something we've overlooked that'll point us in the right direction— and hopefully prove your sister innocent."

"Right now, I'm afraid you're a lot more optimistic than I am," he admitted.

The corners of Susie's mouth curved ever so slightly as she paused in the doorway and looked at him. "You're just finding that out now?" Susie asked him. "I never thought of you as a slow learner, Ryan Colton. Guess I was wrong."

She left him in the corridor, trying to puzzle her last words out.

CHAPTER TEN

"TALK ABOUT PUTTING in long hours. I didn't think you'd still be here."

Ryan's comment was addressed to the back of Susie's head as he paused in the doorway to peer into the lab. He'd been on his way out when he'd doubled back to see if there had been any new findings.

Susie looked up from the high-powered microscope and glanced over her shoulder toward the doorway.

"I could say the same thing about you," she said to Ryan.

Turning back to the microscope, Susie paused for a second to rotate her head from side to side a couple of times. Her neck muscles felt as if they were starting to cramp up. The tension there went straight up to the top of her head and then spread out. It was beginning to interfere with her being able to work.

"It's *my* sister who's in a holding cell as a prime murder suspect," Ryan pointed out, as if that explained it all.

"And it's my findings that made her a prime suspect." Which was why she was still here, searching for something to disprove her previous conclusions. Taking a momentary break, Susie looked at him again. "Any new evidence?" she asked, assuming that was what had brought Ryan to her lab at this hour.

"No," he replied, successfully keeping the mounting

frustration out of his voice. "Any new findings with the old evidence?"

This was beginning to feel like a table tennis match, she thought. Or possibly a stale comedy routine. Susie sighed.

"No." Pushing aside her own wave of frustration that was growing within her, Susie had a possible suggestion for the detective before her. "Maybe you should have another go at Greta."

Bad idea, Ryan thought, her suggestion creating an instant, protective reaction from him.

"And what?" he questioned, wondering just what the woman could be thinking. "Try beating a confession out of her?"

Susie's temper flared, but she clamped it down, cutting Ryan some slack. It had to be rough, having to accuse someone he cared about of murder. "No, I meant have another go at her about her alibi."

Ryan looked at the forensic expert, clearly confused. "I thought you were listening in earlier when I questioned Greta. She has none."

"I *was* listening in," she told him. "That's why I made the suggestion. I think Greta might have an alibi."

Well, that made no sense to him and his expression said as much. "Okay, if she has one, why the hell wouldn't she tell me about it?"

Sometimes Susie wondered how men had wound up being the ones in charge of things. They only thought in a straight line and they couldn't see what was just beneath the first layer.

"Because she's uncomfortable about it, that's why. I was watching her face when you asked her if anyone was with her that night. Instead of answering you right away, she hesitated."

Ryan shrugged his shoulders, not seeing why that was so important. After all, this was Greta, not some crafty, subversive con artist. "Maybe she was just trying to remember if Mark was or wasn't there on the night in question. Or maybe she was just embarrassed to admit that he wasn't there. They could have had an argument and she didn't want to talk about it. There are a hundred reasons she could have hesitated like that."

But Susie wasn't convinced and she shook her head. "Uh-uh, it wasn't that kind of a hesitation."

Why was she playing this game? It was a game, wasn't it? Jerking him around until he wasn't sure what day it was. Maybe he deserved it, Ryan reasoned, but not during a murder investigation and certainly not during one that, at least currently, involved his sister.

"I didn't know 'hesitations' came in kinds," Ryan fired back, unable to keep the note of sarcasm out of his voice.

"*Everything* comes in kinds," Susie countered.

That still didn't make any sense to him, but Ryan decided to give the woman the benefit of the doubt—after all, she was the head of the crime lab and he did have a healthy respect for her skills.

"Okay," Ryan slowly conceded, "then maybe Greta was weighing her options and decided that if she used Mark as her alibi and the prize-winning jerk really hadn't been there that night, she knew he wouldn't lie to save her from a possible prison sentence. He'd look out for his own neck. And that would make her out to be a murderer *and* a liar." The skeptical look in Susie's eyes was still there, which told him she wasn't buying his explanation. "Okay, so what's your big theory?" he asked.

It was really very simple, Susie thought. "I think she's not giving you a name because she's protecting someone."

Ryan's brow furrowed. "Who?" he asked, curious. "The killer?"

She hadn't worked out all the details yet. "Possibly," Susie allowed. "But I think it's more a case of her being with someone she knew she shouldn't have been with."

"'Been with?'" Ryan questioned, still somewhat puzzled. Was Susie saying what he *thought* she was saying? His frown deepened. "Do you mean like in the biblical sense?"

That was one way to put it, Susie thought, amused despite the gravity of the situation that they were discussing.

"Maybe," Susie allowed. "Maybe not. Maybe even in an innocent sense. But the hour had been late, maybe even actually closer to morning than to night, and that isn't exactly something a respectable young woman does when she's engaged to be married to someone else. She doesn't spend time, alone, with a man who isn't her fiancé. Not if she's still intending to marry her fiancé."

Every time he thought about the bastard Greta was marrying, a wave of close-to-uncontrollable anger would wash over him. Greta had been here a number of hours. Nobody had heard a word out of Stanton. It was probably exactly what Ryan thought—Stanton was just interested in covering his own back. That meant that if Greta went down for this murder, Mark didn't want to be caught in the undertow.

"Who still hasn't come to the precinct to find out why she's been picked up for questioning," Ryan all but growled as he pointed out that glaring fact.

She would have to be deaf not to have heard the animosity in his voice. "I take it you don't like the man."

Ryan laughed drily. "And I take it that you have a gift for understatement."

Susie smiled a little at his comment. "Sometimes," she answered, rotating her neck again and moving her head from side to side. It didn't help.

The tension in those muscles just refused to abate. She might as well give up. The next moment, Susie almost jumped when she felt Ryan's hands on either side of her neck.

"Take it easy," he told her, holding her in place rather than dropping his hands and stepping back. "I'm not about to strangle you. I just thought I could help you."

"I don't understand," she said, trying to turn her head to look at him. But his hands remained where they were and they held her in place. "Help me with what?" she asked.

"I can knead some of that tension out of your shoulders," Ryan answered. "Seeing as putting in long hours on my sister's case is what probably made you so tense in the first place, I figure I owe you something for your hard work."

She was about to protest his interpretation of how she came by the tension that was causing this severe ache in her neck, but the next moment, Susie swallowed her words. There was no point in denying what was obviously true. And even if feeling his hands on her instantly brought back memories of a happier time—memories she *really* didn't want to have resurrected—she was adult enough to keep those thoughts at bay.

Because if she did allow herself to go there, to remember all that, angry recriminations would find their way to her lips and she would wind up asking him *why* he had done what he had.

Why had he just decided, out of the blue, that he could live very well without her when she had barely survived without him? Had it all been *that* one-sided? Had she really been that much of a fool, to have loved him with all her heart and soul while he had only stayed with her as long as he had because she had been something different, a new conquest for him to acquire and then just move on from?

She refused to submerge herself in those thoughts, because they had been, and always would be, her own personal, private hell. She had no time for hell. Her work schedule was much too full.

Susie tried to shrug his hands off, but he held her in place.

She heard him whistle softly to himself. "Damn, I've felt softer bricks than what I'm feeling while I try to work your shoulders. Maybe you should see someone professional about that," he suggested. She expected him to laugh then, but he didn't.

"Maybe I just need to solve the case," she countered defensively. "And you need to find more evidence—or go at Greta again and find out if she is hiding something." She rephrased it so that it no longer sounded like a foregone conclusion.

This time, she managed to successfully shrug Ryan's hands off. There was just so much resistance and self-control that one person had before they just succumbed—and that would have been a big mistake.

There was a note of irritation in Ryan's voice when he retorted, "I already told you, I didn't get the impression that Greta was hiding anything."

Turning around from the counter, she faced Ryan squarely. With some of the latest technology on her counter whirling and creating background noise, she gave her former lover a long, penetrating look, as if she was trying to read his thoughts.

"Then maybe you need to look closer," Susie suggested quietly.

His patience, always in short supply, began to evaporate at this point. "The world isn't one great big complicated conspiracy, Howard. Sometimes what you see is what you get."

"And what you see is a guilty Greta?" Susie marveled, surprised. If anything she would have thought things would be the other way around—that she would be the skeptical one he was trying to convince of his sister's innocence. Instead, she was trying to convince *him*.

He didn't want to believe that Greta was guilty, but at this point in the investigation, he really didn't know if his sister was guilty or not. He didn't have anything but his gut to tell him that she wasn't.

And, he thought, *let's face it, I'm not the Pope*. Which meant he wasn't infallible. Sometimes, he added sadly, he was all too fallible.

"I hope to God not," he finally said to Susie in response to her question just before he walked out of the lab.

But instead of leaving the precinct and going home, Ryan made his way through the building to where his sister was being held.

Though his expression didn't change, or indicate what he was feeling, it really did break his heart to see her like that.

Ryan couldn't help thinking that she looked like a lost waif. Despite her height—five-nine—behind bars his sister looked like a lost, frail waif to him.

He was relieved that the uniformed policeman he'd sent with Greta had listened to his subsequent instructions and had put his sister in a holding cell away from any of the other jailed women who were spending the night behind bars, courtesy of the county.

Ryan waited until he had crossed to Greta's cell and was standing right at the bars before he asked his sister, "Did you make your one phone call?"

Greta brightened instantly when she heard her brother's voice. Looking up, she quickly rose from the cot she had been sitting on and made her way over to the bars to get as close to him as she could, under the circumstances.

She shook her head, her dark brown hair moving back and forth across her shoulders like the fringes of a curtain as she did so.

"No," she answered honestly.

Ryan stared at her, stunned.

"No?" he echoed. Was she kidding? *Everyone* used their one phone call. "Why not?" he demanded. "Why didn't you call someone?"

Slim shoulders rose and fell in a helpless, heart-wrenching movement as she shrugged in response to the question. "I couldn't think of anyone to call," she said. It was a lie, but she was too embarrassed to tell Ryan the truth, that Mark hadn't responded to the message she'd left for him. She needed to rethink things, to deal with them once she was out of here. But that wasn't Ryan's problem, it was hers.

God, but he felt like an ogre. After all, *he* had been the one to put her in here.

"You could have called Dad, or Jack." Ryan pointed out her logical choices. "Or you could have at least called Preston, our family lawyer, so he could have posted bail for you."

But Greta shook her head again, vetoing her brother's suggestions. "I didn't want Dad or Jack getting upset— and Preston would have called Dad to let him know what was going on. Dad's still shaken up by what happened to Mother, and finding Kurt dead must have been an added blow to him—and to Daniel," she threw in, since Daniel had worked closely with Kurt just like she had. "I didn't want to add to everything they were already dealing with."

That was thoughtful, but it really wasn't like Greta, Ryan couldn't help thinking. The Greta he had grown up with and knew was feisty. She wouldn't have taken anything lying down and she *never* surrendered, even if it meant getting their lawyer to do the fighting for her.

This woman on the other side of the bars sounded docile and, worse, defeated.

And you're not helping by accusing her of murder, a voice in his head jeered. He struggled to block it out. It wasn't easy.

"Did they bring you something to eat?" Ryan heard himself asking.

The question sounded lame to his own ear, but he wanted to make sure that Greta was eating. In her present state of mind, he wasn't sure of anything when it came to Greta.

She shrugged indifferently. "I'm really not hungry, Ryan."

He wasn't going to let her just waste away. "You have to eat, Greta."

"Maybe later," she told him, "when all this is behind me."

He thought of what Susie had said and tried another approach. "Greta, are you *sure* nobody can vouch for you for that night? Nobody saw you, talked to you, came over for a while?" *C'mon, kid, give me something to work with here.*

"No," she said with emphasis.

He saw a glimmer of a spark in Greta's eyes and thought that maybe Susie had it right. Maybe Greta *was* covering for someone.

"I already told you," Greta insisted. "I spent the night alone. Why do you make it sound as if that's so unusual?" she asked. And then she turned the tables on him by asking, "Did *you* spend the night alone two nights ago?"

He didn't answer her question. What he said was, "I didn't kill Rodgers."

Her chin shot up in a defensive movement, something the old Greta would have done. "Neither did I."

Ryan tried again. He had to break through the wall she had erected around herself. "If you're lying to protect someone, that's all well and good when it's just a matter of destroying your reputation, or not rocking the boat. That's your choice. But it's not just a matter of that, it's bigger. A hell of a lot bigger. This is the *death* penalty we're talking about, kid," he stressed. "You've got to think of yourself, Greta. The first person you owe something to is *you*," he insisted. "And then it's to Mother and Dad. Think of what this is going to do to them, to lose you all because you have some twisted sense of loyalty."

Greta pressed her lips together and for just a glimmer of a second, he thought he had gotten through to her.

But then he heard her say, "I was alone," and his heart sank.

"Have it your way," he said, his voice distant.

With that, he turned on his heel and walked away.

The prison door, separating the cells from the outer corridor, slammed behind him, emphasizing the separation.

Maybe a night in the holding cell would do her good, he thought. Maybe, if she spent the night there, listening to the echoing sounds of catcalls and whatever else transpired there at night, it would scare her into speaking up for herself.

Because he had a feeling, after this second go-round with Greta, that Susie was right about her hunch. He had come away with the same impression: Greta was holding something back.

Whether it was the identity of someone who could serve as her alibi or something else, he didn't know. But the one thing he felt he did know was that Greta was not being completely honest. His sister was holding something back. And if it was something that could ultimately clear her of all this, then he intended to find out just what that "something" was.

He had to make her tell him.

He hadn't meant for it to happen.

He had always prided himself on the fact that no matter what he was feeling, he always had everything under control. Everything was contained to such an extent that no one ever guessed what he was really experiencing inside.

All he had to do was keep walking, blocking his own thoughts until such time as he could deal with them and they were no longer of any consequence.

Once she was married to his brother, then Greta would be, in essence, his sister, which in turn made her doubly off-limits.

Just place one foot in front of the other, walking in a path directed away from her, that was all that he had to do. Place one foot in front of the other and he'd be home free.

But he didn't *want* to put one foot in front of the other, at least not on a path that led away from Greta. Quite the contrary. In fact, the simple exercise had very nearly taken him in the completely opposite direction.

It had almost taken him to her.

More specifically, it had taken him to her house. After some soul-searching, he'd decided to come to alert her to the fact that maybe marrying Mark was not in her best interest, nor was it the smartest thing for her to do at this time in her life. He wanted to tell her that it wasn't just that Mark was small-minded, petty and even jealous of the woman he was going to marry—it was that Mark was openly cheating on her, as well. His younger brother was making no effort to hide it and certainly no effort to stop it.

Greta deserved better and he had really wanted to turn up on her doorstep to tell her so.

But as he got within five feet of her doorstep, he had second thoughts. If he warned her, if he told her not to marry Mark, then she might think he was just saying that because he'd fallen in love with her himself. And maybe she'd be right, he thought ruefully. Pretty funny, considering that he had never even entertained the notion of having another half to add to his own. But though he tried to tell himself it wasn't the case, somehow, when he wasn't looking, Greta had managed to become his other half.

A half he was having trouble envisioning giving up.

CHAPTER ELEVEN

SHE KNEW IT was him.

The second that Susie heard the knock on her front door, she knew it was Ryan.

It wasn't anything unusual about the way he knocked, no unique way of rapping his knuckles against the wood to some inner rhythmic beat that had once been a code known only to the two of them. They hadn't been together long enough at the time to develop something like that.

She just knew.

It was as if something inside of her had been waiting for him. Waiting for this moment.

And now it was here.

Dressed in just the jersey and a pair of cutoff shorts she slept in, Susie quickly made her way to the front door and swung it open.

"Hi." Still holding the door, she stepped back, opening it wider.

The cop in him reacted automatically and he frowned. She hadn't asked who it was and from the sounds he could make out on the other side of the door just before she had unlocked it, Susie hadn't bothered looking through the peephole, either.

"Kind of careless of you, don't you think?" Ryan

asked, coming in. "Just opening the door like that without bothering to see who it was first?"

Her careless shrug had the neckline of the jersey sliding off to one side, exposing a bare shoulder as it hung on her, askew. "I had a feeling it was you."

The simple statement caught him off guard. "Why?" he asked. "Am I that predictable?"

He used to be. For that small island of time that they had been together, his reactions had been very predictable. But he had lost his predictability, not to mention any ability to actually feel something other than anger, since then.

"No, I just had a feeling." Since he had come in, she closed the door and flipped the lock into place, mainly out of habit. "Besides, Conway didn't growl." She nodded toward the black-and-white border collie on the floor, who was lying so flat he almost blended in with the rug. "You might recall, he's generally not too keen on strangers coming up to my door."

Conway had been a puppy back then, one she had rescued from an animal shelter less than a month before they first met.

"I recall he was a lot more energetic back then." Squatting down next to him, Ryan petted the dog. "How old is he now?"

There was affection in her eyes when Susie looked down at her pet. "Conway's almost twelve—and he likes to save his energy for things that count."

"Don't we all, boy?" Ryan said, nodding as he ran his hand along the animal's muzzle.

The dog perked up a little, then licked Ryan's fingers by way of a greeting before putting his head down again.

His tail thumped a few more times against the floor. And then, just like that, the dog was fast asleep again.

Ryan observed the process with fascination. "He really drops off, doesn't he?" he asked the woman who had just knelt down across from him. Amusement curved his mouth.

"Gotta get those naps in when he can," Susie responded.

She reached over to pet her beloved confidant and companion. She had poured out her heart to the dog— and only the dog—when she'd received the letter from Ryan that had broken that heart into a million pieces. And she could have sworn at the time that Conway seemed to sense what she was going through. In the days following her receipt of the letter, Conway hardly left her side. He seemed to know that she was suffering because of the breakup. Because she had no way of calling Ryan to find out why he had written what he had.

Conway had been there when she first learned of the consequences that arose from falling in love with Ryan—and the price she was forced to pay.

Her mother had been privy to that part of it, to the consequences and what came afterward, but at the time that couldn't be helped. Although she dearly loved her mother, some things she would have rather kept to herself. That had been one of them.

Because they were both petting the dog at the same time—a slightly smaller than medium-size dog—it was one of those inevitable things one of them should have foreseen happening sooner or later.

It happened sooner.

Susie's fingers brushed up against his. She pulled her hand back as if she'd touched fire, then chided herself for reacting like a pubescent teenager instead of a mature adult woman with a master's degree in criminology and an entire criminal investigative department to command.

"He's saving up his strength for the more important things," Susie added matter-of-factly, doing her best to cover up her momentary lapse.

She was fairly certain that Ryan had seen her involuntary shiver the second they had inadvertently made contact.

Rising, she deliberately ignored the hand Ryan offered to help her to her feet. For a split second, she avoided eye contact. She was actually looking at the wall above his head as she said, "Since you're here, it saves me the trouble of having to call you."

Ryan's focus returned to Greta and the case and he was instantly alert. "Something new come up?" he asked hopefully.

"Not quite," Susie confessed. She didn't want Ryan getting his hopes up. "Let's just say something new on something old."

What the hell was that supposed to mean? It sounded like some kind of a riddle. "Let's say something a little clearer than that," he suggested tersely.

Susie started again. "After you left the lab, I took another look at the crime scene photos. Specifically, at the victim's face."

He didn't see how that could have helped. "Okay. And...?" Ryan let his voice trail off, waiting for her to fill in the missing words and shed a little light on where she was going with this.

"And the expression on his face was shock," Susie told him. "Pure, unadulterated shock." And what she was going to say to him next was based on that.

"Getting shot in the gut'll do that to a man," Ryan commented wryly.

Ryan wasn't getting it, she thought. Susie gave it another try. "I'm talking about shock like he suddenly realized that something was wrong."

"Something *was* wrong," he said impatiently. "Greta shot him. I still don't see how his expression is some sort of a revelation," he told Susie, waiting for the new twist part.

Realizing that she wasn't making herself clear, Susie gave it one more try. "No, not as in shock that the woman he'd been working so closely with would suddenly turn on him and shoot him, shock as in the person who was shooting him wasn't the person that he thought she was."

Ryan shook his head, as if the simple action could help clear it and make sense of what she was saying. It didn't. "And the difference is…?"

Patiently, Susie explained it to him. "The difference is that the person who shot him *looked* like Greta but wasn't Greta." There was no flash of enlightenment across Ryan's face so she kept on explaining the theory she was developing to attempt to explain what might have transpired. "Your sister's a very pretty woman, but she's not one-of-a-kind-unique pretty. It wouldn't be hard to resemble Greta enough to be able to pass as her—if someone wasn't paying strict attention."

Much as he wished he could just go along with what Susie was saying, the way he saw it, her explanation left out one very crucial—and damning—piece of the puzzle.

"And the DNA?" Ryan pressed. "The DNA *you* verified over and over again? How does that turn out to be the same as Greta's if the person who shot Rodgers and did all those random acts of vandalism *wasn't* Greta?"

"I'm still working on that," Susie admitted, seemingly not as daunted as Ryan thought she might be, given the circumstances. "You'll be the first to know when I come up with something. You want anything to drink?" she offered, moving away from the sleeping dog on the floor in front of them.

What he caught himself wanting was a tall, cool drink of her, but he knew better than to say that and he was grateful that his internal censor had kept the words from reaching his lips. He'd completely lost the right to do anything other than repent when it came to matters involving Susie that were even remotely personal.

"No, I'd better not," he finally told Susie. "I just might not stop at one," he added honestly. "But you go ahead if you want."

She laughed softly, shaking her head at his instruction. "Haven't you heard? Drinking alone is a sure sign of a problem drinker." Not to mention that if she drank, she might let her guard down and say all the things to him that she had kept bottled up within her for a very long time.

"Okay, back to Greta," she declared with feeling in order to keep herself from veering off track and saying or doing something she was bound to regret. "I know what the evidence says, but none of this makes any sense," she insisted. "*Why* would Greta suddenly do all these insane things?"

She faced Ryan squarely now, treating him like a witness rather than a police detective. "Did anything traumatic happen recently to set her off?" she asked him. "You'd know that better than I would. Did your father suddenly decide to cut her off or did your mother get into an argument with her, saying she was making a huge mistake marrying Mark Stanton?"

"No and no," Ryan replied, answering each of the two questions separately.

Susie had more. "All right, did Greta suddenly have some kind of a meltdown?"

Again Ryan shook his head and said, "No."

There was another possible explanation for Greta's sudden unbalanced behavior. "Has she ever been diagnosed with a mental illness?"

"Not that I know of. Greta's the most levelheaded person that I know."

"Then I stand by what I said," Susie reiterated. "Greta's suddenly turning on a man she worked with and actually shooting him just doesn't make any sense. She's not an irrational person."

"Maybe Rodgers caught her by surprise and came on to her," he suggested. "When she rebuffed him, he just came on stronger and wouldn't take no for an answer."

She could see that scenario—all except for the ending that Ryan was heading for. "A simple slap, or even a well-placed jab with her knee comes to mind. Why grab a handgun and shoot him?" she asked. "Greta struck me as someone with a healthy respect for life."

"You think someone's framing her?" Even as he asked the question, he wanted an alternative to Greta being guilty so badly that he seriously began to entertain the idea, even though logically it made no sense at all.

"It'd be tricky, but it could be done. Does your sister have any enemies?" she asked.

Ryan shook his head. "Not that I know of, but I'm not really all that close to her anymore," he had to admit.

Ryan regarded the situation for a long moment, mentally mapping out his next move. "Maybe I'll put that question to her so-called loving fiancé."

"The same man who hasn't been to see her once in the five days she's been in jail, at least not as of an hour ago?" Susie asked, unable to keep the contempt out of her voice.

To satisfy her own curiosity, she had asked to see the precinct's sign-in ledger. No one had been by to see Greta except for Ryan during the entire length of her incarceration.

In Susie's fierce opinion, a leech like Mark Stanton should be kicked to the curb instantly.

Much as it pained him to come out on the side of a man he found himself loathing, in all fairness Ryan had to point out, "I don't think he even knows she's in the holding cell. Greta refuses to call anyone and tell them where she is."

"Being stubborn isn't a bad trait," Susie pointed out in Greta's defense—and possibly her own, as well. "Sometimes, that's the only way things get done around here."

"I never said it was a bad thing," Ryan told her. For just a moment, their eyes met and held and he felt things stirring within him. Things that shouldn't be stirred, not for either one of them.

Ryan abruptly rose to his feet. "Maybe I'd better go."

She knew she should just nod and let him go. That would have been the smart thing to do. Heaven knew it would be for the best because every second Ryan was here like this just seemed to wear down her resistance a little more, even though he probably had no idea what he was doing to her. But she just couldn't keep letting things go. Somewhere along the way, she had to take a stand, draw a line in the sand.

Or yell out the single word. "Why?"

Realizing how shouting that had to sound like an accusation—which, in truth, it was—Susie quickly changed the import of her words by adding, "Did I say something wrong?"

"No, you didn't say anything wrong," he assured her. And then, because she continued looking at him for an explanation for his abrupt departure, he fumbled and told her the truth, something he had meant to keep to himself. Something that, once said, gave him away. "It's—it's your perfume."

Susie looked at him in confusion. "Perfume? I'm not wearing any perfume."

"Cologne, then," he corrected in helpless frustration. "Whatever it is, it's the same one you used to wear, and for some reason, it just seems stronger tonight."

More seductive tonight, he added silently. The truth of it was, the scent he detected was clearly getting to him. It was undermining his senses—making him, in effect, crazy.

Crazy about her.

Or at least more than he already was.

"I'm not wearing cologne, either," Susie informed him.

She made sure she kept busy all the time. Things like remembering to spray on cologne somehow just fell through the cracks. It had never actually made her priorities list to begin with.

"It might be the soap I use," she suggested, unable to think of any other possibility. "It's the same one I've been using ever since I was a kid," she added, thinking that was probably what he was referring to. Nothing else suggested itself to her. "Maybe that's it."

"Maybe," he agreed. Ryan moved toward the door, more for her sake than his own. Susie followed him, remaining much too close to him for his comfort. "Look, I'd better go before…"

"Before?" she repeated. When he made no effort to add any words of explanation to the sentence that was dangling between them, she asked, "Before what?"

Why wasn't he opening the door? Crossing the threshold? Making his getaway? Why did he keep on standing here, as if his feet were glued to the rug?

"Before I do something I shouldn't."

It was a full-out warning to her.

Her brain fairly screamed, *Run!* But her feet remained where they were, firmly planted on her floor. Her heart began to beat a little faster as her eyes met his. Her own voice sounded almost surreal to her as she asked, "And that is…?"

His eyes never left hers. "Do I really have to spell it out?"

It was, she knew, a rhetorical question. Even so, she had to answer, "Yes."

The look in her eyes broke through the last flimsy wall he had surrounding his swiftly weakening self-control.

"Oh, damn it, woman, you should have just let me walk out the door," he told Susie, surrendering to the huge crying need he felt growing within him like some sort of unbridled storm—a storm gaining in breadth and momentum with each moment that went by.

The next second, the yearning within his soul had engulfed him and exploded.

Ryan was as much its prisoner as he was hers.

After pulling Susie to him, his mouth came down on hers and he kissed her the way he had fantasized about kissing her for the past four years, from the first moment their paths had crossed again.

For longer than that.

Very possibly from the moment he had forced himself to write that letter to her, ending, he now fully realized, the best damn thing that had ever happened to him.

Her.

Somewhere in his head, he had attempted to convince himself that his past actions had all been for the best. Just as he tried to fool himself now by saying that all he wanted was to kiss her just one more time and then he could walk away.

But it was a lie and he knew it.

Because kissing her one more time was the reason that he discovered he *couldn't* walk away. Kissing her once made him want to kiss her again.

And again.

And again.

Each kiss was hotter, more ardent, more demanding than the one that had come before it.

Each kiss lasted longer, pulled him in closer, made him want her that much more.

Things became blurred. For now, he felt no shame in the fact that he was aware of kissing her as if his very life depended on it, aware of her softness yielding to him, melding against the hardening contours of his body.

He became aware of his blood heating and rushing through his veins. Became aware that his last ounce of resistance had been shredded into tiny, microscopic pieces. Became acutely aware of the fact that the entire universe began and ended right here, with this woman, inside this kiss.

He heard her breath becoming louder, bordering on being almost erratic.

The very sound excited him almost beyond limits. He hadn't thought that was possible, but then, he hadn't thought that he would ever be able to kiss her again, either.

Drawing his mouth away from hers, he wanted to give Susie a chance to say "no." To push him away the way she should. To put him in his place, which would have been tantamount to hell if he had to be there without her. But she had the right to do that and he deserved anything she wanted to do to him.

He really wanted to give her that chance, to actually *be* noble for once in his life instead of just pretending to himself.

But the second he drew his lips away from hers, the volume of his hunger almost immediately consumed him and he began to kiss every other part of her. Her neck, her cheeks, her eyes. Every available part of her, and more and more of her was available to him as she melted into his being.

Ryan pushed her jersey up over her head, tossing it aside like an inconsequential rag. His eyes feasted on what he had uncovered.

She was, he decided without any reservations, magnificent. His hands felt almost clumsy as they slipped over her breasts, taking possession.

Her sigh of surrender undid him entirely.

CHAPTER TWELVE

THE DOG MADE a noise, as if protesting the fact that he was an unwilling, albeit temporary spectator who had been roused from his sleep by the movements and noises coming from his owner.

The border collie's furry eyebrows rose, first one, then the other. And then, the next moment, Conway's eyebrows had returned to their dormant state, as had he. The dog had gone back into the arms of sleep, content to be there, away from the madness of strange humans.

Susie saw Conway's momentary movement out of the corner of her eye and was grateful that the dog had gone back to sleep. She was afraid that the slightest interruption would cause Ryan to rethink his actions and stop what he was doing—and she didn't want him to stop. She felt as if she was on fire and needed for this to burn through to its natural conclusion.

Having been ignited—admittedly it had taken very little to get her to this heightened, extremely sensitive state—she matched Ryan movement for movement, caress for caress.

Passionate kiss for passionate kiss.

She was well aware that they were swiftly stoking one another's fires and that, very quickly, they would be bringing those fires to their exceedingly logical conclusions.

She wanted this to go on forever. At the same time, her body felt as if it was begging for that final explosion, that final moment where absolutely everything was right with the world and nothing would interfere with that.

Nothing would ever be wrong again.

She'd been dressed skimpily to begin with and Ryan had separated her from her shorts and jersey in less than a heartbeat. Getting him out of his clothes had taken longer, but she was more than a little inspired and there had been absolutely no resistance forthcoming from either his belt or the zipper on his jeans.

Or him.

She couldn't even remember when or how his boots had come off. All she was really aware of, beyond the hunger swiftly gnawing away at her, was that they were both naked, dressed only in their own desires and mingled traces of sweat.

And then, without any further impedance, the hunger burst out in full force on both sides.

Somehow, again without any sort of clear recollection, they had managed to wind up in her bedroom.

That had probably been Ryan's doing, she'd thought later. It was so like him to attempt to give her a small measure of privacy—away from the front window and the dog—and to provide her with some simple comforts. The bed was wide and a great deal more comfortable than the living room floor or even the sofa.

They took turns as to who did what to whom.

It had rapidly turned into a game of one-upmanship. Except that, though nothing was actually said, no audible words actually exchanged, they both knew that it wasn't a game.

But even so there was most obviously an unspoken goal and that was being the one who could give the most amount of pleasure.

That was one of the things she had loved about Ryan. He was a kind, selfless lover, putting her needs above his own. Making her feel cherished and beautiful without saying so much as a single word out loud. It was in the way he looked at her, in the way he touched her. In the way he made love to each and every part of her.

It was the memory of this that she had tried so hard to bury.

And this was what she remembered.

Whenever she had thought of Ryan, she tried to cling to the memory of the pain she had felt when she had read his letter and realized he had abandoned her. Abandoned her just when she needed him most.

But though the pain had been strong, it didn't serve as a barrier, because it dissolved whenever she remembered what they'd had. The glorious way he could make her feel in just an instant. Just because he was there.

As she gave herself up to this wondrous sensation, she knew that no matter where she went, no matter who she met and who she thought she loved, this much would remain constant: that Ryan would always be the love of her life.

The only man she could ever love.

HE LOST HIMSELF in her. He couldn't help it. He wasn't and had never been the kind of man who lived for his next conquest, for the next challenge that crossed his path. Sex had never been a priority for him—except with her. If this had been anyone else but her, anyone else but Susie, he could have stopped it before it had come to this.

Hell, he wouldn't have ever *started* this.

But there was something about this woman that reduced him to a mass of worshipful needs. There always had been, right from the very beginning.

As urgent as these needs were, Ryan managed to hold himself in check enough to go slower than his body demanded. He wanted Susie to know that this was special—that *she* was special. And making love with her in this even tempo was the only way he had of showing her.

But with all his good intentions, there were human limits and he had come to his.

Kissing her lips over and over again, he gathered Susie beneath him. With his heart pounding madly—in rhythm with hers—he raised his head just enough to look at her face, a face that, years ago, had become the center of all his dreams.

He saw her eyes flutter open, as if she could actually *feel* his eyes on her. The moment she looked at him, his eyes held hers.

And then he made them one.

Time froze.

And then, slowly to begin with, they began to move in concert, each mimicking the other as anticipation gave way to sensation and a surge pushed through them both that was beyond description.

Sharing the moment, heartbeats intertwined, arms tightening around each other, they let the euphoria sweep them away.

SLOWLY, EVER SO SLOWLY, the warm mists receded, slipping off into the darkness.

He didn't want to leave, not her, not this magical place they had created together. Even so, he knew he should. There were so many things demanding his attention, demanding his time. Not the least of which was the dilemma his sister was in.

But that all required his getting out of bed. Leaving

Susie. And he didn't want to. Because once he did, once he allowed the world to come in, the moment, *this* moment, would be gone. And he was afraid of losing it, of losing her.

So he lay there, one arm tucked loosely around her, holding Susie to him, absorbing her warmth, breathing in her essence.

"There is a scent, you know," he whispered softly against her hair when she stirred against him. "I don't know if it's your shampoo, your soap—or just you—but there definitely is a scent about you. Honeysuckle and roses," he identified, taking a guess. "Or maybe magnolias," he corrected, then laughed at his own indecisiveness. "Flowers really aren't my strong suit," he admitted to her.

He felt Susie's mouth curving into a smile against his chest. Sunshine spread out along his skin just beneath her lips.

"That's okay," she told him, her warm breath against his chest causing the muscles in his stomach to tighten almost into a knot. "You have a great many other talents."

Raising herself up on her elbow, she looked at Ryan, knowing that she couldn't make too much of what had just happened. It would be like trying to capture an elusive hummingbird by closing her hand over it. That would crush its essence.

Still, she leaned her chin against the hand that was splayed across his chest, her eyes on his, and quietly asked, "What kept you?"

He had no idea why that sounded so sexy to him. Or why just the sight of her smile had another strong surge of desire pulsing through him.

Ryan didn't bother trying to analyze it, or attempting to unravel the mystery of what there was between them that seemed so strong.

He just gave himself up to it.

Cupping the back of her head, Ryan brought his mouth down to hers and caught himself all but devouring her lips.

The rest was all too predictable, and too delicious, to attempt to dissect. He'd much rather just lose himself in the wonder that was Susie.

RYAN SUPPRESSED A groan as he reluctantly opened his eyes. Annoying rays of daylight were attempting to pry their way into Susie's bedroom.

Daylight.

And Conway.

The border collie had obviously decided to check whether his mistress's visitor was still here. When Ryan did open his eyes, he found the dog had his head on the comforter, his snout just barely a few inches away from his own face. The dog appeared to be taking measure of him.

Ryan ran his hand over the top of the dog's head. Conway accepted the tribute.

"I don't remember your dog being a voyeur ten years ago," Ryan said by way of a greeting when he realized that Susie was already awake and watching him.

"He's settled into a routine—my routine, actually— and he's not used to anyone being in my bed but me," she said, trying to explain why Conway was staring at him so intently.

"Good to know," Ryan murmured. His mouth curved just a touch. "He's pretty protective of you."

"He's my security system," she answered, leaning over to give the border collie an affectionate pat on the head. "Right now, I think he's hungry," she guessed.

When Susie had reached over to the dog, the sheet that she had tucked against her had slipped, treating him to a view of her nude upper torso. Ryan found it utterly impossible to look away, despite any fleeting noble intentions on his part.

"So am I," Ryan murmured.

Susie caught his meaning instantly and suppressed a laugh.

"I'm talking about being hungry for food," she pointed out.

"Oh," Ryan acknowledged, showing just the proper note of embarrassment—although in reality he was experiencing something entirely different.

Susie knew exactly what he was thinking.

"You want to use the shower first, or should I?" she asked in an attempt to start her day.

His eyes slid over her body, a look of unabashed lust all but radiating from him. "I was hoping, in the name of conservation, we could take one together."

"Conservation?" she repeated as if the word needed to be closely examined. "Correct me if I'm wrong, but there's no water shortage in this state."

He pulled her over against him. "Pretend," he whispered seductively against her ear.

IT WAS A while before she was finally dressed and able to get into the kitchen to make him breakfast.

Humming softly to herself, padding about barefoot in the kitchen, she had just taken out her cast-iron skillet and opened the refrigerator in a search for ingredients when the doorbell rang.

Susie glanced at her watch. "Who would be on my doorstep at seven thirty in the morning?" she murmured audibly under her breath.

"Only one way to find out," Ryan informed her cheerfully.

"Wise guy," she accused as she wiped her hands on the first towel she picked up.

Walking into the living room, where her evening had in essence begun last night, Susie headed toward the front door.

Realizing that she wasn't going to even bother looking through the peephole—for a CSI, Susie was almost blissfully naive at times—Ryan was right beside her. If there *was* someone unsavory on her front step, he wanted to be there to protect her. He had his doubts about how effective Conway could actually be beyond growling and baring his teeth. Unless, of course, the dog pushed the so-called unsavory type onto the ground and then subsequently fell asleep on him, Ryan thought, amusement curving his mouth.

Her hand on the doorknob, Susie looked toward him, bemused by his close proximity. "Playing bodyguard now?" she teased.

Ryan made no effort to dispel the image. "Why not? Yours is a body that's really worth guarding."

Her smile went all the way up to her eyes before it widened on her generous mouth. "Why, Detective, is that a compliment?"

He laughed, pressing a kiss to the top of her head. "Absolutely."

She'd been teasing, but his answer did warm her heart. For good reason. "That's the first time you ever gave me one, you know."

He was about to contest that, but then, reflecting, Ryan realized that she was right.

"I was an idiot back then," he told her with feeling. And he meant it. It would have cost him nothing to tell her what was in his heart. How she made him feel.

He had allowed too many opportunities to slip by. He wouldn't anymore.

Susie laughed softly as her eyes all but delved into him. "You'll get no argument from me," she assured Ryan solemnly.

He knew she was referring to his having sent her that breakup letter—and at this point, he had to agree with her.

The doorbell rang again, more insistently this time. Whoever was on the other side of the door was now leaning on the button.

The jarring sound went all through Susie and she shivered.

She saw suspicion enter Ryan's eyes. He was staring straight ahead at the door. And then he motioned for her to unlock it, his right hand holding his service weapon drawn and ready.

"Just who do you think is ringing the doorbell?" Susie asked in a whisper, amused. Ryan looked as if he was ready to take down a member of some organized-crime syndicate.

"You can never be too careful," he responded in the same hushed whisper. "Open it," Ryan ordered in no uncertain terms, the expression on his face as dark as she had ever seen it.

Taking a deep breath, Susie flipped open the two locks on her front door. Then, bracing herself, she pulled open the door.

She heard Ryan cocking his weapon at the exact same moment.

The person on her doorstep sucked in their breath at the same time that she did.

And then, seeing who it was, Susie's mouth dropped open.

"Mother!" she exclaimed.

CHAPTER THIRTEEN

SHE HAD A master's degree in criminology, was a thirty-year-old top forensic expert who headed her own CSI team within the Tulsa PD and had managed, through diligent, tireless work, to crack a number of exceedingly difficult cases. Yet, even so, in less than two seconds in her mother's presence, Susie felt as if she was an awkward ten-year-old child in mismatched shoes.

Her mouth was completely dry as she cried, "Mom, what are you doing here?"

Short and petite, Elizabeth Howard's ordinarily bright, sunny face darkened instantly as she gazed right past her daughter's head and straight at the dark-haired young man standing just behind Susie.

"Apparently, having a heart attack. What's *he* doing here?" Elizabeth demanded, then immediately held up her hand, as if warding off her daughter's answer. "No, never mind. Don't say it. I don't want to hear it." Her brown eyes narrowed, boring holes into the object of her fierce anger. "I can figure it out for myself."

"Mrs. Howard," Ryan began, having absolutely no idea what he was going to say to follow up on his opening salutation.

He never got the opportunity even to shakily make an attempt.

Elizabeth, far more diminutive than her daughter,

went after him like a piranha that had been on a forced starvation diet for the past month.

"You have one hell of a nerve, showing your face here after what you've done, Ryan Colton—"

"Mother!" Susie cried, raising her voice in a desperate attempt to drown her mother out until she could find a way to get the woman to subdue her temper.

"No, it's okay," he told Susie. Turning toward her mother, he said, "Mrs. Howard, you have every right to be angry at me."

Elizabeth's brown eyes had narrowed into almost fiery slits. "I don't need your *permission* to think of you as the scum of the earth, a heartless bastard who doesn't even have the decency—"

"That's enough, Mother," Susie warned, an angry edge entering her voice.

There were equal amounts of anger and pity in her eyes, both wrapped in a mother's love, when Elizabeth looked at her daughter.

"No, it's not enough. It'll never be enough," Elizabeth said hotly. "Are you forgetting that he *left* you? Left you and then wrote a Dear John letter to break up with you instead of facing you and telling you in person like a man?" The daggers returned as she turned her glare back toward Ryan. "But then, a real man wouldn't have run out on a woman when she was pregnant with his baby, now would he?"

"Mother!" Susie cried, utterly appalled that her mother would have just shouted out her secret so blatantly after Elizabeth had promised never to say anything to anyone, not even her own husband. This was supposed to have been just between the two of them.

"Wait, what?" Dumbfounded, Ryan stared at the

woman he had just spent the night with. There had to be some sort of a mistake. "You were *pregnant*?" he asked her, stunned.

Elizabeth snorted, not taken in by what she viewed as his act for a moment. "Oh, like you didn't know," she jeered.

"He *didn't* know, Mother," Susie insisted, coming to Ryan's defense.

Just like that, his whole world felt as if it was imploding around him, collapsing in on itself, leaving him to free-float through space like a jettisoned piece of trash. Ryan stared at the woman he thought he knew. "Why didn't you tell me?" he demanded.

He had to ask? Seriously?

Anger became her shield. "I wasn't about to go crawling after you when you clearly didn't want me enough to even write letters to while you were away fighting overseas."

She was bright enough to figure out why he'd had to do it, Ryan thought. "I didn't want you to feel as if your whole life was on hold. I really wanted you to move on."

But none of that, noble or otherwise, mattered anymore.

"A baby," he said, the very word feeling so strange on his tongue. Why hadn't he seen it? Why hadn't she said anything once they had reentered each other's lives? Numb, confused, shocked, Ryan heard himself asking, "What did we have?"

"We didn't," Susie replied stoically, staring straight ahead at the wall above Ryan's head. It was the only way she could even get herself to say the words that were associated with the most awful event that had ever happened to her in her whole life. "I lost her," she finally added, her voice so low that he had to strain in order to hear her.

"Her?" Ryan repeated, feeling shell-shocked and numb at the same time. The words dripped from his lips. "It was a girl?"

"It was a girl," Susie confirmed, her voice only the tiniest bit louder than when she had initially told him about the loss.

Something twisted inside his chest, skewering the organ that was supposed to be his heart. "Oh, God, Susie, I'm so sorry."

Elizabeth's expression indicated that she didn't believe him for a moment. "Yeah, right. Easy to say now that it's all over. I'm sorry, honey," she told Susie. "I don't buy the crocodile tears. He should have been here for you when you needed him."

"You're right. I should have," Ryan said with sincerity to her mother.

There was nothing he could ever say that would make up for what had happened. In all honesty, he had no idea how to ever set things right. Ryan felt as if his very presence was only serving to agitate her.

It was certainly agitating her mother.

"Look, I think that I'd better go," Ryan told her in a subdued voice just before he turned on his heel and walked out the front door.

"Ryan—" Susie began, starting to hurry after him. She was stopped by her mother, who caught her by the arm when she tried to hurry past the woman.

"Let him go, Susie," Elizabeth ordered. "He wasn't here for you when it mattered, and he has no business sniffing around you now."

Susie turned to confront her mother face-to-face. "Mother, I said he didn't know."

Elizabeth frowned. "How convenient. He didn't know because he cut off all communication with you."

Susie sighed. She could see that this argument would go around in the same tired old circles.

Even so, she was bound to defend Ryan, especially after what had just happened last night.

"He had his reasons," she told her mother, in effect defending the very action she had taken apart and scrutinized so many times in her heart herself.

Elizabeth laughed shortly. "Yeah, it's called self-preservation, so that he was free to go tomcatting around anytime he wanted to."

Susie closed her eyes, seeking strength. "Ryan's not like that."

"Honey, they're *all* like that," her mother maintained with authority. "Except your father, of course, but that's probably only because he knows what I'm capable of doing if I ever found out," she said without any particular fanfare.

"Mother," Susie said pointedly, "Ryan lost a child, too."

Elizabeth refused to be swayed or impressed. Most of all, she refused to view anything about the man who had broken her daughter's heart in a favorable light.

Susie could see her mother digging in. Susie had inherited this stubborn streak from her. "They're not all alike," she insisted.

The laugh was a little harsher this time. Elizabeth Howard was not a woman given to illusions. She dealt in reality.

"The one that isn't is on display in the Smithsonian,

under glass," Elizabeth informed her sarcastically. She put her fisted hands on her hips, as if that could somehow help her understand her daughter's flawed thinking. "Why would you even let that man inside your house?" she asked.

Susie paused for a second, trying to find a way to phrase her answer acceptably. What she wanted to say was *Because I love him,* but she knew that would only lead to another argument, which would, in turn, really upset her mother.

So instead, she said, "We were going over a case."

Elizabeth looked at her knowingly. "Is that what they're calling it these days? A case?"

"Mother, it wasn't like that," she said, knowing that if she told her mother the real truth, she would never hear the end of it until the day that one of them was dead. "His sister is accused of murder," Susie emphasized.

Elizabeth appeared to perk up for a moment. "Do you think I could hire her to off Colton before she's sent away?"

If she didn't know any better, Susie would have sworn that her mother was serious. "Mother, please stop talking like a grade-B TV procedural and be serious."

Elizabeth looked at her in all sincerity and said, "I *was* being serious."

Susie threw up her hands. It was no use. "What are you doing here, anyway?" she asked, asking the same question she had put to her mother a hundred years ago, when her mother had first shown up at her door. "And please, this time spare me the dramatics."

"I could say the same thing," Elizabeth told her. "I tried to call you last night and you didn't answer your phone."

She must have accidentally turned it off when she and Ryan had started rocking each other's worlds, Susie realized. Retaining a poker face, she told her mother, "I could have been working on a case."

It was a plausible enough excuse. "That's what I told myself. But then I called again this morning and you still didn't answer."

She remembered turning on her phone this morning. The call must have come in while she and Ryan had been in the shower together.

Sparing her mother the longer version, Susie simply said, "I must have been in the shower then."

She saw the skeptical look entering her mother's eyes. "You must have been," the woman agreed without really agreeing.

Despite this little frustrating episode, she really did hate worrying her mother. She could well imagine how she was feeling. "Why were you trying to reach me?" she asked.

"For no other reason than because I couldn't reach you," Elizabeth told her, falling back on cyclical reasoning. Elizabeth frowned now, glancing toward the shut door and obviously thinking of the man who had just gone through it. "Are you going to be all right?" Elizabeth asked, her voice sounding far more compassionate than it had a moment earlier.

Susie shrugged, as if physically attempting to shed the question. "Why wouldn't I be?"

By the expression on Elizabeth's face, a dozen reasons obviously came flooding back to her. Being a mother didn't just stop after eighteen years. It lasted for a lifetime.

"Alphabetically, chronologically or by order of magnitude?" Elizabeth asked.

In response, Susie leaned over and kissed her mother's cheek. "I love you, Mom. There're times I really want to strangle you, but I love you."

"Ditto," Elizabeth replied, her expression giving nothing away. She debated for a moment before speaking again. "Susie," her mother said in a quiet, firm voice, "I want you to stay away from Ryan."

Susie raised her chin stubbornly. She wasn't going to get pulled into an argument with her mother about this, she wasn't. But she wasn't about to let her mother steamroll over her, either. "Can't, Mom. We work together, remember?"

Elizabeth sighed and rolled her eyes. "All right then, work together," she allowed. "But for heaven sakes, don't play together."

Okay, enough was enough, Susie thought. "Mom, please don't take this the wrong way, but butt out. This is none of your business, really," she told the older woman emphatically.

"I'm sorry, but it is my business," she contradicted. "When the doctor cut the umbilical cord that joined us, she did not cut the part that worried about you, that wanted only the best for you. Sorry, but there's nothing you can do about it. You're stuck with that. And, furthermore, I intend to go on worrying about you and wanting the best for you. The latter, by the way, is definitely not Ryan Colton."

It was getting late, and Susie could practically *feel* the work piling up on her desk even as she stood here. "I've got to go to work," she told her mother, picking up her purse from the table by the front door. "So if there's nothing else—"

Elizabeth held up her index finger. "There's just one thing."

"Yes?" she asked, struggling to suppress her weariness.

"Be careful," Elizabeth warned her, concern etched deep into her features.

"Always," Susie assured her.

"I wish I could believe that," Elizabeth said under her breath. It was still loud enough for Susie to hear. "Call me later," Elizabeth instructed her daughter.

Preoccupied, trying to think of a way to prove Greta innocent, Susie responded to her mother's remark with a murmured "Uh-huh."

Elizabeth would have none of it—and she was not above making threats when it suited her purpose. "Or I'll come over."

She would, too. Her mother had already proven that. "I'll call, I'll call."

"Good girl." Elizabeth paused in the doorway for a moment, looking at her daughter, her only child whom she loved intently with all her heart. "In case I haven't been clear enough, that's an order, Susie," Elizabeth said just before she left.

Susie's sigh was audible even through the closed door after she shut it.

A CHILD.

She'd been pregnant with a child.

His child, and he hadn't even known of its existence until it didn't exist anymore.

The stark reality of that weighed oppressively on him. Ryan hardly remembered getting behind the steering wheel of his car. Barely remembered starting the car and pointing it toward the precinct.

Technically, he had enough time to make a quick pit stop at his house before he went into work. That would give him an opportunity to put on a fresh change of clothes, maybe get something to eat on the fly.

But all those niceties seemed beside the point and of no real interest to him.

A child.

He would have been a father if—

If.

A gut-wrenching, breath-stealing, double-barreled two-letter word that could and did make all the difference in the world to him.

If he had known…

If she had lived…

If.

Ryan blew out a ragged breath. There was no point in torturing himself. He *hadn't* known and now that he did, he couldn't do anything about it to change the circumstances. Couldn't do anything to make it up to Susie, or change the way things had played themselves out.

Last night had shown him that he wasn't over her. Would *never* be over her, and he might as well get used to that glaring fact of life. Some men could move on. Some men actually had more than one love of their life over the course of their existence.

And some men fell just once—and hard—never to experience that wonderful, surging, teeth-rattling feeling again.

He fell into the latter group and it was his misfortune that he hadn't done everything in his power to hold on to Susie, to remain in her life and not allow her to get away, when he had the chance.

Allow?

Hell, he hadn't "allowed," he had pushed, pushed her away with all his might, because he'd thought that was the right thing to do for both her *and* for him. A man worrying about the girl he left back home wasn't razor sharp. He wasn't at the top of his game and it took being at the top in order to attempt survival. Even then, it wasn't a done deal.

So he had chosen to shed everything that might have kept him from making it through the awful experience of war and thus, he had survived.

But survived for what?

To what end?

His life was filled from end to end with work, with making others safe so that they could sleep at night, while he went home to an empty house with an empty feeling in the pit of his stomach.

An emptiness that it seemed nothing, no amount of honor and duty, could fill. Somehow, it didn't seem as if he had managed to accomplish anything at all—other than hurting a woman who might very well have been, if things had gone well, the mother of his child.

The ache Ryan was feeling in the pit of his gut was almost indescribable.

He was here, at the precinct, he abruptly realized as he mechanically pulled into the parking lot.

Ryan couldn't remember how he'd got here.

It was as if the car had somehow known the way, he thought wryly.

Maybe, if he just threw himself into his work until

he could face and deal with what he'd just learned, he'd find a way to eventually come around.

Until then, it would be a matter of putting one foot in front of the other, taking one thought and hopefully linking it up to the next.

Provided he could think, of course. As of this moment, the chances of that were rather slim to none. Right now, his entire brain felt as if it was engulfed in some sort of a dense fog. He was unable to see his way clear to anything.

But then—

Ryan stopped abruptly as he realized, getting out of his vehicle, that he was standing only a few feet away from, and staring at, Susie's car.

Somehow, she had managed to have gotten here ahead of him.

How was that even physically possible? He'd driven here straight from her place.

It was enough to make a man feel as if he was irrevocably doomed.

CHAPTER FOURTEEN

HE SHOULD HAVE gone straight to his desk. He knew that.

But knowing and doing just weren't aligning themselves for Ryan lately. Instead of heading for the elevator and pressing the up button, or even just heading for
the stairs and going upstairs to the homicide division,
the way he did some mornings, when Ryan got to the
stairwell, he went down.

Down to the basement. Where the lab was.

Where *she* was.

He still couldn't believe that Susie had somehow managed to get to the precinct ahead of him. After all, he had
left her condo first, ahead of her. When he'd driven away,
she was still inside, with her mother, presumably still
being quizzed by the woman as to what she could have
possibly been thinking, spending the night with him.

Granted he hadn't driven hell-bent for leather, more
as if the car was on sedatives, but still, he should have
arrived here before she had.

Or at the very least, they should have arrived at the
same time, their paths crossing in front of the entrance
of the building.

Half in disbelief, half drawn as if by some sort of
mystical siren song, he went to the crime lab's main door.

The door was unlocked and standing open, as if his
presence had been anticipated.

Looking in, he saw her. Susie had just slipped on her white lab coat and was about to slide onto the stool right before her favorite piece of equipment—a state-of-the-art, ultra-high-powered microscope.

He saw her shoulders tense ever so slightly and knew she'd sensed him standing there. Because he didn't want to seem as if he was lurking, Ryan spoke up. "What are you doing here?"

Susie didn't look up. Whatever was on the slide seemed to command her full attention. "I work here, same as you."

Well, he hadn't come to gawk, he'd come to tell her something. Rather than retreat and wait until a later time, Ryan forced himself to speak.

"Listen, under the circumstances, if you'd rather have your assistant handling this case..." This wasn't coming out right and he tried again. "What I'm saying is that if you have a problem working with me, I get it. I understand."

Very slowly, Susie increased the magnification, just a whisper of a hairbreadth at a time. "I don't have a problem," she told him crisply. "Do you have a problem?"

"No," he answered. He hesitated, trying to find a tactful way to broach the matter he really wanted to talk about.

"Then let's get to work," she replied, her attention apparently still focused on the microscope in front of her.

He couldn't just pretend that he was still in the dark about her former pregnancy and miscarriage, that nothing had been said. When it came to personal matters, under ordinary circumstances, he tried to avoid direct conversations. He would usually just brush things off to the side until they resolved themselves one way or another.

But this was different.

This was far too important for him to pretend that it hadn't happened—or that he didn't know. They had to get this out into the light of day once and for all—and then hopefully clear the air as best as could be expected.

"Look," he began slowly, his tongue feeling like pure lead, "about what your mother said—"

No!

She raised her head away from the microscope and turned around on the stool.

They weren't going to go there. She refused even to entertain the idea of a discussion about the most sensitive topic of her life. Nothing could be gained from going over that painful territory. Certainly nothing would be changed.

"Never mind about my mother," she told him in a tone of voice he had never heard before. "We've got a lot of work to do if we're going to save your sister." Susie glanced at him when he didn't immediately respond or agree. "You remember your sister, don't you? Really cute, with long brown hair and a can-do attitude? Fortunately for her, she doesn't look a thing like you—ring any bells yet?" Susie asked, peering at his face.

Ryan stifled a surge of irrational anger. "Yeah, it does."

"Good." Susie got down to the salient part of the matter. "Because the more I think about it, the more things just don't gel for me. I don't think she's behind any of this. The first thing we need to do is to find a way to get those murder charges against Greta dropped. And we both agree that she's holding something back," she continued, her voice gaining momentum. "I think she was with someone and she's obviously unwilling to tell us who that was. Would she have confided in one of your brothers?" she asked, looking at Ryan for some kind of insight.

He shook his head. "They would have immediately come forward if she had—at least they would have come to me. Everyone in the family dotes on Greta."

"How about your mother? Would Greta have confided anything—say, maybe prewedding jitters or doubts and why she was having them—to your mother?" Susie felt that the key to Greta's silence had something to do with her pending wedding.

Again, he shook his head. "Everyone had been walking on eggshells around my mother ever since the incident."

That was the way he and the rest of the family referred to the attack his mother had suffered: the incident.

Abra Colton had regained consciousness slowly, and bit by bit, she'd remembered more of the day of her attack. He was fairly certain that his mother remembered everything, but he could see that she didn't want to talk about it. He didn't want to press her yet, not until he had to. But the truth of it was, he was beginning to feel as if he was running out of time.

There were definitely moments when he wasn't crazy about his job.

"Okay, then maybe one of her bridesmaids or her maid of honor would know if she was having second thoughts, or if something was off-kilter for Greta. *Someone* has to know something," she insisted.

Ryan read between the lines. "You think my sister

was fooling around with someone other than her fiancé," he guessed bluntly.

It sounded harsh, but these things did happen. "It is a possibility that can't be overlooked."

She knew Ryan would have said the same thing—if this hadn't about his little sister. But then he was the one who had brought Greta in and put her in a holding cell in the first place. Ryan didn't need to have his duty pointed out to him.

Ryan nodded stoically in response to what she had just said. "Okay, I'll go see if I can get any of her bridesmaids to break the code of silence and talk to me about this—if there is a 'this,'" he qualified.

He began to walk toward the exit and was caught off guard when he saw Susie taking off the lab coat she had just slipped on. The next moment, she had crossed over to him.

"What are you doing?"

The look she gave him said that was clearly self-explanatory. "I'm going with you. Why?"

He nodded toward the microscope as well as the other equipment on the granite counter. "I thought you said you had work to do."

"I do, but you were right. Harold can handle some of it." She knew the man was more than eager to flex his lab muscles. "You need backup," she told Ryan when he continued to regard her quizzically. "More than that, you need emotional support." She allowed a quick, quirky smile to momentarily curve her mouth. "I'd be the one to know all about that."

"Susie—" he began, completely at a loss as to what he could possibly say to her that would make an utterly horrible and painful episode in her life even the tiniest iota better.

"Shut up and walk, Colton," Susie ordered, waving her hand toward the hall and indicating that was where their next steps should take them. When Ryan did just that, moving ahead of her, she addressed his back, adding softly, "You don't have to say anything, you dummy. I understand."

He turned around then, a thousand unsaid things all there in his eyes as he looked at her, possibly searching for forgiveness, if not absolution.

"Susie," he began again, angst, apology and so much more vying for space in his voice.

"You're not walking," she reminded him.

Her tone, although not abrupt, told him she wasn't up for any further discussion of their issue at the moment—maybe never. But right now, it was enough for her to know that he wanted to address it.

Intent carried a great deal of weight with her.

He paused by the elevator. "Maybe I should have another go at Greta before we tackle the bridesmaids."

"Now, *there's* a lovely image," she cracked.

"Maybe if she sees you, she'll be more inclined to talk," Ryan speculated, a note of hope coming into his voice.

Susie gave a noncommittal shrug. "Can't hurt to try."

Retracing their steps back to the elevator rather than leaving the building, they went to the rear of the first floor where the holding cells were kept.

When Ryan requested that his sister be brought to the common area, where inmates were allowed visitors, the uniformed officer, an older man with gray streaks in his hair, appeared to be a little hesitant.

"Something wrong, Sergeant?" Ryan asked. There was nothing unusual about his request. Why was the sergeant acting as if there was glue on the soles of his shoes?

"Not wrong, sir, but the prisoner you requested brought to the common area is already there. She has a visitor, sir."

"You mean someone came by before?" Ryan asked, wanting to get what the officer was saying clear.

"No, now," the sergeant corrected. "She's in the common room talking to—" Pausing for a second, the sergeant looked back at the log to verify his information. "Mr. Stanton."

"Well, what do you know, Mark finally showed up. The lazy SOB certainly took his sweet time about it," Ryan muttered. There was no love lost between Ryan and his brother-in-law to be.

"No, it's not Mark Stanton," the sergeant corrected. "The name on the log is Tyler Stanton."

At the mention of the president of Stanton Oil, Ryan exchanged glances with Susie. Surprise melted into curiosity. Either way, he still needed access to his sister. "I need to see her, Sergeant."

"Very good, Detective," the sergeant obliged. "I'll just tell Mr. Stanton that he has to step aside and wait until—"

"No," Ryan said more forcefully than he intended. It stopped the officer in his tracks. "It might be useful to talk to my sister with Tyler there." Ryan could see that his idea sat very well with Susie.

"Okay, whatever you say, Detective." The sergeant led the way.

Walking into the common area, Ryan took little notice of the other prisoners who were seated at a handful of tables, talking to people from their former daily lives. For the most part, the former group seemed acutely aware that the latter were free to come and go just as they wished.

Ryan's attention was entirely focused on Greta and the man who was seated opposite her. From what he heard as he came closer, Tyler Stanton was taking her to task about something.

The first words Ryan heard were "Why didn't you call and tell me?"

Ryan automatically looked over his shoulder at Susie as a strong feeling of déjà vu washed over him.

"Sound familiar?" he asked her under his breath.

"A lot of people say that in here," she answered crisply, looking straight ahead rather than at him or any of the people at the tables.

"I didn't want to get you involved," Greta stressed in what could have amounted to a very low stage whisper. Her voice was so low that had he and Susie not been almost on top of the duo at the table, Ryan was fairly certain that he wouldn't have heard any of this exchange between his sister and her fiancé's brother.

He heard Susie clearing her throat and had a feeling that she was doing that deliberately, especially when Tyler almost jumped, indicating that he had been completely unaware that there was anyone there, listening to what he was saying to Greta.

When Tyler did realize who was there, his expression took on a whole new demeanor. He looked stunned, and somewhat annoyed, as well. Not at the intrusion, but over what he seemed to regard as an omission.

"You knew better." And then he turned in his chair

to face Ryan. "You should have been the one to call me the second she'd been arrested because you thought—" Tyler regrouped, his thoughts scrambling all over one another. "You can't possibly think that she killed that cowboy she was working with," he said to Ryan.

Ryan began the way he always did, citing the facts. "The evidence—"

Usually mild-mannered, for a moment, Tyler lost his temper, his complexion reddening from anger. "To hell with the evidence. She wasn't at the ranch when Rodgers was killed. She was—"

Horrified and clearly surprised, as if anticipating his next words, Greta cried, "Tyler, don't!" Swinging around to appeal to her brother, she begged, "Don't believe him. I don't know why he's doing this, but he's just trying to protect me."

"She's the one trying to protect *me*," Tyler contradicted.

Ryan sighed. This could go on for hours. "Would both of you just stop trying to protect one another and spit it out? What are you trying to say?" Ryan asked, looking from one to the other.

Susie was unable to hold her tongue any longer. "Isn't it obvious?" It was a statement rather than a question because it was certainly obvious to her. Since last night, it felt like all her thoughts were geared toward seeing relationships where none should have existed. After all, she couldn't help thinking, look at her own situation. She certainly shouldn't have allowed last night to happen, yet there was no way she could have humanly prevented it, feeling the way she did about Ryan. "They were with each other." The look she gave Greta was filled with understanding and sympathy. "And it's Mark you're trying to protect, isn't it?" she asked. Before Greta could answer, Susie continued as she warned the woman, "Don't. If you're attracted to Tyler, then you owe it to yourself to call off the wedding until you're absolutely sure about the direction you want your life to go in."

Ryan laughed shortly. "Well, there you go. Out of the mouths of babes," he said philosophically, indicating Susie.

"But it's not true," Greta cried. "He's making it up to keep me out of jail. Tyler wasn't with me," she insisted. "I was alone."

It was obvious that Ryan wasn't buying her protests. Maybe because he wanted to prove that she was innocent, but whatever the reason, he went with Susie's interpretation.

At the moment, his attention was focused exclusively on Tyler. "Now, just give me the short and sweet version—and remember, I want the truth. Were you with Greta during the time in question?"

"Yes," Tyler replied emphatically.

"Tyler—" Greta pleaded.

Ryan held his hand up, silencing his sister. He was still looking solely at the other man at the table. "From when to when?" he asked, wanting Tyler to pin the time down. He did, after all, need facts to back this up.

There was no hesitation in Tyler's voice as he answered the question put to him. "From nine in the evening until seven the following morning. We were—"

Ryan quickly held up his hand again, this time to prevent Tyler from continuing. "I don't need that part," he said, stopping Tyler before the latter could give him any further details. He might be the investigating detective on this case, but he was still Greta's brother and as far as he saw it, there was such a thing as too much information. At least, in this instance. "Short and sweet, remember?" he asked, referring to the format of the details he had requested. "You're willing to swear to what you just said?" he pressed.

"Absolutely," he said without any reservations.

"Tyler," Greta begged, "if nothing else, think of your reputation." She didn't want to be the reason that people walked way from his company or his family turned on him.

Especially since Tyler was lying.

"My reputation is a pretty paltry thing," he told her, "if it means that you have to sacrifice your life for it."

"Well, seeing as how your reputation for telling the truth in these parts is only second to that of George Washington," Ryan went on to assess, "I'd say that gives Greta a pretty damn good alibi." He turned to look at Greta. "But we're still facing that annoying so-called fact that you were supposedly seen in the area around the time in question. That means the eyewitness is either lying—"

"Or they saw someone who looks like Greta," Susie quickly interjected, tactfully omitting the fact that she had already raised the possibility of someone lying about seeing his sister earlier.

Drawing him away from the table, his sister and Tyler, Susie suggested, "Tell you what, why don't we go and question your mother next?" The second the words were out of her mouth, she saw the hesitant expression in his eyes. She knew he was thinking about upsetting his mother and was reluctant to do so. Ordinarily, she would be, too, but this was definitely not something that fell under the heading of "ordinary." "It's the only way we can start clearing Greta's name and get to the bottom of all this. The more information we have, the better our chances are of finding out what actually happened."

It all made sense. Ryan nodded. "You're right," he agreed.

"Of course I'm right. Tell you what. I'll even bring the eggshells."

He looked at her quizzically. "Come again?"

"You said everyone is walking around your mother as though they're treading on eggshells. I get that," she told him sympathetically. "Some people are more fragile than others. I don't want to upset her, I just want to find out why, according to what you've told me, she looks so nervous around Greta every time they're in the same room together when clearly, from all indications, your sister loves her and wouldn't do anything to hurt her for the world."

Ryan wanted to pin down her reasoning so he knew what he was dealing with. "You think it might be this Greta look-alike who's responsible for the attack?"

"Honestly?" Susie asked. When he nodded, she said, "I think we've had enough questions. It's time to look for some answers. And if we have to turn over some rocks and rattle some cages to do it, so be it. The truth is not always easy to get at, but in the long run, it'll be worth it."

Ryan couldn't have agreed more.

CHAPTER FIFTEEN

IT WAS HER first time at the main house on the Lucky C ranch and Susie had to admit that although she *thought* she was ready, she definitely was *not* prepared for the sight of the 11,000-square-foot brown-and-beige Oklahoma-stone house. Even the outside of the main house was overwhelming.

A circular flagstone driveway lead up to the impressive two-story building. It came with a grand outside staircase that in turn led up to a two-story open foyer.

"Be it ever so humble, there's no place like home," Susie murmured under her breath. She knew the Coltons were wealthy, but this gave wealthy a new meaning, at least for her.

Hearing her comment, Ryan laughed as he haphazardly parked his vehicle at the end of the driveway. "I guess it can be a little overwhelming at first," he agreed.

She slanted a glance in Ryan's direction. "You think?"

At any other time, he might have volunteered to give her a tour of the place, but right now, they both had something more pressing to attend to.

"C'mon, I think I know where my mother is," he told Susie, leading her inside.

"Mr. Ryan, I wasn't expecting you." The surprised greeting came from a silver-haired woman of medium stature. Trim, with gray eyes and her hair pulled back in a severe, tight bun, Edith Turner had been with the family for twenty years, and was in charge of keeping the household running as smoothly as a classic timepiece. It upset the woman greatly that so much turmoil had taken place recently under her watch. Her body posture indicated that she was being even more vigilant than usual.

"I wasn't expecting to be here, Edith," Ryan told the woman by way of a greeting. "Is Mother in the sunroom?" he asked.

Ryan noticed that the housekeeper was scrutinizing Susie, but the woman was much too polite to say anything beyond answering the question she was asked. "Yes, she seems to enjoy spending her mornings there."

Ryan nodded his thanks and made his way to that location.

Susie was right behind him. "She's not very friendly," she observed, glancing back at the woman they left in the foyer.

"She is once she gets to know you," Ryan assured her.

"So I guess she's never going to be very friendly," Susie commented.

Was that just a flippant remark, or was Susie putting him on notice that what had happened last night was a one-time thing, strictly for closure and nothing further?

This wasn't the time, Ryan told himself sternly. He could settle things between the two of them later, once he put this thing with Greta to rest.

"Mother, I brought someone with me," Ryan said as he quietly entered the sunroom.

The woman who had given him life was sitting in a white wicker chair, a delicately crocheted white throw covering her lap and legs to ward off any minor, would-be chill lingering in the air.

At sixty-one, Abra Colton was a remarkably thin, fragile-looking woman who showed no telltale traces of ever having given birth to five children. Thanks to the vigilant efforts of a skilled, faithful, longtime hairdresser, there were no traces of gray evident in her straight, chin-length dark brown hair.

There was an edginess about the graceful woman that was immediately evident to all but the most casual of observers. It had become even more noticeable in the past few months, ever since she had suffered the attack. An attack she'd suffered in her own home, which had robbed her of any feelings of safety she might have clung to. Now she was never safe, never fully at ease.

Despite that, she did appear to be coming around, albeit very slowly.

Abra shifted her gaze from her son to the young woman who was standing beside him. Sharp eyes took immediate measure of Ryan's companion.

"So I see," Abra replied. "Is she your girlfriend Ryan?" she asked.

Rather than have Ryan deal with what would be an awkward explanation at best, Susie stepped up and handled it for him.

"We work together, Mrs. Colton." Susie extended her hand to the woman. "I'm CSI Howard."

After a beat, Abra took the hand that was offered to her. "CSI?" she repeated, looking from the young woman to her son for an explanation.

"Crime scene investigator," Susie clarified. She couldn't help thinking that Ryan's mother was probably the only person in the country who didn't know what the letters stood for, given the extreme popularity these days of procedural programs.

"Oh," Abra murmured.

Susie could almost see the woman visibly withdrawing from them. What was she afraid of? Had seeing them caused her to remember something? Confront something that had been hidden from her until just now? Somehow, she had to get the woman to trust her, Susie thought.

"We need to ask you a few questions," Ryan told his mother patiently, then added, "About when you were attacked."

Abra stiffened visibly, her entire demeanor becoming defensive. "I don't want to talk about it."

"Please, Mrs. Colton, this is important," Susie stressed. She lightly placed her hand on top of Abra's, making contact. The look in the older woman's eyes told her a great deal. "You saw your attacker, didn't you?" she asked softly.

"No, no, I didn't," Abra cried, growing agitated. "Please, don't ask me," she implored. The plea had been directed toward Ryan.

His natural inclination was to back away, to try to curtail his mother's suffering as quickly as possible. But Susie had been right. If his mother remembered anything at all, *saw* anything at all, she had to tell them.

"Did the person who attacked you look like Greta?" he asked her.

Abra's eyes flew open, as if she was startled by the accuracy of her son's question.

"But it wasn't Greta," she cried. "I know my Greta. This woman's face was contorted with hate. Greta doesn't hate me," Abra insisted. "She loves me. She said so." As she spoke, Abra clutched at her son's forearm, squeezing it as her agitation increased.

"Take your time, Mother," Ryan urged calmly. "We're not going anywhere."

Appearing sufficiently controlled, Abra took a moment to gather herself together before continuing. "At first, I thought that maybe Greta was on some kind of mood-altering medication, or possibly taking street drugs. Young people do the stupidest things," she confided sorrowfully. "But when she came to see me at the hospital, Greta seemed fine. She was so upbeat, so concerned about me. There wasn't a trace of hostility at all—I was afraid maybe I was losing my mind," she confided. "And then I was just afraid…" Her voice trailed off. When she looked up at Ryan again, it was to implore him for reassurance. "But it wasn't Greta who did this to me, was it?"

Ryan's hand closed over his mother's in a gesture of protectiveness.

"No, Mother, it wasn't Greta."

For a moment Abra looked content, but then her troubled expression returned. "But then who was it? Who was pretending to be my daughter while she was doing such terrible things?" she demanded as forcefully as she was able.

"That's what we're going to find out, Mrs. Colton," Susie promised.

Abra addressed her solemnly, "Please do."

Taking their leave, neither of them said a word to the other until they were in the hall and out of his mother's earshot.

For a moment, Ryan felt stumped. "So what now?" The question was more to himself than to Susie.

"Now we look for someone who's imitating your sister and find out why she's doing it."

Imitating implied an impostor. That still left them with the same glaring problem that had confronted them from the very start.

"And the fingerprints and blood?" he asked. How did she intend to explain the fingerprints and blood that had been found? Or was that an inconvenience that was being swept under the rug for the time being?

Susie shrugged dismissively. "Maybe someone lifted them and then strategically planted the prints where they would do the most harm. Same could have been done with the blood. It's not difficult to envision that."

"Maybe not hard to envision, but tricky and very difficult to execute," Ryan pointed out. "Greta would have to have had some psycho following her around, lifting and transferring fresh prints and smearing her blood when she wasn't looking." It kept coming back to that, back to Greta's fingerprints and blood. There *had* to be another explanation for that being at the crime scene. "There's no other way that the fingerprints and blood evidence could turn out to be identical?" he asked.

"Well, yeah." As far as Susie knew, there was only one other explanation possible for identical fingerprints. "But your sister would have had to have a twin—twins have identical DNA—and I really think you might have been aware of there being twin girls growing up at your house."

Something she said struck a chord for him. Ryan strained for something in the back in his mind. "Maybe not."

Stunned, Susie stared at him. "You're going to have to explain that."

He was still trying to work it out in his head himself. "Something my father said recently that keeps popping back up in my head. At the time we were talking about Greta being a prime suspect in the stable break-in, and he said something to the effect of having gone through a great deal of trouble getting Greta, so he wasn't about to give up on her now. Not *conceiving* Greta, but *getting* her."

Susie didn't see the problem. "Potato, po-tat-toe," she countered. To her "conceiving" and "getting" could be seen as synonymous.

"Hear me out," Ryan said. "Have you ever noticed that Greta doesn't really look like the rest of us?"

"All of you—including Greta—have dark brown hair." The differences he was referring to were only minor. "So her eyes are hazel green instead of bright green." Or, in his case, magnetic green, she couldn't help thinking. "That's not exactly enough to make her stand out in a lineup—or label her a Colton impostor."

He didn't like the word *impostor* but maybe Greta really wasn't a Colton. "But it is possible, right?" he asked.

"Anything is possible," Susie conceded. "I guess the only way to settle this is to talk to your father and find out if he's just being careless with his words, or if that was actually an unintentional slip on his part."

Ryan nodded. He wasn't looking forward to this, but it was something that had to be done. "Let me take the lead on this, okay?" he cautioned.

There was no way she would have fought him for the right to question his father. That task belonged exclusively to him.

"You're the detective," she told him.

"You don't have to come along if you don't have time. This is probably keeping you from your work," he guessed.

She shook her head.

"Uh-uh, I'm not missing this for the world. I'm not leaving until we get some answers about this that make sense."

Ryan felt the same way.

THEY FOUND BIG J in the den.

The silver-white-haired man's back was to the doorway and he was standing in the middle of the room, right in front of his extensive library. He was regarding the books, appearing to be lost in thought.

For a moment, Ryan thought his father hadn't heard them come in and he was hesitant to intrude on the man. But then Big J spoke and Ryan realized that he knew they were there after all.

"You know, there was a time when I knew what was in almost every one of these books. Now I don't even remember why I got half of them."

He turned around to face them, then addressed his son. "Don't get old, boy. It's a bear. Old age is an unkind thief that can rob you of everything that's important to you."

Ordinarily, he'd let his father go on as long as he wanted to. But there was nothing ordinary about his visit to the ranch.

"Dad," Ryan began, interrupting his father, "I need to ask you something."

"Sounds serious," Big J joked. When neither his son nor the woman with him smiled, Big J's own smile faded. "I guess this *is* serious," he surmised. "All right, what's this question you have to get off your chest?" he asked.

Ryan really had no idea how to ask his father this.

There was no delicate way to proceed, so after a moment, he just plowed in. "Is Greta my sister?"

Big J stared at him as if he had lost a few screws. "Of course she is. Why? Are you suddenly drawing blanks about things, too?" Big J asked, concerned.

But Ryan wasn't finished. "Is she my sister by blood?" he pressed, determined to get the issue resolved once and for all.

Big J stiffened. Instead of answering, he asked, "Why do you ask?"

"Dad, answer the question first," Ryan insisted. "Is Greta my sister by blood, yes or no?"

Big J hesitated, taking so long to answer that for a moment Ryan thought maybe his father had actually forgotten the question—or perhaps was drawing a blank regarding the answer.

But then—finally—Big J uttered a single, bitter-tasting, judging by his expression—word. "No."

Finally!

"I need details, Dad," Ryan requested gently. His father's answer had him reeling, but this wasn't the time or place to deal with that. This was about a murder on the ranch and proving that Greta wasn't the one who did it.

Big J seemed to deflate right before their eyes, gripping the armrests of his chair and sinking into the soft leather cushion as if his knees could no longer support him.

"I didn't know what to do. That last pregnancy took everything out of your mother. She used up her last ounce of strength giving birth to that precious baby girl and the doctor was afraid that the least little thing might just kill your mother. But the baby wasn't strong. She died the next day."

"Died?" Ryan echoed, stunned.

"The news would have definitely killed your mother. You know what she was like. And she was weakened, besides. I had to do *something*. And then I heard a couple of the nurses talking about this woman who had just given birth to twin girls at home because she was too poor to pay for a hospital stay. I hardly knew what I was doing, but I went to see her.

"The house was like a pigsty," he recalled. "And she was a mess. There was no husband around. I offered to pay her fifty thousand dollars for one of her daughters—and her silence. She gave me her word she'd use the money to move away and promised never to tell her other daughter that she had a twin sister. There was nothing else I could do," he added helplessly. "You see that, don't you?"

Rather than Ryan answering, they heard the crashing sound of a china cup hitting the tiled marble floor behind them.

Whirling around, Susie saw her first. Abra Colton had come up behind them and had listened in silence to her husband's story. Pure shock had caused her to drop the cup filled with tea she'd held in her hand.

"Oh, John, how could you not tell me?" the older woman cried.

Big J jumped to his feet, hurrying to enfold his wife in his arms.

To Susie, it looked as if it was actually the other way around, that it was Abra who was holding—and comforting—her husband.

"I was so afraid of losing you," the big man cried. "I had already lost my daughter, I just couldn't stand to lose you, too, and you were so weak then, so very frail." Holding her to him, he kissed his wife's forehead. "I'm sorry I didn't tell you, Abra. I wanted to. So many times, I wanted to," he swore. "But somehow, the time just never seemed right." There were tears in his eyes as he pleaded for her forgiveness. "I'm sorry," he repeated.

Abra was visibly comforting her husband.

"There's nothing to be sorry for. You should never be sorry for being kind," she told him gently, hugging her husband again.

Ryan stepped back and let his parents have their moment. Turning toward Susie, he whispered, "Well, on the plus side, this clears Greta of murder *and* those incomprehensible acts of vandalism she was accused of committing."

It was very obvious that Ryan was greatly relieved his sister was cleared. That was what had drawn her to him in the first place, Susie recalled, the way he was so loyal to his family, even though they might not see eye to eye on a lot of things. Her own family was close and that had always meant a great deal to her.

"Yes," she agreed. "I guess all we have is the minor, annoying little detail of tracking down this obviously evil twin before she does any more damage she could pin on Greta. Your sister isn't going to be safe until this other woman is caught."

That hadn't even occurred to him yet. "I guess I've still got my work cut out for me," Ryan said, thinking out loud.

"We," Susie corrected with emphasis. *"We* have our work cut out for us."

Ryan stopped walking. "Are you telling me you intend to come with me and help track her down?"

Susie looked at him as if she couldn't understand

how he could possibly think anything else. "Just try to stop me."

Tracking down a suspect wasn't her field. "But you belong in the lab."

"I belong anywhere I want to be," Susie deliberately countered.

Ryan knew when he was on the losing end. He raised his hands in mock surrender. "You'll get no argument from me."

"I guess there's always a first time," Susie said wryly.

They were outside of the main house now and heading back to his car when he pulled Susie to him and kissed her. "I'd rather concentrate on second chances," he told her.

She blinked, trying not to appear shaken. "What was that for?" she asked, referring to the sudden kiss.

Ryan felt that his one-word answer covered it all.

"Everything."

CHAPTER SIXTEEN

GRETA HELD HER breath as she watched the police officer unlock the door to her cell. She didn't release it until the creaking door was actually standing wide-open.

"That has to be the most beautiful sound I've ever heard," Greta confided to Ryan as he and Susie stood behind the officer who had unlocked the door.

For a moment, Greta stood in the cell, as if afraid to take another step, concerned that it was all a hoax and that the door would be shut on her again before she had a chance to make it across the threshold.

But the guard didn't attempt to close the cell door again. Instead, he continued to wait, watching her impatiently. With what seemed like a burst of energy, Greta quickly strode out of the cell.

"I'm really free," she cried, her eyes all but tearing up with relief and joy.

"Absolutely," Ryan told her. He smiled at her. The relief his sister had to be experiencing was no greater than his own. Just so that she was clear about the dropped charges, he went over the list of things she had been accused of. "You didn't kill Rodgers, you weren't the one to deface that property on the ranch and you didn't attack Mother."

Greta's eyes widened at the very last part of her brother's statement.

"Attack Mother?" she echoed. "Mother thought I was the one who attacked her?" Even as she said the words, it seemed surreal to her.

"Actually no," Susie was quick to interject, slanting a glance at Ryan. Ryan had a great many good qualities, but tact wasn't always one of them. "What your mother said was that it *couldn't* have been you, even though her attacker had your face and looked like a really angry, deranged version of you."

Greta glanced from the forensic expert to her brother, more confused than ever. "Someone looked like me? I don't understand."

"Believe me, I know this isn't going to be easy for you to hear, but—"

Ryan stopped abruptly when he heard the sound of boots coming down the corridor.

About time they got here.

He saw Susie looking at him quizzically, but he didn't want to say anything more until his brothers had reached them.

All four of them were talking over one another, eager to hug Greta and assure her that they were in her corner no matter what.

"Looks like Ryan finally came to his senses and let you out," Brett said, taking his turn at hugging his sister.

"God, but you're a noisy bunch," Susie commented with a grin.

"We would have hired a brass band if we thought we could get it past the sergeant at the front desk," Jack told her, laughing as he gave Greta a bear hug.

"What are you all doing here?" Greta asked. It was clear that she was really glad to see them, especially now that they were all on this side of the cell. "You didn't have to come."

"Yeah, we did," Eric told her. "Besides, Mr. Detective here—" he jerked a thumb at Ryan "—asked us to come here because he had something to tell us. I figure he wants to get the apologies over with all at once instead of telling us one at a time. Am I right?" he asked, his sharp eyes pinning down his older brother.

"Actually," Ryan replied, deliberately stretching the word out for effect, "no. I called you here to tell you the reason Greta's fingerprints were found at the scene of each crime."

It was obvious from the way they all exchanged glances that the brothers had their own opinions about that.

"Because your lab is second-rate and slipped up?" Jack guessed.

Ryan was quick to come to Susie's defense before she had a chance to say anything herself. "Our lab is first-rate and nobody slipped up."

Brett clearly wasn't convinced that Jack's answer was off-base. "Then how do you explain saying that Greta's prints were found at the scene?"

"Because they were," Ryan answered. His eyes darted toward Greta as he told his family, "Greta's got a twin sister."

Daniel stared at his half brother. "Oh, c'mon, is *that* what you're going with?" he cried in disbelief.

Out of all the others, he had been the one who had remained in Ryan's corner, but even he found this excuse to be completely outlandish and extremely difficult to swallow.

"That's what he's going with because it's true," Susie told Ryan's brothers and sister.

It was obvious that Ryan's explanation was still falling short of its mark.

"And what, Greta's 'twin' is invisible, so the rest of us can't see her?" Brett asked sarcastically.

"Oh, you can see her, and you did," Ryan assured his brother, ignoring the sarcasm. "Mother saw her when she was attacked by her and that other ranch hand saw her arguing with Kurt Rodgers just before Rodgers met his untimely death."

Jack shook his head. "Look, it's nice that you're finally in Greta's corner, Ryan, but even *you* could have come up with a more plausible story than this twin fairy tale."

"It's not a fairy tale, it's the truth," Ryan told them calmly. "You want proof?" he challenged. When his brothers all nodded their heads, the expressions on their faces all daring him to come up with some sort of way to validate what he was saying, Ryan told them, "CSI Howard and I confronted Dad about it and he told us the truth."

"That you're insane?" Jack guessed.

Ryan went on as if he hadn't heard his older brother. "He told us that when Mother gave birth the last time, the baby died the next day. Dad was really worried that the news might send Mother over the edge—she almost died giving birth—so he found someone who had just given birth to a baby girl and offered to buy her. Only problem was, the woman had given birth to *two* baby girls and Dad had to choose which one he was going to pass off as Greta."

Ryan could see that what he was saying had really

shaken his brothers—and Greta—up. But he kept pushing on, wanting to get this all out now.

"The woman promised to take the other girl and disappear. Fast forward twenty-six years, the other twin is no longer 'disappeared,' she's surfaced, and for reasons I can only guess at she's gone on a rampage to discredit Greta and frame her for murder."

"Why?" Eric asked. "Even if we believe this fantastic story you just told us, why go through all this trouble to get Greta discredited?"

Ryan looked at Susie to see if she wanted to take over, but Susie's expression told him that he could continue. She indicated that this was his show.

"Our best guess is that she is angry that Greta got to live the good life while she didn't and she's out for revenge," Ryan answered.

"So you know where this 'other' Greta is?" Daniel questioned.

"Not yet," Ryan told him, adding firmly, "but I intend to find out."

"But if you don't know where this other person is," Jack pointed out, "how can you speculate that you know she's trying to frame Greta to get revenge?"

That part was easy, Ryan thought.

"Think about it," Ryan stressed. "Very few people get to live the way we did and we do. And from what I gathered from just a cursory collection of background information, Greta's and this angry twin's birth mother wasn't exactly up for any Mother of the Year Awards. I'd say that Greta's twin had a rotten upbringing and feels cheated. Why did Greta get to have all the luck," Ryan said, turning to look directly at Greta, "while this twin had to do God knows what to earn a living—not to mention the fact that she probably got battered around a bit by Mommy Dearest."

"But you're just speculating," Eric said, going back to that nagging fact.

"For now," Ryan allowed. "But I've got a hunch that I won't be for long," he promised his brothers as well as Greta. He could see by the look on her face that she was having a hard time absorbing and accepting all of this. "I—we," he corrected, sparing a grateful glance in Susie's direction, "intend to find this woman who's trying to frame Greta and bring her back to face all the charges that had been brought against our sister."

It was clearly a great deal to take in and process. He could see by the expressions on his brothers' faces that some of them were having a more difficult time than others in accepting this far-from-run-of-the-mill explanation.

"And you're sure you're right about this twin thing?" Jack pressed skeptically.

"As sure as all of us are standing here," Ryan said with unwavering certainty to Jack and the others.

Brett shook his head, as if to clear away the cobwebs. "How could Dad have kept this from us for all these years?"

"I'm sure he had his reasons," Greta said softly, coming to the man's defense.

"Yeah," Eric answered. "Mother."

As he said that, it was obvious that a thought had suddenly hit him. It seemed to telegraph itself through the gathering at the same time.

"Does she know? Mother," Brett specified, "does she know, or is she still in the dark?"

"No, she knows," Ryan assured all of them. "She

overheard Dad confessing all this to Agent Howard and me, telling us why he did it."

"How is she?" Jack asked, concern in his voice.

"This is hard for all of us to wrap our heads around," Brett interjected. "The news must have just about killed her."

"Actually," Ryan answered with new respect for the woman who had periodically bowed out of their lives for prolonged amounts of time while they were growing up, "our mother is a lot more courageous than we've been giving her credit for. She seemed genuinely touched that Dad had been worried enough about her to do something completely out of his comfort zone just to spare her grief. When I left the two of them, *she* was the one who was comforting *him.*"

Greta's mouth dropped open at the image Ryan had just created. "You're kidding."

"No, he's telling you the truth," Susie assured her, stepping in again. "It was all rather sweet, actually. They seemed to be completely committed to one another." A fondness flashed over her face. "You don't always see that with couples who have been married as long as your parents have."

Jack apparently wanted to have the matter—and his fears—laid to rest once and for all. "So this means that all the charges against Greta have really been dropped?"

"Each and every last one of them," Ryan declared with more than a small measure of enthusiasm and satisfaction.

"And exactly what do you intend to do about this evil twin—I can't believe I just said that," Eric muttered, shaking his head. He wanted to be sure that Ryan lived up to his word.

"We're going to find her," Ryan said with unwavering confidence. "At the moment, we can't put an APB out on the woman because people are going to keep trying to drag Greta in, seeing as how Greta and this other woman seem to be sharing the same face, but we'll get her," Ryan promised. He was trying to sound nothing but upbeat for Greta's sake.

Daniel seemed to be trying to share that feeling, but he needed a little help in order to try to sell it. "You seem awfully confident about that."

Ryan tried to remember if his brothers had *always* doubted his abilities as a homicide detective like this, or if this was something new.

Humoring Daniel, Ryan explained, "Now that we know *who* we're looking for and what we're up against, yes, I am. Everyone is bound to slip up once in a while—and I'll be there to catch her the second that this woman does slip up."

"Well, I guess it sounds like you've got your next move planned. Is there anything we can do?" Daniel asked.

"Yeah, try to make this up to Greta for me." He smiled at his sister. She would never know how happy he was to find out that he'd been wrong. "I think I kind of came down hard on you, and I'm sorry. If Tyler hadn't come forward—"

"Whoa, wait a second. Back up here," Jack told his younger brother. "Don't you mean Mark? Mark Stanton's her fiancé, not Tyler," Jack reminded him.

"And he was also a no-show as far as coming up with her bail money, or even just standing by her," Ryan told them, scowling. "Rumor has it he didn't want to be photographed coming down to the precinct. The pig *still* hasn't shown his face around here."

Eric tried to find excuses for Mark. "Maybe jails make him nervous—or maybe you do." Eric took his thought a step further. "Maybe the guy's scared of you."

Brett laughed shortly. "I can relate to that," he said, speaking up. "I'm scared of you."

"In what universe?" Ryan scoffed, waving away his brother's so-called revelation.

Jack's raised voice cut through the cross fire of conversations. "What's this about Tyler?" he asked. "Just what kind of an 'alibi' for Greta did Tyler Stanton come through with?"

Ryan glanced in Greta's direction. "Oldest one in the world," he answered.

Jack immediately caught his drift and looked at Greta, almost speechless. "Really, Greta? You and Tyler?"

No, not really. But if she said anything to deny the claim, Tyler Stanton—whose only sin was trying to save her—would be disgraced for lying to the public. She knew how very fickle the public could be. They loved their heroes, loved building them up—and loved tearing them down even more.

So for his sake, she fashioned a nonanswer answer. "I'd rather not talk about it," she told her brothers evasively.

She had no idea why, but Tyler had lied for her. More than that, if that fabrication of his was somehow leaked to the press—it would completely unravel her pending wedding.

Would that be so bad? a little voice inside her head asked.

The closer her ceremony came, the less inclined she was to take part in it.

Moreover, the less convinced she was that she actually *did* love this man with the extremely attractive face. On a scale of one to ten, in the looks department Mark Stanton scored a twelve. But in the soul department, such as when it came to all these small details, or recalling the location of their first date—or even answering her phone calls the night she'd been taken into custody—Mark fell painfully short of the goal.

Mark couldn't even put himself out to pay her a visit, while Tyler, for reasons she couldn't begin to understand, had not only put himself out for her, he'd *lied* for her.

Lied to give her an alibi and keep her from being charged with the murder of Kurt Rodgers.

His lying would have quickly come to light and fallen apart if it hadn't been for Ryan. If Ryan hadn't been so committed to proving her innocent, hadn't grasped at straws, Tyler's act of chivalry would have all been for naught and quickly dismantled.

"Does that mean the wedding's off?" Daniel asked his sister as the thought suddenly occurred to him. By the look on his face, he wasn't exactly consumed with worry for his sister.

"I sure as hell hope so," Susie cried, piping up. The others turned to look at her and it was obvious by the expressions on their faces that they had forgotten that she was even there, a silent witness to their conversation. "Any man who doesn't stand by the woman he's supposed to love doesn't deserve to marry her," she said firmly.

"Well, I don't know what the hell Mark Stanton is thinking—or *if* he's thinking," Brett added with a dismissive wave of his hand, "but I can sure tell you one thing for sure, we'll all stand by you," he told Greta, acting as the group's spokesman.

Greta was taking nothing for granted. It had been that kind of a day. "Even after what you just found out?" she asked incredulously.

"That you've got some evil twin running around, pretending to be you?" Eric asked.

"No," she cried. He was missing the point. They all were. "That I'm not your sister."

"The hell you're not," Jack told her. There was no arguing with his tone of voice. "You grew up with us. You fought with us, laughed with us. You were a part of every day. If that's not what makes a sister, well, then I don't know what does. You're a Colton, Greta. You might as well stop fighting it and just come along peaceably."

There were tears in her eyes as she nodded and said, "I guess that's that, then."

"Yes, it is," Ryan told her with finality, adding with a conspiratorial wink, "Remember, Jack doesn't like to have anyone argue with him."

And no one, apparently, was about to argue with Ryan, either.

CHAPTER SEVENTEEN

TENSION RADIATED FROM every pore of his body. He'd been at this for hours.

And the end result had been fruitless.

Nada. Nothing. Zero.

Annoyed, Ryan pushed the keyboard away so hard it bounced on his desk before impotently coming to a rest, askew.

So far, all the leads he and Susie had come up with hadn't panned out. They'd either led him around in circles or they brought him smack up against a dead end. Like now.

Dead end.

A little like his own life, he couldn't help thinking. At least, his life the way it had been for the past ten years—and especially as of late.

Hard as he was working to find a lead on this faux Greta—and he was working very hard—Ryan's thoughts kept going back to what he had unexpectedly found out, thanks to Susie's mother and her completely unanticipated visit.

The scene with the feisty, combative woman kept replaying itself in his head.

He'd been a father.

For a small inkling of time, he'd been a father, or rather, a father-to-be—and then he wasn't. And it had all happened without the slightest bit of knowledge on his part. And, to add to the insult and pain, all of this had transpired not recently, but almost ten long years ago.

Ten *years* ago.

The very thought just boggled his mind as he turned it over and over again in his head.

If that baby had had a chance to make it and survive, right about now she would have been about nine years old.

The very idea shook Ryan down to his very roots, not so much that he could have been a father but that he actually *liked* the idea of being a father.

Where had that even *come* from? Ryan silently demanded.

He hadn't felt any stirrings or longings when Jack had had a son. Oh, he really loved his nephew, Seth, and looked forward to doing things with him as the boy grew, but watching Jack and Seth together had never made him particularly enthused about offspring of his own. Or even envious.

Yet abruptly finding out the other day that Susie had been pregnant with his baby, and then lost it, filled every single crevice within him with remorse, with deep, consuming regret and with an unbelievable longing. He certainly wouldn't have believed it of himself had anyone told him that this was the way hearing the news of almost having a child—especially so belatedly—would affect him.

But it was true. He, Ryan Colton, actually *wanted* children.

It was a hell of a thing to find out about himself at this stage of his life. Not only did he want children, but he wanted children *with Susie*.

Fat chance of that ever happening. You really messed that one up, the little voice in his head mocked.

Still, that one night they'd had together had brought back all the feelings he'd once had for her—rekindled all the old feelings and brought in a whole truckload of new ones.

And despite the tongue-lashing her mother had given him, Susie had not taken the opportunity to put him in his place or return to that state of polite avoidance that he and she had feigned during their last four years in the Tulsa police department.

Rather than go back to that behavior, Susie had stepped up and let him know that she had his back in this ongoing investigation involving his family's ranch, as well as his sister.

Anyone else might have said that their one night together had been a slip and, more than that, a mistake. Moreover, they undoubtedly would have left him high and dry as far as any forensic and investigative backup might go.

But Susie hadn't.

Susie was there for him and *with* him. That had to mean something, didn't it?

Yeah, she was honorable, probably a lot more honorable than he would have been had the tables been reversed, he thought ruefully.

Ryan switched off the monitor and glared at the darkening computer screen. That mirrored, unfortunately, the state of the investigation right now, and possibly its continuing state in the foreseeable future.

For a second, Ryan chewed on the side of his lip, thinking.

Since Greta was at least out of jail, if not completely out of danger, and his mother was out of her coma and finally on the mend, maybe he could break off a tiny piece of time to get something resolved—between himself and Susie.

If he didn't do this now, it would only continue to bother him, only continue to grow until it became way too unmanageable.

Not that it would be any sort of a cakewalk for him the way things stood right now, Ryan thought, revising his initial assessment of the situation before him.

This was no time for his courage to flag.

If he was going to do this, Ryan told himself, switching off his computer, he would do it right. There were steps to take, procedures to follow and things to prepare.

He felt the palms of his hands growing damp, which caught him by surprise. He was sweating. He, Ryan Colton, a former Marine, currently a detective with the Tulsa PD, who had found himself looking down the barrel of a gun more than once, talked down a killer in his day, all without breaking a sweat, he was perspiring like a high school freshman about to ask his first girl to the prom.

Hell, he hadn't even sweated it out then, he recalled. So why did what he was about to undertake make him feel so nervous now? He was a police detective, for God sakes.

Because if he did this, it would leave him completely exposed, completely vulnerable. Not even the bravest of men relished that kind of exposure.

But he was going to do this right. Because he had everything to win.

Or lose, that same nagging little voice whispered, not missing a single opportunity to gnaw away at his confidence.

RYAN STOOD IN front of the somewhat weathered front door of the narrow two-story house, working up his courage to ring the doorbell. Considered tough and relentless by the people he went after, he found himself on the other side of an extremely rare, unsettling case of nerves. He'd faced down armed felons, not to mention the enemy, comprised of hostile, suicidal soldiers, on foreign soil halfway around the world. He'd done it without flinching.

Yet the thought of facing a petite older woman he literally towered over and outweighed by a third had him hesitating and rehearsing words in his head for what felt like the dozenth time.

He'd already made up his mind and knew he was going to ultimately go through with this whether or not Elizabeth Howard approved and gave her blessing, but he also knew it would go over so much more smoothly if he could get the woman to give him her stamp of approval.

Finally, because he was afraid that Mrs. Howard might suddenly choose to open the door and catch him at a disadvantage, Ryan forced himself to ring the doorbell. His fingertips felt cold and stiff, the way they might if he were the exposed, unwilling target of a sniper wearing night vision goggles at midnight.

The second he saw the front door opening, his heart rate sped up. And then all but stopped altogether.

It was now or never.

"Hello, Mrs. Howard."

Elizabeth Howard's soft, unlined face lost its natural

smile and her expression hardened the instant that recognition set in. One hand remained on the door, holding it in place rather than opening it farther in an unspoken invitation.

There was no invitation in her eyes.

"I have nothing to say to you," she coldly told the man who she felt had broken her daughter's heart and ruined her life.

Ryan forced a smile to his lips. "That's all right, because I have something to say to you and I'd really like you to listen."

Elizabeth said nothing in response. The door remained just the way it was, as did she.

This was not going well, Ryan thought. A couple of years ago, he would have just turned on his heel and walked away. But then, a couple of years ago, he wouldn't have been here in the first place.

He was putting himself on the line, stripping himself bare and was, consequently, utterly vulnerable. But he had no choice. He'd come this far—he had to see this through. "May I come in, please? I'd rather not say this standing out here—and I don't think you'd want me to, either."

Still the woman said nothing, as if she was slowly turning over and examining not just each word, but each letter that went into making up each word. The silence dragged on, all but skewering itself into his chest.

Just when he was about to give up, Elizabeth took a small, measured step back, taking the door with her as she did.

"Make it quick."

He wasn't about to tell her that he couldn't "make it

quick." That this was going to take a little time. But first things first. And first, he had to get inside the house.

Nodding at her, Ryan went in.

SUSIE HAD PUT in an extralong day at the lab, starting earlier than she normally did and remaining far later than was her custom. And she had done it all for a reason.

She'd gone through all the evidence with the proverbial fine-tooth comb, hoping that this time around, she would find a clue that she and the others had missed when they had initially gone over it.

There had to be something, she kept telling herself. There just had to be.

But so far, there wasn't.

Maybe she was just too tired to see it, she finally told herself just before she decided to call it a night and go home. She could always get an early start in the morning—but in order to do that, first she had to *leave* the office.

Putting one foot in front of the other, she did just that.

Dinner turned out to be some leftover something-or-other she had no actual recollection of either buying or eating the first time around. Susie consumed it while standing over the sink, going over the case in her head one last time. When she was working on a case, everything else became secondary.

Everything but Ryan.

The annoying, accusing as well as unsettling thought seemed to just pop up in her head out of nowhere, as if to mock her and remind her that she was not an actual pillar of self-restraint and control.

Susie supposed that she could be forgiven that, seeing as she'd almost had a child with the man and, more than that, Ryan Colton was the only man she had ever really loved.

Oh, she'd been infatuated before, close to head over heels smitten before, but love? Actually in love? That had only happened to her once.

Yes, and then he dumped you, remember?

It wasn't exactly *dumping*, she silently argued. According to Ryan, his reasons for what he'd done had been complicated and he had broken up with her to keep them both safe, especially her.

Now, there was a new one, she couldn't help thinking. But because his excuse was so unique, she had to admit that it probably carried more than a germ of truth. Knowing Ryan the way she did, she could actually believe that *he* at least believed that was the reason he had done what he had.

She, however, couldn't come up with a scenario in which breaking things off between them could even *remotely* be construed as being for her own good. "Good" to her revolved around having Ryan in her world. Having him love her, having him want her.

Having him—

Having *him*, she thought, smiling to herself as her imagination began to take off.

Knock it off, Howard, she upbraided herself sternly. *Stop building a case for something that isn't there, that isn't going to happen. You enjoyed some really good sex, but it didn't come with strings or any terms for renewal. It was hot and it was brief. Get used to it.*

And then get over it.

She was so involved in her thoughts, she almost didn't hear the doorbell. The more emphatic knocking, however, did register.

Feeling a little leery now that she knew there was someone out there attacking people within Ryan's sphere of friends and family, Susie took her handgun with her to the door. Just to be on the safe side.

"Who is it?" she asked, standing a good three feet away from the door. She'd stepped over Conway to get this close. The dog was sleeping and apparently the knocking had done nothing to change the border collie's state.

"Good, you're finally asking that before you open the door," he said with approval.

"Ryan?"

"None other," he confirmed.

Surprised and trying not to notice the way her heart suddenly decided to accelerate, Susie quickly unlocked the door.

"I see you were expecting me," he deadpanned. In this case, he felt that humor was his best defense.

The first thing he noticed when she opened the door to admit him was the way Susie's cheeks were flushed. They did that whenever she was surprised.

The second thing he noticed was the gun in her hand. Her finger was still poised on the trigger, but the muzzle was pointed down.

Her eyebrows drew together in confusion. "What?" When he nodded at the handgun in response to her question, she put it down.

"What happened to your 'security system'?" he asked.

"Conway's had a long day," she said in the dog's defense. The pet's faint snoring could be heard. "What are you doing here?" she asked, closing the door behind him.

He decided to gauge the atmosphere and approach his subject slowly. "I wanted to talk to you."

They'd interacted off and on all day. She'd thought he was as worn-out at the edges as she was. Had he come up with a new angle on his way home?

"About the case?" she asked.

"Yes." It was the first word on his lips, but he didn't want to start off by lying, so he said, "No, not really." Pausing for a moment, more for courage than for dramatic effect, he began, "I wanted to talk about us."

"Us?" she echoed uncertainly.

Ryan looked at her. He couldn't approach this by pussyfooting around the subject, so he dove straight into the deep end. "Why didn't you tell me that you were pregnant?"

Susie blew out a breath, the kind one exhaled when they were punched in the gut. That was how she felt, dealing with this question and its answer.

"Because I didn't want you 'doing the right thing' just because I was carrying your baby," she told him honestly. "If you were going to ask to marry me, I wanted it to be because you were in love with me, not because your family expected you to own up to your responsibilities by marrying the girl you accidentally got pregnant. And, anyway, one way or the other," she added with a careless shrug, "you're off the hook now."

"I don't consider the thought of marrying you as being 'on the hook,'" he told her, clarifying how he felt—or at least thinking that he was.

She shrugged as if the whole thing didn't matter to her one way or another. She'd worked hard to be able to summon this facade of disinterest at will. But even so, it was a struggle for her. "Either way, you're free."

His eyes met hers. "Is that what you really think?" he asked.

She hesitated at first, then fell back on the careless shrug. "Well, yes."

Ryan laughed softly to himself. "Then maybe you're not as smart as I thought you were." Enough with the bandying things back and forth. Time to get down to the heart of why he was here. "I want to marry you, Susie."

The words stunned her for a second, but then she managed to collect herself. It was just talk, nothing more, Susie told herself.

"Why, because you're a Colton and you've got a code to uphold?" she challenged.

Ryan took hold of her shoulders, bracketing her in place. "No, because I'm in love with you and I don't want to face the next forty to fifty years without you right there by my side. I want you *with* me."

Susie's mouth went dry. *Words, just words. He knows how to use them, how to get your defenses down.* "You don't know what you're saying," she told him, dismissing what he had just told her.

The laugh was a dry one. "Funny, that's what your mother said earlier when I went to talk to her."

That caught her completely off guard. "You went to talk to my mother?" Her mother had made it clear in no uncertain terms that she couldn't stand the sight of him. Why in heaven's name had he gone over to her mother's house?

Ryan nodded in response to her question. "Yes."

She had to ask. "Why?"

"To ask for permission to marry you."

To hell with a dry mouth—it fell completely open this time. "What did she say?" As if she didn't know, Susie thought.

"Well, at first I think she wanted to have me drawn

and quartered, and it took some doing, but I finally convinced your mother that I was serious. I told her that ever since I found out about the baby you lost, I couldn't stop thinking about it. I told her that I wanted another chance to have a baby with you. Lots of babies."

Her eyes widened, just like her mouth had. Disbelief and amazement highlighted her face. "And she believed you?"

"Not at first," Ryan qualified. "But I can be very persuasive when I want to be—and I really wanted to be," he added.

She still didn't know whether or not to believe him. It would require ignoring her fear of getting irrevocably hit emotionally. "And you're serious?"

"Never more serious in my whole life," he swore, crossing his heart like a small child might do. He was leaving no base uncovered. "I've made some mistakes in my life, but not a day goes by that I don't regret ending it between us. I didn't fully realize just how much you lit up my world until you weren't there to do it anymore."

Her mind was desperately scrambling to understand and absorb what she was hearing. After first wanting him, then wanting to get over him, she needed to get every single word straight.

"So what you're saying is—"

He answered her in quick succession. "I want to marry you. I want to have children with you. I want to have grandchildren with you and I want to grow old with you—"

"Ryan?" She finally managed to get him to pause long enough to hear her.

He looked at her, afraid of what he might hear, his mind searching for a way to convince her to say yes.

"What?"

"Are you planning on shutting up anytime soon?" she asked him.

Thrown off by her question, Ryan cocked his head, curious. "Why?"

"Because I'd like to kiss you and it's very hard to kiss a moving target," she told him.

"I can shut up," he said in all seriousness.

"Good. Then do it," she told him, throwing her arms around his neck.

He had enough time to enfold her in his arms and bring her closer to him. "Then you'll marry me?"

Her answer was yes. It had always been yes. But for now, she was enjoying the moment and played it out a little longer.

"We'll talk," she promised. "Later."

The last word fluttered across his mouth a microsecond before her mouth met his.

Conway raised his head as if to check them out, yipped his approval once, then went back to sleep.

Susie and Ryan were otherwise occupied. They didn't talk for a long, long time.

EPILOGUE

RESTLESS, THE TALL, willowy-figured young woman paced about the small hotel room like a caged animal longing for freedom.

Freedom, *her* freedom, was coming.

But it wasn't coming soon enough.

Alice could feel the impatience clawing at her throat. She was desperate to implement the last part of her detailed plan.

She was through with playing games, Alice thought with a surge of anticipated triumph. Through with poking a stick at her prey, watching her squirm from a distance. Her strikes had been getting closer and closer to the center of Greta's world, but the excitement of those strikes wasn't enough anymore.

Weren't enough to keep her anger contained.

Not anymore.

She was tired of being patient, tired of waiting on the sidelines, tired of a life of deprivation and living on crumbs while that bitch with her face got to live like a queen.

It wasn't fair!

Why had that man picked her sister and not her? She'd seen that photograph, the only one that existed of the two of them. There hadn't been an iota of difference between them. They'd been babies, not even a week old at the time.

Like two damn peas in a stupid pod.

What had set the two of them apart for him?

Why her and not me? her mind demanded for the hundredth time.

The question echoed over and over again in Alice's head, growing louder. It was so loud it was almost deafening.

Or maybe the question was actually echoing around the room.

Was that her voice she heard?

Abruptly, she stopped pacing in front of the stained dresser. Alice stared at her reflection in the mirror that hung just above it.

They hadn't looked any different then and they didn't look any different now.

Well, maybe she was a little prettier, Alice decided, looking at herself, but not to the point that it could set them apart if they weren't standing side by side.

She had diligently done her homework once she'd found out that she had a twin. A drunken confession from her piece of trash of a mother had opened her eyes to the injustice that had occurred in her life before she ever had any recollection of it. Slurring her words, her mother had actually had the gall to look at her and complain that maybe she'd sold the wrong twin. Maybe she should have kept the other one and sold her because the other one had turned out to be a better daughter.

She'd had to threaten her mother with a broken whiskey bottle to get the rest of the story out of her. But once she'd heard it, she knew what she had to do.

It was all as clear as crystal mountain water to her. She had to find that bitch, find some way to get rid of her.

But first she was going to make her pay. Pay for the miserable life she'd had to endure while her worthless twin got to play the adored little rich girl, even getting her picture in the paper just because she was going to be marrying the brother of some big-time CEO or something like that.

It should have been her.

It was *going* to be her.

All she had to do was kill Greta and take her place. No big deal.

* * * * *

Carla Cassidy is an award-winning, *New York Times* bestselling author who has written more than 120 novels for Harlequin. In 1995, she won Best Silhouette Romance from *RT Book Reviews* for *Anything for Danny*. In 1998, she won a Career Achievement Award for Best Innovative Series from *RT Book Reviews*. Carla believes the only thing better than curling up with a good book to read is sitting down at the computer with a good story to write.

Books by Carla Cassidy

Harlequin Romantic Suspense

Cowboys of Holiday Ranch

A Real Cowboy
Cowboy of Interest
Cowboy Under Fire
Cowboy at Arms
Operation Cowboy Daddy
Killer Cowboy
Sheltered by the Cowboy
Guardian Cowboy
Cowboy Defender

The Coltons of Red Ridge

The Colton Cowboy

The Coltons of Shadow Creek

Colton's Secret Son

Visit the Author Profile page
at Harlequin.com for more titles.

THE COLTON BODYGUARD

Carla Cassidy

CHAPTER ONE

THE JAIL-CELL DOOR clanked shut behind Greta Colton. She turned and grabbed the bars, staring at her brother on the other side.

"Ryan, you know this is all a mistake. I didn't kill anyone. I'm innocent. I didn't kill Kurt." She watched in horror as Ryan turned his back on her and walked away. How could he believe she was capable of murder?

"Ryan, please." She grasped the cell bars more tightly, frantic for him, for anyone, to believe her. "I'm not a murderer," she screamed, but he didn't stop walking away from her.

Greta sat up and looked around, disoriented as to time and place. Her pounding heart slowed. She was safe in her king-size bed in her bedroom. A glance at the clock on the nightstand told her it was just after four in the afternoon.

She was safe beneath her sky blue comforter with the afternoon sunshine drifting through the lacy white curtains at the window. She released a sigh of relief.

The nightmare she'd just suffered had become a familiar one over the past three weeks, ever since she really had been arrested for the murder of ranch hand Kurt Rodgers.

She'd decided to take a short nap after lunch but had slept longer than she had intended. Lately, sleeping had been far easier than being fully conscious and in the present.

The moments before and since she'd been released from jail had been fraught with anger, sadness, lies and questions. It wasn't just Greta who had been through hell but her family, as well.

She got out of bed and walked to the nearby window. From this vantage point she could see much of the green pastures and impressive outbuildings of the family ranch, the Lucky C.

But ranch business was the last thing on her mind. A lie had got her out of jail, ruined her engagement and destroyed her mother's happiness in planning a wedding. For the past two and a half weeks, Greta had been living like a hermit, trying to cope with everything that had happened to forever change her life.

She left the window and headed for the shower in the luxurious bathroom just off the sitting area in her bedroom. It was time for her to face the man who had lied for her, the man who had sworn that on the night of Kurt's murder he was in a hotel room with her in Oklahoma City.

She *had* been in a hotel room in Oklahoma City, but she'd been all alone, certainly not with Tyler Stanton, her future brother-in-law. She definitely hadn't been carrying on a torrid affair with Tyler, as he had implied to the police when he'd offered up the alibi that had ultimately released her from jail.

It didn't take her long to shower and dress in a pair of tailored brown slacks and a russet blouse that she knew complemented her slender figure. She pulled on a pair of brown suede dress boots and slipped inside her right boot the knife her father had given her when she'd turned sixteen years old.

Her father had worried about her having the run of the ranch, dealing with ranch hands who appeared to be good guys but might be a danger to her, so he'd gifted her with the knife for self-protection. He'd also told her not to pull it on somebody unless she had the guts to use it.

When closed, it was a beautiful mother-of-pearl palm-size case, but with a click of a button it became a wicked nearly-five-inch-long weapon. Thankfully, she had never had to use it or even take it out of her boot.

She left the Lucky C by one of the back doors, grateful when she didn't encounter anyone. She didn't want anyone knowing where she was going. Thankfully, the only person in the family who knew she'd been alibied with the lie of an affair was her brother Ryan and a couple of the officers who worked for the Tulsa police force. As far as she knew, none of them had shared that information with anyone else.

So far she'd been spared the humiliating experience of trying to explain to her parents and siblings that she wasn't having an affair, no matter what Tyler had told the authorities.

It was almost seven when she pulled her red Jeep just inside the black wrought iron gates at the entrance to Tyler Stanton's estate. It was an hour-and-a-half drive from the Colton ranch in Tulsa to Tyler's home in Oklahoma City.

Throughout the drive, several times she'd considered turning around and heading back to the ranch. But ultimately, she knew she had to confront Tyler and tonight was as good a time as any. She hadn't spoken to or seen him since being released from jail. She needed answers that only he could give her.

She stopped the Jeep when the impressive sprawling ranch house came into view. It was definitely the living space of a successful man and Tyler was definitely successful. As owner and CEO of Stanton Oil, he was ridiculously handsome and socially sought after for various fund-raisers and events. The few times Greta had been around him, she'd always found him slightly cold and very intimidating.

Why would he risk his good reputation and his relationship with his brother, Mark, by implicating himself in an affair with her?

Thankfully, he must've greased some palms to keep her alibi quiet, for there had been no hint of tawdry rumors floating around. Of course, Mark had heard and had ridden into the Colton house a week ago on a self-righteous horse and declared their engagement over.

She'd spent five days in jail, and for the past week she'd been on the phone canceling wedding arrangements that had been made and praying her mother didn't spiral down into one of the deep depressions that had occurred often through most of Greta's life.

Stalling, she now thought. She was stalling by sitting here and staring at Tyler's house. She put the Jeep into Drive and moved forward, swallowing against the swell of anxiety that tried to waltz up the back of her throat.

She didn't have the answers to a lot of things that had been happening at the Colton ranch, but she could at least get an answer from Tyler as to why he had lied for her.

She parked right in front of the house. Light spilled

from several windows, breaking through the falling darkness of the early-November night.

Tyler had a reputation as a workaholic. It was possible he wasn't even home yet. If he wasn't, then she'd wait. If his household help didn't want her inside, then she'd wait in her vehicle. She'd already put this conversation off for far too long.

Getting out of her car, she fought against the nervous energy that sizzled through her. She had nothing to be anxious about; after all, he was the one who had told the outrageous lie. But Tyler had always made her nervous with his cold blue eyes and hint of disdain when he looked at her.

She straightened her shoulders resolutely and rang the bell, hearing the musical chimes respond from someplace inside. As she waited, she pulled up the collar of her lightweight beige coat against the chilly evening air.

The door opened and she wasn't sure who was more surprised, she or Tyler. She'd expected a housekeeper, but instead a Tyler Stanton she'd never seen before stood in front of her.

The few times they had ever had any interaction, Tyler had always been impeccably dressed. The Tyler before her was absent his suit coat and tie. His white shirt was half-unbuttoned to reveal just enough bare chest to be distracting and his short light brown hair was slightly mussed. His dark blue eyes appeared to take in the whole sum of her with a quick sweep from head to toe.

"Greta, I was wondering when or if I'd ever hear from you. Please come in." He opened the door wider to allow her into a large foyer. "May I take your coat?"

Before she could reply, he had removed her coat and hung it in the nearby closet. He then smoothly ushered her into the great room and offered her a seat on the plush black leather sofa.

It was as if she'd entered an alternate universe. The Tyler she knew was stiff and formal, but this Tyler appeared casual and surprisingly welcoming. "How about something to drink? Maybe a glass of wine?" he asked.

"That would be nice." She finally found her voice.

"Red or white?" He moved to an elaborate built-in bar on one side of the large room.

"White would be fine," she replied.

"How have you been?" he asked and strode across the expanse of the room to hand her a long-stemmed crystal glass of wine.

He sat next to her and set his own glass of wine on the glass-topped coffee table in front of them.

"I've been better," she replied. He sat so close to her she could smell the scent of his spicy cologne, so different from Mark's woodsy favorite scent. "I guess you heard that Mark broke off our engagement."

His gaze held hers intently. "Are you heartbroken over it?"

She hesitated, wondering if she should lie and make Tyler feel bad. "No, I'm only sorry he beat me to the punch," she replied honestly. "I was behind bars for five long days and nights and he didn't even visit me once. Five days in jail gave me a lot of time to think. In fact, I've heard from a couple of my friends that while I was locked up, Mark was making the rounds of his old girlfriends, so I'd intended to break things off with him anyway. But that's not why I'm here."

She paused and took a sip of her wine and then set the glass down. She eyed the handsome man beside her boldly. "Why, Tyler? Why did you lie for me?"

"Because I knew you were no murderer," he replied easily.

"Didn't you hear that my DNA and fingerprints were all over the crime scene? My own brother arrested me." Pain swept through her as she remembered Ryan placing handcuffs on her and putting her into the back of his patrol car.

"I also know they had a hotel receipt to support the fact that you checked into the Regent Hotel on the night that Kurt was murdered, but since you were alone and had no interaction with the hotel staff, that nobody could substantiate your alibi. Besides, I didn't care what incriminating evidence they had. I knew you didn't have it in you to hurt anyone. I lied because you needed an alibi and I knew nobody would question my word."

It was not arrogance in his tone; it was just a statement of fact that reminded her that Tyler was an important, powerful businessman not just in Oklahoma City but in Tulsa, as well.

"Why on earth would you even involve yourself with my problems?" She knew that he and Mark weren't particularly close, so she couldn't believe he'd intervened for Mark's sake, especially given the alibi he provided of being her lover.

Her cheeks warmed at the thought. She had a feeling when Tyler Stanton made love to a woman, it would be more like a total body-and-soul possession rather than just a pleasant sexual encounter.

Tyler leaned toward her, his nearness seeming to suck all of the oxygen out of the air. His blue eyes were piercing, as if wanting to see something deep inside her. "Do you really want to know why I got you out of jail? Why I involved myself in your life?"

She nodded. She'd never noticed before how easy it would be to fall into the depths of his dark blue eyes and how hypnotic his smooth deep voice could be. She leaned toward him, as if anticipating a secret that might change her life and right her world forever.

"Mark was never supposed to take you for himself. That day in April I sent him to meet with you because I had a troubled horse that I wanted your help with. But I also wanted to get you here and hopefully into my bed."

She reeled back, shocked by his words. "What are you talking about? Mark never mentioned a horse to me that first day he came to the ranch to see me." She didn't even want to address the rest of what he'd said to her. She could scarcely wrap her brain around his bold audacity.

"No, I'm sure he didn't," Tyler replied drily. "He simply set out to win your heart for himself and he accomplished that."

He picked up his wineglass and took a sip and then set the glass back down. "Despite my own desire for you, I was happy for Mark when the two of you got engaged in June. My brother and I see eye to eye on few things, but I wanted him to be happy, and if you were his happiness, then I would have never done or said anything to ruin things for the two of you."

"Mark is happiest when he's the center of attention," she replied. "But he only wants positive attention. I always suspected that when I was at home on the ranch in Tulsa and he was at his town house here in Oklahoma City, he was seeing other women."

Tyler said nothing, but in his silence Greta recognized the truth. Mark had never really loved her. He had been in love with marrying a Colton, with all the society-page tidbits about their romance and upcoming wedding. But he'd never truly loved Greta, the tomboy who was happiest wearing jeans and a sweatshirt and working with and training horses.

"I thought that the relationship with you might make a man out of him," he said. "But I guess I was wrong."

"Do you still have that troubled horse?" she asked, eager to turn the course of the conversation.

"I do. She's a three-year-old filly who has had no training and very little human contact. Are you interested in working with her?"

"I might be," she replied. She needed something to focus on besides the fact that the man she'd nearly married wasn't in love with her and she really hadn't loved him. She needed a challenge to take her mind off all the strange and frightening things that had been happening in her life and around the Colton ranch.

"I still have the horse and I still have an intense desire for you. Would you also be interested in sharing my bed tonight?" he asked.

TYLER WASN'T A man who believed in playing games. He believed in going after what he wanted, and he had wanted Greta Colton since the very first time he'd seen her.

It was obvious he'd shocked her with his indecent and unexpected proposal to share his bed. She grabbed her wineglass and downed the contents, her cheeks a becoming pink.

Although she looked lovely now in the tailored slacks that hugged her long legs and the rust-colored blouse that enhanced her hazel-green eyes and her dark brown hair, she had really caught his attention when he'd watched her working with a horse at a rodeo months earlier.

Then her slender figure had been clad in dusty jeans and a T-shirt and she'd commanded the horse with confidence and mastery. That had been the woman who had both captured his desire and intrigued him.

She lowered her glass and tucked a strand of her long wavy hair behind her ear. "You're something else," she finally said. "You make up an outrageous lie to get me out of jail, a lie that ruined my engagement, and now you have the audacity to ask me to sleep with you?"

He smiled. "Sleep wasn't exactly what I had in mind." Her cheeks flushed once again with color, but she made no move to leave. "Greta, we're both consenting adults and don't need to answer to anyone for what we do," he added.

"I don't just fall into bed with any man who asks me," she replied and straightened her back defensively.

"I'm aware of that," he said. "If you were that kind of woman, then I wouldn't be interested in you."

She stared at him and then looked away. "Could I please have another glass of wine?" she asked. "And let's talk a bit more about this horse you have."

He got up and refilled her glass, then sat down again, this time a little bit closer to her…close enough that he could smell the fresh scent of her.

It was crazy—he had never felt such a visceral pull toward a woman before or since that first time he'd seen Greta. He'd initially been disappointed when he realized Mark and Greta had become an item, but he'd also been pleased that his younger brother had found somebody and intended to settle down.

It hadn't taken long for Tyler to realize that Mark had no intention of settling down, wedding or not. Getting engaged and planning a wedding to Greta hadn't slowed

Mark's womanizing ways or forced him to begin to build a future of financial stability for himself and his wife.

"What else do you want to know about the horse?" he asked.

Her gaze danced down to his exposed chest and then quickly moved back up to his face. "Uh...how did you come to own her?"

That quick glance emboldened him. She apparently wasn't completely immune to him. "I was driving to work one day and passed a field where the horse was tethered to a post. She was half-starved and appeared to have been whipped. I couldn't just drive by and forget about her obvious distress, so I stopped at the closest ranch house, and the man living there told me the horse was his. I offered to buy her, and after some negotiation, he agreed. Since then she's filled out and healed from her physical abuse, but neither of my ranch hands have been able to work with her. She won't let anyone near her."

"It sounds like you probably saved her life," Greta replied, more than a hint of approval in her voice.

"If I did, she isn't showing any gratitude," he replied drily. He was rewarded by her short but melodic laugh. "And speaking of gratitude, I haven't heard you thank me for getting you out of jail."

"I am grateful, but I'm not sure I've forgiven you for the particular lie you told. Didn't you consider what it might do to my reputation? What it would do to your relationship with your brother? Didn't you consider any of the consequences of your lie?"

"Nothing has gone public, so your good reputation remains intact." He paused and thought about his brother. "Mark and I have always had a difficult relationship. To be honest, I knew that you'd already told the authorities that you were in a hotel room on the night of the murder. It just seemed easiest for me to tell them that I was in that room with you. I wasn't thinking of consequences. I just couldn't stand the thought of you having to spend another day and another night in that jail cell."

She sighed and took a drink from her glass. "It would have been so much easier if Mark had been the one to come forward and say he was with me that night." Her eyes narrowed. "But he did absolutely nothing to help me. He didn't even come to see me or make a phone call to check on me."

"If all this hadn't happened, then you wouldn't have known that you were about to marry the wrong man," Tyler countered. "Not that I'm suggesting I'm the right man."

She tilted her head slightly and looked at him curiously. "Why haven't you married? You're handsome and successful and I'm sure plenty of women would be happy to become Mrs. Tyler Stanton."

"The women who want to be my wife aren't the kind of woman I'd want for a wife. They want it for all the wrong reasons," he replied. "I got close to marrying once, but it didn't work out and since then I haven't found the right woman. Besides, I work long hours and don't have a lot of time to do the whole dating thing."

"So you just invite emotionally vulnerable women to share your bed for the night and then move on to the next woman." She stared at him boldly.

A small laugh escaped him. "You don't appear to me to be an emotionally vulnerable woman, and no, I don't make a habit of inviting women into my bed. In fact, you're the first who has gotten an official invitation."

She eyed him dubiously.

He leaned closer to her, so close that if he wanted to, he could wrap her in his arms and take full possession of her lush lips with his. It was tempting. It was oh so tempting.

"It's true, Greta," he said and watched her eyes spark with gold and green hues. "I don't invite women into my bed. I wait for them to invite me into theirs. But you're different, and the desire, the passion, I have for you is stronger than anything I've ever felt for any other woman."

Her mouth trembled slightly and he continued, "In all of my life I've never been jealous of Mark, but when he hooked up with you, I was jealous of him for the first time. He had what I wanted…what I still want."

"I should go," she replied in a breathy voice, but she made no move to get up.

"You should stay," he countered. "It's a long drive back to Tulsa. You should stay here with me tonight and then tomorrow morning you can see the horse."

Her eyes looked slightly glazed and he didn't know if it was from the wine she'd drunk too fast or the blatant lust he knew shone from his own.

"Greta, if you want, you can spend the night in one of my guest rooms." It wasn't what he wanted, but he also didn't want to coerce her in any way. He'd laid his cards out on the table and the next play was hers.

"I'll stay," she said slowly. "I'll stay in one of your guest rooms and take a look at the horse in the morning and decide if she's a project I want to take on."

Disappointment winged through him, but he tamped it down. He knew he'd been forward and he really wasn't surprised by her answer. He'd definitely been too open too quickly. It had been out of character for him, but when he'd seen her standing on his front porch, all of his desire for her, which had simmered for so long, had roared to full life.

"Then whenever you're ready, I'll show you to your room," he replied.

"I think I'm ready now." She stood and finished the last drink of wine in her glass.

He got up, as well, and took the glass from her and carried it and his own to the bar. He felt her gaze on his back and cursed himself for being a fool.

He should have just told her he'd alibied her because he'd been sure of her innocence and then told her about the horse he wanted her to work with. He should have never come at her with the open and honest passion that was in his heart and beat through his veins.

"I'll get you a T-shirt to sleep in," he said as he led her down the long hallway. They passed several bedrooms and two baths before he finally turned into a room that was located next to his master suite.

"This is lovely," she said. She offered him a small smile. "My bedroom at home is decorated in shades of blue, too."

"Then you should feel right at home here. There's an en suite bathroom, where you should find whatever you need. There's several new toothbrushes beneath the sink, and if you need something else that you can't find, just ask."

"I'm sure I'll be fine," she replied.

"I'll just go grab a T-shirt for you to sleep in."

He left her standing in the guest room and went into his master suite and to the drawer that held his T-shirts. He pulled one out and for a brief moment imagined her wearing it and nothing else.

He shook his head and shoved the vision aside and then returned to the guest room, where she hadn't moved a foot.

He handed her the T-shirt. "Thanks. This should be more comfortable than trying to sleep in my clothes," she said. She shifted from one booted foot to the other, obviously uncomfortable.

"Then I'll just tell you good-night," he said. "I'm right next door if you can't find what you need or if you change your mind about joining me." Damn, he'd done it again.

"You're very persistent," she replied.

"I am when I know what I want."

"Good night, Tyler," she said.

"Good night." He left the room and she closed the door behind him. He headed back to the great room and to the bar to put the glasses they had used into the dishwasher in the kitchen.

He certainly didn't intend to give up on satisfying his desire for Greta. He'd shocked her tonight, but he could be a patient man and he'd swear there had been more than a hint of interest in her eyes.

Tonight wasn't the end of things with Greta. He had a feeling it was just the beginning. All he had to do was convince her of that fact.

CHAPTER TWO

GRETA LAY IN the center of the king-size bed, Tyler's T-shirt smelling of fresh Oklahoma air and a hint of ocean-breeze fabric softener.

It was still early, just a little after nine, but she'd needed to escape from Tyler. She should've just driven home, but the truth was the wine had gone to her head, as had Tyler's invitation to share his bed.

She'd heard him go into his room just a few minutes earlier. Since it was a Tuesday night, he probably had gone to bed early because he had to work the next day.

They both would have to be up early if he was going to show her his troubled horse before he left for work. The possibility of working with a new horse was exciting. She was in desperate need of a challenge, and training this horse would fit the bill.

She closed her eyes, seeking sleep, but her mind conjured up a vision of the man in the next room. Did he sleep in pajamas or was he naked beneath his sheets? His unbuttoned shirt had given her a tantalizing peek at his bare chest. What would he look like with no shirt? What would he look like naked? A rivulet of heat worked through her. Drat the man anyway.

Mark had never gazed at her with such an unabashed desire. She'd never seen utter lust, such blatant hunger for her, in any man's eyes before tonight.

She'd seen it in Tyler's and she'd be a fool not to admit that he'd stirred something in the very depths of her, a hunger she hadn't known existed.

Mindless pleasure—she knew that was what she would find in his arms. Not love, not a promise for any future relationship. He'd offered her only one night of throwing caution to the wind and having uncomplicated sex with him.

After everything that had happened at the ranch over the past five months, mindless pleasure and uncomplicated sex sounded far too appealing.

She rolled over on her back and stared up at the ceiling, where pale moonlight danced tiny strands of illumination as it filtered through the slight part in the curtains at the window.

She couldn't go to sleep, because she was hot and bothered and curious. She'd known in her head that Mark had been cheating on her long before she had acknowledged it in her heart. She hadn't wanted to believe it, but the signs had been there.

Several times she'd thought of calling off the wedding, but for the first time in her life she'd enjoyed a real relationship with her mother, Abra. They had bonded over picking out flowers and deciding on arrangements, checking out caterers and choosing the size and flavor for the wedding cake.

She'd never seen her mother look so happy, and she'd felt incredibly responsible when Mark had broken their engagement, the wedding plans were called off, and her mother had fallen into one of her bouts of depression. At least her mother hadn't jumped on a jet to head to Europe like she'd done in the past when the depression struck. Of course, her health wasn't as good as it had once been.

Greta rolled over, this time curling into a fetal ball as a vision of Tyler once again filled her head.

She'd always found him incredibly handsome. While she'd seen the effect of his sexy smile on other women, he'd always been very cool and reserved around her.

Tonight she'd felt the force of that sexy smile, the intensity of his midnight blue eyes directed at her, and she'd liked it. She was surprised to discover a want inside her, a desire to throw caution to the wind, abandon her good senses and go crawl into his bed.

Mindless pleasure between two consenting adults. Would it really be wrong? She was on her feet at the side of the bed before she realized she'd consciously made up her mind.

Before she could change it, she walked out of her bedroom and into his. The moonlight in his room was brighter, drifting through a bank of floor-to-ceiling windows on the opposite side of the large room.

He sat up, a dark silhouette in the king-size bed. "Greta? Do you need something?" His voice sounded deeper, huskier than usual. She walked to stand at the very edge of his bed, his features now visible to her.

Hunger. It shone from his eyes and stole not only her power to speak but also momentarily her ability to breathe. He didn't say anything. He lifted the sheet that covered him and she slid in beside him.

"Are you sure?" he asked softly.

"I'm here," she replied.

She tried to tell herself it was the dizzying effect of the wine, the stress of the past five months in her life. She tried to believe that she wasn't herself, that she was acting irrationally, but the truth was she just wanted him to make love to her.

He pulled her into his arms and took her mouth with his in a fiery openmouthed kiss that heated her from head to toe. He continued to kiss her until she couldn't think. At the same time his hands moved languidly up and down the back of the T-shirt, stopping just shy of her bare buttocks.

She ran her hands across his shoulders and back, vaguely surprised by the play of hard muscles beneath his warm skin, muscles that were usually hidden beneath crisp white shirts and expensive suit coats.

He wore a pair of boxers, and those and her T-shirt were the only barriers between them and total naked flesh.

A small moan escaped her lips as his hands moved beneath her T-shirt at the same time his mouth slid down the length of her throat. He nibbled and teased her neck and then sucked one of her nipples through the thin cotton material. Flames of desire flared hot through her.

She reached down, slid her hand beneath the band of his boxers and grasped him. He was fully erect and after that everything happened in a haze.

T-shirt and boxers were gone, leaving them naked and gasping.

He teased and tormented her, stroking every inch of her body. He was confident and masterful in his touch and shot electric pleasure through her.

He followed his heated caresses with his mouth, kissing her in places she'd never been kissed before.

In turn, she did the same, stroking his smooth, muscled back, kissing down his neck and across his broad chest.

She was on fire and only he could put out the flames. She moved her hips against his, wanting…needing him to take her.

When his fingers danced across the place where she

needed him to touch her most, she gasped in fevered delight.

His fingers pressed harder, moved faster against her sensitive center, and a rising, overwhelming tension filled her.

As it peaked she rode the wave of a climax that left her shuddering with the force of the release. He didn't give her time to catch her breath. He moved between her thighs and took her.

He stroked deep and slow, and the rise of her pleasure began to build again. She moaned his name and he increased the speed of his thrusts. Her hips met his as they moved in a frenzy.

They ended together, with her crying with her own climax as he groaned and finished, as well.

When it was over, he held himself above her with his weight on his elbows. His eyes gleamed with the satisfaction of his possession. "I knew you'd be the perfect lover for me," he whispered.

"And I knew this was a huge mistake."

He frowned and rolled to the side of her. "Why was this a mistake? It was just as I imagined it would be... beyond wonderful. We fit together so well."

She sat up and grabbed the sheet to hide her breasts. She couldn't tell him it was a mistake that she wanted to repeat again and again, but that was the truth.

She'd never felt so wonderfully out of control as she had when he'd made love to her. She'd never known the intensity of the electric sensations he'd pulled from her. He'd tapped into a part of her that she hadn't even known existed.

"I'm not in the habit of falling into bed with men I don't love," she finally replied. She certainly wasn't in the habit of falling into bed with men who didn't love her. "I'm not a one-night-stand kind of woman."

"I'm hoping this isn't a one-night kind of thing," he replied.

His words shocked her almost as much as her uncharacteristic actions so far this night. "What exactly did you have in mind?"

He reached up and gently shoved a strand of her hair away from her face. "I was hoping that you'd meet my horse in the morning and agree to work with her. It's too long of a drive for you to come back and forth from Tulsa every day, so I figured you'd move in here, where you'll be available to work whenever you want to. And if you're staying here, why not sleep in my bed each night?"

"Did you manipulate things so that this would all happen?" She gazed at him searchingly. "Did you decide to alibi me knowing that Mark would break off our engagement, that I'd come here to speak to you and that I'd wind up in your bed?"

He laughed, a deep low rumble that she found ridiculously pleasant. "You're giving me far too much credit as a super mastermind." He sobered and his eyes took on that glow that created a new heat to flow through her.

"I waited five days before coming forward with that alibi. I had assumed Mark would do something to help you. When he didn't, I stepped forward. I knew there would be repercussions to my actions, but I certainly didn't anticipate you'd wind up here in my bed. But if I'm perfectly honest with you, it's what I wanted. It's what I've wanted for a very long time."

"You never gave a hint that you were interested in me before."

"I told you that I would have never interfered in your

relationship with Mark if I truly believed the two of you really belonged together. But it was obvious when Mark didn't even bother to visit you in jail that you deserved better than my brother. Marrying him would have been the biggest mistake of your life."

Greta felt as if her head were about to explode. The night had been a surprise on so many levels. She scooted toward the edge of the bed.

"Where are you going?" he asked.

"I'm going back to the guest room, where I probably should have stayed."

"There's no reason you can't finish the night out here," he countered.

"I don't want to make this into anything but what it was, an impulsive sexual encounter with a man I barely know. I won't wake up in your bed, because that makes what we just did into something different." She frowned, knowing he probably didn't understand, but it didn't matter. "I'll just tell you good-night."

She slid out of the bed and found the T-shirt on the floor. She pulled it on over her head and then left his room and went back to the guest room next door.

She went directly to the bathroom, turned on the light and stared at her reflection in the mirror. What on earth had she just done? What had she been thinking?

As if her life weren't complicated enough already, she'd just had mind-blowing sex with Tyler Stanton. And he'd made it clear that he didn't intend for it to be a one-night thing.

What did he really want from her? He certainly couldn't be in love with her. He didn't know her well enough. And she certainly didn't know him well enough to be in love with him. Until tonight she hadn't even been sure if she liked him at all. He'd certainly never given her any indication that he liked her.

She turned off the light and left the bathroom and got into bed, her mind still whirling with questions. To her surprise, she fell asleep almost immediately.

The scent of freshly brewed coffee and frying bacon awoke her the next morning. She was shocked to realize it was after eight, later than she normally slept. She'd expected Tyler to show her the horse and be on the road by this time. He had an important job to get to.

Maybe it was the cook fixing breakfast and Tyler had already left for work, she thought as she dressed in the clothes she had worn the night before.

He'd probably arranged for a ranch hand to show her the horse and then he'd call her later in the day to see if she was interested in working with the wild filly.

Once dressed and with her teeth brushed and hair combed, she followed her nose down the hallway and through the great room to find a large, airy kitchen and Tyler standing with his back to her in front of the stove.

Tight jeans cupped his taut butt and clung to his long legs. He also wore a blue flannel shirt and was barefoot. She'd never seen him so casually dressed and so relaxed. It was definitely a good look on him.

"Good morning," she said.

He whirled around and smiled at her. "Back at you. Coffee is in the carafe—help yourself—and bacon and eggs will be ready in just a few minutes."

"What can I do to help?" She walked to the counter with the coffee machine and an awaiting cup.

"Nothing. Just have a seat at the table and relax."

She poured her coffee and carried it to the round glass-topped kitchen table. "Don't you have household help?" she asked, realizing for the first time that she'd seen no staff since she'd arrived the night before.

"I have the house cleaned once every two weeks by a team that comes in and I have a laundry service that picks up dirty clothes each week, but other than that I don't keep anyone full-time except two ranch hands. I spend so many hours at work that it seemed silly to me to have cooks or maids just hanging around all day with nothing to do."

"Speaking of work, shouldn't you be there now?" she asked.

He forked bacon out of the skillet and onto an awaiting platter covered with a paper towel. "I took the day off. How do you like your eggs?"

"However you make them," she replied. "You have a reputation as a workaholic. Do you often take days off?"

"I can't remember the last time I didn't go into work. But the company can run fine without me. I have a great general manager, and if any problems arise, somebody will call me." He cracked several eggs into a bowl, added a dollop of milk and began to whisk the concoction.

"Mark never had any problems taking time off," she said. "And he's vice president of the company."

"It's a title, not a life calling, for Mark. Mark likes to think of himself as a trust-fund baby. Unfortunately, there was very little trust fund other than the family business. Mark shot through his cash in the first two years after my parents' deaths."

He paused to pour the eggs into the skillet. "Mark has always preferred play over work." There was no censure in his voice. It was just a statement of fact that Greta knew to be true.

Greta sipped her coffee and wondered now how she'd

ever thought she could find happiness with Mark. She'd suspected from the very beginning of their relationship that he was cheating on her. She knew he didn't possess much of a work ethic. They'd had very little in common and had never really talked about what their future together would look like.

But he had been so charming and attentive when they were together, and he'd always managed to sweep away her suspicions about him and other women. Tyler was right. Marrying Mark would have been a terrible mistake.

Greta shunned the limelight and Mark craved it. She loved her work as a horse trainer and he'd been bored by it. Despite their engagement and wedding plans, Mark's interest in her had begun to wane the minute he'd found out she wasn't a blood Colton but rather adopted. A recent fact that had been revealed that she was still trying to come to terms with herself.

"Here we go." Tyler set a plate in front of her and then took a seat next to her at the table with his own plate in front of him.

"Thank you, but you really didn't have to cook me breakfast. You could have just shown me the horse and I'd have been on my way."

He grinned, his blue eyes sparkling in amusement. "But then I wouldn't have the pleasure of your company while I ate breakfast."

"Do you cook breakfast for all the women you sleep with?" she asked, and a faint warmth filled her cheeks.

"All the women I sleep with?" He raised an eyebrow. "If you knew how few women I've slept with over the last couple of years, you'd feel sorry for me and offer to be my lover every single night."

She couldn't help but smile. "You're a piece of work, Tyler Stanton."

"Yes, I am, but what I'm saying is true. I'm not a player, Greta."

"Then what are you doing with me?"

He sobered and gazed at her for a long moment. "To be honest, I'm not really sure, but I like what I'm doing with you so far. Now, eat up before it gets cold."

While they ate, she was grateful that he kept up a light conversation, talking about the changes he'd made to Stanton Oil since his parents had died in a car accident ten years ago. At twenty-two he'd stepped in as president of the company and eventually had appointed his two-years-younger brother as vice president.

"I had to work twice as hard and twice as long as anyone else to earn the respect of my employees. To most of them I was a snot-nosed kid who'd just graduated from college with a business degree but didn't have the age or wisdom to run the company."

"But you proved them all wrong," she replied. She knew how respected Tyler was in the business world.

"It took time but I now enjoy a good relationship with everyone who works for me," he replied with a touch of pride in his voice.

She was vaguely surprised that there was no morning-after awkwardness. He was warm and easy to talk to, showing her a side of him she'd never seen before.

By the time they'd finished eating and she'd helped him with the cleanup, she was ready to see the horse he'd told her about.

He helped her into her coat and then he donned a casual leather jacket and they left the house by a back door in the kitchen. In the distance several outbuildings rose up, certainly nothing like the big cattle operation at the Colton ranch but enough pasture and room for a few horses.

The early-November sun was warm, and as they drew closer, she identified the outbuildings as a small barn and stables. There were two corrals, a large one in the distance and a smaller one with a shedlike structure that would provide shelter from the weather. In the small corral a black Thoroughbred filly danced nervously as they approached.

"Oh, Tyler, she's beautiful," Greta exclaimed.

"And so far completely unbreakable," he replied.

When they reached the fence, the filly backed to the opposite side. She pawed the ground and shook her head in a show of spirited temperament.

The excitement of a new challenge rose up in Greta. "She has good lines. Do you intend to race her?"

"No, nothing like that. I just want to be able to ride her. I want her to trust somebody and find some peace."

Greta looked up at Tyler, surprised and touched by his words. The man continued to keep her slightly off balance. He was proving himself to be nothing like she'd originally thought.

She looked back at the filly and her heart ached with the need to soothe, to cure. The physical wounds the horse had sported when bought by Tyler had apparently healed.

Her coat looked shiny and full, and while she was still a bit on the thin side, she looked healthy. But she was obviously tormented by the abuse she'd suffered at the hands of her human owner and those scars were deep inside her.

"I want to work with her," she said firmly.

"Great!" Tyler smiled with pleasure. "I hear you're one of the best in the business, so I know she'll be in good hands. You know, the easiest way is for you to move in here so that you can work with her whenever you want. It's silly for you to drive back and forth from here to Tulsa."

She knew he was right. Often when she was training a horse, she stayed on the ranch where the horse was located. Besides, things had been so tense at home lately. The idea of a couple of weeks away was definitely appealing.

"I'll drive home now and pack some bags and come back here later this evening," she finally said. She didn't know if her decision was a mistake or not, but as she looked at the filly, she knew with certainty she wanted to help her, to train her to trust again.

He nodded. "I have two ranch hands. Bill Naters takes care of upkeep and lawn work and whatever else needs to be done. He's here off and on. Raymond Edwards is here full-time during the days and works mostly in the stables and with the horses. Just tell him whatever you need and he'll see to it that you get it. You can usually find him either in the stables or in the barn."

They began the walk back to the house. "Should I expect your return by dinnertime?" he asked once they were back in the house and she had grabbed her purse to leave.

She looked at her watch. "Yes, I should be able to make it back here by early evening."

He opened the front door and together they left the house and headed toward her Jeep in the driveway. "We'll go out to dinner. Do you like steak?"

She smiled at him. "I grew up on a cattle ranch. I cut my teeth on a T-bone."

"Dumb question," he replied with a charming grin.

"There's a great steak place not far from here. How does that sound for dinner?"

"Wonderful," she replied. Dining out was definitely better than just the two of them eating in. She still felt more than a little bit vulnerable where he was concerned and she was determined to make sure that he understood that the arrangement between them was strictly professional from here on.

Last night had been an anomaly that she didn't expect to be repeated, no matter how much she might entertain a weakness for a repeat.

She opened the Jeep door, but before she could get inside, he took her by the arm, twirled her around and pulled her close against his chest.

"What are you doing?" she asked, both loving and hating the instant responsive heat his nearness evoked.

"Just one more thing before you go," he murmured softly.

"What's that?" she asked breathlessly.

"This." He slanted his lips down to capture hers in a kiss that seared her from head to toe.

Someplace in the back of her mind she knew she should jerk away…halt the kiss…do something to stop the insanity. Instead her arms automatically reached up to circle his neck and she leaned into him as the kiss deepened.

When he finally released her, her heart pounded too fast. She murmured a quick goodbye and slid into the safety of the Jeep.

It was only when she was on the road and headed toward Tulsa that she allowed herself to think about Tyler and that deep, unexpected kiss.

It had been a definite sign that despite their night together, he still wanted her. And as crazy as it was, she still wanted him, too.

She'd never indulged in a strictly physical relationship before, but that was what this was…desire built on nothing more than some kind of wild chemistry between them.

The sane thing to do was to drive home and not return to Tyler's place. But she hadn't felt quite sane in months. Besides, she desperately wanted to work with the horse that showed such distrust of people. There was also a desire for her to be away from her own home, gain some distance from everything that had been happening there.

Work had always centered her and it had been too long since she'd utilized her talents as a trainer. For the past couple of months she'd been busy planning a wedding that was no longer going to take place.

Working with the horse at Tyler's place would be a good escape for her. She no longer had to play the socialite and appear at public events in fancy designer dresses with Mark and her parents. It was a role she'd never been comfortable in.

Surely when she returned to Tyler's later this evening, she'd be able to make him understand that what had happened between them last night wasn't going to happen again.

CHAPTER THREE

TYLER WATCHED THE horse he'd named She-Devil when he'd first brought her home and realized just how temperamental, how emotionally damaged, she was. She remained backed up against the opposite side of the corral, her body tensed as if she was expecting something bad to happen to her.

Raymond Edwards, his ranch hand, joined him at the corral. "I saw you had Greta Colton out here. Is she going to work with the filly?"

"Yes. She left for Tulsa to pack some bags and will be back here sometime later this evening."

"Good. I'm glad she's on board. She's one of the best trainers in the area. If anyone can help that poor tormented soul, she can," Raymond said.

"I told her you'd be available for whatever she needs," Tyler replied.

"Of course."

Tyler clapped the thin, wiry cowboy on his shoulder. "You're a good man, Raymond."

Raymond smiled at him, revealing a missing eyetooth that had been knocked out in a bar fight when he'd been young and stupid. "You're an easy boss. I'm heading into the stable now to clean out the stalls. I look forward to learning from Greta."

Tyler nodded and watched Raymond disappear into

the stable. Raymond didn't live on the property. For the past five years he'd worked for Tyler, he'd arrived each morning at dawn and left around six. Tyler kept four saddle horses and Raymond saw to their needs and kept the stable and riding equipment meticulously clean and maintained.

With a final glance at She-Devil, Tyler turned and headed back toward the house. Greta. His brain instantly filled with a vision of her. He'd been surprised to see her on his front porch, but nothing had surprised him more than her appearing in his room the night before.

He'd wanted Greta Colton long before Mark had ever met her. He'd sent Mark to meet Greta with the specific intent of getting her interested in his filly and close to him.

The moment he'd first seen her she'd stirred something inside him. Even after making love to her last night, he hadn't had enough of her. He wanted more.

Once Mark had become engaged to her, Tyler had tried to spend as little time as possible around her, although there had been occasions when they'd all been together. Still, Tyler had kept himself distant, not wanting to ruin anything for his younger brother by giving away his own feelings about her.

Since the age of nineteen, when their parents had died, Mark had struggled with life. He'd squandered what little inheritance he'd received, and when he'd been flat broke, Tyler had offered him the position of vice president of the family company, along with a generous salary and few real responsibilities.

But Mark liked the good life and he rarely made it from payday to payday. When that happened, he'd come to Tyler for extra money, and it happened frequently.

Tyler entered the house by the back door, poured himself a cup of coffee and sat at the kitchen table. There were times he thought his brother hated him. Mark hated Tyler's success, hated having to come to him for a handout. Mark had known of Tyler's desire to meet Greta from the beginning. When they first met, his brother hadn't mentioned the wild horse but had wooed Greta right into a relationship and eventually an engagement. Tyler suspected a lot of Greta's allure for his brother was because Mark knew Tyler was interested in her.

Tyler hadn't alibied Greta to ruin her relationship with Mark, although he'd known the odds were good that would happen. He'd alibied Greta because he couldn't stand the thought of her being behind bars and he knew she didn't have it in her to kill anyone. Most important, when he discovered that Mark hadn't even visited Greta in jail, let alone attempted to help her in any way, Tyler had known he had to step forward.

He hadn't seen or spoken to his brother since Greta's release from jail, but he had heard rumors that Mark wasn't crying in his beer and instead had been making the rounds of old girlfriends and partying it up. He must have found a sugar mama because normally by now Mark would be asking for an "advance" on his paycheck.

Thankfully, nobody's heart appeared to have been broken by Tyler's false alibi and the subsequent broken engagement. He'd accomplished what he wanted to do by getting Greta released from jail and last night he'd held her in his arms and made love to her.

It had been magic. Making love to her had been everything that he'd fantasized about and more. He had no driving desire to find a wife and build a future with her. He just knew he wanted Greta again…and again.

She not only drew him physically, but she also intrigued him. He wanted not just to know her body but to get into her mind, as well. She appeared to be so different from the superficial social-climbing women who normally surrounded him.

He didn't know exactly where this would all lead, but for the first time since his parents' deaths, he was willing to let fate take over and just go along for the ride. For the first time in a long time, he was allowing emotions to lead him rather than carefully planning and using his head.

He finished his coffee and then headed for his bedroom. As he made the bed, he thought of how passionate she'd been, how eagerly she'd responded to his every touch the night before.

After making the bed, he checked in with his office and was glad to hear that there were no fires that needed to be put out. It would be a long day awaiting Greta's return.

Tyler had few friends. Taking over the family business and making it successful and seeing to Mark's welfare had taken up most of the time when young men hung out at bars or sporting events and built friendships.

Thankfully, he had one good friend, the rancher next door. Derek Underwood was three years older than Tyler, but the two had struck up an unlikely friendship that Tyler cherished.

He returned to the kitchen and punched Derek's number into his cell phone. Derek answered on the second ring. "I was wondering if you wanted to come over and drink a cup of coffee and shoot the bull with me for a little while," Tyler said.

"You're at home? On a Wednesday morning?" Derek replied in surprise.

"I took the day off," Tyler said.

"I'd better look outside to see if the sky is falling."

Tyler laughed. "You want to come by or not?"

"Sure, I'll be there in ten minutes."

The two men hung up and Tyler made a fresh pot of coffee. By the time it had finished brewing, Derek was at his back door. On the surface the two men were exact opposites.

Derek's wardrobe consisted solely of worn jeans and flannel shirts. Some days he shaved; some days he didn't. His dark brown hair was long and shaggy and appeared to have not been acquainted with a comb for years.

"I hired Greta Colton to come out here and work with She-Devil," Tyler said as he poured them each a cup of coffee and joined Derek at the table.

Derek frowned, his bushy brown eyebrows nearly meeting across the bridge of his nose. "Are you sure that's a good idea? I have a good friend in Tulsa who is fairly friendly with the Coltons, and lately it seems there's a lot of drama going on with that family."

"What kind of drama?" Tyler asked. He knew about the murder of a ranch hand and Greta's arrest, but he hadn't really kept up with what was happening to the Colton family.

"Greta's mother was attacked in her bedroom and was in a coma for a little while. They've had fires set in some of their outbuildings and fencing torn down. Then there's the mystery of the murder of Kurt Rodgers. I've even heard rumors about Greta being on drugs."

Tyler stared at his friend in surprise. He hadn't heard anything about the problems at the Colton ranch. Mark certainly had never mentioned anything unusual going on there. Of course, Mark had been more interested in getting his photo in the paper with his lovely fiancée.

"Sounds like foolish gossip to me," Tyler scoffed.

Derek shrugged. "Maybe. All I know is that from what I heard, where Greta goes, trouble follows. I mean, even her own brother had her arrested for murder."

"Greta couldn't kill anyone. I don't know how her DNA got around the crime scene, but it wasn't there because she killed somebody."

Derek took a sip of his coffee and eyed Tyler over the rim of the cup. He set the cup back down and leaned back in the chair. "I heard you alibied her for the night of the murder. Is it true that she was with you that night?"

Tyler hated lying to anyone, especially a good friend, but he knew he had to stick to his story, not just to protect Greta but also to protect himself. "Yeah, it's true. I was at the Regent Hotel for a business meeting, and when the meeting ended, I wandered into the bar. She was there and we shared a couple of drinks and one thing led to another and I wound up in her room for the entire night."

Derek narrowed his eyes. "If that's what you say."

"That's what I say," Tyler replied firmly. "And where did you hear about the alibi?"

"I've got a friend in the police department in Tulsa. He told me and then warned me that if I repeated it to anyone, he'd shoot me."

"If you repeat it again, I'll shoot you," Tyler replied with a grin.

"At least you're getting the best when it comes to a trainer for She-Devil."

Tyler nodded. "Greta is moving in here to work. She should be arriving sometime this evening and will stay as long as it takes."

"Rumors or not, if I were you, I'd sleep with one eye open," Derek said wryly.

Tyler laughed. "I'm sure it will be fine."

The two visited for about a half an hour, talking about ranching and local news, and then Derek left to go back to his chores.

Tyler placed the coffee mugs into the dishwasher and thought about what he'd just learned about the events at the Colton ranch.

Burning buildings, downed fencing, an attack on Abra Colton and murder… It was a lot to take in.

Where Greta goes, trouble follows.

I've even heard rumors about Greta being on drugs.

Those two sentences of Derek's played and replayed in Tyler's head. He knew she was a talented horse trainer, but what didn't he know about the woman he'd made love with the night before, a woman he'd invited to live with him in his home?

"MOTHER, YOU HAVE to cheer up," Greta said.

Abra Colton sat in a chair next to a window in the sitting area of the master suite and stared listlessly outside.

After years of barely knowing her mother, who had spent much of her children's growing-up years traveling the globe, in recent months Greta had finally begun to develop the kind of relationship she'd always wanted with her.

Abra had thrown herself wholeheartedly into Greta's wedding plans. Her smiles had come more often and her eyes had sparkled with life. There had been no killer migraines, no need for her to take to her bed for days on end of rest and quiet.

Now she released a weary sigh, her thin frame absent any energy as her fingers idly toyed with the fringe on the bottom of a lavender throw that covered her shoulders. She turned and gazed at Greta. "But you would have made such a beautiful bride."

As usual, Abra was perfectly groomed, every dark brown hair perfectly combed into a chin-length bob, but her eyes held such sadness it broke Greta's heart.

She sank down on her knees next to her mother's chair. "But surely you wouldn't have wanted me to marry a man who couldn't bring me happiness," Greta said softly.

"Of course not," Abra replied quickly. "I just thought Mark was a much better man than he turned out to be."

"That makes two of us," Greta said. "Mother, just because this wedding fell through doesn't mean I'll never have a wedding at all, and when the next time comes, I want you by my side and planning every detail with me."

Abra forced a sad smile. "So much has happened in the last couple of months. The wedding was the one good thing to take my mind off everything else." She patted Greta's hand absently. "Don't worry. I'll be fine, dear. I just need a little bit of time."

Greta rose to her feet. "I'm getting ready to leave for a job. I'll be in Oklahoma City for the next couple of weeks or so." She didn't tell her mother specifically whom she would be working for or where she would be staying, and she was grateful when Abra didn't ask.

She left her mother's room and headed to her father's study. She wondered how much of Abra's depression was due to the cancellation of the wedding and how much was because she'd recently learned that Greta wasn't her biological daughter and the baby girl she'd given birth to twenty-six years ago had died after only one day of life.

Greta found her father at his desk in the opulent over-size room. He didn't hear her approach and for a long moment she stood in the doorway and simply looked at him.

At sixty-six years old, John "Big J" Colton was still like a force of nature. He was the life of any party, with a loud, booming voice and a bigger-than-life presence.

Although his hair was now silver white, his green eyes still sparked with a lust for life. He'd been the rock of the family when his children had been growing up, and Greta knew the anguish he'd suffered each time Abra had gone away for one of her convalescing trips.

He must have sensed Greta's presence, for he looked up from whatever he'd been reading and his face lit with a smile.

"Greta, my darling girl." His eyes filled with the affection and love that had got Greta through life despite her mother's many absences.

Big J had been the one constant in Greta's life. "Are you working hard?" she asked.

His grin widened and his eyes twinkled. "Hardly working is more like it."

"I just wanted to let you know that I'm heading off to Oklahoma City for a couple of weeks."

"Work or play?"

"Work. I've been hired to train a horse."

"Good. I think some time away from here is best for you until Ryan and the rest of the police get everything under control." He eyed her with a touch of worry. "You'll stay in touch?"

"Of course," she replied. "You can always reach me on my cell phone. And you'll keep an eye on Mother?"

Big J's gaze softened. "Absolutely. She's a bit sad right now, but I'm sure she'll rally."

"I feel guilty about the wedding being called off,"

Greta confessed. Of course, the wedding hadn't been the only recent blow Abra had received, along with the rest of the family.

"Nonsense." Big J waved his hand dismissively. "The last thing I'd want for you is to be married to a shallow womanizer like Mark Stanton. You know I never really warmed up to him. Never forget that no matter what has happened, you're a Colton through and through and you deserve the very best."

Sudden tears misted her eyes and she quickly blinked them away. "Then I'll just get on the road. I'll be in touch." She left the room before the tears did more than blur her vision.

She loaded her Jeep and headed away from the huge mansion on the hill that was home. Abra had designed the house and Big J had given in to her every whim, which had resulted in an 11,000-square-foot home furnished to make a statement…and it screamed, "We have money."

Greta had always been more at home in the pastures than in the house. She'd been right beside her five brothers as they'd all grown up, climbing trees and fences, scooting through cattle chutes and riding bareback on some of the biggest, fastest horses on the ranch.

The past couple of months of prewedding activities had been miserable for her as she'd donned frilly dresses she wasn't accustomed to, picked out pink ribbon and lace and flowers for the wedding and visited various caterers, all in an effort to please her mother.

The whole pink-and-white wedding scene hadn't been her thing, but she'd gone along with it all, being somebody she wasn't to make Abra and Mark happy.

Although she was sorry for the way things had turned

out and that Abra had fallen into one of her depressive states, there was also a sense of freedom that she could once again just be herself.

Before leaving the house, she'd showered and changed into a pair of jeans, a burnt-orange blouse and a brown suede jacket. She had no idea what the dress code was for the restaurant Tyler had mentioned, but she'd packed a couple of less casual things just in case.

As she got closer to Tyler's, a little bit of nervous energy jumped through her veins. She wasn't nervous about working with the horse. In fact, she was excited by the challenge. The black filly had called to her, touching something inside her that was impossible to ignore.

It was definitely the man himself who made anxiety bubble up inside her. Despite the fact that she'd showered not so long ago, she imagined she could still smell the scent of his expensive cologne clinging to her skin, still feel the heat of his hands on her naked skin.

It was early dusk when she pulled into his driveway. He opened the front door, as if he'd been standing there staring out and waiting for her all day.

"You made it back," he said as she got out of her car. "And I have reservations at the restaurant in thirty minutes, so your timing couldn't be more perfect."

The force of him, the very energy he exuded, had her half-breathless before she'd even opened her back door to get to her suitcases.

"Here, let me take those." He carried the two suitcases to the front door, with her hurrying to catch up with him. Once she did, he headed down the hallway until he reached the guest room she'd stayed in the night before. "In here? Or in there?" He gestured toward his room.

"In here," she said firmly and walked into the guest room. He placed the two suitcases on the floor.

"You can unpack later. We should probably go ahead and head out to the restaurant," he said.

"Should I change clothes?" she asked, although he was casually dressed in a pair of jeans and a long-sleeved white shirt.

"No, you're fine." He smiled at her. "I'm just glad you're here."

With the same momentum that he'd put forward in bringing her inside, he took her back outside, and before she could even catch her breath, she was ensconced in the rich leather passenger seat of a sleek silver sports car.

"This place is a little hole-in-the-wall, but it's become so popular you have to make reservations even on a weeknight," he said as they pulled out onto the highway.

"You mentioned it was a steak house. I'm definitely a steak-and-potatoes kind of girl," she replied.

"Good. Then we should get along just fine."

"I never asked you this morning what the horse's name is." She wanted to keep the conversation focused on the reason she was there.

"She-Devil," he replied.

Greta shook her head. "That will never do. Does she respond to that name?"

"She doesn't respond to anything."

"Then we have to find her a new name, something that doesn't have such a negative connotation."

He slid her an amused glance. "I suppose you want to call her Sugar."

"That's perfect," she replied. "And by the time I get finished with her, she'll be as sweet as sugar."

"You sound pretty sure of yourself."

"I know what I'm good at," she replied.

Again he flashed her a grin. "I like confidence in a woman."

They passed a strip mall and he turned into the parking lot. At the end of the line of businesses was a restaurant named Cattle Call.

"Like I said, it's a bit of a hole-in-the-wall, but the steaks are out of this world," he said and angled into an empty parking space at the side of the building.

"I like hole-in-the-wall kind of restaurants," she replied. "Besides, it's the quality of the food that counts."

They got out of the car and entered the crowded restaurant, where the hostess greeted Tyler by name and led them to a two-top table in the back that was a little more secluded than the other tables.

The scent of grilled meat filled the air, and while the place was full of people, the level of noise was relatively low and made conversation between them easy.

The hostess handed them each a menu and then with a bright smile told them their waitress would be with them soon and left the table.

"It smells delicious in here," Greta said as her stomach rumbled with hunger. She hadn't eaten anything since breakfast that morning. "You must be a regular since the hostess knew who you were by name."

"I eat here two or three times a week. It's on my way home from work, so I usually pop in for dinner." He didn't bother picking up the menu.

Greta opened hers and peered at the offerings. It took her only a minute to make up her mind. The waitress, a pleasantly plump woman with a name tag that read Brenda, greeted them and took their drink and dinner orders.

"A friend of mine stopped by today and told me there

have been some rough times at your place lately," Tyler said once the waitress was gone.

"We've had some issues," she replied, unsure what he'd heard and how much to tell him.

"My friend told me a lot of the issues seem to revolve around you." He held her gaze intently.

Greta sighed. She'd been raised to keep family matters in the family and not involve outsiders unless necessary. Certainly Mark, as her fiancé, had known some of the problems that had occurred. "Mark didn't ever mention anything about it to you?"

"Mark only speaks to me when it serves his purpose and that's usually when he needs money," Tyler said drily.

The waitress returned with their drink orders, a glass of wine for Greta and a scotch and soda for Tyler. When she'd left once again, Greta decided to tell Tyler everything. She wanted him to trust in her, and who knew what kind of rumors his friend had told him? Besides, she needed to talk about it with somebody other than a family member, to vent some of the fear and uncertainty that she'd been living with for what seemed like forever.

"It all started soon after Mark and I got engaged in June. My mother was attacked in her bedroom and the doctors had to put her into a medically induced coma. Everyone thought it was some kind of a botched robbery attempt. Soon after that I received in the mail a copy of Mark's and my official engagement picture that ran in the paper. My face was x-ed out in the photo. I thought it was probably from one of Mark's old girlfriends, but it still made me feel a bit uneasy."

"I can imagine that would be unsettling," Tyler replied.

She nodded. "At the same time, odd things were happening around the ranch—a fire was set in one of the outbuildings, tires were slashed on some of the farm vehicles and fencing kept getting torn down."

She stopped talking as the waitress arrived with their meals. She continued once the waitress had left, feeling as if she'd held everything in too tight for too long and it was a relief to talk to somebody who had no horse in the race, so to speak.

"Thankfully, my mother came out of the coma and returned home, and she and I continued with the wedding planning." Greta frowned and took a sip of her wine. "Although my mother seemed happy, something was different between us. She was different with me, but I thought it had something to do with the head injury she'd sustained. Then one day when I was here in Oklahoma City, my brother Daniel called me and asked what I was doing hanging around the ranch. I told him that I was here and it was impossible that he'd seen me there, but he insisted he'd seen me. That's when I think most of my family started to worry about me."

She laughed self-consciously. "I'm doing way too much talking and not enough eating. Let's eat while it's hot."

"You have to talk and eat. I feel like you're forcing me to walk out in the middle of an intriguing movie." He picked up his fork and steak knife and she did the same.

The steak cut like butter and melted in her mouth, but her head was filled with what she hadn't yet shared with Tyler. The rest of what she had to tell him, she hadn't really processed completely herself.

She ate several bites of the steak and baked potato and then continued talking. "Then my DNA was found at several crime scenes around the ranch, including where

Kurt was murdered. As you know, I was arrested and you got me out of jail. As soon as I returned home, my mother told everyone that it was me who had attacked her, but it wasn't me. She said the woman looked like me but she looked crazy and wild. And that's when my father made his big confession…" Her voice trailed off.

Tyler leaned forward. He held a piece of steak on his fork suspended between his plate and his mouth. "His big confession?"

She nodded. "He told us that after giving birth to all her boys, my mother had finally given birth to the girl she'd always wanted. But the baby only lived for a day and then died. He'd learned from a nurse that a young woman had just given birth to twins at her home because she couldn't afford the hospital bills. Believing that losing her daughter would send my mother over the edge forever, he met with the other mother and arranged to buy one of her twins for fifty thousand dollars. That's how I became a part of the Colton family."

Tyler gazed at her with vague surprise. "It must have been a shock to learn about the circumstances of your birth at your age."

"A shock not just for me but for the entire family." She took another drink of her wine and tried to stanch a chill that threatened to invade her. "I know now that I have a twin sister and I think she's found me. I don't believe she's looking for a happy reunion. I think maybe she wants to kill me."

CHAPTER FOUR

TYLER STARED AT HER, stunned by what she'd just told him. A dead baby, another one bought to replace it? And an evil twin sister to boot? It sounded like something out of a bad B-rated movie. "What makes you think she wants to kill you?"

"If she wanted a real happy reunion, she would have just knocked on the front door and introduced herself. Instead it was her DNA found at Kurt's murder scene. It was her DNA found all around the ranch where bad things have happened."

"What would be her motive to kill you?"

"I have no idea. I've never met her. I don't know anything about her. I just think she must be crazy. I believe the only reason why she hasn't managed to hurt me so far is because for the last couple of months I've been on the move between the ranch and Oklahoma City for the wedding plans."

Tyler digested everything she had told him. Was she really in danger? "Did you tell anyone outside your immediate family that you were going to be staying at my place?"

"No, I didn't even tell my immediate family exactly where I was going. I just told them I had a job in Oklahoma City. Thankfully, nobody asked me to be more

specific. They're used to me being gone and not knowing exactly where I am, especially when I'm working."

"Then you will be safe at my place," Tyler replied.
Any concerns he had entertained throughout the afternoon about Greta due to the conversation with Derek
had been laid to rest.

He gazed at the woman across from him as she focused on her food. She appeared more relaxed than she
had when she'd first arrived. She also looked lovely with
her slightly wavy dark hair falling to her shoulders and
her hazel-green eyes emphasized by long, lush eyelashes.

"It must have been a bit traumatic at twenty-six years
old to learn that you weren't a biological child," he said,
trying to read where she was at emotionally with everything that had happened to her.

She looked up at him and smiled. "More than a little
traumatic, but the family rallied around me and insisted
that I was every bit as much a Colton as any of them."

"Did you expect anything else from them?"

"Not really. But it's funny—when I heard that I had
a twin sister, I was surprised and yet I somehow wasn't
surprised. Since the time I was little, I always felt that
something was missing, that a piece of me was absent.
When I found out that I had a twin sister, that missing
piece suddenly filled in." She laughed. "I know I sound
crazy."

"On the contrary, I believe in the twin connection.
I've seen too many news stories about separated twins
who find each other and finally feel whole for the first
time in their lives."

"Knowing about her has explained the empty feeling I've always had, but I'm not eager to meet her if she

really is responsible for Kurt's death and my mother's injuries." Her eyes darkened.

An unexpected protectiveness surged up inside Tyler. He'd had no idea what Greta had been dealing with over the past couple of months, and he wished he'd been by her side to ease some of the pain she must have suffered through everything.

He definitely had a feeling she'd downplayed just how difficult the past few months had been for her. First all the incidents on the ranch, then her arrest for a murder she didn't commit. The finding of her DNA all over the place… She'd been through hell, and apparently, it wasn't over yet if what she'd said about her twin's intentions were really true.

Still, he'd satisfied his curiosity and desire to make love to her. But he was vaguely surprised that even after all she'd just told him he still wanted more.

One thing was certain. His brother wouldn't have been a source of comfort for her. Mark was too self-absorbed to understand or empathize with other people's feelings.

"What about your real mother? What do you know about her?" he asked.

"Just her name, Tamara Stewart."

"Do you have any interest in finding her? In getting to know her?"

She looked at him ruefully. "She sold me for fifty thousand dollars when I was two days old. She's not somebody I have any desire to know," Greta said. "Although I suppose I wouldn't mind asking her some questions about my twin to try to find out why she seems to hate me." She took a sip of her wine. "Besides, they aren't my family and they never could be. The Coltons are my family."

"Tell me about them," he said, hoping to pull some light back into her eyes, which had grown so dark.

"Growing up with five brothers wasn't easy," she said. "They teased me unmercifully. I don't think there's an outbuilding on the property that I wasn't locked into or tied up in." A twinkle of memories sparked in her eyes. "The bottom line is they were my heroes and I wanted to spend all my time with them, proving that whatever they could do, I could do just as well."

He smiled at the vision of her as a young girl, tagging after her big brothers to prove herself as tough as they were. "Other than Ryan, who I know is a detective, do they all work on the ranch now?"

"My oldest brother, Jack, is the manager. Brett also works on the ranch. Eric is a trauma surgeon. Daniel is actually a half brother, but he's a whole brother in my heart. He's enjoying a lot of success with a horse-breeding program he started. So other than Eric and Ryan, the ranch is definitely a family affair."

"But you're close to all of them."

"We've had our ups and downs through the years, but yes, we're all very close."

After they had finished their meal and the waitress had removed their plates, they lingered over coffee. "I wish Mark and I were closer, but we were never really close even before our parents' deaths."

"I think part of what made all of us so close was that our mother wasn't around very much when we were growing up. She spent most of our childhoods away from the ranch, and when she was at home, she was always in bed with a headache and we were allowed only minimal contact with her."

"That must have made it hard on your father," Tyler observed, fascinated by each tidbit of information he learned about her and her family.

She smiled, a warm, open gesture that pooled heat in the pit of his stomach. He wanted to lean across the table and capture her kissable lips with his, breathe in that warmth that her smile exuded. He tamped down the impulse.

"I don't know how he did it, but my father managed to run a hugely successful cattle operation and at the same time was always there when any of us needed him. Of course, we had a variety of nannies to help out, and our housekeeper, Edith, was like a second mother, but the glue that held us all together was definitely my father."

A wistfulness welled up in Tyler. There had been many days over the past ten years that he missed his father. Daniel Stanton had been not only loving but a friend and mentor, as well.

"Shall we head back to the ranch?" he asked, unwilling to dwell on the tragedy that had occurred years ago.

"I'm ready whenever you are," she agreed and took the last sip from her coffee cup.

He paid the tab and then they got back into his car for the short drive home. The scent of her filled the air, a scent of freshness combined with a hint of vanilla and orange. It was so different from the expensive, heavy perfumes other women he'd dated had worn. He found it incredibly evocative.

"We haven't really talked about the conditions of me working for you," she said.

He was thinking about how to get her back into his

bed that night and she was obviously thinking about work. He tried to adjust his thoughts. "I figured room and board and whatever fee you normally charge."

She told him her usual fee. "But that's negotiable depending on my success with Sugar."

He grinned at her use of the new name. "Aren't you always successful?"

"I have to admit there have been a couple of unbreakable horses in my past. They were just too damaged to ever trust human beings again. Thankfully, those are few and far between. I have a feeling given a little time, Sugar and I are going to become great friends and then we'll make sure you're her friend, too."

By that time they were back at his house. "Why don't you unpack and get settled in, and then when you're done, we'll finish the night off with a glass of wine in the living room," he suggested.

"Sounds like a plan," she agreed. She disappeared into the guest bedroom and Tyler went into the kitchen and sat at the kitchen table, his thoughts on Greta and everything he'd learned over dinner.

It sounded as if she and her family had been through the wringer over the past couple of months and yet she appeared to have weathered everything very well.

Beneath the cheerful attitude she displayed, did a well of emotion exist that she hadn't tapped into? Time would tell. He was only grateful that she'd apparently forgiven him for the lie that had not only got her out of prison but also broken her engagement to his brother.

Although he hadn't spoken to Mark since providing the alibi, he had seen him twice at popular restaurants, each time with a different woman on his arm. He didn't appear to be too upset over the loss of Greta. Greta might not know it, but he'd actually done her a favor. She would have never been happy married to Mark.

It was nine thirty when he and Greta carried glasses of wine into the living room for a nightcap. "I'm assuming you'll be returning to work tomorrow?" she asked when they were settled on the sofa.

"That's the plan," he replied. "And I'm assuming your work with She-Sugar won't require me at first."

"Nice save," she replied at his stumble over the horse's new name. "And no, for the first week or two, depending on Sugar, it will be just me and her working out together."

He took a sip of his wine and gazed at her. What were the odds of having her in his bed that night? It was impossible for him to sit next to her, with her heavenly scent surrounding him, and not want her again.

He couldn't help but remember the silkiness of her skin, the fire of her kisses as they'd made love the night before. She'd been an eager participant, giving as well as receiving. She'd been everything he'd dreamed of and more…and he definitely wanted more.

"Earth to Tyler." Her voice interrupted his thoughts. "You looked like you drifted off there for a minute."

"Sorry, I did," he replied and focused on the sweet curve of her lips. "I was just wondering if you'd want a repeat of last night."

Her cheeks immediately flushed with color and her eyes widened. She took a sip of her wine and then carefully placed the glass on the coffee table and looked at him. "What, exactly, do you want with me, Tyler?"

She'd asked him the question before, but he hadn't given her a real clear answer, because he hadn't had one. He still didn't have one.

He gazed at her for a long moment before replying. "To be honest with you, I'm not sure. I know I'm tremendously drawn to you physically and I'd definitely like to get to know you better. I've wanted that for a long time, but beyond that, I don't know."

She averted her gaze from his once again. "I appreciate your honesty."

"But you didn't answer my question." He waited until she looked at him again and then he smiled. "You know what you're good at and I know what I'm good at."

She laughed, a musical sound that only increased his desire. "Does that ego get in your way much?"

"I try not to pull it out too often," he replied lightly. But his lightness of tone didn't last but a moment. "Make love with me again, Greta. Let me hold you in my arms again and kiss you until you can't think straight."

He could tell by the expression on her face that she was conflicted and he pressed on. "Don't overthink things. Just let it happen. There is no right or wrong to this. I want you again and I believe that you want me, too."

Her eyes filled with an emotion that had his blood simmering. "I do want you," she confessed softly.

He didn't say another word. He stood and took her hand and pulled her up from the sofa, and together they walked down the hallway to his bedroom.

She'd officially lost her mind. That was Greta's first thought when she awoke in the guest bedroom the next morning. She'd made love with Tyler and again had refused to stay in his bed through the night, as if that somehow mitigated the fact that they were acting like horny teenagers with no self-control.

He'd told her he wanted to get to know her better, and she'd like to get to know him better, too. But they'd got it all backward, making love first and getting to know each other later.

She had never allowed physical attraction to lead her in a relationship. She'd always allowed her heart and her head to be in charge of her hormones.

But when Tyler looked at her with such hunger, when his lips curved into that sexy smile, she became powerless to deny him whatever he wanted…because she wanted it, too.

It was time she fixed things, refused any more physical contact with Tyler until she at least decided if she really liked him or not. So far she found him surprisingly warm and charming, but she'd really known him for only two short days.

She hadn't forgotten that the times she'd encountered him while she'd been with Mark, he had struck her as cold and not particularly interested in her presence.

Will the real Tyler Stanton please stand up? she thought as she scooted out of bed. She grabbed a pair of jeans, a blue flannel shirt and clean underwear for the day, intending to spend most of the daylight hours in the corral with Sugar.

Minutes later as she stood beneath a hot shower spray, she couldn't help but think of being in Tyler's arms, of his kisses and caresses, which had formed such an intense fire inside her, a fire she'd never felt before.

They fit together perfectly in the bed, but she had no idea how well they'd fit together out of bed. Things had happened so fast. Everything had been pleasant between them so far, but it was early in the game and she really had no idea what to expect in day-to-day life with him.

"You'll find out soon enough," she muttered as she stepped out of the shower and grabbed a fluffy fresh-smelling towel from a cabinet.

At least Tyler would be at work today and she would be able to focus her sole attention on the horse renamed Sugar. To Greta there was almost nothing worse than somebody who abused a helpless animal, unless it was somebody who took the life of an innocent human being.

Once she'd dried off and dressed, she stared at her reflection in the mirror and thought of the twin sister she'd never met.

It was obvious from the fact that Abra had thought it was Greta who'd attacked her, and that Daniel had believed he'd seen Greta at the ranch when in reality she'd been in Oklahoma City, that her sister was an identical twin.

Greta had seen heartwarming shows on television about the reunion of separated twins. The reunions always resulted in joy and love and new extended families. Why hadn't that happened for her? She would have welcomed her twin sister into her life, enjoyed the friendship and love of somebody she'd shared a womb with through nine months.

She didn't even know her twin's name or much of anything about their biological mother. All Big J had been able to tell them was the woman's name was Tamara Stewart and that she had sold him the baby. He'd met her only once, in a small house someplace on the west side of Tulsa near the hospital.

He hadn't been able to remember the address or the specific neighborhood of the house. He hadn't even remembered that much about the woman. He either hadn't paid attention or had forgotten the details from that day so long ago. All he knew was that he'd been so desperate to replace the baby Abra had lost that that was all he'd really cared about. He hadn't wanted Abra to suffer the grief of finding out that her baby girl had died.

Greta knew her brother Ryan was investigating and attempting to locate Tamara in an effort to get a handle on her daughter, who had become a threat to both Greta and her adopted family.

She turned away from the mirror and tried to clear her mind. There was nothing she could do about her twin sister. She needed to focus on greeting Tyler this morning and letting him know that from now on, there was going to be no more physical interaction between them.

She had to be strong and not allow his smooth talk, his gorgeous blue eyes or his sexy smile to change her mind. She was here to do a job, and if in the process they got to know and like each other, it would be a bonus. But she wasn't going to be persuaded to sneak into his room for a bout of mind-blowing lovemaking again.

Feeling strong and looking forward to the day of work with the horse, she left the bathroom and headed for the kitchen. She found Tyler seated at the kitchen table, a newspaper folded and laid to the side of him and a cup of coffee before him.

Clad in a navy business suit, a white shirt and a navy-and-silver-striped tie, he looked like the man she'd been accustomed to seeing on the rare times they had run into each other when she'd been with Mark.

The only difference was the warm smile that lit his handsome features when she walked into the room. "Coffee is made, but you're on your own for breakfast this morning."

"That's fine," she replied. She poured herself a cup

of coffee and joined him at the table. "I suddenly feel terribly underdressed for coffee."

"You look gorgeous in denim and flannel," he replied.

"And you look handsome in your power clothes. I know you're probably ready to head into work, but before you go, I need to talk to you for just a minute."

"I've got something to discuss with you, too. But you go first," he said.

She raised her chin and looked into the depths of his eyes. "I am not going to sleep with you again."

His lips rose in a rueful smile. "You haven't *slept* with me yet."

She huffed out a sigh of frustration. "You know what I mean. I'm here to train your horse and that's it. I'm not going to be your nightly toy to play with at will. If you want me again, then we have to get to know each other first."

He looked at her in obvious amusement. "So you want me to court you."

She eyed him with a narrowed gaze. "Are you making fun of me?"

He laughed. "Not at all. I'm just trying to get clear on what you want or what you need from me."

"I'm not arguing that there isn't some sort of crazy physical attraction between us, but I won't settle for that. We don't really know each other. I want to get to know you out of bed, and I want you to get to know me that way, too."

He sobered and nodded. "As much as I'd love for you to be my bedtime toy every night, I respect your wishes. I'd like to get to know you better. That's part of what I wanted when I first saw you so many months ago."

He took a sip of his coffee and set the cup back down.

"Greta, I understand that we rushed into things fast and furious and you want it to slow down. I can be slow and patient." His eyes twinkled. "I promise I won't try to cajole you into my bed again. I'll wait until you ask me to make love to you again."

"You sound sure that I will," she replied.

"That's hope you hear in my voice." The twinkle in his eyes disappeared and he picked up the folded newspaper next to him. "And on a much less pleasant note, the issue I wanted to talk to you about is this…" He opened the newspaper to a prefolded page and shoved it across the table in front of her.

Greta looked down in horror at the photo of her and Tyler kissing by the side of her Jeep. The caption read Cattle Princess Jilts One Brother for Another.

CHAPTER FIVE

IT WAS AFTER nine when Tyler finally left the house and Greta headed out toward the small corral. Tyler had suggested that it was probably Mark who had taken the picture and given it to the newspaper. The accompanying story had been tawdry and filled with misinformation and salacious half facts.

Tyler had tried to calm Greta down, but she'd been both furious and embarrassed. She knew her father had a subscription to the Oklahoma City paper. How was she supposed to explain all this to him…to the rest of the family?

She breathed in the fresh morning air as she walked briskly to the corral, telling herself that the article and photo didn't really matter. But she was surprised to find herself hurt by Mark's betrayal, if, indeed, he was responsible for the picture and the column of gossip.

When she reached the corral, she remained outside the wooden enclosure. There was no way she could go in and begin to introduce herself to Sugar until she relaxed herself. The horse would immediately pick up on any anger or anxiety Greta carried with her, and at the moment Greta had both bubbling hot inside her.

A short dark-haired man came out of the barn to greet her. He introduced himself as Raymond Edwards. "Yes,

Tyler told me you'd be around," she said. "It's nice to meet you. I'm Greta Colton."

"I know who you are, Ms. Colton. I know of your work," he said respectfully.

"Please, make it Greta," she replied and turned her attention to the horse backed against the far railing. "And I don't know if Tyler told you or not, but from here on, that horse's name is Sugar."

Raymond grinned. "If you can make that filly sweet as sugar, then I'll know your reputation as a miracle worker with horses isn't overblown."

"Time will tell," Greta replied. The two chatted for a few minutes, talking about rodeos they had both attended and mutual acquaintances in the horse business, and then Raymond returned to his work in the barn, leaving her to sort out her mood.

The photo had been such a shock. Why would Mark want to do something like that? Why would anyone do that? Something so ugly? Why make her out to be some kind of a slut when he was the one who had left her to languish in a jail cell while he wined and dined old girl-friends?

It was mean-spirited and so unfair, and it only made her more grateful than ever that the wedding had been called off before she'd married such a man.

Did Tyler possess that kind of mean streak, too? That was the problem. She didn't know him well enough to discern all of the facets of his character.

She knew how well he kissed. She knew how his surprisingly muscled body felt against hers. She'd seen his charm and sense of humor, but that was only a part of who he was. She had no idea what other parts made up his sum.

She drew in deep cleansing breaths and released the air slowly, calming herself as she watched Sugar shake her head and paw the dusty reddish-brown earth. She pranced beneath the shed and then along the back fence as if staking out her territory.

The first thing Greta needed to do was make the horse understand that the territory was hers only if a human allowed it. Sugar had to understand she wasn't the boss.

Finally calm and with the negative energy gone, Greta opened the gate and Sugar froze. Her ears flicked backward and she flared her nostrils. "Hey, girl. Hey, pretty Sugar," Greta said as she stepped into the fenced area and closed the gate behind her.

Greta began to walk around the corral, never attempting to get close to Sugar, who moved to keep a healthy distance between them.

For an hour that was all she did…walk the territory that Sugar had believed was her own. She talked to the horse sometimes in a soft whisper and other times in a loud voice.

Sugar had to get used to the different tones of human voices. She had to learn not to spook by a shout.

Greta walked slowly and methodically, making sure not to get too close to the horse. She never lost track of the fact that with a single kick or with a sudden lurch or lunge the horse could seriously hurt or kill her. She always respected the size of the animals she attempted to gentle.

After an hour she returned to the house, where the newspaper was still on the kitchen table. She reread the article and then took great pleasure in shredding the whole paper into tiny pieces that she then threw into the trash.

She'd just fixed herself a glass of iced tea when her cell phone rang.

"Is she saddle ready?" Tyler's deep voice asked when she answered.

Greta laughed. "No, I think I need another hour or so."

"I just thought I'd check in with you. You were pretty upset when I left this morning."

"I just purged myself of my upset by tearing the newspaper into tiny little pieces and throwing it away," she replied.

"Then you're doing okay?" There was genuine concern in his voice.

"I worked with Sugar for an hour. I'm inside having a glass of iced tea and then I'm going back out to the corral. I'm doing fine now," she assured him.

"I'm planning on being home around six tonight. Shall we do dinner out?"

"It's up to you, but I don't mind cooking something here," she replied. She definitely wasn't too keen to be out at a restaurant tonight with Tyler when their kiss-fest had been broadcast in the newspaper that morning.

"You can cook?"

"I'm certainly not a master chef, but I can get a decent meal on the table," she replied. Many nights, she'd cooked for Mark in his condo because he hadn't wanted to spend the money to go out to eat unless it was a special night and he thought their picture might be taken by some reporter.

"I'll leave that decision up to you," he replied. "I don't want you to feel responsible for anything but training the horse."

"And I'm about to head back out there now," she replied. She didn't want him to think she was just lazing around inside the house while he was gone.

"Then I'll see you around six," he replied.

They said their goodbyes, and before heading back outside, Greta checked the refrigerator freezer to see what she could pull together for dinner. It was obvious by the slim offerings that Tyler ate out a lot. She spied a package of four pork chops wedged beneath a frozen pizza and threw them on the counter to thaw and then headed back outside.

BINGO.

Alice stabbed a dirty fingernail into the newspaper that held the photo of her twin sister kissing Tyler Stanton. Greta Colton—cattle princess and living the life that was meant for Alice.

Hatred shot through her as she stared at the image of her double. Why had Big J chosen Greta to take the place of his dead daughter? Why hadn't he picked her? He should have picked her.

She pulled her hat down lower over her forehead as the café waitress came over to refill her coffee cup. "Can I get you anything else?" the waitress asked.

Alice shook her head. She was in a little dive on the outskirts of Tulsa, a place she knew her sister and any of her high-society friends or family would never be caught dead.

Still, she'd pulled her hair up beneath a hat and wore a pair of fake eyeglasses in an effort to disguise herself from anyone who might have seen Greta either in person or in the morning news.

The waitress left and Alice stared back at the newspaper. Over the past couple of days she'd lost track of Greta's whereabouts.

Alice had lain low after she'd killed the ranch hand, and in the span of the past couple of days she'd realized Greta's Jeep was missing from the family garage and she'd had no idea where she'd gone.

She'd been frantic to find her. How could she right the wrong of the past if she didn't know where Greta was?

She smiled down at the newspaper article. But now she knew exactly where she was located, at Tyler Stanton's home in Oklahoma City. All Alice had to do was conduct a little research and she'd learn the location of that home.

Then she and Greta could have the family reunion Alice had always dreamed of, the one where she killed the woman who looked like her, the woman who had stolen the life Alice should have had.

It was five minutes after six when Tyler pulled into his garage at home. Thoughts of Greta had plagued him throughout the day and now he was eager to get inside and see her once again.

He tried to tell himself that he was just anxious to find out how things had gone with Sugar, but that wasn't the whole truth. He just wanted to see her again, make sure she was really okay after the morning surprise of the newspaper article.

He was interested in her work, but he was equally interested in the woman. He was surprised by her adamant declaration that she wasn't going to share his bed again.

The few women he'd dated in the past had been far too eager to keep him in their beds, using their sexual wiles to attempt to entice him into marriage. But he'd known in his heart that it wasn't love that drove them but rather the desire to be married to the money and status that Tyler possessed.

Greta's determination for them to get to know each other on a different level only made him respect her. He shut off his car engine and entered the house by the door that led into the kitchen.

She wasn't there, but the tantalizing scent of cooking meat and simmering vegetables greeted him. He couldn't remember the last time he'd come home to the scents of a home-cooked meal. It was nice. It was a welcome he embraced.

He shrugged off his suit jacket and loosened his tie. It had been a rather stressful day with meetings and the concern about the volatility of oil prices and constantly changing regulations. It was good to get home and put all that behind him for the rest of the evening.

He walked from the kitchen through the great room and met Greta coming out of the spare bedroom. "Oh, I didn't hear you come in," she said in surprise.

"I'm in," he replied and tried not to notice how charming she looked. She was still clad in her jeans but had changed into a different long-sleeved red flannel shirt.

Her dark hair looked soft and touchable as it fell to her shoulders in rich, thick waves. He had to fight against the automatic physical desire to run his fingers through her hair and pull her close against him.

"I was just cleaning up for dinner," she said.

"It smells delicious."

"I'll have it on the table in about fifteen minutes," she replied.

"Good. That will give me a chance to get out of this monkey suit."

They passed each other and he caught a whiff of her fresh, clean slightly citrusy scent and again fought off a desire to take her into his arms and kiss her until they were both breathless.

He shook his head as he entered his bedroom, surprised that after two nights of making love to her he still wanted her as badly as he had the first night, when she'd appeared in his doorway clad only in his T-shirt.

She'd looked like a goddess in that shirt, with her coltish long legs bare and the thrust of her breasts visible. The moonlight had painted her features in a silvery patina that had been enchanting.

But he intended to stick to his words. He wouldn't attempt to get her into his bed again, at least not overtly. Seduction was still on the table, although the ball was ultimately in her court. He was vaguely surprised that he was eager to know her mind as well as he'd learned the contours of her body.

He changed into a pair of jeans and a long-sleeved beige polo shirt, looking forward to a leisurely dinner and some relaxation with the woman who had been in his thoughts all day. He also wanted to know how the day had gone with Greta and Sugar.

By the time he reached the kitchen, she had the table set and the food on the plates. "Just in time," she said as she sat in the chair she'd sat in for coffee that morning.

"Hmm, pork chops, corn and fried potatoes—it all looks delicious." He sat down across from her.

"I didn't have a lot to work with. Your freezer speaks of a man who rarely eats at home."

He nodded. "The Cattle Call isn't the only restaurant around here where people know my name. It just seems like a pain to cook for one."

"If you want me to cook dinner each evening while I'm here, you should probably make a trip to the grocery store tomorrow and buy what you like to eat," she replied.

He picked up his fork but kept his gaze focused on her. "I feel like I'm taking advantage of you."

"Nonsense," she scoffed. "Taking advantage of me would have been you asking me or expecting me to cook. Instead I offered. Now, eat while it's hot."

She picked up her fork and cut into her pork chop. He did the same. He took a bite of the savory meat and smiled. "Delicious." He felt the stress of the day slowly melting away.

For the next few minutes they ate in silence. He was glad that she wasn't the kind of woman who felt obliged to fill every silence with chatter. This was the comfortable silence of two people taking the time to savor their meal.

It was only when they were halfway through that she asked him about his day. "Actually, I had a busy day, lots of meetings and little fires that required my attention. That's unusual. Most days I just sit in my office while everything hums smoothly around me. What about you? How did things go with Sugar?"

"Pretty much as I expected. She's intelligent and doesn't seem to be aggressive, which is a good thing."

"I would imagine that working with aggressive horses can be pretty dangerous."

"Definitely," she agreed. "Even great trainers sometimes get hurt or killed by not respecting the animal they're working with." Her eyes sparkled and it was obvious she loved what she did. "The secret is to use specific training methods for specific cases. No two wild or traumatized horses are the same and you can't use a one-size-fits-all kind of training." A faint blush colored her cheeks. "Sorry. I'm sure that's more information than you wanted."

"Please, don't apologize. You're passionate about what you do and I find that very attractive in a woman."

"Attractive or not, it's who I am," she replied. "What about you? Are you passionate about your work?"

"Definitely. I feel an almost obsessive responsibility to Stanton Oil. The company was started by my great-grandfather and has grown and prospered with each generation."

He frowned thoughtfully. "My father made it clear from the time I was young that I was the heir and Mark was the spare to the Stanton Oil throne. I think the family dynamics helped make Mark into the irresponsible, entitled man he has become."

"How so?" she asked in open curiosity.

"The more my father doted on me, the more my mother did on Mark. She overcompensated by giving him everything he wanted. He never had to earn anything—it was all just given to him. My father made me work hard for his respect. Looking back, I think it was a little unhealthy for both of us."

"I don't care what his childhood was like. If he gave that photo of us to the newspaper, then he has a mean, vindictive streak in him. I haven't called anyone in my family to see if they saw the paper. I don't know how to begin to explain it to them."

"Tell them the truth, that you're working for me and we had a moment between us…a moment we're attempting to build on. They know you didn't jilt Mark. I'm sure they also know what kind of woman you are and you're nothing like what the article implied."

She smiled in obvious gratitude. "Thanks. I didn't realize I needed to hear that."

"Today's news will be forgotten by tomorrow. The social pages have painted me as an arrogant, womanizing bastard over the years." He frowned. "The *Oklahoma Star* social-page editor is known for exploitive, sensationalized stories. She should be working for a tabloid instead of a legitimate newspaper."

They finished the meal talking about more pleasant topics, the unseasonably warm weather, their favorite foods and what he intended to pick up at the grocery store before coming home from work the next day.

They cleaned up the dishes together, and each time their shoulders bumped or they brushed against one another, a slight sizzle shot through Tyler's veins. It was ridiculous how easily she could stir up a healthy dose of lust in his veins.

"Wine in the living room?" he asked once the kitchen was clean.

"Actually, there's still enough daylight that I'm heading back out to the corral for a while," she replied. She smiled at him ruefully. "Besides, that wine-in-the-living-room thing has been dangerous for the last two nights."

He grinned at her. "I told you the ball was now in your court. If you want to kick it into my bedroom, I don't have a problem with that."

"Of course you don't," she replied drily.

Minutes later when she headed out the back door, Tyler followed her and tried not to notice how her jeans cupped her perfect bottom and fit down her long legs.

She went directly to the corral, opened the gate and

stepped in. Sugar stood in the center of the area and didn't move. This was already a change from the horse's normal behavior. Whenever Tyler or Raymond even opened the gate, Sugar always darted directly to the back of the corral, as far away from them as possible.

Greta walked around the edge of the corral, her strides long and confident. Sugar remained in the center, moving only to keep eyes on the stranger in her domain.

Tyler leaned his arms on the top of the corral, content just to watch Greta move. With her long legs and slender figure, she moved with the grace of a dancer. She'd stop occasionally and looked at Sugar for long moments, talked to her and then continued her walk around the perimeter of the corral.

The evening air smelled of rich earth and held the crispness of autumn. He dreaded the coming of winter. It had been on a wintry night when his parents had been killed on an icy highway in a ten-car pileup. Winter always brought with it a bittersweet cache of memories and a renewal of loss despite the years that had passed.

He shoved these maudlin thoughts away and focused back on Greta. It had been nice to come home not only to the scent of dinner filling the air but also to the presence of another person in the house.

Lately he'd become acutely aware of the silence when he was home, resulting in his working later and later hours in an effort to avoid the utter quiet of his private life.

He'd tired of the fund-raisers and charity events he was invited to attend, even though he knew he could find a willing female to share a couple of hours of meaningless conversation.

Twilight had fallen and the air had grown nippy by

the time Greta finally left the corral. "The first thing I need to teach Sugar is that I won't hurt her with my presence," Greta explained when they walked back to the house. "She also has to know that she's a guest in my territory instead of the other way around."

"Makes sense to me," he replied. "Coffee?" he asked when they reentered the kitchen.

"No, thanks, I'm good."

"Want to head to the living room and sit for a bit before bedtime?" he asked.

She looked down at her dusty jeans. "Actually, before I sit anywhere, I need to head to the shower." She bent down and pulled off first one and then the other of the dusty cowboy boots she wore. Something clattered to the floor.

"Is that what I think it is?" he asked as she picked up the pearly-white item.

"If you think it's a knife, then it's exactly what you think it is." She tucked it into her back pocket.

"All this time I've spent with you and I didn't know I was hanging out with somebody who was armed and dangerous."

"Keep that in mind for future purposes," she replied with a teasing light in her eyes. "Now, I'm going to head to the shower."

"I'll wait for you. I'd like to ask you some questions about your work."

She appeared surprised. "Oh, okay. I won't be too long."

She disappeared from the kitchen and took some of the life, some of the energy, in the air with her. He thought about making coffee for himself, then nixed the idea and instead headed into the living room.

He sank down into the lush leather of the sofa. When would he hear from Mark? There was no question in his mind that it had been his brother who had taken the picture and then given it to the paper. It definitely had Mark's stink on it.

There was also no doubt in Tyler's mind that it had been an attempt at humiliating not only Greta but Tyler, as well. It had not only reflected Greta in a bad light but also painted Tyler as a man with no familial loyalties and no respect for his brother.

Tyler leaned his head back and closed his eyes. He supposed it was true. He had little respect for Mark, who at thirty years old had yet to accept any adult responsibilities and make his own way in the world.

But someplace deep inside his heart he loved his brother and he had hoped that Mark had made a true heart connection with Greta and was ready to grow up.

Tyler would have found another trainer to work with Sugar and remained cool and distant to the woman he'd secretly lusted after. He would have respected their relationship for as long as they were together.

He refused to feel guilty about pursuing Greta now. He was sorry only that this would probably widen the rift that had always existed between the two brothers.

His brain shifted gears. The knife that had clattered to the floor from her boot had surprised him. It shouldn't have. She went to a variety of ranches where she worked with mostly men. He was glad that she carried some form of self-protection, although he had trouble imagining her using the knife on anyone.

She'd certainly have no need to use it here. Neither of his ranch hands would dare try to attack her in any way, and in any case, they were both good men with a set of upstanding morals. Tyler wouldn't hire any other kind of man.

He smelled her before she entered the room, that evocative scent of citrus and vanilla. He opened his eyes and straightened as she entered the room.

She'd changed into a pair of soft black fleece sweatpants and an oversize T-shirt that was black with gold lettering advertising a Tulsa feed store.

"Thank goodness you didn't change into a diaphanous silk gown for lounging around," he said.

She laughed. "Diaphanous silk just isn't my style." She curled up in the corner of the sofa opposite him. "You don't really want to know more about my work, do you?"

"Absolutely. I find what you do fascinating."

"Mark always found it a bore."

"I'm not my brother."

"What do you want to know?" she asked.

"When did you know that you wanted to be a horse trainer?" he asked.

"I'm not sure it's something I consciously decided on. When I was about twelve, my father noticed that I had a special affinity with horses. Whenever he bought one that was difficult, he'd have me work with it and he told me I should be a horse trainer. He told me I had something rare in that I seemed to be able to get into the mind of a horse, to understand their needs and turn them into friendly animals that enjoyed human contact."

She told him that when she got older, she'd studied horse training and worked with several trainers in the area to learn different techniques and philosophies.

While Tyler was fascinated with the conversation, equally as captivating was the way her hazel eyes sparkled and her voice took on the lilt of enthusiasm and joy. She absolutely captivated him.

"Dad eventually set me up on the ranch with my own corral to work in and a nearby small barn to hold what I needed for the horses I trained."

She was both charming and refreshing as she talked about her work, and he was disappointed when she looked at the clock on one of the bookshelves and realized it was almost eleven.

"It's time for me to call it a night," she said. "I want to get an early start in the morning." She rose from the sofa. "Good night, Tyler, and thank you for allowing me to ramble on as long as I did."

He stood, as well. "I enjoyed every minute of it. Sweet dreams, Greta."

He watched her head down the hallway to her room. He didn't expect her to appear in his room tonight. As much as he'd like her to, she'd set the new rules and seemed determined, and he would just have to abide by them.

He checked the doors to make sure they were all locked and then headed to his own room. Her bedroom door was closed, but he could easily imagine her snuggling into her bed beneath the light blue sheets and the navy comforter.

Cotton. She definitely was a cotton kind of woman. She wouldn't wear a spaghetti-strap low-cut silk nightgown to sleep in. She probably had a cotton nightshirt. Still, even imagining her in that simple garment evoked a sexy image in his brain.

Within minutes he was in bed and staring up at the ceiling as he waited for sleep to overtake him. Tyler had experienced only one serious relationship in his life.

Three years ago he had met Michelle Willoughby at a charity event. He'd found the petite blonde to be not only charming and beautiful but intelligent, as well.

He'd pursued her with a single-mindedness that had resulted in an engagement after three months. He'd been ready to marry and start a family and he'd decided Michelle would make a good wife. His decision to marry her wasn't so much a heart decision as a head decision. But ultimately, the relationship hadn't lasted.

Had he already made the same mistake with Greta? Moving too fast, pursuing too hard? Time would tell. She'd already drawn a line in the sand, telling him that things had moved too fast. Now he had to be patient and just let things happen naturally between them without his pushing.

If she had the time to really get to know him, would that result in some kind of a love connection or would she just be a horse trainer he'd made love to for a brief period of time?

CHAPTER SIX

GRETA FELL ASLEEP almost the minute her head touched the pillow. She dreamed of riding Sugar. Tyler was by her side on his own horse, his smile challenging her as they raced across a vast pasture.

Cool autumn air exhilarated her as her hair flew wildly around her head and a sense of freedom winged through her with the powerful animal beneath her.

She threw back her head and laughed when she pulled just ahead of Tyler. His laughter rode the breeze with hers, mingling with it to make beautiful music.

She drew in deep breaths, tasting the scent of the approach of winter and the wood smoke that drifted from a nearby farmhouse.

The smoke grew thicker, darker and she started to choke. She tried to cough but couldn't. The smoke was stuck in the back of her throat.

Panic washed over her. Her throat completely closed off and she couldn't take a breath. Her eyes snapped open and she realized she wasn't dreaming.

Somebody was on top of her. That same somebody's hands were wrapped tightly around her throat. *This isn't a dream*, her brain screamed. *This is real! This is happening right now.*

In the moonlight that drifted in the window, Greta saw her attacker's face. It was the same face she saw in her own mirror each morning, except this one was twisted with the rage of the crazed.

Greta kicked and bucked, attempting to dislodge the woman from on top of her. She clawed at the hands that wrapped so tight around her throat that she couldn't get air.

Even as she grew dizzy from a lack of oxygen, instead of having the automatic instinct to attempt to tear the hands from her throat, she reached her hands up and tried to jab at the woman's eyes.

Once.

Twice.

Greta finally managed to make contact and her twin jerked back and her hands momentarily slipped from their grip on Greta's throat. Greta screamed, an ear-piercing alarm loud enough to wake the dead.

The woman...her twin...froze and then sprang off the bed and to the open window. With a quick glance backward, a glance filled with hatred, she then disappeared into the night as Greta's door crashed open and the overhead light clicked on.

Tyler stood in the doorway clad in a pair of black boxers. His gaze first shot to her and then to the open window. "Are you okay?" he asked with urgency.

Greta nodded and reached a hand up to her throat, where she could still feel the pressure and the sickening heat of the hands that had attempted to strangle her. "It was her... It was my twin," she finally managed to gasp and then began to cry.

Tyler quickly moved to the window and peered out. "There's nobody there now." He closed the window and locked it and then moved to the bed and pulled her into his arms and held her tight. "It's okay. You're safe now. I'm here now and she's gone."

As full comprehension of what had just happened slammed into her, Greta cried harder, unable to stanch the fear that still coursed through her.

She clung to Tyler, unable to believe what had just happened. What if she hadn't been able to scream? What if Tyler hadn't heard her? She'd already been dizzy due to a lack of oxygen. Within seconds she might have been completely unconscious and then she'd have been dead.

This thought only made her cling to Tyler more tightly as she continued to cry. Her sobs eventually subsided to embarrassing hiccups. Tyler loosened his grip on her and she unwound her arms from around his neck.

"Sorry. I'm not usually a big crybaby."

"It's okay. I don't mind a crybaby now and then," he replied gently.

"I didn't hear anything," she said when the hiccups finally stopped. "I was dreaming and in my dream I started to choke and then I woke up and she was on top of me and trying to strangle me."

Tyler took her chin and nudged it upward to eye her throat. His eyes were a darker blue than she'd ever seen as he gently swiped his fingers across her skin. His action instantly dispelled the fire of rage and malevolence that had lingered there.

"How did she even know...?" Her words drifted off as the answer to her question revealed itself. "The picture in the paper... That's how she knew where I was. She knew I was here with you because of that photo."

Tyler stood, his features stoic. "You can spend the rest of the night in my bed. I'll stay awake and keep an eye on things. First thing in the morning you pack your bags. You won't spend another night here." His voice was brisk and all business.

"Where will I be going?" she asked.

"Back home to Tulsa and I'll be going with you. I'm not letting you out of my sight until this woman is behind bars."

"What about my work with Sugar?" she asked. The entire world had turned upside down in the space of a heartbeat.

"We'll figure it all out in the morning. I should call the authorities and make a report."

"Please don't," she said hurriedly. "I've already had more publicity than I want and there's really nothing they can do. Besides, Ryan is already working on trying to find her with the Tulsa Police Department. If we're going back there, I'll just let Ryan know about this latest incident and he can deal with it from his end."

She shivered as a deep bone chill overtook her. It had been surreal to open her eyes and see her hazel eyes, her own face staring down at her.

"Are you sure? It wouldn't take long to file a report."

She shook her head. "I'm positive. I'll talk to Ryan tomorrow and he can take it from there."

"Come on. Let's get you settled in my room," Tyler said. He helped her out of bed and threw an arm around her shoulders and then led her into his room, where he turned on the light and gestured her toward the bed.

The clock on the nightstand indicated that it was just before three o'clock. She got into bed and watched as he pulled on a pair of jeans, his socks and his shoes and then grabbed a T-shirt from the closet and pulled it on over his head.

He then went to the top drawer of his dresser and

pulled out a handgun. He smiled at her grimly. "I might be a businessman, but I'm also an Oklahoman and I have a gun. I'm going to call Raymond and Bill to come over and help me keep an eye on things around here. Get some sleep, Greta. You have nothing to worry about for the rest of the night."

She believed him. He looked bigger, meaner and thoroughly capable with his dark blue eyes, determined expression and a gun in his hand.

This was the Tyler Stanton she'd known in the past, confident and in control with a slightly dangerous edge to him. She was more than comfortable to let him be in charge. How many people had met this man across a conference table in the boardroom? She bet it was an experience they never forgot.

He waited until she was snuggled beneath the sheets that smelled of his familiar scent and then he grabbed his cell phone, turned off the light and left the room.

She heard his deep voice speaking to somebody on the phone before he moved out of hearing distance. She closed her eyes, but sleep was as distant as the lights of New York City.

Over and over again her mind played that moment when she'd left her dream behind and come awake to terror. Greta had always been a sound sleeper, but she couldn't believe her twin had managed to get through a screen and open the window without awaking her.

She must slither like a snake, move as quietly as a shadow. Greta shuddered once again and pulled the comforter more tightly around her.

The minute Big J had confessed that he'd bought her as a baby and that she had been one of two, everyone had realized it hadn't been Greta's DNA all over the ranch where trouble had happened. It had been her twin's.

With that new knowledge, her detective brother had begun to search for the whereabouts of Tamara Stewart, Greta's birth mother, in an effort to find out more information about Greta's twin.

It had been twenty-six years since Big J had met the woman and bought a baby from her, twenty-six years when Tamara Stewart could have married and moved anywhere in the world.

Greta only hoped her brother managed to get some answers before her twin got another opportunity to vent her hatred, a hatred Greta wished she understood. This was her last thought before she finally fell asleep.

She awoke just after dawn. The house was quiet and she snuggled deeper into the sheets, surrounding herself with Tyler's scent.

She didn't want to get up and face the day. She hated the fear that now resided deep inside her. They had all realized that Greta's twin had probably been responsible for all the damage and mischief that had occurred around the ranch.

They all agreed that it had been the twin who had attacked Abra so many months ago and had killed the ranch hand Kurt Rodgers, but last night had been the first time she'd come for Greta.

Reluctantly, she got out of bed, knowing she couldn't put off the future, whatever it might hold, any longer. She crept out of the bedroom and stopped in surprise as she saw Tyler sitting in a straight-back chair in the hallway just next to the bedroom door.

He was sound asleep, his gun in his lap and his sensual mouth slightly agape. Her heart tightened as she realized he'd apparently spent the night in a chair just outside where she'd slept in order to make sure he kept her safe from harm.

She remained frozen, unsure if she should go back into the bedroom or try to creep past him without awaking him. Before she could make a decision, his eyes opened and he smiled. "Good morning. It looks like we made it through the night."

"You must be exhausted," she exclaimed. "You can't have slept well in that chair."

He grabbed his gun from his lap and stood, then stretched with his arms overhead, the action forcing the bottom of his T-shirt to creep up to expose a bit of his taut bare belly.

He dropped his hands and eyed her purple nightgown with an angel seated on a gold half-moon on the front. "I knew you were a cotton kind of girl," he said with a small smile. The smile left his lips as his gaze locked with hers. "Are you okay? Did you get some sleep?"

She nodded. "I slept, but I'm not sure I'm a hundred percent okay."

"You'll feel better once we get you out of here."

"What, exactly, are the plans?" she asked.

"Why don't you get dressed and I'll make the coffee and we'll figure everything out then," he replied.

"Okay." Her heart beat slightly faster as she entered the guest room where she'd been attacked. With the light of day creeping in the window, which was closed and locked, the room held no hint of the life-and-death drama that had occurred the night before.

She grabbed her underclothes, a pair of clean jeans and a brown flannel shirt. She headed into the bathroom, where she showered as quickly as possible and then got dressed.

By the time she went into the kitchen, the coffee was made and Tyler sat at the table with two cups of the fresh brew already poured. He'd changed into a long-sleeved flannel shirt, as well, his a blue pattern that emphasized the color of his amazing, beautiful eyes. He also wore his gun in a holster on his belt.

She sat and pulled one of the two cups before her and wrapped her fingers around it, seeking its warmth to ease the chill that hadn't quite dissipated from the night before. "Now, what are the plans?"

"We pack up and take you home. You'll be safer there not only with your family around but with me there, as well. I'm hoping your family will welcome me as a guest for a while?"

"Of course they will, but what about your work? You have responsibilities here," she protested.

"I've given myself vacation leave. I'll be close enough that I can drive back here if necessary, but I'm not letting you go without me." He gave her a sexy smile. "I haven't gotten to court you long enough yet."

"And what about my work with Sugar? I'd already started making some headway with her."

"You mentioned that you had a corral where you work with horses."

She nodded. "It's pretty much like the setup you have here."

"Then we'll get her into a trailer and bring her with us." He took a sip of his coffee.

Greta frowned, thinking of all the reasons why Tyler shouldn't come home with her and yet feeling surprised to realize how badly she wanted him beside her. It was crazy after spending such a brief time with him, but she couldn't help it. Right now he represented safety to her.

"Can you get Sugar into a trailer?" she asked worriedly.

"Raymond and Bill can use a chute and get her in. She won't be happy, but she'll survive."

Greta took a drink of her coffee and wondered if she would survive the inexplicable wrath of a so-far-elusive sister who seemed to have the ability to stay undercover and move as if she were a ghost.

IT TOOK A little over two hours to get everything ready to prepare to leave the house. Tyler instructed Raymond and Bill to trailer Sugar and then called his general manager at Stanton Oil to let him know he would be in Tulsa for an indeterminable amount of time.

He then called Derek to let his neighbor know he would be gone, and Derek assured him he'd keep an eye on the place. While Tyler was making his phone calls, Greta was packing her bags.

With the necessary calls made and business taken care of, Tyler went into his room to pack what he thought he would need for his time in Tulsa. He hoped the Colton family would welcome him, although he knew he carried the baggage of being not only Mark's brother but also the man who had been pictured in the paper kissing Greta. And a fine kiss it had been.

He'd just have to make them understand that he was there for Greta's safety and nothing more. The vision of opening her door the night before to see her sitting in bed, eyes wide in terror, her throat red and the cold wind of the night blowing through the open window, would sit with him for a very long time.

What if she hadn't been able to scream? What if Tyler hadn't awoken? He would have found her dead in the bed this morning. He shoved the thought out of his head, unable to abide that particular image without feeling sick to his stomach.

At a little after nine o'clock Tyler's powerful black pickup truck was in the driveway with Sugar in the horse trailer hooked behind it. "I just had an idea," he said to Greta when they stepped outside with their bags in hand.

"What's that?" Her worried gaze shot to the horse.

"Why don't you ride with me and we'll leave your Jeep here in the driveway. Maybe that will throw off your evil twin and she'll think you're still here. At least it might work for a little while."

"Okay," she agreed after a moment of hesitation.

"I'll pack the bags," he said.

She dropped hers next to his and then walked to stand a couple of feet from Sugar's trailer. "It's going to be all right, girl," she said. "I know you're scared, but we're going to take you someplace nice and you'll be just fine."

She had nearly been killed last night and yet she was concerned for the mental welfare of his horse. She had to be traumatized and yet she worried about how traumatized Sugar might be by riding in the trailer.

It only made him want to keep her safe from harm more. She wasn't the typical socialite he'd thought she might have become when she'd been with Mark. She wasn't like any other woman he had ever met or dated. He had no idea where their crazy relationship might be headed. He knew only a ferocious sense of protectiveness for her that he couldn't deny.

They were on the road by nine fifteen. "I gave my

father a heads-up that we were on our way to the ranch while I was packing," she said.

"So he knows I'm with you?"

"He knows and I'm sure by now everyone at the ranch knows."

"And?" He shot her a quick glance, picking up on something in her voice.

"And I'll admit he has some reservations about you, but ultimately, he trusts my judgment."

"I didn't expect to be greeted with warm fuzzy hugs," he replied. "As long as they don't make me sleep in the barn or the stables, I'll handle the fact that they have some reservations about me."

"It's just that with the breakup with Mark so fresh, I think they all believe I'm rebounding with you to hurt Mark. You know that's not the case."

He gave her a quick glance. "To be honest, it never crossed my mind. But you don't strike me as the vindictive kind of woman who would consciously seduce me to hurt my brother."

"Ha! I don't remember being the one who did the seducing," she exclaimed in protest.

He cast her a quick grin. "And a fine seduction it was."

Her laughter was music to his ears. He didn't want her to think about last night and how close death had come to her. He didn't want her to dwell in a place of fear, although he knew she had to harbor a simmering terror deep in her heart.

She'd been attacked, and the bad guy—or in this case, the bad woman—hadn't been caught. There was no sense of safety this morning, only the hope that maybe they'd buy themselves a couple of quiet days by fooling her sister into believing she was still at his place.

Despite what had happened and the circumstances of their leaving his house, the drive to Tulsa was pleasant. They talked about the passing scenery, the coming of winter and inconsequential things he hoped dispelled some of the residual terror she'd suffered the night before.

He asked her to tell him more about her siblings, knowing that he would probably meet them all at one time or another while he was at the ranch.

She told him about Eric, the trauma surgeon who had found love with Kara Sheppard after witnessing her being struck by a hit-and-run driver. He learned that Jack had a five-year-old son, Seth, and that Greta was particularly close to Tracy, the woman who had become the love of Jack's life. Tracy was currently pregnant with a baby girl.

Greta told him that Brett was married to Hannah and the two of them had just had a baby boy named Alexander and Daniel had been working his horse-breeding program and recently married his assistant, Megan.

Finally, there was Ryan, who was not only actively working the investigation into the trouble at the ranch and finding Greta's biological family but was also in love with a forensic expert named Susie.

"I think it's going to take me a while to get them all straight," he said and then added, "So you're the only one who hasn't found true love."

"After the debacle with Mark, and with a killer's target on my back, finding love is the very last thing on my mind," she replied. "Horses are so much less complicated than human beings." She paused a moment.

"And with everything else that's going on, I'm worried about my father."

Tyler looked at her in surprise. "Worried about what?"

"On the surface he's still the bigger-than-life figure that he's always been, but I've noticed little things that make me believe he's losing some mental capacity."

"Do you mean like dementia or Alzheimer's?"

"I hope not, but yes. There's a hesitation about him, a blankness in his eyes sometimes that makes me worry." She twisted her fingers together in her lap.

"Have you spoken with your brothers about it?"

"A little bit, but not much. Jack has basically taken over all the ranch duties and responsibilities. I'm just so used to Dad being the one to take care of us all and he's always been so good at taking care of my mother."

"Greta, right now you have to think about taking care of yourself," Tyler said gently. "I can't imagine being in your head with everything that seems to be swirling around in there."

She smiled ruefully. "It's definitely chaotic in there."

"The best thing you can do for yourself is let go of as much of the chaos as possible. Ryan is taking care of the investigation into Kurt Rodgers's murder and finding your twin sister. Your family will rally around your father and support him. All you need to focus on is working with Sugar and staying close to me so that I can keep you safe from harm."

She reached a hand up and rubbed the center of her forehead, as if attempting to erase a headache. "You're right," she said and dropped her hand back to her lap. "My brain is on overload right now. I won't work with Sugar today. She'll need some time to get settled into the

new surroundings and I can spend the afternoon showing you around our place."

"Sounds like a good plan," he agreed. He hoped that
for at least a day or two her twin would be fooled into
believing she was still at his house. He only hoped he
wasn't making a mistake by taking her back to the home
where too many bad things had already happened.

CHAPTER SEVEN

GRETA HAD THOUGHT that arriving home would bring her a sense of renewed peace and security, but it didn't. This was where her sister had attacked her mother, where her twin had committed arson and mischief and had killed Kurt Rodgers.

Still, there was some comfort in knowing that not only would Tyler and her brothers be around, but so would any number of devoted and loyal ranch hands. She'd have plenty of people watching her back here, and at least now they knew for sure who the enemy was and what she looked like.

After they'd entered the impressive gates that led to the Colton estate, she pointed him past the house and toward the small corral. Her first priority was getting Sugar out of the trailer and into her new home.

Tyler backed the trailer up to the corral gate and by that time two of the Colton ranch hands had appeared. Greta and Tyler got out of the truck.

"Hey, Damon... Michael." She greeted the two men with easy friendliness. "This is Tyler Stanton. He's going to be staying here for a while." As the men exchanged handshakes, she moved to the trailer. "And this is Sugar, my newest challenge."

Both men kept a healthy distance from the trailer. They knew how possessive Greta was when she was working with a particular horse. "She's a beaut," Michael said.

"She's a mess," Tyler replied.

"If anyone can turn her around, it's our Greta," Damon said with obvious pride.

Greta flashed him a smile and then moved to the back of the trailer. She opened the back and Sugar exploded out backward. She raced around the corral, her nostrils flared in displeasure as she kept her distance from the trailer.

Tyler got back into the truck and pulled it away from the wooden structure. Greta shut the corral gate and watched the beautiful horse as she acted out her unhappiness. Within minutes she had calmed enough to walk the perimeters of the corral, obviously curious about this new place where she found herself.

"I see the barn you mentioned," Tyler said when he rejoined her and pointed to the barn near the corral.

"My father went a little overboard," she replied. "It's way bigger than I needed since it's dedicated to hay bales and feed and equipment only I use for the horses I work with here." She looked back at Sugar. "She should be fine now," she said more to herself than to him.

With the horse settled in, Greta rode with Tyler to a place where he could unhook the trailer and park his truck. They then grabbed their bags and headed for the house.

They entered through a side door that led into a large mudroom and from there headed into the huge kitchen, where Maria Sanchez, the main cook for the family, was in the process of preparing the noon meal.

Greta made the introductions and then they moved out of the kitchen and through the formal living room, to the large staircase that led up to her bedroom and several guest rooms.

They had reached only the bottom of the staircase when Edith Turner appeared. Edith had come to work for the Coltons when Greta was six years old. She not only ran the household smoothly and still mothered the children who had grown up in her presence, but she had also had a special touch when dealing with Abra and her frailties throughout the years.

"I prepared the guest room as you asked," she said, her gray eyes warm as her gaze lingered on Greta.

"Thank you, Edith. And this is Tyler Stanton."

Edith sniffed and the warmth in her eyes disappeared in a single blink. "Another Stanton," she said. "If you're anything like that lowlife of a brother of yours, I'll see to it that the maids short-sheet your bed."

Greta gasped, Edith blushed and Tyler laughed. "Believe me, my only reason for being here is to see to Greta's safety and well-being. Don't judge me for the sins of my brother."

Edith harrumphed. "Time will tell," she replied curtly. "I just want you to know I have my eyes on you."

"I don't know what got into her," Greta said moments later when she and Tyler reached the top of the stairs. "I've never seen her act that way with a guest."

"She's obviously very fond of you," Tyler replied good-naturedly. "And I haven't had my bed short-sheeted since I was twelve and Mark snuck into my room to do the deed."

Greta led him into the room next to hers. "This is where you'll be staying." The room had a king-size bed and an adjoining bath and was done in beige tones and black. As with all the guest rooms, it was both large and beautifully decorated.

"Nice," he said and dropped his bags to the floor. "And where are you?"

"Next door."

"I want to see." He took her two bags out of her hands.

Greta had slept with Tyler twice and yet she felt oddly shy as she took him next door and into her private quarters. She'd chosen to decorate the room in shades of blue that made her feel as if the beautiful Oklahoma sky were inside.

The king-size bed sported a sky blue comforter with a blue-and-white bed skirt. Gauzy white curtains hung at the windows, allowing in plenty of sunshine.

A built-in bookcase held not only a large flat-screen television but also miniature statues of horses and books about horses and training.

There was also a sitting area with two blue chairs in front of a white marble fireplace. Many a wintry evening she'd sat in one of those chairs, reading one of the books about horse training.

He set her bags on the floor and nodded as if satisfied. "Now when I'm so lonely in my bed next door, I can imagine you in here, covered in sky and sheets that I guess will have your scent in them." He released a deep, overly dramatic sigh.

She nudged him in the ribs with her elbow. "You're incorrigible."

"Only with you," he replied lightly. Their gazes met and the teasing light in his eyes shifted into something else, something that threatened to steal her breath away.

She took a step backward away from him. "Come on. We've got some time before lunch for me to show you around."

He followed her down the stairs and she marveled that with a single look he could cause something to shift inside her, a force of desire to rise up. She'd hoped that here, in her own territory, he wouldn't have such power over her, but she was obviously wrong and that meant she had to take care.

She probably should have put him in another of the guest rooms farther away from hers, but when she'd thought of him spending the night in a straight-back chair to keep her safe, she'd wanted him close to her.

"I'll introduce you to the rest of the gang at lunch," she said as they went back down the stairs. She led him back through the kitchen and then the mudroom and out the side door. "So this is our ranch."

Tyler stood for a moment and surveyed the landscape before him. "I knew you all ran a big operation here, but I had no idea it was this big."

"That huge building you see in the distance is our main office and sales barn. We have a sales ring, twelve pipe stalls, a wash bay and a tack room. If we walk up that hill, you'll see our working pens. There's also a smaller breeding barn. That's where Daniel is working on a new program that is proving to be quite successful. Then there's the bunkhouse, the equipment-and-hay shed and the cabin, which was originally built for the ranch manager but now Daniel lives there." She paused to take a breath.

"Wow, I had no idea there was so much here."

"And I haven't even mentioned the stables or the old house," she said.

"The old house?"

"It was the original homestead. It's located about two miles south of here. It's over a hundred years old but in decent shape. Jack lives there now with his pregnant wife, Tracy. As you can see, there are also lots of other smaller sheds and such around." She frowned suddenly. "Plenty of places for somebody to hide."

Tyler placed an arm around her shoulders and drew her closer against him. "And plenty of people looking after you."

She smiled up at him and then stepped out of his embrace. "You're right. I can't allow her to fill me with fear of my own home. I need to live my life and hope that Ryan and the police department get her behind bars sooner rather than later."

"That's the spirit," Tyler replied.

"We'd better head back inside. Lunch should be served in just a little while and we both have unpacking to do." With a final glance around, Greta led him back into the house.

There was no time to unpack. By the time they got inside, Maria was bustling to get the food in serving dishes and the sound of voices drifted from the dining room.

Greta steeled herself, wondering how her family would react to her guest. She would know immediately if any of them were displeased, although they would all be polite in Tyler's presence. She would be able to tell by subtle body language or facial expressions how they really felt about him being here.

"Prepare yourself," she said softly as she took him by the arm and led him into the dining room, where her mother and father and her brother Brett and his wife, Hannah, were also present.

Greta made quick introductions, and while nobody said anything untoward, Hannah gave Greta a look that indicated a private girl talk was definitely in order later when they were alone.

Hannah had given birth to a baby boy less than a month ago. His name was Alexander and he was spending his mother's lunchtime with one of the maids. Hannah was definitely a hands-on new mom and had refused to hire a full-time nanny, but baby Alex was usually cared for by a maid during family mealtimes.

Within minutes Daniel and Jack had arrived, making the lunch bunch complete. Although both men lived close enough to go home for lunch, Jack in the old house and Daniel in a cabin near the breeding barn, they usually came to the main house for their noon meal.

It was a bit chaotic as everyone took their seats. Edith had placed Tyler across the table from Greta and next to Jack, who definitely had his suspicious-big-brother role on when he was introduced to Tyler.

Initially, the talk revolved around the ranch as Jack, Daniel and Brett dominated the conversation by discussing business with Big J.

As always, Jack and Brett bickered good-naturedly about the ranch. Brett accused Jack of hanging on to the past and Jack replied that Brett wanted to make changes too fast. It was a common argument between the two.

When Maria had brought out all the food, a hot chicken salad and various side dishes, the men fell silent and the women had a chance to visit.

Greta was pleased that her mother appeared a little brighter than she had been when Greta had initially left for Oklahoma City. It was definitely nice to see her mood lifting rather than following the initial plunge into a real depression.

"How's my little nephew?" Greta asked Hannah, who was seated next to her.

Hannah smiled. "Wonderful. He's such a good baby. He's already sleeping through most of the night."

"He's smart as a whip," Brett said proudly. "I swear the other night I heard him say 'Good night, Daddy' when I put him in his crib."

Everyone laughed. "And I'm sure he'll be toddling around within the next week or two," Jack teased.

"I wouldn't doubt it," Brett replied with a glint of laughter in his eyes.

"After lunch I need to unpack and then I definitely want to get a new-baby-smell fix," Greta said to Hannah. "There's nothing like the smell of a sweet baby."

"Ha! He doesn't smell that sweet all the time," Brett replied, once again making everyone laugh.

"And maybe when you get a chance, you can explain to me what you're doing with him," Hannah whispered and gazed at Tyler, who was asking questions of the men about the ranch and its workings.

Greta nodded, but she honestly didn't know how to explain what she was doing with Tyler. She wouldn't tell Hannah about her intense sexual attraction to him or that when he looked at her with such intensity, he made the whole crazy world fade away.

She couldn't explain that something about Tyler made her feel safe amid all of the madness that had been her life in recent months.

"I've decided to have a big Thanksgiving Day feast here," Abra announced when there was a break in the conversation. "I'll take care of all the arrangements and it will be a wonderful family gathering."

"Sweetheart, that sounds wonderful," Big J replied enthusiastically. "I can't remember the last time the whole family was together for a holiday."

Greta exchanged a worried glance with her brothers. Abra had never been the kind of mother who planned family gatherings. Rather, she tended to shun them, finding the chaos and all of the people overwhelming. The only time she had planned a gathering had been for Greta's engagement party.

"You know we'll all pitch in to help," Hannah said.

Abra shook her head. "Thank you for the offer, but this is something I want to do all on my own." She gazed across the table at her husband fondly. "It's past time that I step up to my place in this family. Besides, I'm looking forward to it. I've already started planning the menu."

"That's great, Mother," Greta replied with a bit of forced cheer. Although her mother's state of mind had always been a worry, maybe she was taking this on to replace all the planning she'd been involved with for the wedding that was not taking place.

Greta was at least pleased to see a new spark of life in her mother's eyes, a lilt to her voice that had been absent for so many years of Greta's life. Maybe her mother was finally finding the strength to face life that had always been elusive before.

After lunch she and Tyler parted in the hallway, each going to their own rooms to unpack and get settled in. As Greta unloaded the clothes she had taken to Tyler's, she replayed the lunch in her head.

Tyler had been at his very best, charming and warm and openly curious as to how and why things were done at the ranch. He'd easily won over Big J, and both Daniel and Brett had seemed to warm to him.

She hadn't missed the wariness in Jack's eyes as he'd interacted with Tyler, a wariness that hadn't vanished by the end of the meal. Jack, like Greta, had bought into

Mark's facade of a loving fiancé. Even if it wasn't fair, Tyler would have to go a long way to overcome the sins of his brother as far as her older brother was concerned.

If Greta were honest with herself, she would admit that she harbored more than a little bit of wariness about Tyler despite all the positive qualities she'd seen in him so far.

He'd been kind and protective. He'd shown a warmth and a sense of humor that was far too attractive. So far he had given her a vision of the kind of man she'd imagined she'd eventually marry.

But Mark had given her many of those same things. He'd charmed her with sweet talk and ideas of future and family. He'd also passed the brother test and had endeared himself to her parents. He'd made her believe she was the only woman on earth who was right for him. She'd swallowed it all hook, line and sinker.

And she'd been so wrong about him.

She wanted to believe that Tyler was exactly the kind of man he'd shown her so far, but she couldn't forget how easily she'd been fooled by a Stanton before and she refused to be fooled again. *Fool me once*... she thought as she hung up the last of her clothes in her closet.

She believed Tyler wanted to keep her safe from harm. She also recognized that his physical desire for her was very real, as was hers for him. But she wasn't willing to put her heart on the line so easily again.

If Tyler Stanton wanted a real relationship with her, he was going to have to work hard for it. If he just wanted hot sex and a tamed wild horse from her, then he'd get half of what he wanted while he was here at the ranch.

In the meantime, nothing in her life had changed. She still had a mother who she feared might be in for a fall by taking charge of the whole Thanksgiving-feast idea. She had a father who she was afraid was struggling with a loss of his mental acumen and a sister she'd never met who had tried to kill her once and who she feared would make another attempt. The next time she just might succeed.

TYLER UNPACKED HIS duffel back in the guest room, pleased at how well he'd got through lunch. The only person he felt he hadn't managed to win over at all was Jack.

Greta's eldest brother had the bright green Colton eyes and they'd held a level of suspicion and distrust each time they'd met Tyler's gaze.

Typical big-brother protection, Tyler thought. He couldn't blame Jack for not trusting Tyler given the circumstances and his relationship with Mark.

It was obvious that Jack was an alpha male and the man in charge of the ranch. Daniel and Brett had seemed more laid-back than their eldest brother. It was equally obvious that Daniel was passionate about his horse-breeding program, and Tyler looked forward to learning more about both it and the ranch operation while he was here.

When he was finished unpacking, his thoughts were still on Greta's brothers, particularly one of the two who had not been at the lunch table.

Greta hadn't said anything about talking to her brother Ryan, but Tyler knew they needed to report what had happened the night before at his place.

Tyler had met Ryan Colton when he'd come forward to alibi Greta. Tyler had no idea if at the time Ryan had believed him or not, but the alibi had got Greta out of jail and that was all that was important.

Tyler sat on the edge of the bed and pulled his cell phone from his pocket. It took him only minutes to call the Tulsa Police Department and be connected with Detective Ryan Colton. He told Ryan that he and Greta were at the ranch and needed to make a report. He got no further than that when Ryan said he'd come immediately to the ranch.

The minute he hung up the phone, Greta appeared in his doorway. "Ah, I just finished talking to your brother Ryan." He got up off the bed. "He's on his way here to take a report about what happened last night."

Her eyes darkened and she nodded. "Thanks. I should have called him earlier. I just hope my twin still thinks we're at your place in Oklahoma City."

"Unless she saw us leave this morning, there's no reason for her to believe we're not there. That might buy us a day or two of time before we have to worry about her showing up around here." He wanted to take that darkness out of her eyes, replace it with something bright and shiny.

"What are the plans for the afternoon?" he asked. He gave her a mock leer and then looked at his bed.

The darkness in her eyes instantly lifted and she released a small laugh. "We'll be heading back outside to get you some fresh air to blow whatever thoughts you might entertain in that direction right out of your brain."

"If you insist," he replied, pleased with his mission accomplished. The darkness was gone, replaced by wry amusement that sparkled in her beautiful eyes.

Minutes later they headed toward the small corral where Sugar eyed their approach with ears flickering and nostrils flaring.

"If we don't go any farther than here, Ryan will be able to find us easily when he arrives," she said.

"I don't think we should go farther than here ever until your evil twin is behind bars," Tyler replied as he surveyed the land. At least the only structure close to the corral was the barn.

Tyler didn't want to venture any farther on the property where there would be more places for somebody to hide and lie in wait for an opportunity to get to Greta.

Once again the November sun was warm on his back and he couldn't help but notice how the sunshine sparkled in Greta's long hair, making him want to touch it, to feel those silky strands flow through his fingers once again.

"You should go back home," she said. She looked at him somberly. "This isn't your fight. You have your work… your life to get back to. This isn't even your business."

He studied her intently, admiring the gold flecks in her hazel-green eyes, the slight upthrust of her chin and the slight tension that emanated from her.

"I'm not going anywhere, Greta, not unless you want me to go," he replied. "This is my business. I made it my business when I took you to my bed, when I realized I care about your safety. My business runs fine without me and I don't have much of a personal life to get back to. I'm here for you unless you tell me otherwise."

Her chin lowered and some of the tension dissipated. "There are plenty of men here at the ranch, including my brothers." She turned to look at Sugar and propped her arms on top of the fence. "But to be honest with you, I do feel safer with you here."

She didn't look at him again, but her words touched him. "I'll be here until the danger has passed or until you ask me to leave. Or until your brother Jack kicks me out," he added with a touch of humor. He moved next to her and put his arms on the top of the wooden fence.

She gave him a quick smile. "Jack is a tough guy. He's had to be as the oldest of the family and especially with everything that's been going on around here and my father handing him the reins of the ranch."

"Daniel seemed especially nice," he observed. "I'm interested in learning more about his breeding business."

"Daniel is the product of an affair my father had with a nanny while my mother was away on one of the convalescing trips. His mother was half-Cherokee and she died when he was ten, and Daniel came to live here with us. Although all of us kids loved the fact that we suddenly had another brother, my mother ignored him and he struggled for years to fit in here."

"He seems to be comfortable now," Tyler said.

"He's as much a brother to me as Jack or Brett and I love his wife, Megan. In fact, I'm close to all my sisters-in-law. After growing up with five brothers, I love having females finally in the family."

"I wonder if I'll still be here for the Thanksgiving feast."

"Surely not. That's still almost two weeks away." Once again her eyes darkened. "I have a feeling whatever is going to happen with my twin is going to happen very soon. She failed last night, but I imagine she won't waste any time coming for me again."

Tyler placed his hand on the butt of his gun. "Don't worry. You're under the protection of a lethal gunslinger."

She eyed him wryly. "Have you ever even fired that thing?"

"Only on a firing range," he admitted. "But I hit the targets every time."

Once again her eyes were somber. "Could you shoot a woman?"

"Absolutely, if she was trying to hurt you." He said it firmly and without hesitation. He would do whatever it took to keep Greta safe.

They fell silent, both of them watching Sugar as she watched them. What was it about Greta Colton that evoked such a fierce protectiveness inside him?

Was it guilt over the way his brother had treated her? Was it just the natural instinct of a man who had taken possession of a woman twice and still had a hunger for her?

He didn't know the answer. He knew only the driving need to be her personal bodyguard until any danger had passed. He would stand in front of her and use his body as a shield if danger came at them.

This was the first time that something felt far more important than his work at his company, and that alone was something strange and inexplicable for him.

The slam of the side door turned their attention from the horse. Ryan stood just outside the door and waved for them to come inside.

Once again he felt the palpable tension that filled Greta. "I know Ryan was the one to arrest you. Are you two okay now?" he asked as they headed for the house.

"Initially, Ryan took a lot of grief for my arrest from the rest of the family and I'll admit I was both angry and confused when I was arrested. But he was just doing his job, and unfortunately, all of the evidence he had pointed to me. We're fine now. I'm just dreading having to talk about what happened last night."

"Just remember that last night is over and you're still here," he said. "You survived and live to tell the tale."

She cast him a quick grateful smile and then they

reached Ryan. He greeted them both, Tyler with a handshake and Greta with a quick hug.

"Let's go down to the basement to talk," he said as they entered the house.

The basement was obviously a place for the Colton clan to hang out and relax. It was fully finished, with comfortable furniture, a huge flat-screen television and a pool table.

Floor-to-ceiling windows and walk-out glass doors showed a view of a huge patio area and a swimming pool that was covered for the winter.

It was easy for Tyler to imagine how beautiful the outside area would look in the summer with the sparkling pool water surrounded by blooming flowers. It was also too easy to imagine Greta in a bikini with the sun bathing her body.

He and Greta sat on a sofa and Ryan sat in a chair opposite them and pulled out a pen and pad. "You said you had a report to make. I was going to touch base with Greta today anyway, but let's get to the report first."

Greta told Ryan about waking up by being strangled. Tyler listened to her go over the events as they had occurred and a knot formed in his stomach as he again imagined what would have happened had she not managed to scream, had he not awoken to rush to her room in time.

"It was her, Ryan. It was my twin sister. She jumped out of the window just as Tyler ran into the room," Greta said, her voice trembling.

Tyler reached over and took one of her hands in his. Cold. Her hand was icy cold, as if the telling of the story had given her an arctic chill inside her very soul.

"Did you call the Oklahoma City Police Department?" Ryan asked. "Make a report with them?"

"No," Tyler replied and released Greta's hand. "We figured it wasn't necessary for them to come out and take evidence in an effort to identify the intruder. We know who it was and so thought it should be reported to you."

Ryan nodded and scribbled on his pad. When he looked up again, his gaze went to Greta. "I've managed to dig up some information."

Greta leaned forward, her body once again tense. "What kind of information?"

Ryan hesitated and then stood enough so that he could pull several folded pieces of paper from his back pocket. "This is the original birth record for Tamara Stewart, issued by a Dr. Richard Cummings. It indicates the birth of twin girls." He handed the piece of paper to Greta and then continued. "Two days later the same doctor issued a death certificate for one of the baby girls."

"That would be me," Greta said softly.

"Actually, we can assume that death certificate was for Mom's baby girl that died. Dad must have greased some palms to make this all appear as legal as possible. The doctor had to be crooked in order for it to all work." Ryan frowned.

Tyler watched Greta carefully, knowing that what she was hearing was heavy emotional baggage, but her features were schooled in neutrality, as if they were discussing a topic that had nothing to do with her at all.

"Is there more?" she asked.

Ryan gave a curt nod of his head. "We found a death certificate for Tamara Stewart Bailey. She died of a drug overdose in a motel room in Lawrence, Kansas, last April."

Greta took the piece of paper and stared down at it. "In April, and our problems started here at the ranch around the beginning of June." She looked back at her brother.

"I'm only guessing here, but I think maybe at some point just before she died, she must have told her daughter about you for the first time."

"That makes sense," Tyler said. "Otherwise, why wouldn't the twin try to find Greta sooner?"

"Exactly," Ryan agreed.

"Tamara Stewart Bailey," Greta said slowly. "So she was married at the time of her death?"

"She was a widow. Tom Bailey, her husband, died of a drug overdose three years ago, so he's a definite dead end as far as getting any information about your twin," Ryan said.

"So we don't know any more now other than my birth mother was a drug addict and is now dead," Greta said flatly.

"That's not exactly true." Ryan held one more piece of paper in his hand. "This is a copy of a short obituary that appeared in the Lawrence, Kansas, newspaper after Tamara's death. It indicates that she is survived by one daughter, Alice Stewart."

Greta took the paper from Ryan and stared at it for a long time. "Alice." Her voice was a mere whisper. She looked up at her brother and then at Tyler. "My monster now has a name and her name is Alice," she said, fear simmering in her voice.

CHAPTER EIGHT

ALICE.

The next morning when Greta stared in the bathroom mirror as she finished up getting ready for the day, her twin's name played and replayed in her mind.

Alice.

Her twin sister.

Alice. Her potential killer.

They shared the same DNA and had shared the same womb for nine months. How twisted had Alice's life been to turn her into a killer? Greta didn't believe Alice had been born that way; if she had been, Greta surely would have some bad impulses or criminal thoughts. And she didn't. She never had.

They might be twins but they were obviously nothing alike on the inside. It had to be a nature-versus-nurture kind of thing. Greta had been raised in the bosom of a loving family.

Even though her mother had been distant and often unavailable, Big J and Greta's siblings had assured her of her value, her worth as a person. What had Alice's childhood been like being raised by a drug-addicted mother? Or had Tamara Stewart become a drug addict after Alice was grown?

She turned away from the mirror and left her bathroom. At this point in time it didn't matter. Alice was a killer and she'd placed a big target on Greta's back and that was all Greta had to stay focused on.

Tamara Stewart Bailey. She couldn't grieve for a mother she never knew, a mother who had sold her just after birth. Had her mother been a drug addict then? Lured by Big J's money to sell a precious baby and spend the cash on her habit?

She couldn't feel sorry for a twin sister who now harbored such hatred in her heart. There were always choices, and at some point in her life Alice had chosen to go bad.

Even if she had been raised by a drug-addicted mother, plenty of other people had suffered the same kind of circumstances and had made choices to rise above the adversity of their childhoods.

Clad in a pair of comfortable jeans and a forest green sweater, she left her room and was surprised to find Tyler's bedroom door open and him not inside. Where could he be?

It was still fifteen minutes or so before breakfast time. She headed down the stairs and peeked in the dining room, where the table was set for the morning meal but nobody was there. Where was Tyler?

She approached the kitchen and heard the sound of voices. Although Maria Sanchez prepared the family's lunch and dinner, she went home after her duties were done. Edith was always in charge of breakfast for the family.

There had been a time when Greta had been a young girl that she'd often sit at the kitchen island and watch Edith work or help with small cooking tasks that Edith would oversee. Over the years Edith had become like a surrogate mother to Greta.

It was a bit of a shock to walk to the kitchen door and peer inside to see Tyler seated at the island, a cup of coffee in hand. Dressed in jeans and a navy long-sleeved shirt, he looked perfectly at ease.

"My mother made the best French toast in the entire state of Oklahoma," Tyler said to Edith, who was removing a baking sheet of golden biscuits from the oven. "She said the secret was in the cinnamon."

Edith placed the biscuit pan on a warming pad and shook her head, not a silver hair moving from the tight bun she wore. "Not cinnamon," she replied. "Vanilla. The secret is in knowing just how much vanilla to add to the egg mixture. When you taste my French toast, you'll forget all about any you've ever eaten before."

"I'll just have to trust that you're right for now."

"I'll see to it that you have my French toast tomorrow morning," Edith replied, rising to the challenge she obviously felt had been thrown down.

"I look forward to eating it. French toast is one of my breakfast favorites," Tyler replied.

"What's going on in here?" Greta asked as she entered the kitchen. Tyler greeted her with one of his amazing smiles and she couldn't help the ridiculous thump of her heart in response. How could a simple smile do that to her?

"Your guest is bothering the cook," Edith replied, but there was a twinkle in her eyes that indicated Tyler was working his magic charm on her.

"I'm just playing nice to make sure my bed doesn't get short-sheeted in the near future," he replied.

"If you continue to behave yourself through today, then you're good for another night," Edith replied. "But

I'm not making any promises about the future. Now both of you get out of here and let me finish up my work."

Tyler stood and grabbed his coffee cup and carried it with him as they left the kitchen and went into the dining room. Tyler sat in the chair he'd sat in the day before for meals while Greta beelined to the silver coffee server on the buffet side table and got herself a cup of coffee.

"How are you doing this morning?" he asked.

Greta knew she'd been fairly quiet the day before after Ryan had left. She'd had so much to process, so many things to think about. "I'm much better this morning. It's amazing what a good night's sleep will do." She sat in the chair opposite his, where she'd sat the day before. "Did you sleep well? I know it's tough sometimes to be in a strange bed."

"I slept like a baby once I finally went to sleep. I have to confess I was awake for a little while worrying about you. You got hit with some pretty heavy stuff yesterday." His eyes radiated with a touch of worried concern.

"I'm still processing it all, but at least I now have some answers that I didn't have before." She took a sip of her coffee, refusing to dwell on the thoughts she'd had earlier about her birth mother and her twin sister.

"By the way, have I said that you look ravishing in green?" he asked.

She cocked her head to one side, pretending to think. "No. I don't think so. I'm pretty sure I would remember you saying something like that."

At that moment Abra and Big J entered the dining room, followed closely by Brett and Hannah, and breakfast was placed on the table.

"This crazy old brain of mine—I'm afraid I've forgotten your first name," Big J said to Tyler.

Greta's heart cringed. There had been a time when her father never forgot a name or a face. Tyler reintroduced himself. "Greta is training a horse I own," he added.

"Ah, that's my girl." Big J's gaze was warm and loving as he looked at Greta. "You won't find anyone better. She's half-woman and all horse whisperer."

Tyler's eyes glittered as he looked at her, the expression on his face letting her know that as far as he was concerned, she was definitely all woman.

Greta focused on her plate as a small wave of heat swept through her. Drat the man for being able to make her all hot and bothered in the middle of a family breakfast with just a wicked glint in his eyes.

With all the emotional turmoil that had whirled around inside her the night before, it had been a tempting thought to sneak from her own room into his to find a temporary respite in the warmth of his strong arms.

Thankfully, she'd successfully fought off the impulse, knowing that it would only be taking a step backward in what she wanted in their relationship right now.

He still confused her. She still didn't quite trust the warm, caring personality he had shown her so far. She had been fooled so easily before and she didn't want to get her heart involved with Tyler Stanton.

But it was impossible not to admire the way he interacted with her family. It was difficult not to notice how easily he'd charmed everyone he'd come into contact with so far.

Was it a calculated act simply to draw her back into his bed? If so, he was going to a lot of trouble for sex. Or was this really who he was at the core? And she still wasn't sure what she wanted from him…what exactly they were doing here together.

Stop overthinking things, she told herself as breakfast finished up. She just had to let things happen and see where they led.

She was eager to get outside, empty her brain of complex thoughts and get some work done with Sugar. Even damaged horses were definitely less complicated than human beings.

Twenty minutes later an armed Tyler followed her outside. He might have been a high-powered businessman, but as his narrowed gaze shot around the area of the small corral and beyond, he looked more like an undercover bodyguard on duty.

She breathed in the scent of home, the fragrance of fresh air and sweet hay and horseflesh. She immediately felt more centered. Despite the fact that she knew it was possible danger might be near, she felt safer here than any other place in the world.

Sugar greeted her presence at the corral gate with a snort and a shake of her head, as if to say "Don't bother me." Greta carried in her jacket pocket two bright orange carrots, although she didn't expect the horse to get close enough to her today to take them from her.

"She doesn't look any friendlier today than she did yesterday," Tyler said as he leaned into the corral fence, one foot on a lower rung.

"Patience, Mr. Stanton," Greta replied. "The most important attribute a trainer can have is a tremendous amount of patience."

"I'm learning that's a pretty good trait for a man to have, too."

She smiled at him. "Definitely."

He grinned and leaned over and gave her a light peck

on her cheek. Despite the fact that it was quick, she felt the impact of his warm lips sizzle through her.

"What was that for?" she asked.

He shrugged. "I just felt like it. I said I'd wait for you to invite me into bed, but I didn't promise I wouldn't ever kiss you again. That was just a prelude to the kiss I'd like to give you when we have a little more privacy."

"Shut up," she replied. She didn't even want to think about his kisses. She pointed down to her dusty black cowboy boots. "Don't forget the little friend that rides in my boot. I'm an armed and dangerous woman."

He laughed, obviously pleased that he'd got a rise out of her.

"I'll warn you that watching me work is going to get boring very quickly," she said in an effort to get the conversation back on the matter at hand. She wanted to focus on Sugar, not the hot sugar he offered her with one of his kisses.

"Trust me, I don't find watching you do anything boring," he replied.

"Then you haven't known me long enough," she replied and opened the gate and entered the corral.

As she expected, Sugar moved to the far side of the corral, putting as much distance as possible between herself and Greta. "Hey, girl. Hey, Sugar," Greta called out, and with that she let all thoughts of anything else except the tormented horse fall away.

TYLER'S ATTENTION WAS torn between watching Greta with the horse and any activity by another human being near the corral.

Once again he was struck by Greta's gracefulness as

she walked the perimeter of the corral, forcing Sugar to keep moving in order to maintain distance between them.

Sometimes she walked slowly and then would increase her pace. At times she stopped completely and stood still in the center of the small enclosure. She spoke sweetly and softly to Sugar and then would yell unexpectedly. It was almost always the same words. "Hey, girl. Hey, Sugar. We're going to be friends."

While Tyler still entertained more than a small dose of lust for her, he realized he also wanted to be her friend. She was surrounded by chaos, facing danger, and yet she seemed to be refreshingly uncomplicated. There wasn't an ounce of drama queen in her and he'd known more than his share of drama queens.

He felt at ease with her, as if he didn't have to be anything but himself. He'd spent so many years forcing himself to be a CEO and boss in the boardroom and a smooth and polished partner for charity events. Away from that world he was discovering parts of himself that had lain dormant for far too long.

He jerked his gaze to the left and his hand fell to the butt of his gun as he saw somebody approaching in his peripheral vision. He relaxed when he saw it was Jack. His shaggy dark brown hair was hidden beneath a black cowboy hat. His piercing green eyes pinned Tyler in place.

"Tyler," he said in greeting.

"Good morning, Jack," Tyler replied.

Jack looked at Sugar. "Nice piece of horseflesh," he said.

"We'll see if your sister can work her magic," Tyler replied. He had a feeling Jack wasn't here to talk about Sugar or Greta's training skills.

"Greta does have the magic touch," Jack replied. "What are you doing with her?"

Tyler turned and eyed the man. "Is this a 'what are your intentions toward my sister' conversation?"

"Maybe." Jack shoved his hands in his pockets. "Your brother certainly wasn't much of a stand-up kind of guy."

"I'm not my brother," Tyler replied with a hint of coolness. "And if you really want to know what my intentions are with your sister, I'm not going to blow smoke up your behind. At this point the only thing I can tell you is that I like her and I like spending time with her, but I also want to make sure she stays safe. She was attacked in my home and I feel personally responsible for that and for her."

Jack held his gaze for a long moment and then grunted as if in satisfaction. "I never did much like anyone blowing smoke anywhere," he replied.

"I know you all have jobs around here and can't keep an eye on Greta every time she peeks her head outside the house. I also know that she's a woman who won't be relegated to spending days on end inside the house." Tyler placed a hand on the butt of his gun. "I can keep my sole focus on her while I'm here."

Jack glanced down at Tyler's gun. "Have you ever shot that thing?"

Tyler sighed in frustration. "What is it about you Coltons that you think just because I wear a business suit during the day that I don't know how to shoot a gun?"

Jack pulled his hands from his pockets. "Just asking, that's all."

"Trust me, I know how to shoot and I wouldn't hesitate using my gun to protect Greta from anyone who might want to harm her."

Once again Jack eyed Tyler. "Then it's good to have you here. I'll see you at dinner tonight. My wife, Tracy, and our son, Seth, plan to eat at the big house this evening."

"Then I look forward to meeting the rest of your family," Tyler replied.

With a nod of his head, Jack turned on the heels of his boots and headed away from the corral. Tyler watched him go and felt as if he'd just passed the big-brother-Colton test.

He turned his attention back to the tall, slender woman who now stood in the center of the corral, one hand outstretched with big, thick carrots on her palm.

Sugar stood some distance from her, as still as Greta as they eyed each other. Tyler could swear that they were communicating with each other through eye contact or some sort of psychic connection.

They remained in those positions for at least twenty minutes and finally Greta dropped her hand to her side and came back to the gate.

"She didn't go for the carrots," he said as Greta left the corral.

"I didn't expect her to," Greta replied. "Probably not today and possibly not tomorrow, but eventually, her curiosity will overcome her fear and she'll take the carrots from me. I saw you talking to Jack. Did he give you a hard time?"

"It was a big-brother moment," Tyler replied. "He wanted to know my intentions toward you."

She winced. "Sorry about that."

"Don't be. I'd be concerned if I were in his position. It appears I'm living under Mark's shadow."

"Mark didn't cast a shadow big enough for you to live

under," she scoffed as they headed back to the house. "None of my brothers know how often I thought about calling off the wedding plans over the last couple of months."

"Then why didn't you?"

She stopped walking and frowned. "For the first time in as long as I can remember, my mother was happy. She and I were sharing a new kind of relationship...closer... warmer, as we planned the wedding. I didn't want to ruin things for her."

"So you were willing to sacrifice yourself for your mother's happiness?" he asked.

"I guess the way things turned out, I'll never know." She continued walking. "After lunch I'll work again with Sugar."

"And what do you plan to do between now and lunchtime?" he asked.

"Do you play chess?" she asked.

He grinned. "There's nothing I like better than capturing a queen."

Minutes later they were in the basement seated at a table with a chessboard between them. "My dad taught me how to play chess when I was twelve," he said, a bit of nostalgia filling his heart as he remembered those special times with his father.

She looked at him intently. "You miss him."

"I do," he replied. "There was so much more he could have taught me about being a boss, about being a man and what it takes to be a father."

"You want children?" she asked.

"Definitely. Ideally, I'd like at least a son and a daughter. What about you?"

"I want children. The more, the merrier," she replied and made her first move on the chessboard.

He made a return move, imagining what their children might look like. He'd want them to have her dark hair and maybe his blue eyes. He'd want them to possess his business sense and her inner strength, his sense of responsibility and her love of the outdoors and soft heart. They'd be terrific kids.

"Tyler? It's your move," she said, interrupting the crazy thoughts that had momentarily danced through his head. At the moment he had no plans to marry Greta, let alone have children with her.

"By the way, what are we playing for?" he asked as he made his next move.

"For fun," she replied.

"Oh no, there has to be a prize," he protested. She eyed him warily. "A kiss. If I win, then I get a kiss. If you win, then you get a kiss."

She laughed and shook her head. "Then it's a win-win situation for you."

"And for you," he returned, making her laugh once again.

"Okay," she agreed with the light of challenge in her eyes. "A kiss it is, then, but the most important thing is who wins the game," she replied, displaying a competitive nature that he found totally hot.

Tyler quickly learned that Greta had a teasing, sexy side to her that she pulled out as he tried to focus on the game. She flipped her hair and ran a finger over her lower lip, a wicked glint in her eyes that told him she knew she was being a flirty distraction.

Tyler was competitive, but it quickly became obvious that she was an intelligent player, and he found that as sexy as anything else she was doing.

"Checkmate," she said in triumph.

Tyler stared at the board in disbelief. "You cheated," he exclaimed.

"You know I didn't," she replied vigorously.

"Yes, you did," he protested. "You cheated by distracting me with your beautiful face and with the way your sweater makes your eyes so green. You distracted me by subtly flirting with me."

She laughed. "Now you're just making excuses for losing. I beat you fair and square."

"Okay, I concede," he relented. "You won fair and square and now it's time for me to take my punishment." He stood and walked around the table to where she sat.

She raised her face as if in anticipation of another peck on the cheek. There was no way he would be satisfied with a mere peck. He'd had that earlier in the day and it had only made him hungry for a different kind of kiss.

He took her hand and pulled her to a standing position and then wrapped her in his arms. Her eyes darkened in hue just before he took her lips with his.

She stood perfectly still for a moment, but when he deepened the kiss by pulling her more firmly against him and swirling his tongue with hers, she wrapped her arms around his neck and leaned into him.

Kissing Greta was like nothing he'd ever experienced before. Her mouth was sweet and hot and stoked a hunger inside him for more. He had a feeling if he kissed Greta a thousand times, it wouldn't be enough... It would never be enough.

She broke the kiss, dropping her arms from around

his neck and wiggling out of his embrace. She took two steps back from him as if afraid he might grab her up in his arms again.

"Another game?" he asked, eager to repeat what they'd just shared.

"Definitely not," she replied, her gaze not meeting his. "I think I'll go up and check in with my mother before lunch. Feel free to turn on the television and make yourself comfortable."

Tyler watched her go, his blood heated as he wondered if she'd ever come to him for lovemaking again. He'd told her he wouldn't invite her to share his bed again, that the next time they made love, it would be because she initiated it.

He almost wished he were the kind of man who broke promises, who went back on his words. He realized that as much as he desired her, he needed even more badly for her to want him.

CHAPTER NINE

GRETA STOOD IN the center of the small corral, her hand outstretched with carrots on her palm. Although she kept her gaze focused on Sugar, her head was filled with Tyler and that kiss.

That kiss had shaken her to her very core, had reminded her of how wonderful it was to be in Tyler's arms, how magical it had been making love with him.

It was her own fault. She had agreed to the silly terms of the chess game. She'd known it would end in a kiss, but she hadn't expected the fire of desire to roar through her so viscerally.

Last night at dinner he'd continued to charm the family, including Jack's pregnant wife, Tracy, and their five-year-old son, Seth. Seth always lightened any meal with his easy laughter, and Tyler had told several fun stories of his youth in an effort to bond with the little boy.

Tyler was in her head, but he was also making headway into her heart, and that scared her. She definitely had some trust issues where Tyler was concerned, issues she knew came from her relationship with Mark and her uncertainty as to what exactly Tyler wanted from her.

The warm, charming man who so far fit so seamlessly into her family and whom she'd always viewed as a businessman with ice in his veins. She knew Mark and

Tyler shared a contentious relationship. Was it any wonder that she had trust issues where Tyler was concerned?

The one thing she was certain of was that he had her back. She had no doubt that he'd do whatever he could to keep her safe from harm. Each time she glanced at him, his hand was on the butt of his gun and his gaze scanned the surroundings. She definitely felt as if he had become her personal bodyguard.

All thoughts of Tyler shot out of her head as Sugar took two tentative steps closer to her. The horse was still a good fifteen feet away, but those two steps were progress.

"Come on, girl. Come and see what I have for you. Drop those defenses and trust me," she said aloud.

The two remained in their positions for the next half an hour, and finally, Greta dropped her hand and moved to the gate, where Tyler awaited her.

"Did you see her?" Greta asked in excitement. "She came closer."

"I saw. Do you have any idea how beautiful you look with your cheeks pink from the cold and happiness sparkling in your eyes?"

She felt her cheeks warm. "You have to stop saying things like that to me."

"Why? I thought women liked compliments."

"I feel like you're trying to seduce me." Her cheeks grew even hotter.

"I am. Isn't that what men do when they desire a woman?"

He looked so handsome in his jeans and long-sleeved black shirt. His light brown hair was slightly mussed by the breeze and his cheeks were slightly reddened by the cold.

"You're going to a lot of trouble for sex," she replied and looked down at the ground.

He placed a hand beneath her chin and gently nudged her face up so he could meet her gaze. "This isn't all about sex, Greta. I can't tell you what it's all about, but I know it's about more than just sex."

She searched his eyes, looking for a lie, but found none there. "You're just so different than I always thought you were."

She started walking toward the house and he fell into step beside her. "Different how?"

"Warmer, more human. You live alone in a big house and have a reputation for being a bit of a shark. You always seemed like an island, perfectly satisfied in your own company and not needing anything but your business world. Whenever I was around you with Mark, you always acted like you didn't even like me."

"I liked you too much. That's why I had to keep my distance from you. I'll admit that when I'm at work, I have to be the man in charge. I have to be confident and strong and make tough decisions. That's part of who I am, but it certainly isn't all that I am."

He grasped her arm to halt their progress before they reached the door to go inside. "When I get home to my big house, it resounds with a silence that is unnatural and has become increasingly uncomfortable. I'm thirty-two years old. I'm at a place in my life where I want to fill that silence with a woman's voice, with the sound of laughter and meaningful talks." He released his hold on her arm.

"You said you came close to getting married once. Tell me about that woman." His words had touched

Greta, but he hadn't said that the woman he wanted to fill his silence was her.

He looked around where they stood. "Why don't we go inside and we can talk more."

She nodded her agreement and a few minutes later they were back in the basement, Greta seated in a chair and Tyler on the sofa across from her.

"Her name was Michelle," he said, picking up the conversation where they'd left off. "She was beautiful and bright. She was socially polished and would have made a perfect corporate wife. We dated for several months and then I asked her to marry me and she agreed. We were engaged for a month when she broke it off."

"Were you heartbroken?" Greta asked, remembering that he'd asked her the same thing when he'd learned that she and Mark weren't together.

"Initially, I was a bit hurt, but then I realized I'd picked her with my head, not my heart. I liked her, I admired many things about her, but I wasn't in love with her. I've never been in love. I don't know what love feels like, but I realized quickly that it wasn't what I had with Michelle."

"I thought I knew what love was," Greta said, thinking of those early months with Mark. "But I was so wrong. Mark was my first real relationship, and as you know, that didn't go so well."

"We both dodged a bullet," he replied.

"It would seem so," she agreed. She just didn't know if Tyler was another bullet she needed to dodge.

The day passed much as it had the day before. Lunch was pleasant and then Greta returned to the corral to work with Sugar. She remained in the corral for two hours and several times Tyler received calls on his cell phone.

She assumed they were business calls and guilt suffused her, as she knew that she was keeping him from his work at Stanton Oil. But when she finally left the corral and mentioned it to him, he assured her that everything was running smoothly without him and there was no reason for him to leave the Colton ranch to go back to Oklahoma City and his office.

Dinner was also pleasant. Her mother chatted about her big plans for the Thanksgiving Day event, showing an animation that was surprising yet wonderful. Brett and Big J talked about various ranching topics and Tyler added to the conversation by asking questions about the family business that entertained Greta's father.

After dinner everyone went their own separate ways and Greta asked if Tyler would like to watch a movie. He agreed and she led him to the media room upstairs.

"I suppose you want to watch some sappy romance movie," Tyler said as he settled into one of the plush theater seats.

The media room had been Big J's baby, with a huge screen, theater seats and surround sound to give a real entertainment experience.

"And I suppose you want to watch some action movie with killer robots or aliens," she replied and picked up a remote control.

"I'll watch whatever movie you pick out if you start up that popcorn machine," he replied.

"It's a deal." She got up and turned on the machine that would spill popcorn for them to enjoy during the movie.

Within minutes the air filled with the scent of fresh

popcorn. Greta filled two bags and grabbed two sodas from a refrigerator that was hidden behind plush curtains and they settled in.

"It's been years since I've been to a movie," he said. "And this is some setup you all have here. I feel like I'm in a real theater."

"It's all my dad's doing. We have movie night every Friday. My dad loves it when the family all gathers here to watch one of his favorite flicks." She picked up the remote, punched in several numbers and settled back in her chair as the opening of an old black-and-white John Wayne movie filled the screen.

Tyler gave a small laugh. "Why am I not surprised?"

"There's nothing better than the Duke's movies."

"Shh," he whispered. "John Wayne is in the house."

Greta grinned at him and then focused her attention on the big screen. Over the years she had seen all of the John Wayne movies and countless other Westerns dozens of times, but she never tired of them. They represented security and family tradition that was heartwarming, and most important, the good guys always won.

They were halfway through the movie when Tyler finished his popcorn and placed an arm around her shoulders. She immediately felt like a sixteen-year-old on a first date as a flush of excited warmth swept over her. It was ridiculous, she told herself. It was ridiculous how easily he could stir her with the simplest touch.

His heady scent overrode the smell of the popcorn and filled her head with the memory of making love to him. It also imbued her with a sense of safety, of protection from all evil.

Alice.

The name jumped into her head, bringing with it a chill that made her lean closer to Tyler and consciously focus her attention on the movie unfolding. The last thing she wanted was for thoughts of her twin to ruin a good movie with a hot man.

When the first movie ended, they decided to watch a second one despite the fact that it wouldn't end until after eleven. Greta was reluctant for the evening to end, and apparently, he was, too.

They refilled their popcorn bags and settled back in for more John Wayne. Once again when Tyler had finished with his popcorn, his arm went around her shoulders and he pulled her closer.

"If you try to cop a feel, I'll put on a sappy romance movie," she warned.

His perfect teeth flashed with his smile in the semi-darkness of the room. "To be honest, it hadn't crossed my mind, but now that you brought it up…"

"Just try it, buster," she retorted.

He laughed and squeezed her shoulder. It all felt so natural, she thought. The teasing, the simmer of sexual tension between them, the laughter—nothing felt forced or alien.

Despite the fact that she had known him for such a brief period of time, in some ways it seemed as if he'd been by her side for years.

The movie ended and it was as they were leaving the media room that Tyler's cell phone rang. He frowned and pulled his phone from his pocket. Before he even answered it, Greta had a bad feeling. Phone calls that came this late at night never brought good news.

She watched Tyler's face intently. There was no clue as to what he was hearing. His features remained passive as he listened and then told whoever was on the other end of the line to call the police and get a report made.

"What's happened?" she asked once he'd hung up.

"That was my neighbor Derek. I'd called him before we left my place and asked him to keep an eye on things for me while I was gone. He was on his way home from a local bar tonight and decided to drive up and check things out at my house."

"And what did he find?" she asked, her voice slightly breathy with an anxiety that knotted in her stomach.

"Your Jeep with all the windows broken out and all four tires slashed. I would guess that Alice now knows you aren't there any longer and the car in the driveway was just a ruse."

She stared at him as a chill started deep in her soul and worked its way out to the tips of her fingers and toes. "Then that means she's probably either on her way here or already here."

Tyler didn't reply. He pulled her into his arms and held her tight. They both knew that danger had once again just moved intimately closer.

RYAN WAS AT the house just after breakfast, and as with last time, he, Greta and Tyler went down to the basement to talk privately.

Tyler and Greta sat on the sofa and Ryan in the chair facing them. "I had the Oklahoma City Police Department fax me over a copy of the report they made last night." He looked at Tyler. "There was no damage to the house." He turned his gaze to Greta. "But your Jeep was trashed. They pulled no fingerprints off the vehicle and didn't find what was used to smash in the windows, although they assume it was some kind of bat."

"Even if they had found fingerprints, they would have matched mine," Greta said. "You know it was her. You know it was Alice."

Tyler was pleased by the strength in her voice. Last night she had been frightened and it had been difficult for him to leave her at her bedroom door to face the demons in her mind all alone. However, she'd rallied and found that inner strength he admired and it showed in her eyes.

"We're working under the assumption that it was Alice," Ryan replied. "If she followed you to Tyler's place, then it's a good guess that last night she realized you weren't there and took out her rage on your Jeep. I would also say it's a good guess that she'll be on her way back here."

"Or is already here," Greta said grimly.

Ryan's forehead wrinkled in obvious frustration. "She moves like a damned shadow. We haven't been able to find out where she stays or how she's getting from place to place. There's been a rash of stolen vehicles around the area and we can only assume that might be how she's moving around. There's no vehicle registered in her name in any state."

"So what is your suggestion for Greta?" Tyler asked.

"My suggestion would be for her to leave the state and go far away from here until we apprehend Alice." He cast a fond look at his sister. "But I know she won't do that."

"You're right. I won't," Greta replied firmly. "This is my home and I have work to do here."

"Training Sugar is far less important than your safety," Tyler said.

"That's not the point," Greta protested. "I refuse to

be chased away from my family by some nutcase twin sister with a grudge."

"We all know it's more than just a simple grudge," Tyler countered. "She tried to kill you that night at my house. She climbed through a window in the dead of night and tried to strangle you."

She raised a hand to her throat and her face paled. "Trust me, I remember it all too well."

"I think the best thing to do is for you to keep doing what you're doing," Ryan said to Tyler. "Stay close to Greta and I'll make sure the ranch hands know to keep an eye out for somebody who looks like Greta lurking around the ranch who might be acting suspiciously. I also think you shouldn't wander too far from the house. Stick around your corral and your barn so that the ranch hands aren't confused."

"Got it," Greta said.

"If you do leave the ranch, make sure you stay in public places. Alice is too smart to move on you where there will be witnesses," Ryan said. "I'm sure she has no desire to get caught, and when or if she tries to attack Greta, it will likely take place where there are few to no witnesses."

"I'm not sure I understand what Alice's endgame is," Tyler said. "God forbid, even if she succeeds in hurting Greta, she'll always be a fugitive on the run."

"I can't begin to guess what her endgame might be." Ryan stared down at the floor for a moment and then looked back at Greta. "I'm sorry I ever doubted you."

Greta smiled at him, her eyes gleaming with sisterly love. "You've already apologized to me at least a dozen times. You were doing your job, Ryan, and all the evidence pointed to me. We didn't know I had a wicked twin running around."

"Arresting you was one of the most difficult things I've ever done," Ryan said as he stood.

Greta got up from the sofa and walked over to her brother. She wrapped her arms around his waist and they hugged, and Tyler found himself wishing he shared that kind of sibling caring with Mark. He also wished Greta would hug him with such sweet emotion shining from her eyes.

They broke their embrace and Ryan looked at Tyler once again. "Keep her safe, Tyler, and we'll keep hunting for Alice. Sooner or later she's going to make a mistake and we'll get her behind bars."

"I'm hoping sooner rather than later," Greta said with fervor.

Together they all left the basement, and once Ryan was gone, Greta was eager to get outside to see Sugar. "Just let me get my gun," Tyler said.

"And I'm going to grab a jacket," she replied.

They parted ways to go to their separate rooms. Tyler hooked his gun and holster onto his belt. Ryan's words rang in his ears and the responsibility for Greta's welfare weighed heavily on his shoulders.

Keep her safe.

This was the most important job he'd ever had in his life and he didn't want to screw it up. He could relax when they were in the house together, but he had to be on his toes when they were outside.

"Ready?" Greta appeared in his bedroom doorway, a brown suede jacket now covering her chocolate-colored T-shirt.

"Ready," he replied and gave her a reassuring smile.

They stopped by the kitchen, where Greta grabbed several fresh big carrots, and then they headed to the corral. Sugar stood by the gate, as if eagerly anticipating Greta's appearance. But the moment the horse saw them, she backed away to her usual distance.

As Greta entered the corral, Tyler cast his gaze in every direction, a taut tension forming a small knot in the pit of his stomach.

Where was Alice now? Was she hiding someplace on the property just waiting for the right moment to strike? Would he be up to the task if she did come out of nowhere to attack Greta? Would he see the danger coming before it was too late?

He couldn't imagine anything bad happening to Greta. The thought made him heartsick and his gut twisted into knots. He placed a hand on the butt of his gun.

He hadn't been this afraid when he was thrust into the position of running Stanton Oil at such a young age. He hadn't been this afraid for himself or, more important, somebody else.

"Come on, Sugar. Come and see what treat I have for you." Greta's voice filled the air. Her hair moved with the breeze, the dark wavy strands acting as if they had a life of their own.

She was in her element, and he suspected when she was in that corral, she thought of nothing else except building a relationship with the animal that shared the space with her.

This was the Greta Colton who had enchanted him months ago, before she'd met Mark. The jean-clad tomboy who exuded confidence and competence had captured his attention, and he'd been sick when he'd realized Mark had made his move on her.

He frowned as he thought of his brother. He still hadn't heard from Mark. He knew from speaking with his manager at Stanton Oil that his brother hadn't been into work since Greta's arrest over a month before.

Tyler should call Mark, but he was reluctant to stir up things. There was no question in Tyler's mind that Mark knew Tyler was now with Greta. If Mark had been behind the photo in the paper, then it was obvious he was in a hateful snit. Mark hadn't really wanted her, but he didn't want his brother to be happy with her either.

Happy.

Tyler was vaguely surprised to realize that he was happy in Greta's company. He didn't know if he'd ever been truly happy before. Certainly his work gave him a lot of satisfaction and he had nights at home where he was at peace, but true happiness had remained elusive until now.

He had no idea if this feeling of happiness would last or what it meant in the grand scheme of his life. He touched the butt of his gun again. He knew only that for right now keeping Greta safe was the most important job he would ever have and he just hoped he was up to the challenge.

ALICE HAD A PLAN.

She had been livid when she'd realized her sister wasn't at Tyler Stanton's place, and she'd vented her rage on Greta's vehicle. She'd spent the entire night venting the mindless fury that had overwhelmed her, but she'd finally managed to get herself under control enough to think rationally.

It hadn't taken a rocket scientist to guess that Tyler Stanton had taken Greta home to the bosom of her family. Her family…the family Alice should have had.

Of course, she'd already been filled with impotent wrath after her failed attempt to strangle Greta. If she'd just had another minute before Greta screamed, she would have managed to achieve her goal.

It had taken her most of this morning to find a vehicle she could steal to get from Oklahoma City to Tulsa. She hoped the owner of the old pickup she'd "borrowed" didn't notice it was missing from the barn until she'd got to the Colton ranch.

She'd found a special bonus in the glove box. She'd been delighted to discover the handgun. She now gripped the steering wheel more tightly. Another twenty minutes and she'd be close enough to the Colton ranch to ditch the pickup.

Excitement soared through her at the thought of arriving at the ranch. Once there, it wouldn't take her long to find out if, indeed, Greta was there.

If she was, then Alice was ready. She'd shoplifted from two different convenient stores on the drive, taking bottled water and enough food to keep her going until the perfect time she could act.

Her supplies from those stores sat in bags on the passenger seat. But in the back of the pickup was a real reunion surprise for her sister.

It was all coming together, all the plotting and planning to finally see the demise of the twin sister who had been living the life that was meant for Alice.

Their reunion would be so special because only one of them would walk away and Alice was determined that person would be her.

CHAPTER TEN

IT HAD BEEN seven days since Greta's Jeep had been destroyed, seven long days of looking over her shoulder and jumping at shadows.

Greta definitely had a feeling that Alice was near. She knew her twin was watching and waiting for the perfect opportunity to strike. Greta didn't know if what she felt was just normal fear of a known threat or some kind of inexplicable twin connection that let her *feel* her twin's presence nearby.

Greta now stood in the center of the small corral. It was late afternoon and Sugar stood as close as she ever had to Greta, who held the tantalizing carrots in her hand.

Still, as pleased as she was about the daily progress she'd made with Sugar, she couldn't help but think about Alice and an ever-present danger she had yet to face. The worst part was that she knew deep in her heart that sooner or later she would face that danger.

Tyler had now not only experienced a Colton family movie night but also met the last of her brothers when Eric and his wife, Kara, had stopped by one evening.

Kara had recently opened her own restaurant after being a personal chef for years, and the new establishment appeared to be a rousing success. Tyler had charmed them as easily as he had the rest of the family.

During the past week her relationship with Tyler had only deepened. When she wasn't working in the corral, they spent their time together playing cards or pool and talking.

They'd shared pieces of their pasts, thoughts about their futures and fears about the present. He touched her whenever possible, pushing a strand of hair away from her face, grabbing her hand when they walked and sneaking unexpected kisses that kept her off balance and in a constant state of simmering anticipation.

She was falling in love with him and she couldn't do a thing about it. She had no idea exactly how he felt about her, didn't know if she was headed for heartache at the hands of another Stanton, but she couldn't help the depth of her growing love for him.

She shoved thoughts of him aside as Sugar took yet another step closer to her. Greta studied the horse's body language and was pleased to see no tension, no fear at the moment in the magnificent animal.

"Sweet Sugar," she murmured softly. The horse eyed her with her big brown eyes, hesitant yet still not appearing afraid. It was now just a matter of the horse allowing her natural curiosity to overcome the hesitation.

Greta held her breath, her heart beating just a little faster as Sugar took another step and leaned her head forward, her nostrils flaring as she sniffed the air.

"Come on, sweet baby. Take the carrots," Greta urged and fought her own impulse to move toward Sugar. It was important that she not make a move that Sugar might find aggressive. That would undo all of the progress Greta had made. Sugar had to come to Greta on Sugar's own terms.

And then it happened. Sugar stepped up close enough

to take one of the carrots from Greta's hand. Sugar chomped it down eagerly and then took the other carrot, leaving Greta empty-handed.

A wild sense of success swept through her even as Sugar backed away from her. Greta turned back to look at Tyler, who gave her a wide grin and a thumbs-up sign.

She left the corral, and once she was outside, she threw her arms around Tyler's neck with a laugh. "She finally is starting to trust."

Tyler picked her up and twirled in a circle, then set her back down on the ground. "Your patience is finally paying off."

Greta released her hold on him and nodded. "Now the real work can begin. I'll work with carrots for another couple of days, then start with some apple slices, and finally, we can introduce her to you and some equipment."

Tyler fell into step with her as she headed for the barn next to the corral. "I think we should go out to dinner tonight to celebrate your success," he said.

They entered the darker barn interior, which housed stacks of hay bales, along with an equipment area and bins of grain. She sat on one of the bales of hay and stared up at him with concern. "Do you really think leaving the ranch and going out is a good idea?"

"I think it's a great idea. We've been cooped up for almost two weeks now, and Ryan said as long as we're in public places, you should be safe. We could go to Kara's restaurant."

"That sounds nice," she agreed. "I haven't been to her restaurant since it opened, but according to the publicity she's been getting, it's *the* new place to dine in Tulsa."

"Maybe you can call her and use the family connection to make sure we can get a table around seven."

"I'll do that." Greta stood and started to pick up one of the bales of hay, unsurprised when Tyler stepped forward and lifted it into his arms.

"Feed trough?" he asked.

Greta nodded and together they walked to the small shed that sheltered Sugar. Through a back door Tyler set the bale on the floor and Greta not only filled the trough for Sugar to eat but also added fresh water to the water trough. "I'm hoping to get her to go willingly into one of the barn stalls before the first snow flies," Greta said.

"That's still weeks away, and now that you've had a breakthrough, hopefully, things will move more quickly."

"That's the way it usually works," she agreed.

Two hours later she stood in front of her closet, trying to decide what to wear out for dinner. She'd spoken to Kara and she'd assured Tyler and Greta a table at seven.

While Greta was looking forward to an evening out, especially at her sister-in-law's restaurant, there was also a part of her that was afraid to go out.

Alice had become an omnipotent monster in her mind. Although there had been no sign of her around the ranch and no fires, downed fencing or other indications she was here, Greta felt her nearness.

Hiding…waiting…looking for a window of opportunity to strike again. Would it be tonight? Tomorrow? Ryan had checked in the day before with the news that there was still no news on Alice's whereabouts. None of the ranch hands had reported seeing anything unusual.

She finally grabbed a deep-coral-colored dress from her closet. Her mother had picked it out for one of the many wedding showers she had anticipated Greta might attend.

Although it was more her mother's style than Greta's with its flirty skirt and ruffled V-neckline, she decided she might as well get some use out of it and it might be nice to be a little more feminine tonight.

She laid the dress on the bed and then went into the bathroom to finish up her makeup. She usually skipped the makeup thing altogether if she was just hanging out at the house or working outside, but tonight she pulled out all the stops, mascara, a touch of blush and lipstick. After all, this was a night of celebration that deserved a little extra effort on her part.

She put her knife in her bedside stand. There would be no place to hide it in the dainty high-heel shoes she wore. Besides, she had a feeling Tyler would have his gun with him.

He'd had it with him almost every moment of every day that he'd been here. He wouldn't plan a night out without carrying.

She and Tyler had agreed to meet in the foyer at six thirty, and as she came down the stairs, she saw not only Tyler but her mother waiting for her, as well.

They were talking and for a moment didn't see her coming, but before she reached the bottom step, her mother saw her and clapped her hands together in pleasure. "Oh, Greta, you look so beautiful. Now, that's my girl without her usual jeans and sweatshirts."

"That's not a girl," Tyler said, his eyes gleaming in obvious approval as his gaze swept her from head to toe. "She's definitely all woman."

Greta reached the bottom of the stairs. "Stop it— you're both going to make me blush."

Abra reached for her and kissed her on the cheek.

"You look positively lovely and I hope the two of you have a wonderful outing this evening."

"Thanks, Mother." Greta was both surprised and delighted by her mother's kiss. Abra had never been an affectionate parent. A loving caress, a sweet kiss had been rare when Greta was growing up.

"We'd better go," Tyler said with a quick glance at his wristwatch.

"I had Tyler's truck brought around to the driveway, so it's just outside," Abra said.

"Thank you. Then we'll see you later," Tyler said. He looked powerful and confident in a black suit, blue shirt and a black-and-blue tie. His handsomeness nearly stole Greta's breath away, and as they walked down the outside stairs that led to the driveway, she felt unaccountably shy.

He helped her up into the passenger seat of his big pickup truck and then circled the vehicle to slide into the driver seat. "As beautiful as you look tonight, I'm sorry we don't have a limo to ride in."

"I don't need a limo. I'm perfectly satisfied with your monster truck," she replied.

He started the engine and looked at her once again. "Have I told you that you look gorgeous?" His eyes glowed in the light from the dashboard and flooded her with familiar warmth.

"Thank you, but don't get too used to it. You know I'm a jeans-and-T-shirt kind of girl at heart," she reminded him.

"I realize that, but it's nice to occasionally see another side of you."

"I haven't mentioned how well you clean up. You look

very handsome, Mr. Stanton. I hope there is a gun underneath all that expensive suit-jacket material."

He flashed her a smile. "Never leave your home without it," he replied. His smile fell. "Try not to worry. Try to enjoy the night, Greta. Don't even think about her. Let's just celebrate a great day and your success with Sugar." He put the car into gear and they were under way.

Even though he told her not to worry, not to even think about Alice, Greta couldn't help but notice that as they drove, his gaze went frequently to the rearview mirror. He was obviously concerned about being followed.

How could she not worry when the man who had told her not to appeared to be worried, as well?

THE PARKING LOT at Kara's restaurant was filled to capacity and Tyler was grateful that they'd been assured a table, with the crowd. Thank goodness for family connections, he thought. They walked into the entrance, where a group of about a dozen people stood waiting to be seated.

Tyler grimaced once he saw an unexpected yet familiar face. Greta stiffened next to him as Mark approached them, a small smirk curving his mouth. "Well, well, if it isn't the happy couple," he said.

"Hello, Mark," Tyler said evenly and fought the impulse to wrap an arm around Greta and pull her close to his side. "What are you doing here?"

"I've been in Tulsa for the last week or so and I assume I'm here for the same reason you are, to try out a new popular restaurant."

"Rumor has it that the food is terrific," Tyler replied, trying to keep the conversation civil.

"That's what I hear." Mark paused a moment and a

smirk once again lifted his lips. "Tell me, brother, are you enjoying my sloppy seconds?"

The blood of rage rushed to Tyler's head. He surged forward, halted only by Greta taking hold of his arm and gripping it tightly. "Mark, stop it," she said with a toughness that surprised Tyler. "Your brother has done nothing but help me when I needed help while you were missing in action. It's done. You were the one sneaking around behind my back seeing other women when you were supposed to be committed to me."

Kara appeared by the hostess stand and motioned to them. "If you'll excuse us, our table is ready," Greta said and forcefully tugged on Tyler's arm.

Tyler allowed her to pull him along, afraid that if he remained in hitting distance of Mark, he'd punch his face, brother or not. Knowing his luck, somebody would catch him punching his brother on a cell-phone camera and it would feed a scandal that publicly had gone away in the past week.

The utter disrespect and repulsiveness of Mark's words still burned inside him when they were seated at a two-top in a relatively secluded part of the restaurant.

"Let it go, Tyler," Greta said once their drink orders had been taken. "I already have."

"He disrespected you," Tyler said in a half growl.

"Consider the source. Besides, he disrespected himself with his own ugliness," she replied. "Thank God I didn't marry him."

Tyler drew in a deep breath and released it slowly in an effort to release the anger that still gripped him. He didn't want to allow the interaction with Mark to ruin the night of celebration.

By the time the waitress arrived with Greta's glass

of wine and his scotch and soda, he'd managed to get himself under control. Thankfully, Mark and whoever he had with him had been seated out of view.

The only reason Mark would be in Tulsa would be a woman. She was probably somebody Mark had met while he'd been here for Greta and making wedding plans.

He consciously shoved away thoughts of his brother and focused on the woman across from him. The color of her dress brought out the green in her hazel eyes and the slight plunge of her neckline gave a tantalizing hint of her breasts.

He raised his glass toward her. "Here's to Sugar eating carrots and me being lucky enough to be sitting across from the most beautiful woman on earth."

She smiled and raised her glass to clink it with his. "How can I not toast to the success with Sugar and a little bit of baloney?"

He laughed, but for only a moment. "I do feel lucky to be the man taking you to dinner."

"And I feel lucky to be here with you, too," she replied.

She picked up her menu and he did the same, knowing the waitress would return soon to take their orders.

"The roast beef with pickling spices sounds interesting," he said.

"I'm thinking Swiss steak with parsley new potatoes," she replied. She closed her menu. "I'm sure whatever is on the menu is wonderful. Kara is a talented cook and this restaurant has been her dream for a long time."

The waitress appeared to take their orders, and while they waited for her to return, they talked about the decor and the positive reviews the place had received from local food bloggers and critics.

"Your family is so terrific," Tyler said once they'd been served and had begun to eat. "They make me wish I had a big family."

She smiled. "Things can get pretty chaotic at times when all of us are together." Her smile faltered. "Which is why I'm so surprised that Mother is planning such a big feast next week. This will be the first holiday that we're all in one place with her being in charge of everything. In the past whenever we all got together, she'd retire to her room until everyone had gone home."

"She seems to be handling it all very well so far."

"I know. I have to admit she keeps surprising me. As my father gets a little bit weaker, my mother seems to be getting stronger."

"There's obviously a lot of love between them," Tyler said. "Maybe your mother knows a time will come when she needs to be the caretaker and she's rising to the challenge. That's what people who love each other do."

"Did your parents have a good marriage?" she asked.

"For the most part," he replied and thought back to when his parents had been alive. "I think the only thing they really fought about was Mark. My father thought my mother babied him too much."

"The two of you are so different sometimes it's hard for me to remember that you're brothers," she replied.

"I feel sorry for him," Tyler admitted. "Maybe my mother unknowingly set him up to fail."

"Life is about choices. I feel about Mark kind of like I do about Alice. No matter where you come from, no matter what your background is, when you're an adult,

you decide what kind of person you're going to be."
Greta took a sip of her wine.

"You're right," Tyler agreed. "Mark continues to make
bad choices in his life and it's obvious Alice has chosen a wicked path. But enough talk about them. Surely
we can think of more pleasant things to discuss. It isn't
every night we're out celebrating."

"You're right. We can always talk about how bad you
are at chess," she said teasingly. Her eyes sparkled and
a familiar surge of desire rose up inside him.

"I just let you win because I'm a gentleman," he replied.

She laughed. "If that's what you need to tell yourself."

"I'm always up for a rematch if the stakes remain the
same." He watched the faint sweep of a blush fill her
cheeks and knew she was remembering the kiss they'd
shared. He certainly hadn't forgotten it.

"I'd hate to have to beat you again and confirm the
fact that you are a big loser," she replied. "No more chess
games for me."

It was all so easy with her. He didn't have to be on
guard. He didn't have to measure each and every word
or think about consequences. He could just be himself
and that was enough for her. There was such a refreshing sense of freedom with her.

They were halfway through their meal when Kara
stopped by their table. Her blue eyes sparked with pleasure. "How is everything?"

"Absolutely delicious," Tyler said.

Greta smiled warmly at her sister-in-law. "Kara, the
whole place is beautiful and the food is magnificent.
You should be so proud of yourself."

"I couldn't have done it all without your brother's support. Eric has been wonderful about the whole thing. I've never been so happy in my entire life. I married the man of my dreams and am doing what I love to do."

"You deserve it all, Kara," Greta replied. "Thank God Eric was there when you needed him and you found each other to love."

"Thanks, and now I need to make the rounds of the rest of the tables and then get back into the kitchen. Enjoy the rest of your meal and I'll see you next week for Thanksgiving."

"What did you mean when you said Eric found her when she needed him?" Tyler asked curiously after Kara left.

He listened with interest as Greta explained that Kara had been in the witness protection program after witnessing a murder in New York City. The killer had made threats on her life while in prison.

Kara had been moved to Tulsa, but when she sensed danger from the man assigned to keep her safe, she'd run and then had been struck in a hit-and-run accident that had been witnessed by Eric. He'd called for an ambulance and, in the meantime, done what he could to take care of her injuries.

"The man in prison was killed by another inmate. Kara is now safe from her past and can embrace her future with my brother."

"Sounds like a fairy tale. Trauma surgeon falls in love with patient and lives happily ever after."

"You don't believe in fairy tales?" she asked.

"I haven't seen any in my life so far," he replied.

"I don't know about fairy tales, but I definitely believe in happily-ever-after," she said.

"I don't know how you can still be a believer after your relationship with Mark."

"Mark was a toad that I accidentally mistook for a prince. Eventually, I hope I'll find that man who will give me a fairy-tale ending of my happily-ever-after."

"So despite your tomboy penchant, you're still a romantic at heart," he teased.

"My first dream for myself was to become a good horse trainer and I've accomplished that. It's just been recently, since my brothers have all found love, that I've become more of a romantic at heart. You can't be surrounded by so much love and not want it for yourself, as well."

"Then you're in the market for a husband," he said.

"I'm not actively seeking, but I'm open to possibilities," she corrected. "Now, tell me more about your business."

It was obvious to him that it was an effort to change the topic, that they'd drifted into an area of conversation she wasn't comfortable pursuing.

They topped off their dinner with dessert and coffee, and Tyler talked about his work and then Greta told him how all of her brothers had found their wives. Each story was as interesting as the one before.

It was after ten when Tyler finally asked the waitress for their tab, only to be told that it had already been taken care of by management.

Tyler started to argue, but Greta stopped him. "It's obviously a gift from Kara. Don't take away the joy of her giving from her. We'll just be sure to thank her the next time we see her."

As they left the restaurant, there was no sign of Mark at any of the tables. One encounter with his brother had been quite enough for the night. Tyler feared that seeing him again would only reignite the rage he'd experienced at Mark's slur on Greta's character.

He was feeling mellow and relaxed, and he didn't want that mood spoiled by anything. He threw an arm around Greta's shoulders as they left the building and went out into the chill night air.

"This has been so nice," she said as they walked to where his truck was parked.

"A little rocky at the beginning, but I definitely enjoyed having your company all to myself." He gazed around, making sure that nobody was loitering nearby.

"I'd think you'd be sick of me by now," she replied. "You've been stuck like glue to me for almost two weeks."

"How time flies when you're having a good time." He smiled down at her, grateful for the bright moonlight that painted her features in lovely silvery tones.

They paused at the passenger side of his truck and he couldn't help himself. He took her in his arms and kissed her deeply, longingly.

She responded, raising her arms around his neck and opening her mouth to allow him to deepen the kiss. She tasted of sweet desire and a hint of chocolate mousse.

They ended the kiss when he heard people approaching one of the cars parked near them. He opened the passenger door and helped her inside, and then he walked around the car to get into the driver seat.

"That was an almost perfect ending to a perfect evening," he said and started the truck engine.

"I don't even want to hear what would make it a perfect ending versus an almost perfect ending," she retorted drily.

He grinned at her. "Ah, we've reached that point where you can now read my mind."

She returned his grin. "Not really. You're just that predictable on certain subjects."

"Is being predictable a bad thing?" he asked.

"Not necessarily. I think in most cases it could be a good thing," she replied.

At that moment the back truck windshield shattered and a thump resounded as a bullet struck the dashboard.

CHAPTER ELEVEN

"GET DOWN," TYLER YELLED urgently as he glanced in the rearview mirror and cursed beneath his breath. He stepped on the gas.

He didn't have to tell her twice. She unfastened her seat belt in record time and hit the floor in a crouch in front of her passenger seat.

Another bullet slammed into the dash and Greta emitted a small scream in response.

"Just stay down," Tyler commanded, his voice filled with tension. "The shots are coming from the car behind us. Dammit, I should have been paying more attention."

He swerved to the far left and then to the right, obviously in an effort to avoid another bullet hitting them. Greta's heart beat a frantic rhythm of terror as it felt as if they careened out of control.

She knew who must be in the car behind them. Alice. Who else could it be? Who else would be shooting at them? Why was this happening? What was wrong with her twin? What if she managed to shoot Tyler? What if she blew out all their tires and they crashed? A million different horrific scenarios shot off like a flash show in Greta's head.

Her fear wasn't just for herself but for him, as well. At the moment Tyler was as much at risk for death as she was, and she wanted to somehow shield him, to protect him. It wasn't fair that he was at risk. She knew she was the ultimate target.

A sharp ping took out the rearview mirror on the truck's driver side as Tyler increased not only his erratic moves from lane to lane but also his speed.

Greta was thrown from side to side as the thrum of the powerful truck engine revved faster and faster. A glance at the speedometer nearly took her breath away.

He was driving at breakneck speed. If anything got in their way, they would both be dead on arrival. By nature Greta wasn't a big crier, but the sheer terror of the situation had her weeping uncontrollably.

He slowed only to make a sharp right-hand turn and after that he applied the brakes even harder and finally rolled to a stop.

Greta peeked up just enough to see that they were in front of the Colton house. She released a trembling sigh and tried to stanch her tears.

"She didn't make the turn into the entry," he said, his tone grim. "She flew on by the ranch entrance. Let's get you inside the house as quickly as possible. Wait for me to come around and get you." There was a stone-cold command in his voice that she had no desire to disobey.

She watched tearfully as he got out of the truck, his gun immediately filling his right hand. He was at the passenger door in an instant. When he'd opened it and she'd crawled out and stood, he placed an arm around her and then used himself as a shield just behind her as they raced up the stairs to the front door.

Once inside, they both leaned against one of the foyer walls, Tyler catching his breath as she swiped more tears from her eyes.

Edith appeared in the doorway and took one look at them. "What's happened?" Her voice was full of concern.

"Call Ryan," Tyler managed to say, and then he reached for Greta and she went willingly into his arms, needing his strength, his warmth to remind her that she, that they, had survived.

It was over, at least for now. They were inside the house and they were safe. She hugged him tight and he returned the hug. She finally raised her face to look at him. "I just learned something new about you," she said.

"And what's that?" He gently shoved strands of her hair away from her face, an action that had become familiar from him. His gaze remained intent on her face.

"When you want to, you can drive like the proverbial bat out of hell," she said.

"Only when it involves bullets," he replied.

Her legs began to shake as residual terror soared through her. "Come on. Let's get you to the family room, where you can sit down," he said, apparently anticipating her need to get off her unstable legs.

He led her through the formal living room and into the family room, where she collapsed onto the sofa while he paced the floor in front of her.

She could tell he was angry. His back was ramrod straight, and now that his gun was back in its holster, his hands fisted and unfisted by his sides. His features had a hard, dangerous edge to them that she'd never seen before except when she thought he might punch his brother in the nose.

"Tyler?"

He stopped pacing and looked at her and his features relaxed, but for only a second. "It was all my fault," he said before she could say anything more. "I got caught up in the moment with you and forgot to be on guard duty." His hands fisted once again.

"It's not your fault," she countered. "It was just a car driving behind us. How could you have known that the person in that car was going to start shooting at us?"

He began to pace again. "I let the car get too close to us. I should have been paying more attention. She was practically on our back bumper when she shot the first time."

"She must have followed us to the restaurant," Greta said thoughtfully. "She waited while we ate and waited until we were on the road in the dark."

"Obviously." His self-anger was rife in the sharp single word. "There were several cars on the road behind us as we drove to the restaurant, but none of them were close enough that I was concerned."

Edith appeared in the doorway. "Ryan is on his way," she said. "Can I get either of you anything? Maybe something warm to drink?"

Greta forced a smile at the housekeeper who had been such an integral part of her life. "Nothing for me, Edith, but thank you."

"I'm good, too," Tyler said.

Edith left the doorway and once again they were alone, with Tyler's anger the palpable third occupant in the room. He began to pace once again.

He was like a wild caged tiger. Back and forth, back and forth he walked with tension radiating off him in waves.

"Tyler, please sit down," she finally said. "You're making me more nervous than I already am."

He flung himself on the sofa next to her and she grabbed one of his hands in hers. "Instead of blaming yourself, you should be congratulating yourself for getting us both home safe and sound."

His jaw muscles knotted. "That was just by sheer luck. I should have seen the danger coming before it was right behind us."

She squeezed his hand. "Stop it, Tyler. One enemy is all we need without you turning yourself into your own enemy."

He drew in a deep breath and his shoulders lost some of their rigidity. "Thanks—I needed to hear that." Even though he smiled at her, she still felt the tension that filled his body.

Or perhaps it was her own tension she felt. There was no question that she'd been terrified during the harrowing ride, unsure if they would die either by being shot or by crashing off the road or into another vehicle.

She could pretend that she was over it, but she wasn't. It was all still too fresh in her mind…the unexpected shatter of the back window, that sick thud of the bullet in the dash.

"Your truck is ruined because of me," she said with a touch of miserable guilt.

"My truck is messed up because of the bullets that were shot by somebody else. I have insurance, but to be honest, that's the last thing on my mind right now. I keep thinking of all the things that could have gone wrong." He tensed up once again.

"But they didn't go wrong and we're here and we're okay," she said with a forced smile.

He returned her smile and squeezed her hand and at that moment Ryan arrived.

Ryan took the report, his features grim as he asked questions. She was surprised that Tyler was able to identify the sedan that had been behind them as either black or dark blue, and then he and Tyler went outside to check out the damage to Tyler's truck and to see if Ryan could get one of the bullets out of the dashboard for evidence.

Greta curled up into the corner of the sofa, grateful that it was too late for her parents to be up and around. The last thing she wanted was for them to worry about how close danger had come to her tonight. And it had come far too close.

For the past week Greta's mother had worked on menus and seating charts, with autumn-colored floral table arrangements and everything to make this Thanksgiving Day one to remember. Her smiles had been frequent and she appeared filled with a happy energy.

It was certainly the first time Greta ever remembered her mother taking charge of a family gathering. That responsibility had always fallen on Edith's shoulders throughout the years.

Greta rubbed the center of her forehead where a tension headache was just beginning to blossom. She'd love to dwell in thoughts of turkey and dressing, but she couldn't sustain any pleasant thoughts as she thought of how close the threat had come to them tonight.

Alice was here, someplace on the ranch, and she was apparently watching their every move. She was cunning and patient, a lethal combination. And now they knew she had a gun.

She looked up as Tyler returned to the room alone. "Ryan got what he needed from me and now you look like you're ready for bed," he said.

"I am," she agreed. "All this danger and bullets flying is exhausting and I'm fighting off a headache."

He frowned. "Anything I can do?"

"No, I'm sure I'll be fine once I get to bed."

He took one of her hands and pulled her off the sofa. "Everything will look much brighter in the morning," he said.

"You promise?"

"I wish I could," he said ruefully. "But we can hope."

They parted ways at their bedrooms and Greta went directly to her bathroom. She undressed and pulled on her nightshirt and then scrubbed the makeup off her face, all the while trying to keep the new inner chill from sweeping over her entire body.

When her face was clean, she brushed her hair, staring at herself in the mirror. But instead of her thoughts being filled with the woman who looked like her, a woman who, in all probability, had been behind the attack on them tonight, her thoughts were filled with Tyler.

He'd been by her side throughout each and every day. He'd stood patiently for hours by the corral as she worked with Sugar. He'd laughed at her jokes when they weren't that funny and seduced her with a simple touch or an unexpected lingering kiss.

Tonight his first thought had been for her safety. Even as they'd walked up the stairs to the front door of the house, it had been his back that might have been hit by a bullet.

She wanted him. She'd wanted him every night that she'd slept alone since they'd been back at the ranch. But tonight she wanted him more than ever, and with the taste of potential death in the back of her throat, she needed him to remind her how wonderful it was to be alive.

She spritzed a bit of perfume across the top of her head and then left the bathroom and went directly to his doorway. She felt no hesitation, no doubt whatsoever as to what was about to happen.

His door was cracked a bit and she opened it. "Tyler?" She stood in the threshold of his bedroom.

She heard the rustle of sheets. "Yeah?"

"It's time."

"Time for what?" he asked.

"Time for me to invite myself into your bed."

"Then what are you doing way over there?"

She nearly ran to his bed, where he awaited her with open arms. The minute his arms wrapped around her, she knew she was where she belonged and the timing was right.

This night wouldn't be like the two nights they'd previously shared together. It wouldn't be about pure lust and chemistry, at least not for her.

This time her heart was involved. She didn't know to what extent; she knew only that this was about so much more than an uncomplicated sexual release.

When his lips took hers, it wasn't with ravenous hunger but rather with a tenderness that was far more arousing. He kissed her for what seemed like an eternity, his hands running up and down her back as if her cotton nightshirt was the most erotic material he'd ever felt.

Their tongues moved together in a slow dance and she felt as though the music would never end. And there was music in the soft sighs that escaped her lips, in the murmur of his sweet words as his lips drifted down her throat.

Despite the lateness of the hour, she had never felt so wide-awake, so wonderfully alive. Her skin leaped to life with his touch and it wasn't long before she sat up to allow him to pull off her nightshirt.

His hands seemed to be everywhere, palms gliding over the tips of her breasts, fingers sliding over her stomach and down to her upper thighs.

She relished every caress and returned the favor by clinging to his strong biceps and then moving her hands across his broad back. His skin was warm, almost feverish, and banished the chill that had invaded her body hours before.

She gasped in delight as his mouth teased first one of her nipples and then the other, the electric sensations zinging throughout her body and sparking at her very center.

Everything was different this time and she knew it was because it wasn't just a physical experience for her anymore. Whether he knew it or not, for her it was a heart-and-soul connection. She had no idea what was in his heart or in his soul for her, but at the moment it didn't matter.

And she was so in the moment. His fingers once again danced across her thighs, teasing and tormenting her as they got closer and closer to intimately touching her.

Then he was there, his fingers making magic as they moved in a rhythm that accelerated until she was gasping and the crashing waves of her release washed over her.

His mouth took hers again and he gazed down at her, his eyes glowing in the slash of moonlight that crept through the part in the curtains. "You are so beautiful," he whispered. "You are beautiful both inside and out."

She replied by reaching down and grasping his hardness in her hand. He moaned as she moved her hand slowly up and down the shaft of his arousal.

She loved the feel of him and the sound of his obvious desire. She wanted him to want her time and time again. She wanted him to love her.

She froze for a moment as the depth of her feelings for him was revealed to her. She loved him. She didn't know when it had happened, but it was there, burning in her heart.

He took advantage of her pause and rolled between her thighs. Slowly he entered her and she closed her eyes as exquisite sensations rushed through her. He filled her up, made her whole, and she wanted him to stay connected to her forever.

He began to move his hips against hers and her pleasure became mindless bliss. His breathing grew more labored as he increased the depth and quickness of his movements.

She grasped his firm buttocks, silently urging him on as a new tension rose inside her. And then she was there once again, her climax shivering through her while at the same time he reached his own release with a cry of her name.

Greta.

She'd never liked her name as much as she did at that moment.

They remained locked together, his weight held on either side of her by his elbows. He stared down at her for a long moment and then leaned down and gave her a kiss so tender, so caring it sprang unexpected tears to her eyes.

He finally rolled off to her side and turned to face her. He drew a finger down the side of her face, a sweet gesture that shot a new warmth straight to her heart.

"I suppose you're leaving me now," he whispered.

In response she turned over and spooned herself against his warm body. "I'm not going anywhere," she said.

He threw an arm around her and nuzzled her neck, and that was the last thing she remembered before she fell asleep in his arms.

WAKING UP WITH Greta Colton in his arms filled Tyler with emotions he'd never had before. She was curled against him, the scent of her hair filling his nose, and he didn't want to move a muscle that might awake her and send her out of his arms.

It was still dark outside the window, although he had a feeling dawn was just a few eye blinks away. He still had plenty of time to enjoy the warm naked curves against him.

He closed his eyes again. Sated and content—that was what he felt at the moment. He'd been surprised when she'd decided to spend the night in his bed.

Something had changed and he had a feeling it was gratefulness and the closeness of death that had brought her to him the night before and kept her in his embrace throughout the night.

He didn't care what the reason. He was only happy to have the experience of making love with her again and now of waking up beside her. Her sleeping presence next to him evoked a new sense of protectiveness, especially as he thought of the night before.

Ryan had agreed that the shooter in the car had probably been Alice. How could one young woman stay hidden from the authorities for so long? Did she have help? A partner? Or was she just a very smart lone wolf determined to create havoc?

He had a feeling the latter was true. He couldn't imagine a woman filled with such rage trusting or wanting a partner. He also couldn't imagine what she hoped to accomplish with Greta's death. What could possibly be behind her wrath toward a sister she'd never met before?

He couldn't begin to delve into the head of a killer. He had faced many tough sharks across the table in the boardroom and had always come out on top, but they had been savvy businessmen, not cold-blooded killers.

And now they knew that Alice had a gun. The ante had been upped and the stakes were higher than ever.

He fought the impulse to tighten his arm around Greta, afraid of awaking her from whatever dreams she might be having.

He was out of his area of expertise. If Alice had wanted a battle in the boardroom, then he'd have been confident of his ultimate success. But it had been sheer luck and the power of his big-engine truck that had saved their lives last night.

Last night wouldn't be the end of things. He imagined that failure would only feed Alice's killing rage. They wouldn't be out of the woods until she was in jail, facing a multitude of charges that would keep her locked up for the rest of her life.

And once that happened, what would happen between him and Greta? What did he want to happen? Certainly he didn't want to stop seeing her, but he also wasn't sure if he was ready to offer her something more lasting.

He wasn't sure he believed in love...or marriage. Eventually, he wanted those two plus children, but was he ready for it now?

Certainly he had been lonely when he'd met Greta, and being with her filled up a place in his heart that had been empty for a very long time. But was that real and lasting love? He just didn't know what true love felt like and he didn't want to make a mistake. She didn't deserve him making a mistake.

Dawn lightened the room when she stirred and turned onto her back, displacing his arm from around her as she stretched like a kitten just awaking. She opened her eyes and looked at him, a soft, sleepy smile curving her lips. "Good morning."

"Good morning to you," he replied.

She stretched again and then sat up, holding the covers up to hide her naked breasts. "I can't believe how well I slept."

He grinned at her wickedly. "You more than earned it after last night."

She returned his grin. "Then you should have slept very well, also."

"I did."

She reached down and grabbed her nightgown from the floor. "And so a new day begins." She pulled the gown over her head and then slid out of bed.

"It's still early," he said, slightly disappointed that she was ready to leave the warmth of the bed, the warmth of him next to her.

"I thought I'd get in a little bit of time with Sugar before breakfast. I'm going to shower and dress. Meet you back here in thirty minutes?"

"I'll be ready." He watched her leave his room and then got out of bed and headed for his own shower. Time to prepare himself for another day of being on edge each time they stepped outside the door, of watching for anyone who might present any potential danger.

Tyler hadn't mentioned to Greta that last night Ryan had told him not to take Greta off the ranch again, a command that Tyler had easily agreed to with the taste of fear still lingering in the back of his throat.

There were too many variables when they left Colton property. At least here all he had to worry about were a couple of outbuildings some distance away, her barn and her corral. Still, the fact that Alice apparently now had a gun in her possession simply upped the challenge.

"No carrots this morning?" he asked forty minutes later when they stepped out into the cold morning air.

"No carrots," she replied. "I don't want Sugar to expect treats all the time. I need her to bond with humans, not with carrots."

"Makes sense," he agreed.

He watched as she opened the corral gate. He took his usual position with his back to the house and facing the corral and outbuildings.

Would an unexpected attack come today? Would it come tomorrow? The inability to guess what might happen next was frustrating as hell.

He watched as she walked to the center of the corral and Sugar came toward her. She was making good progress with the horse. He only wished Ryan and his coworkers would make progress in pinning down a killing twin sister.

Thankfully, Greta had only about forty-five minutes in the corral and then they went inside to clean up for breakfast. Breakfast was a lively affair with Big J regaling them with stories of the past and how hard he'd worked to make the Lucky C into the successful cattle business it had become. "Thank God I managed to buy out my brother so that I could run the ranch the way it was supposed to run," he exclaimed. "Before that hap-

pened, the ranch was in near ruins and now look at it."
Pride lit his features.

"Hard work always pays off," Tyler replied.

"Damn straight," Big J replied.

"Are you planning on being here for Thanksgiving?"
Abra asked Tyler when Big J had wound down.

Tyler looked at Greta, unsure how to answer. If Alice
was captured tomorrow, then there would be no reason
for him to remain here. Sugar could be moved back to
his corral and Greta could continue to work with the
horse on whatever terms she decided.

"He'll be here for Thanksgiving," Greta replied for
him.

"Good. I'd already placed him on my seating chart,
but I wanted to make sure," Abra replied. "I'm planning on setting up two long tables in the basement for
eating. The dining room just won't hold our big family
anymore."

"That sounds great, Mother," Greta replied.

"It's going to be a hell of a good day," Big J boomed
enthusiastically. "There's nothing better than having the
entire family around." He looked at Tyler. "You should
start your own family. You aren't getting any younger."

Tyler laughed. "It's on my to-do list."

"Speaking of to-do lists, I got Tyler's horse to take
carrots from me yesterday and I plan to try some apple
slices later today," Greta said.

"Hmm, speaking of apples, do you have apple pies on
that menu list of yours for next week?" Big J asked Abra.

She smiled at him fondly. "How could I not, knowing that apple pie is your favorite?"

The two exchanged glances of love that made Tyler's
heart squeeze tight. What was it like to have the same

woman smile at you across a table for nearly forty years? What was it like to bind your heart with another to share a lifetime of experiences, of joy and disappointments?

Tyler hadn't got a chance to enjoy seeing his parents' marriage grow and endure. He couldn't imagine him and Mark ever bonding enough to enjoy each other's families.

Whether they knew it or not, the Colton family all shared something special, a love and respect for one another that Tyler suspected was rare.

He mentioned that fact to Greta after breakfast when they headed back out to Sugar's corral. "Trust me, we've all had our ups and downs," she said. "Jack and Brett butted heads about the running of the ranch but finally worked out their differences. Nobody really believed Daniel would be successful with his breeding program but he's proved us all wrong. Everyone was angry with Ryan when he arrested me. I think because our childhood was fairly dysfunctional with my mother gone so much of the time, we all bonded closer than a lot of siblings. We fight hard when we fight, but thankfully, we love each other harder."

"Your mother seems to be holding up quite well," he observed.

"She does. It's strange—when she was attacked and put into a medically induced coma, I swear my father aged ten years overnight. But since she got home from the hospital, she seems stronger and happier than she has ever been in her life. She used to be so cold and status conscious, but I see no sign of that now."

Greta opened the corral gate, and as always, Tyler's gaze shot around the area as his hand automatically fell to the butt of his gun.

Where was Alice?

The question haunted him. Was she sleeping in some flophouse motel room where she didn't have to show identification and paid in cash? Or was she in the backseat of the car that had followed them last night, plotting a new way to get to Greta?

His worst fear was that she was right here on Colton land. There were a thousand places for a woman to hide here on the property. She could be hidden in any of the barns or in an infrequently used outbuilding, and even the ranch hands wouldn't see her as they went about their usual chores.

He hadn't been able to give Ryan much information on the car that she'd driven the night before. But hopefully, some sort of bulletin had gone out to be on the lookout for a crazy female killer driving a dark sedan and wielding a gun.

He refocused on Greta in the corral. Sugar refused to take the apple slices, although she danced close to Greta and then backed away in uncertainty.

"I really didn't expect her to take the apple slices," Greta said almost an hour later when she left the corral. "They're smaller than the carrots and something completely different. Maybe this afternoon or tomorrow she'll respond better."

They turned to see Ryan coming toward them. He looked more tired than Tyler had ever seen him. With the grim set of Ryan's mouth, Tyler knew he wasn't bringing good news.

Sensing that Greta might need some emotional support, Tyler placed his arm around her shoulders and pulled her closer to his side.

"Ryan, what's up?" Tyler asked.

"I just thought I'd stop by and let you know that Joe Baker made a report this morning that his black Ford Taurus had been stolen. He hadn't been out all day yesterday and so doesn't know the exact time it disappeared."

"A Ford Taurus... That sounds about right," Tyler replied.

"We found the vehicle an hour ago abandoned not too far from here. We'll try to pull prints to confirm that it was stolen by Alice, but at this point I think we can all assume it was her."

Greta leaned a little closer to Tyler. "And you said it was abandoned not far from here?" she asked.

"About a mile or so." Ryan's lips pressed together in a taut line.

"Then that means she's definitely near," Greta said in a soft voice that simmered with fear. "That means she's probably here right on the property now."

"I think she's been here off and on since the night your tires were slashed in my driveway," Tyler admitted. "Joe Baker...does he live near here?"

"Two ranches over." Ryan scanned the landscape, his green eyes narrowed. "Just stay close to the house." He looked at Tyler. "I wish I could be here 24/7 to make sure Greta stays safe. I also wish I could place a full force of officers out here to keep her surrounded, but I don't have the power to do either."

"That's why I'm here," Tyler replied. "I'll do everything I can to make sure she stays safe from harm."

"I hope you're up to the job," Ryan said.

Tyler tightened his arm around Greta. He hoped like hell he was up to the job, too.

CHAPTER TWELVE

IT WAS THE day before Thanksgiving and Greta and Tyler came in from their early-morning work with Sugar to a kitchen that smelled like apple-and-cinnamon heaven.

"Edith, you look like a floury queen of beauty," Tyler teased as he eyed the woman with her flour-dusted apron.

"Too bad I'm not making malarkey pie. I'm sure you'd be tasty surrounded by a good crust," Edith quipped.

Tyler laughed and Greta shook her head with a bright smile. It was good to see her smile. While the work with Sugar was progressing nicely, too often a dark fear appeared to overwhelm the bright green-gold of Greta's eyes.

The past week had brought no further showdowns with Alice, nor had it brought any news about her exact whereabouts, either on the ranch or off it.

The tension of danger yet to be released was definitely in the air whenever they were outside. Each time they stepped out the door, a tight knot of worry fisted in his stomach.

He knew Greta felt it, too. It showed not just in her eyes but in her body language as she walked to the corral, even in the private time they spent together. She was a little quieter than usual, a bit more skittish.

Twice more since the night they'd been shot at, she'd

come to his room and they'd made love. Each morning that he'd awoken with her, his fear for her grew deeper and more profound.

He couldn't imagine anything bad happening to her under any circumstances. He didn't even want her to suffer a hangnail or a stubbed toe. But if something happened to her under his watch, he wasn't sure he'd ever get past it.

"Smells like Dad's favorite," Greta said.

Edith nodded. "Apple pies this morning, and then when Maria comes in, she's baking up the cherry and pumpkin pies."

"Something for everyone," Tyler replied. "My personal favorite is pumpkin. What about you?" he asked Greta.

"Guess I take after Dad. I love apple, but cherry is a close second."

"Good information, but I have more work to do. Scoot, both of you. Out of here," Edith exclaimed. "I have more important things to do besides stand around and chat about pies."

Greta and Tyler left the kitchen and went into the family room, where Brett and Hannah sat, apparently waiting for breakfast time. Hannah held baby Alexander in her arms and Greta quickly beelined for the blue bundle of baby boy.

With a small laugh Hannah handed the baby to Greta, who sat down beside her sister-in-law and cooed to and stroked the baby boy's fine hair.

Tyler watched, enchanted by Greta's obvious maternal instincts. It was easy to imagine that the little boy she held in her arms were theirs.

For a moment his brain went on a fantasy vacation.

He visualized a beautiful round-bellied Greta, her face glowing with the life she carried. He could imagine his hand on that belly, feeling the first kicks of life.

He smiled inwardly as he thought of a frantic ride to the hospital, the antiseptic smell of a delivery room and him coaching Greta to deliver their child.

He snapped his attention to the here and now. Was this love? The flight of fancy into a future filled with a particular woman pregnant with your child? The desire to be a part of her birth experience and raise a precious baby together?

"You think he'll keep those blue eyes?" Greta asked.

"My doctor said not to count on it. It's an even bet whether they'll eventually be brown like mine or green like Brett's," Hannah replied.

"I'm hoping for brown like Hannah's," Brett said as he smiled affectionately at his wife.

"And I'm hoping for the Colton green eyes," Hannah returned.

Greta raised the baby up closer to her face and drew in a deep breath. "I swear if anyone ever figured out how to bottle that sweet baby scent, they'd make a fortune." She handed Alexander back to his mother.

"Speaking of fortunes, how are you managing to be away from the oil business for so long?" Brett asked Tyler.

"Thankfully, I am lucky enough to have great people who work for me," Tyler replied. "My general manager has checked in with me daily and the business runs like a well-oiled machine that rarely needs my actual presence. To be honest, I haven't taken a vacation for the last ten years. This time here has been a welcome change."

"You can't feel like you're on vacation here," Greta

replied. "You're babysitting me and we're both definitely on edge."

"And you're definitely not a baby," Tyler retorted.

"But you know what I mean," she said.

At that moment the maid came in to get the baby so that breakfast could begin. Abra was more animated than Tyler had ever seen her, almost manic as she ticked off the details of the Thanksgiving meal the next day.

"Sounds like we're going to be eating for a week," Tyler said when she'd gone over the menu.

Abra smiled at him. "Feeding five strapping young men and their wives and you and Greta and making sure everyone gets their favorite dish requires a lot of food."

That started a rousing discussion about everyone's favorite Thanksgiving dish. Brett and Big J argued good-naturedly about the merits of sweet potato casserole and Hannah jumped in to say that she loved the cranberry salad.

The discussion about food continued through the rest of the meal, and afterward Greta and Tyler headed upstairs for a little downtime before heading back out to the corral.

He followed her into her bedroom and sat in one of the blue chairs in the sitting area of her room. He hadn't forgotten the conversation they hadn't finished when breakfast had begun.

She sat in the chair across from him in front of the fireplace, which was laid with wood awaiting her request for a live fire.

"Mother was definitely wound up," she said and then frowned. "I hope tomorrow goes exactly as she's planned."

"There's no reason to believe that it won't," he replied. "But right now I want to tell you that your comment about me babysitting you bothered me."

"I'm sorry, but it's true. I feel like you got roped into this not only because we'd slept together, but also because my sister attacked me at your house and my brother put the responsibility on your head."

"Trust me, I wouldn't be here with you if I didn't want to be," he replied. "I'd tell you to get somebody else to watch over you and I'd be out of here." He leaned toward her. "You need to understand, I want to be here for you."

"You just like sleeping with me." She averted her gaze from his.

"You're right—I do like sleeping with you. But I also love to watch you working with Sugar. I love hearing the sound of your laughter. I like learning new things about you and sharing time in your company."

She looked back at him and studied his face for what seemed like an eternity.

"Greta, I love sharing pieces of our past and being in the fold of your family," he added.

She paused a long moment, her gaze lingering on him. "Okay, then," she said and stood. "Let's go ahead and head out to the corral. Sugar is going to get introduced to you."

"Are you sure you aren't rushing things?" He also stood.

Her eyes went dark. "It's time to step things up," she replied. "I want to finish Sugar's training as soon as possible. I want her saddle ready for you." She started for the door, but he stopped her by grabbing her arm.

"What's going on inside that beautiful brain of yours?" he asked.

"Nothing," she replied quickly...too quickly.

"Greta, I know you too well. Something is bothering you."

She released a tremulous sigh. "It's the waiting. It's the wondering when Alice is going to come for me. I want to make sure that Sugar is comfortable with you before something bad happens. I want to make sure that Sugar is okay with you if I'm no longer here." Her voice shattered a bit on her last words.

"Oh, honey." He pulled her into his arms and tight against his chest. "You aren't going anywhere. Nothing bad is going to happen to you. You'll have all the time you need with Sugar and with me."

She snuggled into him and he felt a shiver sweep through her. He hadn't realized until this moment just how much the tense anticipation of an attack from Alice had been weighing on her mind. It irritated him that he hadn't seen it, because he felt it in himself.

"You know that sooner or later she's going to strike again," she said, her voice half-muffled as she buried her head in the hollow of his throat.

"And I'll be ready," he said firmly. "I've got this, Greta. As long as we stay together and remain smart, she'll never have a chance to get close to you in any way."

She finally looked up at him. "And how long are you willing to do this? She's shown us that she has patience. What if she doesn't do anything for another week…or a month…or a year?"

He shook his head. "Right now we take things day by day. That's all we can do." He cupped her face with his hands and a swell of emotion pressed tight against his chest. At the moment she was so fragile.

How he wanted to find the right words to lay her

fears to rest. He wanted to remove the darkness from her eyes forever. But he didn't have the words to soothe her fears, and as she stepped out of his embrace, a hint of the darkness still remained.

"Of course, you're right. I can only deal with this day by day. I don't know what will happen in the future and I only have the here and now. Let's head out," she said briskly.

Minutes later they were back at the corral, where Sugar greeted Greta at the gate. During the past week the horse had allowed Greta to stroke her nose and her neck and run her hands over various areas of Sugar's body. The bond of complete trust had been established.

"Come inside with me," Greta said. "She has to get used to not only you but men and people in general."

Tyler nodded and opened the gate. He stepped inside and immediately Sugar backed up, putting distance between herself and Tyler. At least she didn't back up to the far side of the corral, he thought.

Even though he was inside the wooden enclosure, he remained vigilant as to what was going on outside the corral. He couldn't give Sugar his complete, undivided attention, because he was determined to see danger coming before it arrived.

Thankfully, Greta instructed him to walk the perimeter of the corral, just as she had done the first time she'd worked with Sugar.

That allowed him to remain focused on his number one task of protecting Greta. The conversation they'd just shared had shown him that Greta suffered from dark thoughts she hadn't talked to him about…thoughts where she was killed by Alice…thoughts where she was no longer on this earth.

She worked with a sense of urgency, fearing her own death at any given moment.

Tyler had refused to allow his thoughts to go that dark, but now it was as if somehow their conversation had drawn the darkness closer.

IT HAD BEEN a long day, yet Greta found sleep elusive. It had also been an emotional-roller-coaster kind of day for her. She had no idea why she'd had so little control over her emotions lately, but they had been all over the place.

It had started when she'd held baby Alexander in her arms and wondered if she'd ever have an opportunity to hold her own baby. Or would Alice take her life before she ever got the chance to experience marriage to the man of her dreams and the joy of pregnancy and the miracle of birth?

Her emotions had once again reeled out of control when she and Tyler had had the brief conversation in her room that morning.

It was mostly due to her foolish, foolish heart. When he'd talked about loving her laughter and loving spending time with her and all the other wonderful things he'd said, she'd anticipated that he would end his statement with a declaration of love for her.

I love you. She hadn't realized how much she'd wanted to hear those words from him until they hadn't come. Rather than make her feel better, what he'd said had given her a heartache to go along with the fear that had been a constant companion.

It was stupid. She was stupid for allowing herself to fall in love with him. But during the weeks they'd spent nearly every minute together, she'd thought they'd fit together so perfectly, not just physically but on an emotional and intellectual level, as well.

They shared the same sense of humor and he fit so seamlessly into the family. They wanted the same things out of life. He'd spoken of loving so many things about her, but he hadn't said that he was in love with her.

She turned over on her back and stared up at the darkened bedroom ceiling. Tonight she had no desire to sneak next door and sleep in his arms. That would be the ultimate act of a fool.

She realized she had to somehow begin to distance herself from him. She had to find a way to deal with him and not love him anymore. At the moment that felt like an impossible thing to do. How did you make yourself fall out of love when the man you were in love with hadn't done anything wrong?

Tyler had been protective and supportive and had proved himself to be everything she wanted in a man. She certainly didn't want any false proclamations of love from him. She didn't want him to tell her something he didn't feel. She just wished he were as much in love with her as she was with him.

With a deep sigh of frustration she sat up and turned on her bedside lamp. She couldn't fall asleep with her brain spinning so fast.

There were times in the past she'd found herself unable to fall asleep for one reason or another and had discovered that playing a game or surfing the web sometimes made her sleepy.

She pulled her tablet from the drawer in the nightstand and swiped her finger across the surface to wake it up. She had several horse-trainer bloggers that she followed and she went to those pages first, always eager to learn something new that would help her better work with horses.

She read the blogs and found nothing of real interest and then on impulse decided to do a search on Tyler Stanton. Tons of results came up.

She started checking out each site and was surprised to learn that he'd been named Businessman of the Year for the past two years by the Oklahoma City Chamber of Commerce. He was also heavily involved in many charities and sat on the boards of several. Many of the hits she'd received were about Stanton Oil, with full histories of how his great-grandfather had started the company.

There were pictures of him and a variety of women attending social events. The women were all beautiful, decked out in designer gowns and with a polished appearance that Greta knew she'd never be able to attain no matter how hard she tried. She just wasn't that woman and had no desire to be.

Was this the kind of woman he was looking for as a wife? The socialite who would be an asset as a corporate wife? A woman who didn't own a pair of dusty jeans or cowboy boots but could throw a flawless cocktail party or business dinner?

Was he playing with the tomboy as a change of pace, only to ultimately choose the kind of woman she could never be? Her heart squeezed tight at the thought.

There was no question in her mind that he cared about her; otherwise, he wouldn't have been here. He wouldn't have been playing her bodyguard if he weren't somehow emotionally involved with her, but to what level?

Maybe she was expecting too much too fast. Just because she'd recognized and embraced her love for him didn't mean he was at the same emotional place as her.

It had been less than a month since they'd begun any kind of a relationship. Maybe he just needed more time to fall in love with her.

She was overthinking things, focused on Tyler perhaps in an effort to not think about her twin sister and what might or might not occur.

She was about to close down the tablet when another site about Tyler caught her attention. She clicked on it and saw the official announcement of Tyler's engagement to Michelle Willoughby.

Michelle Willoughby was a stunning blonde. She had dainty features and appeared petite. No colt-like long legs on her, Greta guessed. Her eyes were blue and her lips were red and she exuded self-confidence.

The engagement announcement included a follow-up article, and when she clicked on that link, she gasped in surprise.

The article was dated two weeks after the engagement announcement and the headline read Brotherly Love: The End of an Engagement. It was accompanied by a photo of Mark and Michelle sharing a passionate kiss outside an Oklahoma City nightclub.

There was no article attached, but the photo said it all. Greta stared at it for a long time, her brain once again racing with thoughts…very negative thoughts.

She shut down the tablet and placed it back in her drawer and then shut off her light and curled up on her side. It was obvious from what she'd just seen that Mark had been responsible for the breakup of the relationship between Tyler and Michelle, a fact Tyler hadn't mentioned to her.

And Tyler had played a hand in the breakup of her and Mark's relationship. He hadn't known at the time he bailed her out of jail that she had already decided to break things off with Mark.

Was she Tyler's revenge against his brother?

Had he formed a relationship with her because it was some sort of payback for Michelle and his broken engagement? The possibility thundered in her heart and made her sick to her stomach.

Had it all been lies? All the words of caring, the sweet seduction in his eyes, in his kisses—had they all been a calculated effort to avenge a wrong done to him in the past?

Was she just a pawn Tyler had used to get under Mark's skin? She wanted to confront him right this minute, but she knew he was asleep, and besides, she needed more time to process what she'd just learned.

Her first instinct was to be angry and she didn't want to wake him up in the middle of the night for a wrathful confrontation. That wasn't her style. She needed to calm herself and think things through before having a rational discussion with him.

She'd talk to him first thing in the morning and hoped that if he lied to her, she would be able to discern it in his beautiful blue eyes.

She must have finally fallen asleep, for when she opened her eyes, she looked at her clock on the nightstand and saw that it was almost six, earlier than she usually awoke.

There was no way she was going to go back to sleep, as her head immediately began to spin with thoughts of Tyler and what was the best way to approach him and have the conversation she needed to have.

Would he confess that he'd just used her as payback? Or would he tell her that his feelings for her were real and had nothing to do with an engagement that had happened a couple of years ago?

She got out of bed and dressed in her jeans and a rust-colored flannel shirt. What she needed was a little time alone to get her thoughts together. Surely she'd be safe just going from the house to the corral for a few minutes to see Sugar. She pulled on her brown suede jacket and left her room.

Tyler's bedroom door was closed and she crept by it as quietly as possible. She definitely didn't want his company until she was ready to face him…and she didn't feel quite ready yet.

She wasn't sure if it might be better to talk to him after the Thanksgiving Day meal planned for three that afternoon. She didn't want to in any way ruin things for her mother, who had worked so hard to assure a successful family gathering.

Maybe it would be best to just hold it all in until after the festivities were over and all the members of the extended family had gone home.

Thankfully, she saw nobody as she stepped out of the door and into the cold predawn air. She looked around, checking for anyone in the area, and then made a beeline to Sugar, who greeted her at the gate with a soft whinny.

"Hey, girl," Greta said softly and stroked the velvet of her nose. At least she didn't have to worry about Sugar having ulterior motives. She had fallen in love with the horse and the feeling had become mutual.

The sun had yet to make an appearance, but the sky was pink and orange in the east, a heralding of the imminent sunrise. She decided to go ahead and fill the hay bin so that Sugar would be taken care of for the day. She might even add some grain as a special dinner for Sugar for the holiday.

She'd told Tyler she'd be busy this morning helping her mother with any last-minute details, and once the family arrived, she'd have no time to be out at the corral.

She stepped into the barn and was just about to grab a nearby hay bale when Alice stepped out of the shadows, a gun in her hand. "Hello, sis. Have you missed me?"

"Alice." The name fell from Greta's lips at the same time a wave of horror overtook her.

CHAPTER THIRTEEN

"So you know my name," Alice replied and motioned Greta deeper into the barn with the barrel of her gun. "I'll warn you, if you scream, I'll shoot you right now."

Greta stared at her. It was bizarre to stand in the near darkness of the barn and look at a face that was exactly like her own.

Alice had the same build as Greta, tall and slender. Her hair was also worn in the same style as Greta's, dark waves that fell to her shoulders. She wore filthy jeans and a stained pink sweatshirt.

"It's nice to finally meet you," Greta said, glad that her voice didn't betray the utter terror that nearly gutted her.

"Don't lie to me," Alice replied sharply. "I'm sure I was the last person you wanted to meet this morning or on any other morning."

"Why, Alice? Why have you done the things you've done? Why have you tried to kill me?"

Greta had little hope of anyone rushing to her rescue. When she'd left her bedroom, she'd closed the door behind her. Even if Tyler awoke early, he wouldn't bother her as long as her door was closed. She usually didn't make an appearance for the day until after seven. It was far too early for anyone to know that she was missing from her bed.

She knew that she was in deep trouble, but she wanted answers. She wanted to understand why this was all happening. Why did Alice hate her so much? How could she without even knowing her?

"Why have I tried to kill you?" Alice repeated the question. Her eyes narrowed. "Because it should have been me. Your father chose the wrong twin to bring home, and for the last twenty-six years you've been living the life I should have had."

"But killing me won't change that," Greta protested desperately. "Why don't you put the gun down and we can talk about things." Greta's heart beat rapidly and her knees shook unsteadily with fear.

She'd been so foolish to come out here alone. She should have never taken such a chance.

"Talk about things?" Alice emitted a harsh, ugly laugh. "There's nothing to talk about. Get to the back of the barn. I have a little surprise for you." She wielded the gun like a lethal pointer. "And you can't tell me that if I don't do what I'm here to do, everything is going to be wonderful. I've already killed a man and there's no way two of us can coexist in this world."

A little surprise for you. Those simple words had fired a new sense of terror inside Greta. The surprise could only be a bad one.

Alice stepped close enough to prod Greta with the barrel of the gun. She was near enough for Greta to see the shine of madness in her hazel-green eyes, smell and feel the evil that emanated from her.

Greta stumbled over a bale of hay as she moved backward. "It was just a matter of fate that he took me," she said desperately. "Nobody is to blame except our birth mother, who decided to sell one of us."

"Our birth mother is dead," Alice said flatly. "And what a fine mother she was. I'm sorry you didn't get to experience my childhood of being dragged from one seedy motel room to another, watching dear Mother smoke crack or do whatever drug she could get her hands on. I wish you'd been there to be hungry, to be cold…to be so afraid of what might happen next."

Tears sprang to Greta's eyes. "I'm sorry, Alice. I'm so sorry you had to go through that."

"It's okay. I'm young and I have plenty of time left to enjoy the good life. At least it was nice of dear old Mom to tell me about you before she croaked. Take off your clothes."

"What?" Greta stared at her, fear still pounding her heart at a sickening pace. Surely she had misunderstood.

"You heard me. Strip down to your underwear."

"But why?"

"You won't need clothes in that." Alice pulled a flashlight from her back pocket and shone it on a pine box shoved in a corner of the barn's very back wall.

Greta nearly fell to her knees. It was not just a simple pine box. It was a coffin—her coffin. "Alice, please don't do this." Hot tears began to splash on Greta's cheeks.

"It's my turn. You had enough time as a Colton. Now it's my time. Get those clothes off before I lose my patience and just shoot you now."

Greta's fingers trembled violently as she clumsily unfastened her flannel shirt. At the same time Alice managed to work her pink sweatshirt over her head without ever moving the gun pointed at Greta's center.

She tossed the sweatshirt aside and grabbed the flannel shirt from Greta. "Now the jeans," she said as she put on Greta's shirt.

Now it was clear in Greta's head exactly what Alice's sick plan entailed. She was going to put Greta in the pine box to die and then she intended to become Greta, taking over her family and her life.

"It will never work," Greta said in desperation as she pulled off her boots and then stepped out of her jeans.

The knife in her boot called to her, but the old saying about a fool bringing a knife to a gun battle played in her mind. There was no way she could get her hand in her boot, pull out the knife and use it against the power of the gun Alice gripped in her hand.

And there was no question that Alice would shoot her if she felt it necessary. If she did, she might get caught, but Greta would definitely be dead.

Still, once she was clad in Alice's sweatshirt and jeans and Alice was in her clothing, Greta stepped back into her boots, grateful that Alice didn't seem to want them, too.

"You'll never pull this off," Greta said. "Within minutes everyone will know you aren't me."

"Ah, dear sister, you underestimate me," Alice returned with a confident smile. "I've been hanging around here for a long while. I've seen you with your hot boyfriend, Tyler. I've studied your family and I know all that I need to know to get by. Now, stop wasting my time and get into the box."

Greta balked, her entire body trembling at the very thought of being inside the wooden enclosure and nobody having any idea she was there.

Tyler. Her heart cried his name. She should have awoken him. She should have told him she was going outside. She should have told somebody. She'd been so stupid.

"Move it," Alice said harshly. She jabbed the gun in Greta's back and after a brief hesitation Greta did as she was told.

She sat in the box and tears once again began to flow. She didn't know what to do or how to help herself. Maybe she should scream and hope that when Alice shot her, she'd somehow survive a bullet. Before the thought took full form in her head, Alice shoved a red handkerchief in her mouth, effectively gagging any scream Greta might have released.

"Lie down," she commanded and forcefully shoved Greta backward. Her back and head slapped against the bottom of the box and at the same time Alice grabbed a piece of wood and slammed it down.

It fit perfectly over the coffin, and apparently, Alice jumped on top of it, for when Greta pushed against the wood, there was no give.

Despite the gag in her mouth, she screamed as the sound of a hammer pounding nails into the top resounded in her head. She kicked her feet and banged on the sides with the backs of her hands and on the top with her fists. Her ineffective screams and the pounding seemed to go on forever.

Then complete silence.

IT SEEMED TO take forever to get the bitch in the box, but in actuality it had taken only about fifteen minutes. Alice left the barn and hurried toward the house, hoping to sneak inside and into Greta's bedroom without meeting anyone along the way.

Eventually, after Greta was dead and Alice had established herself firmly as her sister, Alice would figure out a way to get rid of the coffin. She'd make sure it would never be found and hopefully after enough time passed people would just assume that Alice had moved on.

She knew which bedroom was Greta's, for she'd seen her twin standing at the window several evenings while Alice had been sneaking around the ranch and watching the house.

Thankfully, nobody was in the kitchen as she entered the house, and she raced up the stairs and into the room that would now be her own. She got inside and closed the door and then looked around in awe.

Clean and luxurious, the room was like no other Alice had ever been inside in her life. She kicked off her shoes, pulled off her socks and sank her feet into the plush beige carpeting.

Heaven.

She was in heaven.

She went to the closet and opened the door and stepped inside. Fancy shoes sat in cubbyholes, designer dresses hung in a row and jewelry lay out on a small island as if to be grabbed at a moment's notice.

The closet was as big as many of the bedrooms Alice had lived in as a child. She flipped through the dresses, reverential of the designer names as her fingers lingered on silks and satins. Hers. They were now all hers.

She finally left the closet to check out the bathroom. She could easily imagine herself in the whirlpool tub surrounded by the scent of bath oils or fragrant salts. The nearby shower was enclosed by etched glass, a beautiful alternative to a long hot soak in the tub.

The sink was surrounded by plenty of blue-and-white swirled countertop, a perfect place for a lady to put on her makeup or admire herself in the lit mirror.

She returned to the bedroom and sat in one of the two

chairs in front of a white marble fireplace. It was easy to imagine Greta curled up in one of the chairs on a cold wintry night with a fire warming her.

A swift anger shot through Alice. It should have been her being raised in the bosom of a loving family. It should have been her enjoying all the luxury that came with being a Colton.

The minute her mother had confessed that Alice had been a twin and the other baby had been bought by a wealthy Colton, Alice had spiraled down the rabbit hole of wrath.

She tamped down her anger. This winter it would be the new Greta enjoying the warmth of a fire, wearing the fancy clothes and high heels. This winter it would be the new Greta enjoying the holidays with loving family members.

She got up from the chair and undressed from the clothes she'd taken from Greta. She'd changed into them just in case somebody had seen Greta leave the house and knew how she'd been dressed.

A nightshirt was on the unmade bed and Alice took off her bra and panties and pulled it on over her head. She immediately smelled a fresh, citrusy scent that was appealing.

It was Greta's scent. And now it was hers.

Alice crawled into the bed, where the sheets were soft and the pillow still held the imprint of Greta's head. She fit her head into the depressed place and breathed a deep sigh.

She'd done it. After months of planning and waiting, hoping that a time would come when she could do what needed to be done, she felt a sweet sense of success roar through her as she snuggled deeper into the bed.

She knew there was a big family gathering planned for that afternoon. It was amazing what she had learned by staying hidden and listening to the gossip of ranch hands.

It was Thanksgiving Day and nobody on earth was more thankful than Alice right now. She was exactly where she belonged and her twin sister would suffer a slow and agonizing death by suffocation.

The mistake of the past had finally been righted. She closed her eyes and fell into a peaceful sleep, knowing she was where she had always been meant to be.

TYLER SLEPT LATER than usual. He awoke at about seven, and instead of jumping right out of bed, he turned over on his back and remained in a state of relaxation he hadn't known for the past couple of weeks.

Greta had told him last night she intended to spend the morning helping her mother with whatever needed to be done to make the day a rousing success.

There would be no corral visit today, no outside activity and no reason for Tyler to strap on his gun and be on guard. He found himself looking forward to the family getting together, to being a part of something bigger than himself.

Work had always fed his ego and been his reason for being and had given him the satisfaction of being part of something outside himself, but he realized now that work wasn't enough…would never be enough now that he had spent so much time with Greta and the Colton clan.

Greta. As always when he woke up alone in his bed, he missed her snuggled against him. He missed the warmth of her body and the scent of her. And as always when he woke up first thing in the morning, no matter whether she was with him in the bed or not, he was eager to see her smile and to spend time with her.

He also loved to see her interact with her family. She was loving with her brothers and their wives and a soft puddle of goo when it came to baby Alexander and five-year-old Seth. Despite the unusual circumstances, he was honored to be sharing this holiday with her and her family.

He finally roused himself from bed and dressed casually in jeans and a long-sleeved ribbed shirt. He'd change into something a little less casual this afternoon. Greta's door was closed when he left his room, indicating that she either was still asleep or had already left the room to help out in the kitchen or in the basement, where the meal would take place.

He headed to the kitchen for a cup of coffee and a chat with Edith. The housekeeper had definitely warmed to him and he to her as he realized how much she had done for Greta and her brothers when they had been young.

The heavenly scent of cooking turkey filled the air as he got closer to the kitchen. It was possible Edith wouldn't have time for his early-morning teasing. She might be busy with all the cooking that had to be done that day, unless Maria had come in earlier than usual to work.

He entered the kitchen to find Edith sitting on one side of the island, a cup of coffee in her hand. A second cup was ready to be consumed on the opposite side of the island.

"I heard you coming," she explained and pointed to the awaiting cup.

Tyler sat in the stool opposite her. "Thanks. Have you seen Greta yet this morning?"

"Not a sign of her yet. It's still early. I'm sure she'll be up and around soon."

Tyler cupped his fingers around the warm mug. "It wouldn't hurt her to sleep in a little bit. She's been under a lot of stress lately."

Edith took a sip of her coffee and eyed him over the rim. She set the cup back down and released a sigh. "At least you've been here for our girl. She might act like a tough tomboy who can gentle the biggest of beasts, but she has a heart as sweet and soft as anyone I've ever known."

"I'm aware of that," Tyler replied.

"Are you going to marry her?"

Tyler nearly spewed a mouthful of coffee across the island at the unexpected question. "I… We…uh… We've only known each other a little under a month. We're certainly not at a place that we've talked marriage."

"You should. You're good for each other and she's in love with you," Edith said firmly.

"Oh, I don't know about that…" His heart skipped a beat.

"I do," Edith replied. "I've known that girl since she was little. Your brother wasn't good for her and I saw plenty of doubt in her eyes when they were together. But when she looks at you, all I see is her love for you and there are no doubts at all in her eyes."

"We're just enjoying each other's company," he replied and tried to ignore the look Edith gave him that told him she thought he was an ignorant boob. "We haven't even known each other a full month yet."

"True love doesn't watch a clock," Edith replied curtly.

"I figured you'd be bustling around here this morning with all the cooking that would be going on," he said in an effort to change the topic of conversation. He couldn't quite wrap his head around the possibility that Greta was in love with him.

"I've got the turkey baking and a big ham ready to go in. It's too early to do much of anything else right now," she replied. "By the way, there's no official breakfast this morning. I've put out sweet rolls and bagels and fruit on the buffet in the dining room so everyone can just help themselves."

"Sounds good," he replied. "So this is the calm before the storm."

"Maria will be in early and then the real work begins."

"Is Abra up and around?"

Edith shook her head. "I imagine she'll be making an appearance in another half an hour or so. She's truly excited by today and has done so much work to make sure you all enjoy a wonderful holiday."

"Is she doing okay? I know Greta has worried that this whole feast thing would be too much for her."

Edith smiled. "She's doing wonderfully well. This has been so good for her."

"I know she was disappointed when Greta's wedding was called off."

Edith scowled. "Yes, she was disappointed to stop planning a beautiful wedding for her only daughter, but the last thing Abra would want is for Greta to be in a loveless marriage. Abra and Big J have weathered many a storm throughout their marriage, but the one thing that got them through the years was their great love of each other."

"They're lucky to have each other," Tyler replied.

"Yes, they are." Her eyes grew distant. "I was also lucky enough to have a wonderful husband who I went home to each day after my work was finished here. Sadly, he passed a little over a year ago."

"I'm sorry to hear that," Tyler said.

Edith's smile held a touch of sadness. "Thank you, but I have wonderful memories of loving and being loved. I sold the house we had in town and moved in here. The Coltons are my only family now and I love them all fiercely."

There was a warning in her eyes and he knew it was directed at him. It was the silent communication of a woman who loved Greta warning him not to hurt her. Surely Edith had to know that was the last thing he wanted to do.

A few minutes later Tyler sat across from Brett at the dining room table. Before him was a small plate with a bagel slathered in cream cheese and a combination of fresh strawberries and blueberries.

"Where's your better half?" Tyler asked.

"Sleeping in a bit," Brett replied.

"It must be something in the air. Greta is still asleep, too."

Brett unpeeled a banana. "They're fortifying themselves for the chaos ahead," he said good-naturedly. "And trust me, there will be chaos. Six men, six women and throw in a couple of grandkids and it becomes total bedlam at some point."

Tyler grinned. "Actually, I'm looking forward to it. Last year I ate Thanksgiving dinner alone in a restaurant."

"That stinks." Brett ate his banana in three big bites

and then moved on to the palm-sized cinnamon roll still on his plate.

"It would be a real Thanksgiving Day blessing if Ryan arrived with the news that evil twin, Alice, had been caught and was now behind bars," Tyler said.

Brett scowled. "I don't believe in violence against women, but I wouldn't mind wrapping my hands around her throat for a minute or two. Aside from the hell she's put Greta through, Kurt Rodgers was a good man and she killed him in cold blood."

"I just want her caught so that Greta doesn't have to be afraid anymore," Tyler replied. How badly he wanted to take away her fear, let her go about her life without looking over her shoulder or entertaining the kind of dark thoughts that stole the shine from her gorgeous eyes.

She's in love with you.

Edith's words played in Tyler's mind even after Abra and Big J joined them at the table for the continental breakfast. Tyler lingered over coffee, trying to focus on the conversation while his brain whirled with Edith's assessment of Greta's feelings toward him.

Edith had to be mistaken. Greta wasn't in love with him. She might enjoy his company. He knew for sure that she was grateful for the protective role he played in her life, but love? He didn't think so.

But what if she was in love with him?

His heart fluttered and then fell. He carried the burden of keeping her safe very seriously, but the idea of also being responsible for her heart scared him to death.

Was he in love with her? It was a question he'd grappled with over the past week or so. Certainly his feelings for Greta were like nothing he'd ever felt for a woman before…but was that love…the kind of love that would sustain them through a lifetime together?

Initially, he'd believed himself in love with Michelle, but after their relationship had ended, he'd realized he hadn't really loved her in the way it took to build real lasting happiness.

"The big day is finally here," Big J said, his booming voice pulling Tyler from his thoughts. "Are you ready for all this wingding, sweetheart?" He looked across the table to Abra.

She smiled serenely. "You don't have to worry about me. I'm more than ready. There are some odds and ends to attend to, but nothing I can't handle."

"Greta told me last night she was going to get up and help you with whatever needs to be done, but I guess she's still asleep," Tyler said.

"Let her sleep," Abra replied.

"She's usually such an early riser," Tyler said.

"She'll get up when she's ready. She's been through a lot over the last couple of months. We've all been through too much." Abra used her fork to eat a strawberry.

"I wish I could have seen into the future twenty-six years ago." Big J's voice was softer than usual, his expression troubled. "Everything that has happened is all my fault."

"Nonsense," Abra said with a loving look. "You did what you did out of love for me and you gave me the daughter I wanted so badly."

"Nobody could have guessed how this all would go down," Brett replied. "Who knew that this Alice would grow up to be such a crazy wild woman? Maybe Ryan will bring some good news with him today."

"We can only hope," Tyler replied with more than a touch of fervor.

After breakfast he went back up to his room and made a call to his manager at Stanton Oil. Tyler was working a skeleton crew for the day, allowing as many of his employees to be at home with their families as possible for the holiday.

His manager, Bruce Bridges, assured him that everything was running smoothly. They talked for a few minutes about the business and then ended the call.

Tyler looked at his watch. Almost nine and still no peep from Greta's room. A sudden shot of fear went off inside him. Almost nine and nobody had seen Greta since last night.

Was she really sleeping in this late or was it possible that somehow Alice had got to her in the night? How could Alice have managed to get into a second-story window? He didn't know, but what if she had?

Was Greta either gone from her bed or dead in it? His fear rose to a ringing alarm.

He grabbed his gun, even as he knew that if something had happened during the night, it was probably already too late for his weapon.

Tension raced through him as he left his room and stood outside Greta's closed door. He raised one hand and knocked loudly.

"Yes?"

The sweetly familiar voice cast a rush of relief through him and he stuck the gun in the back of his jeans waistband. He cracked open the door to see her in bed. She stretched with her arms overhead, revealing the familiar purple nightshirt she usually wore to bed.

"Hey, you, it's after nine. I figured I'd better check in on you. It's unusual for you to sleep so late," he said.

She gave him a sleepy smile and curled back into the sheets. "I don't know why but I'm just so tired this morning."

"I thought you were going to get up early and help your mother."

"I was, but I figured she'd need my help closer to the time of everyone arriving. I just feel like lazing in bed for a little while longer."

"Then I won't bother you," he replied. "Rest up—you deserve it—and I'll see you later." He closed the door and returned to his room.

He sank down on the edge of his bed and waited for the burst of adrenaline that had momentarily suffused him to pass. She was safe.

She was just tired and he couldn't blame her after all the tension, the sense of imminent danger she'd lived with over the past three weeks.

Besides, she was right. Abra didn't really need her help right now. Later there would be last-minute things to attend to where Greta could help her mother.

He stood and placed the gun in the top drawer in the nightstand, thankful that, at least for today, he wouldn't have to touch it again.

Today Greta would be surrounded by family members and would enjoy the thankfulness of being alive to enjoy a holiday filled with laughter and love.

CHAPTER FOURTEEN

THE BOX WAS DARK.

Greta had never been afraid of the dark before, but this darkness was like death, so deep and so profound and seemingly impossible to escape.

Thankfully, after several attempts, she had managed to spit out the nasty gag Alice had shoved in her mouth and draw in deep breaths of air.

She pounded on the top and sides of the coffin-like box, screaming for help. But she knew nobody ever ventured near her barn unless she needed one of the ranch hands to add more hay bales or feed.

Besides, all of the ranch hands wouldn't be on the property today. By now their morning chores would be done and most of them would have left the ranch to spend the holiday with family. Her father had always been generous in allowing time off for special days as long as there were enough volunteers to take care of the daily chores.

Even knowing this, she continued to kick and punch and scream until she was gasping for breath. As she paused, she suddenly realized that her air source was limited. The top of the box fit perfectly, pounded down tightly to impede any flow of additional oxygen.

Eventually, she would suffocate, and with this horrifying thought in mind she remained motionless and began to take shallow breaths as she tried to think of how to get out of this deadly mess.

It was her own fault she was here, she thought bitterly. She'd been a fool to venture out on her own. But she hadn't been quite ready to confront Tyler about what she'd read the night before. She'd just wanted a few minutes to clear her head. The need for those minutes alone had been her complete undoing.

She had known that Alice was just waiting for an opportunity, and Greta had given her a perfect one. As she ran her fingers along the side of the wood that enclosed her, she marveled at the planning that had been done for this.

Alice would have had to buy or build the box and then sneak it into the back of the barn. It felt as if it would be heavy, but apparently, the strength of madness had made it possible for her to do what she wanted.

And now Alice was probably eating breakfast with the family, wearing some of Greta's clothes and living the life she'd dreamed of since learning of Greta's existence.

Meanwhile, Greta was in a death box, smelling the filth of Alice's sweatshirt as she slowly suffocated.

Could Alice pull off the impersonation? Greta thought it just might be possible despite what she'd said to Alice. Alice had been around the ranch for months, watching and listening and learning how to *be* Greta.

Tears coursed down her face and it was impossible for her to raise a hand to wipe them away. Certainly Alice probably had enough information to fool not only her family but Tyler, as well.

Tyler. He would nuzzle Alice's neck with his sweet lips, give her the unexpected kisses that had stirred Greta so deeply. At the moment Greta didn't care if she'd been Tyler's revenge against his brother or not. All she cared about was the love for him that filled her heart, a love that would die with her in this pine box.

Her knife!

Was it possible that she could reach down into her boot and maneuver it to make air holes? She reached her arm down as far as possible and tried to pull her leg up enough that she could grasp the knife in her boot.

The first time she tried, her knee banged into the top of the box, and while she managed to touch the knife's handle, she couldn't grab hold of it. She tried a second time with the same result.

Frustration forced her to relax back and she began to cry once again. She couldn't reach it. The box was too tight. It was just too hard. Her fate was sealed and there was nothing she could do about it.

Stop it. Stop it right now, a little voice in the back of her brain commanded. She had never been a crybaby and now definitely wasn't the time to turn into one. Besides, crying took up too much energy and too much of the air in the box.

She'd faced huge angry beasts and tamed them into gentle riding horses. She'd become one of the most respected horse trainers in the four-state area by the sheer force of her will to succeed.

She'd grown up with five rough-and-tumble older brothers who had challenged her every day of her young life. She wasn't a quitter. She never had been and wasn't going to turn into one now.

She needed her knife and she had to keep trying to get it, no matter what body contortions she had to go through given the tight enclosure surrounding her.

She finally managed to grasp the knife on her fifth try. By then she was exhausted. She remained unmoving for several long minutes, once again drawing in slow, shallow breaths as she clutched on tightly to the precious knife.

Finally, she pushed the button that would extend the blade and began to hit it against the wood next to her right thigh.

Thud.

Thud.

With each hit of the knife it became more difficult to pull the blade back out. The wood was thick but finally she broke through. A pinprick of light appeared. She carefully moved the knife from one hand to the other and began the process all over again.

She made three tiny holes before exhaustion forced her to stop. Once again she relaxed and breathed, her hand clasped tightly around the knife.

She knew with certainty nobody would be coming into the barn today. She'd told Tyler the night before she wasn't going to work with Sugar today.

Three tiny holes.

Would that give her enough extra air to survive until somebody eventually came out to the barn? What if Alice made some excuse not to work with Sugar tomorrow? Would Tyler buy whatever excuse she came up with?

Even if they came into the barn tomorrow, Tyler wouldn't see the pine box behind the hay bales in the darkest corner of the barn.

Three little holes.

She knew in her heart they weren't enough. She'd run out of air long before tomorrow. She squeezed her eyes tightly closed as the true horror overwhelmed her. She was going to die today and nobody would even know she was missing.

GRETA FINALLY MADE an appearance downstairs just after noon. Tyler was surprised both by how long she'd remained in her room and by the dress she'd chosen to wear for the holiday gathering.

He was seated in the family room playing a game on his cell phone when she appeared, a vision in pink ruffles and dramatic high heels.

"Wow," he said as he rose from the sofa.

"Wow what?" she replied.

"Wow you. You look positively ravishing," he exclaimed, somehow shocked by her overdressed appearance, but he assumed she'd pulled out all the stops to please her mother on this special day.

"Thank you," she replied. "And you know I love it when you wear blue. It shows off those beautiful eyes of yours."

After breakfast Tyler had changed into a pair of black dress slacks and a light blue dress shirt. "You never told me you like me in blue before."

She smiled. "I guess I just thought it to myself." She walked past him, trailing behind her familiar scent. "I'd better find Mother and see what I can do to help. I lazed in bed for so long and then took a sinfully long bubble bath. Do you know where she is?"

"I think she's in the basement. Greta, are you sure you're okay?"

"Of course—why wouldn't I be?" She waved a hand. "I don't want to think or talk about negative things today.

It's a day to give thanks and I refuse for my good mood to be doused by bad topics of conversation."

"Gotcha," he replied. He watched as she headed for the basement stairs, a pink concoction of cheer. Good. He was glad that she intended to entertain only positive thoughts for the day. He planned to do the exact same thing.

He thought about following her downstairs but decided mother and daughter could use some bonding time together without his presence.

He sank back down on the sofa in the family room and pulled out his cell phone and once again began to play a game. Normally, he wasn't much into phone games, but he had one that he'd downloaded and at the moment had nothing else to do to occupy his time.

When he'd wandered into the kitchen earlier, he'd asked if there was anything he could do to help, but both Edith and Maria had shooed him right out.

Now the air in the house smelled of cooking heaven, with a scent of a variety of foods all mingling together to keep his stomach growling in anticipation.

He'd been downstairs once to the basement, where Abra had been overseeing the setting of the tableware on white tablecloths. Each table sported a centerpiece of orange and gold flowers, along with candles the color of red maple leaves.

Abra appeared to be calm and in her element as she moved candles an inch one way or the other on one table and then straightened a centerpiece on the other table.

They had chatted for a bit and then Tyler had gone back upstairs. He knew eventually, Big J or maybe Brett would appear, ready for the festivities to begin.

The next time he glanced at his watch, it was after

one. He figured the rest of the family would probably arrive around two since the meal was to be served at three.

He was looking forward to getting to know Eric and his wife better. He'd met them only the one time they'd come for dinner and so had had only general first impressions of the trauma surgeon and Kara. Besides, he owed Kara a big thank-you for the dinner he and Greta had shared in her restaurant.

Greta.

She'd looked like cotton candy in her pink dress and he'd immediately wanted to taste her. He hoped tonight she would join him in his room. He wanted to hold her in his arms once again, taste the sweet heat of her lips and make love to her until dawn.

Would his hunger for her ever be sated? He couldn't imagine a day or a night that he wouldn't want her. Once again he was thankful that for at least today he didn't have to worry about her safety. There would be no trips to the corral, no reason to leave the house.

He looked up from his phone as Brett came into the room. He was dressed in a pair of dark blue dress slacks and a beige dress shirt.

"Ready for the onslaught?" he asked as he sat in the chair opposite Tyler.

"Ready. I'm glad to see you aren't wearing a tie. I wasn't sure how formal everyone would be."

"The last time I wore a tie was at my wedding and I told Hannah then not to expect to see me in one again until my funeral," Brett replied with a grin. "Did Greta finally get out of bed?"

"Finally. She's downstairs helping your mother with last-minute details, although when I went down to the basement earlier, it looked like Abra had everything under control."

"It's great to see Mother finally being strong enough to really be the matriarch of the family." His gaze grew distant. "As kids we hungered for her to really be a mom, but it was all too much for her. It's nice to share an adult relationship with her now and realize that she loved us all—she was just fragile. But each day that passes, I see her getting stronger and it's a welcome sight."

"Cherish every minute of it," Tyler said, thinking of his own parents' early demise. "You never know what unexpected tragedy could change things in the blink of an eye."

"At least this afternoon the only thing we have to worry about is eating too much turkey and stuffing and making ourselves sick."

"Amen to that," Tyler agreed.

Big J entered the room, and as usual, the talk turned to ranch business. Tyler asked questions about everything from the feed they used for the cattle to the ordeal of getting the cattle to slaughter.

"You keep asking questions and before long we'll turn you into a cattleman instead of a suit-wearing muckety-muck," Brett joked.

Tyler laughed. "I'm afraid I'm destined to be a suit-wearing muckety-muck, but I've got enough land that I wouldn't mind keeping a few head of cattle, as well. That way I'd have the best of both worlds."

The conversation was interrupted as Hannah came into the room, carrying baby Alex in an infant seat. "So is the little man going to enjoy dining with the grown-ups today?" Tyler asked.

"Absolutely. I don't want him to miss his very first Colton Thanksgiving," she said.

"It's your first Colton Thanksgiving, too," Brett reminded her. "In fact, it's the first for all of our wives."

Big J took the infant holder and held it in his lap, talking softly to the baby, who stared at him as if entranced. Big J finally glanced up at Tyler and grinned.

"Raising kids is tough work, but having grandkids is nothing but joy," he said.

"That's because you get to give them back to their parents when you're finished with them or if they start to get fussy," Brett said drily and then laughed as his father held out the infant carrier to him.

Greta appeared in the room. "There's my darling girl," Big J said.

"If you want to get a little baby love, you better hurry," Brett said. "He's got that look of a long winter's nap coming on."

"That's okay. Let him sleep," Greta said as she sat on the sofa next to Tyler.

Tyler looked at her in surprise. "I've never known you to pass up a little baby loving."

"Normally, I wouldn't, but I also don't want to keep him awake from his nap and have him crabby during dinner," she replied easily. "And the basement looks absolutely beautiful. There isn't a fork or spoon out of place and Mother has gone upstairs to change her clothes."

"You definitely dolled up for the day," Brett observed as he handed the baby to Hannah.

Greta shrugged. "It's a special day and I knew it would please Mother. Besides, sometimes a girl just wants to be girlie."

"All I know is that she looks positively gorgeous,"

Tyler replied. He smiled at her and she returned his smile with a hint of heat in her eyes that definitely fired through him.

Their last conversations had been so filled with darkness and the thought of potential disaster that it was a refreshing change to see her so upbeat and a bit flirty.

Maybe tonight she would come to him, come to his bed and make it a true holiday to remember. His blood heated in anticipation.

The arrival of Jack's family was announced by Seth running in and giving his grandfather, then Brett and finally Tyler each a fist bump. "I'm going to eat all the mashed taters today," he proclaimed.

"You're going to have to fight me, partner. Thumb fight," Brett announced.

Seth raced over to him and grabbed his hand as Jack and Tracy came into the room. Jack rolled his eyes. "Let me guess—you're fighting over either the mashed potatoes or the apple pie."

"Taters," Seth quipped as he moved his little thumb in a desperate effort not to be captured by his uncle's much bigger thumb.

Tracy and Hannah immediately began talking about pregnancy and Jack mentioned that Tracy had refused to make him breakfast that morning, knowing that he would overeat this afternoon.

Greta was quiet beside him and he shot her a quick glance. She watched her family with a soft smile curving her lips.

"This is nice," he said as he leaned over to her.

"Yes, it's very nice," she replied.

"But you're very quiet."

She released a contented sigh. "I'm just taking it all in."

He reached over and took one of her hands for a moment, hoping she wasn't thinking that this might be her last Thanksgiving for the rest of her life. He squeezed her hand and then released it.

By the time Daniel and Megan, Eric and Kara, and Ryan and Susie arrived, there was plenty to take in. The room was filled with Coltons and the conversation whirled fast and furious.

Abra joined the fracas, clad in an emerald green dress that enhanced her attractive features and still-lovely figure. Big J jumped up from his chair, his eyes glowing with love. "You look beautiful, darlin'," he said.

She smiled. "Thank you, and sit down. I'll just perch here on the end of the sofa next to Tyler." She sat down next to him and then proceeded to smile as the talk turned to old times and inside jokes and ribbing of one person or another that resulted in laughter.

This was the way family should be, Tyler thought as he felt the love that imbued the air. This was what he'd never had, would never have, with his own parents or Mark.

He was vaguely surprised by Greta's continued quietness. Although she appeared at ease, he wondered if she'd managed to really put away her troubles and push the thought of Alice and danger out of her mind completely.

He considered reaching out once again to grab her hand in his. Would he find it warm or cold with inner fear in spite of the safety of her surroundings?

She'd been unpredictable by getting out of bed late this morning, by not coming downstairs until after noon and by keeping unusually silent now.

To be honest, he was just a little worried about her.

Maybe all the stress of the past couple of months had finally caught up to her.

He couldn't help but think of how fragile Abra had been through the years. Was it possible that Greta was far more emotionally fragile than he'd believed?

Under so many horrible circumstances she had shown such inner strength, but had those moments been only a show? A bravado she wore for him and anyone else but which crumbled when she was all alone?

The only thing he could do was watch her carefully as the day progressed, and if he thought she was at a breaking point, then he would pull her away from the family crowd and upstairs for a little quiet time.

GRETA HAD LOST all track of time. It was as if she'd been in the box for days rather than for hours. She'd managed to make two more tiny air holes, but she felt as if she was slowly suffocating to death.

Despite the cold of the day, the box had become hot, increasing the smell of her own fear and the stench from Alice's clothes.

Was the family eating the big feast now? Were they all gathered in the basement enjoying a turkey dinner with all the trimmings, laughing and joking with each other?

Was Alice sitting in Greta's chair, next to Tyler, laughing at his silliness, enjoying sweet potato pie and stuffing and gravy?

Apparently, Greta had been wrong. Alice was good enough at impersonating her to fool not only her family but also the man she loved.

Her heart beat a slow rhythm. She'd long ago stopped fighting to try to get out of the box, finding the lid too securely in place.

A weary resignation filled her, along with a depth of sorrow she could scarcely absorb. Alice had won. She'd achieved her revenge. She'd apparently managed to impersonate Greta with success, and in doing so, she'd stolen Greta's family, the man she loved and her very life.

For Greta it was all over except for the last final breath.

CHAPTER FIFTEEN

THE HUM OF chaos continued at three when the big group moved from the family room down to the basement. Dainty handwritten placards indicated where each person would sit. Abra and Big J were at the ends of one of the tables, with Jack, Seth and Tracy on one side and Eric, Kara, Brett and Hannah on the other side.

Tyler and Greta were seated at the second table, with Daniel and Megan and Ryan and his wife, Susie. Both tables were laden with food, and Edith and Maria stood on duty to replenish anything that might run out.

"I wish I had great news to really make this a day of thanks," Ryan said as he picked up a platter of turkey and passed it to his wife.

"Ryan has been working day and night on trying to find Alice," Susie said. Susie was an attractive woman with blond highlighted hair and pretty features. Tyler also knew that she was a forensic expert and that she and Ryan were planning to sneak off on a honeymoon sometime in early December.

He only hoped before they left, they managed to get Alice arrested and in jail, where she would no longer be a danger to Greta. He looked over to the woman next to him, hoping the brief chatter about her twin hadn't upset her.

She appeared positively serene, if not a little disconnected from the conversation. He leaned close to her. "Are you doing okay?" he asked with a hint of concern.

She gave him the smile that never failed to shoot a little thrill through him. "I'm doing great. I refuse to think about her. I'm just counting my blessings for being here with my beautiful family." Her eyes shone more gold than green. "I'm just happy today."

"I want you to be happy every day," he replied.

"Hey, quit whispering and pass the gravy," Daniel said to Tyler.

As they all began to fill their plates, Tyler was surprised by how much food Greta piled on hers. He'd shared enough meals with her to know that while she had a healthy appetite, she'd never been one to make a glutton out of herself.

She must have seen his glance of surprise, for she smiled ruefully and looked down at her plate. "I know, I'm being a total pig, but I skipped breakfast this morning and I feel like I haven't had a good meal for weeks."

A discordant chime went off in his head, one he consciously ignored. If she wanted to pig out on Thanksgiving, who was he to say anything. His plate was certainly filled with plenty of food. It just seemed out of character for her.

You're being crazy, he told himself. He'd seen her first thing this morning in her bed. Her bedroom was on the second floor of the house, impossible for Alice to get into.

The fact that Greta had made herself a full plate and had been a little quiet today didn't mean anything. He certainly didn't want to cause a scene with the family because Greta was a bit off and had piled her plate too high.

Once the food had all been passed, Abra clicked a

fork on the side of her water glass and stood. "I'd like to say a few words before we eat," she said. "First of all, I'd like to thank my husband, who has loved me through the worst of days, and my children, who have forgiven me for not always being here when they needed me."

She paused, her eyes shiny with tears. "I've been around the world and back in my lifetime, but I never knew until recently that my true happiness is here with my family. And now, bless this food..."

"And let's dig in," Brett quipped, making them all laugh. Abra sat down and the conversation lowered as everyone began to eat.

Another alarm rang in Tyler's head as he watched Greta wolf down the food with little attention to couth or manners. He ticked off everything that had happened with her since the morning.

She'd stayed in her room ridiculously late. She'd passed up an opportunity to get hold of baby Alex for a quick squeeze of baby love. She'd chosen to dramatically overdress for the day and now ate in a fashion that was totally out of character for her.

Each incident by itself could be attributed to other things, but as he added them up, his heart beat just a little bit faster.

Was the woman seated next to him Greta? She looked like Greta. She even wore the same citrusy scent. If it wasn't Greta, then how in the world and exactly when had Alice managed to take Greta's place?

That was the part that stumped him. It seemed absolutely impossible that the impostor was now in the house and living in Greta's world.

The food he'd managed to consume so far congealed

in the pit of his stomach as doubts plagued him concerning the woman seated next to him.

Greta or Alice?

Was he overreacting? Was he overthinking things?

If she was Alice, then what had happened to Greta? This thought sent a shock wave of horror through him. Nobody else appeared to notice his troubled state of mind. Nobody seemed to see anything in Greta to raise suspicions.

Was it possible he was going off the deep end? That the stress of trying to keep her protected had him becoming a paranoid fool?

He frowned thoughtfully. There had to be a way to know the truth. Now that doubts had appeared in his head, he couldn't just ignore them.

He leaned over toward her. "How about a game of chess later? You know how much I love beating you."

"And you know how much I love losing to you," she replied.

At that moment Tyler's brain exploded inside his head. "Then you're on," he replied. He forced a smile and then stared down at his plate, unseeing.

She wasn't Greta. He knew now with every certainty that the beautiful woman in pink seated next to him wasn't his Greta. He waited a frantic few moments to allow the conversation to continue around him and then he glanced across the table at Ryan.

Tyler's heart suddenly pounded so hard in his chest he felt as if he were on the verge of a heart attack. "Hey, Ryan, could I talk to you for a moment?" Tyler nodded his head in the direction of the stairs. He was grateful that none of his inner turmoil sounded in his voice.

"Now?" Ryan asked and gazed at Tyler curiously.

"It will just take a minute. I just thought of something I needed to show you." Tyler wiped his mouth with his napkin and then stood. It took every ounce of his control to saunter casually to the stairs and wait for Ryan, who appeared a bit irritated by the interruption of his meal.

When Ryan reached the bottom of the stairs, Tyler looked at Alice, who didn't appear suspicious and continued to shovel food in her mouth. Tyler motioned Ryan halfway up the stairs to make sure they wouldn't be overheard.

"That's not Greta at the table," Tyler said urgently.

"What are you talking about?" Ryan asked.

"I'm telling you that I don't know how or when it happened, but that's not Greta in there. It's Alice." Tyler quickly told Ryan about the alarm bells he'd heard ringing in his head, ending with the question about chess.

"Greta beat me and then she swore she wouldn't ever play a game with me again. That woman is Alice, and I don't know where Greta is…" Tyler's voice broke as he lost control of his emotions.

"You're sure?" Ryan asked.

"I'm positive," Tyler replied, the frantic beat of his heart not slowing at all.

"Stay here. I'll be right back. I've got my gun and cuffs in my car parked out front." Ryan raced up the stairs and Tyler leaned against the wall, unable to hold himself up as fear surged up inside him.

He wanted to be wrong. God, he wanted to be so wrong. But he felt it in his soul that he wasn't.

How long had Greta been gone? When had Alice managed to make the switch? How had this happened? He felt as if he couldn't draw enough air. A sense of panic he'd never experienced before jumped inside him, making him feel half-nauseated.

He wanted to run back down the stairs and strangle Alice. He wanted to wrap his arms around her slender throat until she gasped and confessed what she'd done with her twin sister.

His panic mingled with rage and he was grateful when Ryan returned, a determined, steely glint in his eyes. Tyler started down the stairs, but Ryan grabbed him by the arm to stop him.

"You have to be positive about this," Ryan said. "I had to place handcuffs on my sister once before and it was one of the most painful things I've ever done in my life. If you're wrong about this, then I swear I'll cuff you and take you down to the jail for lying to a police officer."

"I'm not wrong, Ryan. And we're wasting time. We need to find out what she's done with Greta and pray that it's not already too late." His own words made him feel sick once again.

"Let me do what I need to do to make sure about all this," Ryan said. He tucked his handcuffs in his back pocket and put the gun in the back of the waistband of his pants. "Just sit back down at the table and act natural."

Act natural? How could he act natural when he believed he was sitting by a killer? A sick evil twin who wanted to destroy one of the most beautiful people on the face of the earth?

Tyler followed Ryan back down the stairs and slid into his chair at the table. Alice/Greta gave him a beatific smile. "Everything okay?"

"Just fine," he said and forced a smile to his lips.

"Actually, I was just telling Tyler about the time I

locked you in the old outhouse and I didn't realize there was a big black snake in there with you," Ryan said to her.

"That was so scary," she replied.

Ryan stared at her for a long moment. "There is no old outhouse on the property and that never happened," Ryan exclaimed and pulled his gun to point it across the table at her.

"Ryan," Susie gasped.

"What are you doing, Ryan?" Alice half rose, her eyes wide in panic as they shot toward the glass door across the room that led outside and then to the stairs that might provide her an escape.

"Don't even think about it," Tyler said and reached over and gripped her firmly by the arm.

"What's going on?" Daniel asked when Ryan left his chair and went around the table and pulled Alice up to her feet.

"What's wrong with you two?" Alice asked, obviously attempting to play innocent.

"Ryan," Abra said uncertainly.

"What the hell," Big J boomed.

"Where is she?" Tyler asked urgently as Ryan grabbed her arms and pulled them behind her back and cuffed her wrists.

The whole room exploded in an uproar as men jumped to their feet and Abra cried out in surprise. Tyler was focused on only one person, the woman who stood behind him.

"Where is Greta? Damn you, what have you done to her?"

"I don't know what you're talking about. I'm right here." She feigned confusion. "Ryan, let me go. Get these cuffs off me."

Tyler grabbed her by the shoulders, wanting to shake her teeth right out of her head. "It's over. We know you aren't Greta. Where is she?" His fingers tightened as a renewed sense of panic seared through him.

"You'd better talk," Ryan said. Even though she was cuffed, he still had his gun out and pointed at her. "You've been on my last nerve for months."

"If you shoot me, you'll never know where she is," Alice scoffed, all pretense gone.

"Dammit, what have you done to her? Where is she?" Tyler shook her until Ryan physically pulled him away.

Abra wept softly and all five brothers were on their feet, their expressions grim and bodies taut with the need for action. Tyler felt as if his head might explode.

He should have said something sooner. He should have questioned her the minute she'd waltzed down the stairs in the elaborate pink designer dress. He should have known the truth before now.

"You'd better talk," Ryan said, his eyes narrowed to dangerous slits. "If you don't talk, then you're no use to us. A jail cell is better than a grave." He visibly tightened his grip on his gun.

"Okay, let's play a game of hide-and-seek," she said, her eyes filled with a mad glee. "I've hidden Greta and you all have to find her. I'll give you one clue. She's someplace here on the property."

"I'll get the men together to search the office and that area," Jack said curtly and headed for the stairs.

Daniel was right behind him. "I'll search the breeding barn."

Brett and Eric followed their brothers, vowing to check every outbuilding on the ranch.

Alice laughed, the sound of her madness ringing in

the air. "It's too late. You're all too late. She'll be dead long before you find her. She's probably already dead."

"Unless you intend to tell us exactly where she is, then just shut up," Ryan snapped. "I'll call for a patrol car to get her out of here and then I'll help with the search."

Edith hovered near Abra. "They'll find her," she said to the weeping woman. "We'll get our Greta back safe and sound."

"I'll order the maids to check the entire house," Maria said.

Tyler was in a momentary state of shock, but Maria's words jerked him to action. "I'll check out her room."

He raced up the stairs to the main floor and then on up to the second level. Had it been Alice or Greta he'd seen in bed that morning? Had Alice somehow managed to sneak into the house and confront Greta while she was asleep?

He hadn't heard any noise coming from her bedroom that might indicate a fight. But Alice had a gun. There probably hadn't been a fight.

It's too late.
She'll be dead long before you find her.
She's probably already dead.

Alice's horrific words had him taking the stairs faster than he'd ever moved in his life. They implied that Greta had been alive when Alice had left her. She had to be still alive.

Greta's bedroom door was closed and he slammed it open and rushed inside. It took him only one quick glance to see that the room was empty.

Fear drove him into the bathroom, where he checked closets and cabinets, deathly afraid of finding Greta stuffed in some small enclosure, her body bloodied and limp.

He opened her closet door and walked inside the large enclosure. Once again he opened cabinets to reveal folded sweaters and a shelf of underclothing. He checked the floor behind the long dresses that would make a perfect hiding place for a body.

No, he wasn't searching for a body, he thought desperately. He was looking for Greta, an alive but probably terrified Greta. He was about to leave the closet when he noticed the shelf where she always put the dusty boots she wore when working with Sugar was empty.

He once again looked in all the shoe cubbies and then went to the side of her bed. No boots. No Greta and no boots. Sugar. Had she got up that morning to see Sugar before anyone else was awake?

He left the bedroom at a run and nearly tumbled down the stairs as he made his way to the side door and burst outside. It was another beautiful autumn day, but Tyler scarcely noticed as he raced to the small corral where the black filly was enclosed.

Why would she take a chance to venture outside alone? She knew the danger and had been afraid. If she'd come out here, then she must have been somehow lured. Nothing else made any sense.

It took only a second to see that Sugar was alone in the corral and from there he ran into the nearby barn. "Greta!" He called her name in desperation, hearing her name being called all over the ranch.

"Greta, are you here?" Nothing appeared to be out of place compared to the last time he'd been inside the barn. He sank down on a bale of hay, the sound of her name ringing all around the property as her brothers and others searched for her.

It's too late.

She's probably already dead.

Alice's words played and replayed in his head. If Alice's intent all along had been to step into Greta's shoes and take over her life, then why would she keep Greta alive? In Alice's mind there was space for only one twin and that twin was Alice.

Tyler lowered his head to his hands and began to weep, something he hadn't done since the day he'd buried his parents. The loss was as deep, as profound, as any he'd ever experienced and he wasn't sure how he would go on living without her in his life.

CHAPTER SIXTEEN

GRETA'S EYES SNAPPED OPEN. She had no idea if she'd fallen asleep or had become unconscious. Despite the fact that it was a late-November day, the interior of the box had become hot...too hot.

Between the stifling heat and the lack of fresh air, she didn't have the strength to make any more holes in the wood with her knife. She didn't have the strength left to do anything but wait for death and she knew it was coming soon.

She closed her eyes once again. She was tired...so tired. Each breath was labored and the heat made her want to just go back to sleep and maybe she just wouldn't wake up and that would be the end of it.

She'd been a fighter all of her life, but now she had no fight left inside her. She'd tried everything she could think of to survive, but it hadn't been enough.

Taking slow, shallow breaths, she felt the darkness rising around to claim her once again. Wait...did she hear something? She opened her eyes and held her breath. Every muscle in her body tensed.

There...she heard it again. It was definitely the noise of somebody in the barn and it sounded like somebody crying. "Help," she cried, her voice strained and weak from the screaming she'd done earlier.

She hit her fists on the top of the box. "Help me—I'm in here."

Silence.

Had she only imagined the noise? Had she become delusional and didn't recognize it? A sob escaped her as she pounded on the top of the box again. Was she making noise that could be heard anywhere besides inside the coffin? Inside her own head?

"Greta? Oh my God, Greta." The deep familiar male voice ended on a sob. "I'm here. Just hang on—I'm going to get you out of there."

Tyler. He'd found her. He was going to get her out. He was here to save her. As she heard the sound of nails being pulled out of the wood, she began to cry.

She was going to survive. This ordeal was over. Had they caught Alice? Or was she still running loose, only to be faced yet again?

Greta couldn't think anymore. Tyler ripped off the lid and she rose up, gasping for the fresh air even as she continued to cry.

He reached down and lifted her into his arms. "Thank God." He said the words over and over again as he carried her from the back corner of the dark barn and into the light of late afternoon.

"I've got her," he yelled. "I found her."

Greta was limp and sweaty, and Tyler held her tight as he headed for the house and men came running from all points of the ranch.

He carried her around the pool area and into the basement, where her mother immediately rushed to their side and her brothers appeared one after the other, along with their wives.

"Are you all right?" Abra asked, and Big J placed

an arm around his wife, his face pale as he gazed at his daughter.

Greta nodded, her arms still around Tyler's neck as he continued to hold her tight in his arms. "Where is she?"

Nobody had to ask twice who the "she" was to whom Greta referred. "She's in a jail cell," Ryan replied. "She'll never see the light of day again."

Greta motioned for Tyler to set her down on her feet. "It was my fault. I did something so stupid." She told them all about her early-morning visit to see Sugar and the confrontation with Alice.

"Thank goodness I had my knife in my boot," she said and smiled at her father. Her smile faltered as she shuddered with the memory of those moments in the dark, in a box she'd truly believed would be her coffin. "With the knife I managed to make a few holes. I think without them I would have suffocated within the first hour."

She shivered and looked at Tyler. "The knife is still in the box. When you lifted me out, I dropped it."

"We'll see that you get it back," Jack said.

Abra placed an arm around her. "Why don't we go upstairs and get you into a nice hot shower."

Greta looked at the beautiful tables with plates half-filled with food. "I've ruined your Thanksgiving Day meal," she said miserably.

"Nonsense," Abra replied briskly. "It wasn't right before. You weren't here. Now, we'll get you cleaned up and changed and then we have a real reason for giving thanks."

Greta leaned into her mother, finding it astonishing that for now Abra was her strength. She allowed herself to be led upstairs by both Abra and Edith.

"It was Tyler who knew she wasn't you," Abra said

once they were in Greta's bathroom and Edith was setting the temperature in the shower. Abra frowned. "I should have known it wasn't you when you appeared wearing the pink Versace dress that you hated and I forced you to buy because I thought it was so lovely."

"I would have worn it to please you. She was good, right? She fooled everyone for a while. Thank goodness Tyler figured out the truth."

"She was good." Abra's eyes grew dark. "She was quiet, but we just assumed it was because of everything you'd been through." Her eyes lightened. "At least it's all over now for good. She's in jail and will never be a threat to you again," Abra said.

By that time the shower was ready and Greta was more than willing to shed the clothes her twin had worn before stealing Greta's.

Greta stepped into the shower and allowed the water to wash away the dirt and sweat of her near-death experience. It was over. It was truly, finally over. Alice would never be a danger to her again.

She cried, her tears mingling with the shower water. They weren't tears of residual fear but rather the tears of relief that she would never have to look over her shoulder again. She was finally safe from the twin who had wanted her life, who had wanted her dead.

Knowing that the family awaited, she cut her shower short and found that her mother had laid out a pair of tailored black slacks and Greta's favorite brown-and-black sweater on the bed.

No pink fluff, no flounces or ruffles. Abra had known her daughter would find comfort in the kinds of clothes she'd chosen. Greta's heart constricted with a renewed burst of love for her mother.

She dressed quickly and then went back into the bathroom and blew her hair partially dry. She stared in the mirror and saw only her own reflection, not a shadow of a look-alike twin she had to fear.

As she turned away from the mirror to leave the room and rejoin her family, she remembered why she had ventured out so early that morning.

Tyler and Michelle.

Mark and Michelle.

She shoved the thoughts away. She refused to allow anything to ruin her dinner with her family. She'd been through enough that morning. She'd get a chance to talk to Tyler later.

Besides, with the danger now gone, everything between them had changed. He no longer had to be her bodyguard. He could return to his home in Oklahoma City and together they could figure out what was best for Sugar.

In the meantime, she had a Thanksgiving family dinner to attend and she was starving for both the love she knew would be in the room and the food that would grace her plate.

WHILE GRETA WAS UPSTAIRS, Edith, Maria and the rest of the women flew into action, removing everyone's plates and replacing them with another set of china.

Food platters were refilled, dishes warmed up, and by the time Greta entered the basement, it was as if the previous meal had never taken place.

A shudder shot through Tyler as he saw her in her slacks and sweater and without any fear lingering in her eyes. Fear still lingered inside him…the fear of loss that had overwhelmed him when he believed they wouldn't find her alive.

As she sat down next to him at the table, he wanted to touch her, wanted the softness of her sweater beneath his fingers. He needed some physical connection with her to assure himself she was really okay.

He reached his hand beneath the table and grabbed one of hers. Her slender fingers entwined with his and she smiled at him. How could he have ever mistaken Alice's smiles for Greta's?

She let go of his hand as everyone took their seats and Abra stood. "We've already blessed the food and I've told you all how much I love you, but I want to say a special thanks that we have our Greta back where she belongs, and hopefully, she'll never have to be afraid again." Tears filled her eyes as she sat once again.

Greta got out of her chair and stood. "And I bless the day that I was brought into this family." She smiled fondly at her father and then gazed around the tables to everyone. "I can't imagine my life not being here with you all. I can't imagine not having the love that has given me such strength for my entire life."

Tears glistened in her eyes. "You never truly appreciate what you have until you think it's going to be taken away."

"Enough toasting," Big J boomed, his eyes misty with emotion. "Let's get the food going again. I still have room for more turkey and stuffing before I have my apple pie."

Greta sat back down as everyone laughed. The food flowed around the tables again and finally a peace settled inside Tyler's heart. The danger had passed and Greta sat next to him, safe and sound.

Without the tension that had tightened his gut for what had felt like an eternity, the food had never tasted so good, the company had never been so entertaining and Greta had never looked so beautiful.

Tyler never wanted the festivities to end, because he knew his place here now was moot. There was no more reason for him to remain on the Colton ranch. It was time for him to go home. The only question was if Greta would be with him.

It was after seven when the extended family members began to leave. Ryan and Susie were the first to go and Tyler knew Ryan probably couldn't wait to interrogate more completely his new arrestee. He could close the book on Kurt's murder and a variety of other crimes in the area.

Daniel and Megan were the second couple to leave, and soon after, Eric and Kara left, as well.

Jack, Tracy and Seth were the last to leave, with Seth making a final round of fist bumps to his grandpa, his uncle Brett and Tyler.

As Brett and Hannah headed up the stairs and Abra and Big J retired to their room, Tyler followed Greta up the stairs to her room to talk.

The minute he sat down across from her in the chairs in front of the marble fireplace, he was overtaken by a sense of anxiety. What if she didn't want to come back to his place? What if she wanted to stay here and have him find another trainer for Sugar?

"I left the house early this morning because I needed to get my thoughts together and I wasn't ready to speak to you," she said.

He looked at her in surprise. "Why didn't you want to speak to me?"

His stomach twisted in knots as she gazed away from him. Whatever she was about to say, she didn't want eye contact with him and that wasn't a good sign.

His heart tumbled inside his chest, aching in a way he'd never known. Had she decided now that she had her life back, she didn't need him in it?

"Greta?"

She finally looked at him, her eyes troubled as she held his gaze intently. "Tell me again why you and Michelle broke up."

Of all the things she might have said to him, this wasn't even on his long list. Once again he stared at her in surprise. "We broke up because we both realized marrying each other would be a mistake. She wasn't really ready to settle down and be a wife and mother. We'd both acknowledged that we'd gotten caught up in a whirlwind, and when it stopped blowing and reality set in, we knew we weren't right for each other." He shifted positions on the chair. "Why are you asking me about this now?"

"Because when I couldn't sleep last night, I decided to do a little internet surfing, and eventually, I did a search on you." Her eyes had gone nearly straight-up green and her beautiful lips pressed together in a tightness he recognized as suppressed anger.

He frowned and searched his brain, trying to figure out what she might have seen that would make her angry with him. "What's going on, Greta? Tell me what you found that has you angry."

She hesitated a moment. "A photo of Michelle and Mark kissing outside a nightclub with the headline something like One Brother Jilted for Another." She leaned back in the chair, as if needing to distance herself from him. "Did Mark steal Michelle away from you? Is that why you pursued me? To get revenge on your brother for stealing Michelle?"

He stared at her in disbelief. "Is that what you really think of me after all the time we've spent together? That photo of Mark and Michelle was taken after she and I had broken up."

Her long-lashed eyes gazed at him dubiously.

"It's true, Greta. Michelle didn't jilt me for Mark. I've never lied to you about anything. I wanted you long before Mark even met you. Mark stole nothing of value from me when he started dating Michelle. Besides, I don't play any revenge games. I'm here because I care about you. Now what we have to figure out is where we go from here."

Once again her gaze left his and she stared at some point in the distance. "I thought I was going to die today," she said softly. "I will always be grateful to you for finding me, for saving my life. But now the danger is over and everything has changed."

His heart thundered. He didn't want things to change, especially not between them. "Nothing has really changed at all," he countered. "Except for finally, you don't have to be afraid."

She tucked a strand of her hair behind her ear and released a deep sigh. The sound was not so much one of relief but rather one of deep sadness and his heart beat even faster with tension.

She looked at him again. "But I am still afraid. As much as it breaks my heart, I can't work with Sugar anymore, because I can't be with you anymore."

The entire world crashed down on Tyler's head. "Why?" The single word ripped from his throat. This wasn't what he wanted. This wasn't the way he'd thought things would go when Alice was no longer a threat to her life.

"I know you enjoy my company and you like the sound of my laughter. I know you love to make love with me and like being around my family. But the problem is I've fallen completely in love with you, Tyler. And I'll never be satisfied with the status quo between us."

"But I... I don't want it to end like this," he said.

She smiled at him softly. "Wrong answer, Tyler. And now I'd like to rest, so if you'd shut the door behind you, I'd appreciate it."

He stared at her, unable to process the happiness of finding her alive to her now shoving him away. He needed to say something, to do something to change what was happening, but he was at a loss as to what, exactly, she needed from him.

"Just go, Tyler," she said wearily.

He got up and stumbled from the room like a zombie, his brain frozen by what had just occurred. There would be no more sounds of her laughter, no more nights snuggled together beneath the blankets.

He wouldn't see her smile at him from across a table, watch her graceful elegance as she worked with Sugar in the corral. He wouldn't share long talks about their futures, their dreams or anything else ever again.

She loved him and she obviously wanted more from him than he offered. She probably wanted him gone sooner rather than later. He headed downstairs and slipped out the side door and headed toward the corral.

Sugar pricked up her ears at his approach but didn't run from his presence as he threw an arm across the fence post and fought back the rise of emotion inside him.

First thing in the morning he'd grab a couple of ranch hands to help him load up Sugar in the trailer. It was time for him to get back to his real life, time to return home and to his position at Stanton Oil.

He just didn't understand why the idea of going home shot a hollowness through him that pierced clear through to his ribs.

HE WAS GONE before breakfast.

Greta got up and dressed, and as she passed the bedroom where he'd stayed, she saw none of his items left behind. She knew then that he was already gone.

It was better this way. She headed downstairs for breakfast. No last-minute goodbyes, no false promises to stay in touch. It was a clean cut that only bloodied her heart.

Breakfast was unusually quiet without Tyler's endless questions and quick wit. Greta was aware of her mother and Hannah watching her closely…too closely, as if they were seeking an outward sign of her ravaged heart. Even Edith eyed her with a narrowed gaze, as if seeking to peer into Greta's very soul.

She refused to give them anything. She smiled easily and put on an impenetrable facade to let everyone know she was okay. She had survived a killer twin sister. She would survive Tyler Stanton.

It was only later in the day when she stood by the empty corral that she allowed her true heartbreak to surface. She'd known to be wary of Tyler from the first minute she'd stepped into his home, but somewhere over the past weeks her defenses had dropped and he'd crawled directly into her heart.

She loved him with all her heart and soul, and now

that she knew her feelings weren't reciprocated, she didn't know what to do with the love that still burned inside her.

She hoped he found a good trainer to work with Sugar. The fact that the trainer wouldn't be Greta only added to her heartbreak. She had fallen in love with the horse and would have liked to see her transformation to completion.

But she'd made the right decision. She couldn't continue to train Sugar and work at Tyler's house. She couldn't continue to make love with him and sleep in his arms and still respect herself knowing that he wasn't in love with her.

She'd hoped when they'd spoken last night… It didn't matter what she'd hoped, because it hadn't happened. He hadn't suddenly pulled her to her feet, wrapped her in his arms and proclaimed himself hopelessly in love with her.

In fact, he'd stared at her as if horrified to discover her true feelings about him. The look on his face when she'd declared her love for him would haunt her for a long time to come.

She stepped away from the corral and eyed the nearby barn. She'd nearly died in there. Alice had almost won. Even looking at the building caused a small sense of panic to sweep through Greta.

She straightened her shoulders and took a step forward. It wasn't Alice's barn; it was hers. She had to push past the anxiety that gripped her as she thought about going inside.

She had to reclaim the space as her own, and the only way to do that was to go into the building and not give Alice power over her ever again.

Placing one foot in front of the other, she slowly approached the barn. She paused at the doorway. This was the place where she kept her equipment, where she kept feed for troubled horses.

Was the pine box still there? If so, she wanted it taken out immediately, if not sooner. This was a good place and there was no room for a coffin in it.

The smell of sweet hay greeted her as she went inside. She headed for the dark corner and breathed a sigh of relief when she saw the space was empty.

Obviously, somebody had already removed the box that had been meant to be her coffin. She sank down on one of the nearby bales of hay and released a tremulous sigh.

It was over. Alice was in jail and would probably be there for many years to come. The danger had passed. Her barn was once again a building meant to feed the horses she loved.

Tears misted her eyes as she thought of Tyler. *Buck up, girl*, she mentally told herself. After all, she was a Colton and Coltons were strong no matter what they faced.

Still, even telling herself that didn't halt the tears that ran down her cheeks as she thought of Tyler and the love he didn't have for her.

CHAPTER SEVENTEEN

TYLER WALKED INTO his quiet house and tugged at the tie that clung around his neck. For the past three days he'd been back on the job at Stanton Oil. Tonight he'd grabbed Chinese takeout on the way home from work. He tossed the bag on the table and then stared out the back window, where Sugar was in the corral.

He knew he should go out to the corral and walk the perimeter as he'd watched Greta do. He should be working with the horse to get her used to his presence. But every time he looked at Sugar, a vision of Greta filled his head and he couldn't make himself go out there to interact with the horse.

He took off his suit jacket and slung it over the back of a kitchen chair and then sat at the table and began to unload the food he'd brought home.

Staring at the waxed boxes, he decided he didn't want food. What he needed was a good stiff drink and some company. He pulled his cell phone from his pocket and punched in Derek's number. He'd never liked to drink alone.

"I've got a scotch and soda waiting with your name on it, if you're interested," he said when Derek answered. "I've also got a ton of Chinese food I just brought home and I'm not hungry."

"A scotch and soda and free Chinese? I'm so there," Derek replied. "See you in ten."

While Tyler waited for Derek to arrive, he pulled down the bottle of scotch, grabbed the tonic and two glasses, and set them on the table. He then added forks and two plates. Even though he had no appetite, he knew that Derek would chow down on the Chinese offerings.

It was exactly ten minutes later that Derek appeared at the back door. "I see you got rid of the wreck of a Jeep in the driveway," he said as he shrugged out of his denim jacket and sat at the table.

"Yeah, I had it towed to a shop with the instructions to fix it and return it to the Colton place." Tyler fixed the two drinks and then sat across from his friend.

Derek studied him. "You look like hell," he said.

Tyler ran a hand through his hair self-consciously. "I haven't been sleeping well since coming back home. I didn't realize it showed."

"Trust me, it shows." Derek helped himself to the sweet-and-sour chicken and then grabbed a spring roll to add to his plate. "So what gives? Problems at work?"

"No." Tyler cradled his drink glass with his hands. "Work is fine."

Derek speared a piece of chicken with his fork and popped it into his mouth. He chewed and continued to look at Tyler. He took a sip of the scotch and set the glass back down. "Are you worried about that crazy chick having a get-out-of-jail-free card?"

"No, nothing like that," Tyler replied. He stared down into his drink glass. "I just didn't know it would be like this…you know…without Greta."

Derek stared at him. "She's why you aren't sleeping?"

Tyler gave a curt nod of his head. "I've tried to put her

out of my mind, but I can't. I miss her smile. Her laughter echoes in my brain. I feel sick to my stomach with the need to just see her. I spend all of my time wondering what she's doing, how she's feeling and if she's okay."

He looked down in his drink, embarrassed by his display of emotions.

"Man, you've got it bad," Derek said. "What did she do? Kick you to the curb?"

Tyler glanced at Derek and shook his head. "She told me she couldn't be with me anymore because she's in love with me."

Derek frowned. "Bro, you aren't making any sense. Did you tell her you are in love with her?"

"No, I…" Tyler stopped talking and stared at Derek. "Is what I'm feeling love? This sickness in my heart, the hollow ache that I have without her?"

"Sure sounds like love to me," Derek replied and ate another piece of chicken.

Tyler took a large gulp from his drink. Love. Each and every moment he'd shared with Greta flashed through his brain. Love.

He'd been such a fool, waiting for some sort of sign from heaven when all the time the signs had been right there in his heart. He was helplessly, hopelessly in love with Greta Colton.

"Derek, you're a genius," Tyler exclaimed.

"Huh?" Derek grabbed another spring roll and ate it in three quick bites. "The real question is now that you know what's going on, what do you intend to do about it?"

"First thing in the morning I'm going to get my woman," Tyler said. He frowned as a niggle of new anxiety twisted his stomach.

What if she wouldn't have him now? What if after three days of his absence she'd realized that she really wasn't in love with him at all?

Derek left after consuming most of the Chinese food and three drinks. That night Tyler tossed and turned, eager for dawn to break so he could be on the road to Tulsa.

The minute the eastern sky began to lighten, he was up and dressed and in his car headed for the Colton ranch. He now recognized the depth of his love for Greta burning in his heart. It was tempered only by the possibility that she'd mistaken gratitude and friendship for love and had now sorted out her true feelings for him.

The miles couldn't clip off fast enough to suit him, and more than once he had to consciously pull his foot off the accelerator to drive at a safer pace.

He'd like to be at the Coltons' place before breakfast. He couldn't wait to proclaim his love for her and prayed that he was headed for a new future with the woman he loved by his side.

When he turned into the impressive gates that led up to the Colton home, his nerves were on edge like never before. He was both giddy and a little sick to his stomach.

Instead of heading up the stairs to the front door, he walked around to the side door and slipped through the mudroom and into the kitchen.

Edith stood at the oven with her back to him. "How's my favorite housekeeper?" he asked.

She whirled around, a spatula in her hand. Her eyes narrowed and she raised the cooking implement as if she'd like to whack it over his head. "What are you doing back here?" she asked.

"I forgot something when I left."

"A spare sock? A tube of toothpaste?" Her voice dripped with disdain.

"No, Edith. Nothing like that." He drew a deep breath. "I forgot to take the woman I love with me." He walked over to Edith, picked her up in his arms and twirled her around. "I'm in love with Greta and I can't live another day without her." He laughed with a newfound freedom and set Edith back down on the floor.

"It's about time you came to your senses," Edith said, her eyes twinkling with happiness.

"Where is she? I need to see her now."

Edith poked a silver hair that had sprung loose back into her tight bun. "She's out in her barn. She's been out there for the last three days, cleaning and moving hay bales and keeping herself busy."

"Thanks," he said. "And, Edith, your French toast really is better than my mom's." He didn't wait for a response, but hurried back out the door and into the early-morning sunshine.

GRETA LIFTED A bale of hay and stacked it on top of another one. She had spent the past three days rearranging the hay to make certain there were no dark corners that weren't filled with the bales.

She knew Alice wasn't a threat anymore. She understood that she was perfectly safe now, but the efforts in the barn were a panacea for her broken heart.

Work had always centered her—at least, that was what she'd always believed, but as she moved hay bales and polished leather and did a thorough cleaning of all her equipment, she felt no more centered than she had the morning she'd awoken to Tyler's absence.

She missed him desperately. She tried to hide it when she was inside the house with other members of her family, but here in the barn she allowed her heartbreak full rein to ache.

She finally stopped to take a break and plucked a piece of hay from her hair. Her jeans were dusty and her jacket had taken on the appearance of a porcupine, with hay sticking out helter-skelter.

Sitting on a hay bale, she couldn't help but think about Tyler. Had it all been just a stupid game to him? Had his kisses really meant nothing?

She'd half expected him to call and attempt to get her back on the ranch and working with Sugar, which she knew deep in her heart would lead to her sharing his bed.

Even though she would have told him no, she might have been persuaded in spite of herself. The fact that no calls had come from him only deepened the hurt. She'd told him she loved him and he'd walked away so easily.

She'd never forget the stunned look on his face after she'd bared her heart and then the way he'd stumbled out of her room to get away from her. Not a word. He hadn't uttered a single word as he'd left.

As always, thoughts of him formed tears that she swallowed hard to control. She wasn't a crybaby and what was done was done. With a renewed burst of energy, she stood up and began moving hay bales once again.

"Hello, Greta."

She froze, her back to the entrance of the barn. Was she now suffering some sort of auditory hallucinations? She'd certainly envisioned him in her mind often enough since the day he had left.

She finally turned around and there he stood in all his

glory. Clad in jeans and a blue shirt and a black leather coat, he looked sexy and handsome and her heart broke just a little bit more. "What are you doing here?"

He sat down on a nearby bale and gestured for her to do the same. She remained standing. "A funny thing happened on the way to my future," he said. She remained quiet, staring at him as if he were a ghost. "I saw a woman working with a horse and I fell in lust with her. Then craziness set in and I found myself spending almost all of my time with her, living with her family and experiencing feelings I'd never felt before."

Was he going where she thought he might be going with this? She didn't want to entertain a modicum of hope. She couldn't stand another fall.

He patted the hay next to him. "I sat on one of these on the day we were searching for you, and when we couldn't find you, I cried for the first time since my parents' funeral. I cried because I couldn't imagine a world without you in it. I couldn't imagine my life without you."

The hope she'd fought so hard against minutes before seeped into her heart. Still she said nothing. He had taken her easily before. If he still wanted her, then he was going to have to work for her.

"I've never been in love before," he continued, his gorgeous blue eyes holding her gaze intently. "I knew I loved your company. I knew I loved everything about you. Then I went home and spent three long days and nights without you. There wasn't a minute that passed that I wasn't thinking about you, wanting just to talk to you, to see that smile of yours that melts my heart."

He stood and took two steps toward her. "Greta, it wasn't until last night that I realized everything that I felt for you was love. I'm so in love with you and I don't want to leave here again without you by my side. I need you, Greta. I need you in my life forever."

She trembled as tears of happiness moistened her eyes. "You really mean it? You have to be sure, Tyler."

He took two more steps and stood just in front of her, his familiar scent surrounding her, his gaze filled with tenderness and love. "I'm sure, Greta. I've never been so certain of anything in my life. I want to marry you. I want to have children with you. You're the love of my life and I can't go back home without you."

"Why aren't you kissing me now?" she asked.

With a burst of laughter he gathered her into his arms. He took a finger and gently swept a strand of her hair back from her face. "Does this mean you'll come home with me?"

"Yes. I can't imagine being anyplace else but with you." She barely got the sentence out of her mouth before his lips took hers in a kiss that seared her body with fire and touched her soul with love.

When the kiss finally ended, she stepped back from him and ran toward the front of the barn. "Where are you going?" he asked as he ran after her.

"To pack. Now that I know where my future is, I'm ready to get to it."

"Run faster," he called from behind her.

She laughed as her heart sang with the song of his love.

GOLDEN OAKS PSYCHIATRIC CENTER was located on the outskirts of Tulsa. It was a three-story brick building with many windows and all of them covered with thick black steel bars. It was a facility for the criminally insane.

Tyler parked in a space in the lot, shut off the engine and then turned to look at her. "Are you sure you want to do this?"

"Positive," Greta replied.

It was the second week in December and Alice had been remanded to the psychiatric hospital until she was deemed sane enough to stand trial.

The past couple of weeks at Tyler's house had been magical. Not only had she made so much progress with Sugar that she was now able to brush her and had introduced her to a variety of riding equipment, but her relationship with Tyler had only deepened.

When she'd heard from her brother Ryan that Alice was here, she'd taken a couple of days to come to the decision she wanted to see Alice one last time.

They got out of the car, and as they walked to the front entrance of the building, Tyler grabbed her hand and gave it a firm squeeze.

She had always been a strong woman, but Tyler's support, his love, had only enhanced her strength. She didn't expect this visit to be particularly pleasant, but it would stamp a final closure in her mind and she needed that in order to fully embrace her future.

A security guard opened the door for them and Tyler was instructed to sit in a small waiting room while Greta was taken to a room to meet with Alice.

The room was like an interrogation room in a police station. There was a long table with a chair at each end and a security camera in one corner of the ceiling.

"Don't try to make any physical contact with the patient. Don't take anything from her or pass her anything," a male nurse instructed her. "The door will remain open and I'll be just outside if you need me."

He disappeared, and while she waited, Greta filled her head with thoughts of her wedding, which was to take place in less than a week, two days before Christmas.

It had been Tyler's idea to get married so quickly, although she certainly hadn't protested. They both knew it was right, that their hearts were entwined together in a way that would last forever.

She sat up straighter in the wooden chair as the nurse escorted Alice into the room. "Well, look who's here," Alice said as she flung herself into the chair on the opposite side of the table from Greta. Her ankles were shackled, as were her wrists in front of her.

"If it isn't the twin sister who stole my life," she said.

"Hello, Alice," Greta said calmly. "I just wanted to see how you were doing."

"How do you think I'm doing?" Alice's eyes narrowed. "I should be sitting where you are. I should be wearing those nice clothes you have on. I should be luxuriating in your life."

"Are you being treated well here?" Greta asked in an effort to keep things positive. Although it was difficult to think positive as she looked at Alice, whose hair hung in oily strands and who was clad in a set of bright orange cotton scrub-like clothes.

"Treated well? They feed me and I've got a bed, and when I get upset, they give me a shot that knocks me out." Her voice was as calm as Greta's. "Things could be worse, but things could have been so much better. Why couldn't you have just died? Maybe then Big J would have come back and taken me."

"You can't dwell on what might have been," Greta

replied. "It was just a matter of fate, Alice. Neither of us had a say in what happened."

"Screw fate," Alice yelled and slammed her palms down on the table. "I could have had it all if your boyfriend hadn't been so smart and you had just died in that box. My whole life would have changed. I'd be you. I want to be you." Her voice rose with each word until she was screaming.

The nurse stepped into the room. "Alice, calm yourself or we'll have to calm you."

"I don't want to be calm," Alice screamed. "I want her dead. There should have only been one of us and it should have been me. It should have been me!" Sheer madness shone from her eyes as she leaped up on the table and crawled toward Greta. Greta jumped out of her chair and backed up.

The male nurse was joined by another nurse. It took them only seconds to get Alice off the table and the female nurse plunged a needle into her arm.

Alice's eyes almost immediately fell shut and her body slumped into unconsciousness. The man picked her up in his arms and carried her from the room.

The female nurse walked around the table and placed an arm around Greta's shoulders. "I'm sorry," she said. "Your sister is a very sick woman."

Greta nodded. Although her heart hurt for the twin and all that might have been between them, she knew she wouldn't be coming here again. There was nothing she could do to help Alice.

The nurse escorted her from the visiting room to the waiting area, where Tyler immediately got to his feet, his forehead furrowed with concern. "That was fast. Are you okay?"

"I'm fine."

Together they left the building and it wasn't until they were outside that Tyler pulled her into an embrace. "Are you really all right?"

She nodded. "We won't be coming back here. I'll always wish for a different ending for Alice, but she's truly sick. I don't know if she suffered mental illness before she found out about me, but she definitely believes right now that only one of us can exist and she doesn't want it to be me."

"Then she's where she belongs." Tyler led her to his car.

"I won't go back there, because I think seeing me hurts her," Greta said once they were in the car and headed home. "She got so worked up they had to sedate her."

"She's done a lot of terrible things, Greta."

"I know."

"Did you find what you were looking for by visiting her?"

Greta took a moment to examine what was in her heart. Peace. It radiated through her, along with closure on a horrible part of her life, a terrible threat that had affected not only her but her family, as well.

"Yes, I did." She smiled at him with all her love. "I closed the book on one chapter of my life and now I feel free to embrace the new chapter that is my future."

"Are you planning on keeping your maiden name even after the wedding?" he asked.

She looked at him in surprise. "Goodness, no. I'm ready to become Mrs. Greta Stanton."

"You just made my heart swell," he replied.

She laughed. "You make my heart swell every time you look at me."

She settled back in the passenger seat and drew in a breath of sheer joy. She had the love and support of an amazing family and the love and passion of an amazing man. This was true and lasting happiness.

EPILOGUE

ABRA HADN'T EVEN blinked an eye when Greta had insisted she wanted the wedding to take place in her barn. In turn Greta had agreed to holding a reception dinner afterward at a local community center and making the colors of the wedding pink and white.

Abra had sprung into action to make both the wedding and the reception happen without a glitch. She'd had little time to get it all together, but she'd managed to pull it off.

Greta now stood at the side door, clad in a wedding dress that was her mother's dream. Frothy lace and crystal beads transformed Greta from her tomboy status into a feminine cake topper, but Greta had to confess that seeing her mother's eyes light up at the sight of her was well worth it.

"You look so beautiful," Abra exclaimed as Edith fussed behind Greta with the dress train.

Greta kissed Abra on the cheek. "And thank you for everything you've done to make this day so special."

"At least you let me have the pink-and-white color scheme. I know you agreed to that just to please me." Abra smiled.

"It's almost time," Edith said.

A flutter of nerves shot through Greta's stomach. "Where's Dad? He needs to be here to walk with me."

Brett appeared at the back door, handsome in a black tux. "Everyone is in their place. The music is set to begin in just a minute and I'm here to escort Mother."

Big J stepped into the mudroom. He was also clad in a black tux with a pink handkerchief peeking out of his pocket. He stepped around Greta's train and stood before her, his eyes misty as he gazed at her.

"My beautiful daughter," he said, his voice deeper than usual. "You have been such a big part of the family and I've been proud of you every day of my life. I find myself reluctant to give you away." He looked at her with an unusual sharpness in his eyes. "You're sure about this…that Tyler is the one."

"I've never been so sure about anything in my entire life. He's my happiness."

Big J kissed her gently on the cheek and then reached up and arranged her short veil over her face. "That's all that is important."

From that moment on, everything happened in a haze for Greta. Her sisters-in-law were her bridesmaids and her brothers their counterparts in the wedding party. Tyler had asked Ryan to be his best man, as Mark wasn't invited to the wedding.

The sound of the wedding march began and still Greta remained in a fog as she and her father walked the distance from the house to the barn.

Thankfully, the late afternoon was unusually warm for December, and inside the barn her mother had arranged for heaters to warm the guests attending. Despite the unconventional wedding venue, Abra had invited all of Tulsa's society bigwigs and a few reporters to attend.

As they passed the corral, Sugar whinnied. Greta glanced at the horse, who sported a big pink bow behind each ear. She smiled inwardly, knowing that Tyler must have brought the horse in from his place when he'd arrived earlier in the day.

It was so right that Sugar would share in their wedding day. The horse had been much of what had brought them together. Her mind snapped out of the fog and into the moment.

They stepped to the threshold of the barn and paused a moment. Abra had worked magic. The hay was gone, replaced by rows of folding chairs. Pink and white floral arrangements were displayed on columns here and there.

Although Greta took it all in briefly, her heart swelled with love as she saw the man she was about to bind her heart to forever.

Tyler stood by the minister. He was tall and handsome in his black tux, and the smile on his face, the light in his eyes filled up the entire barn.

She wanted him today and every day for the rest of her life and she saw her own dreams reflected in his eyes. The ceremony was short and then she was in his arms, kissing him after the minister pronounced them husband and wife.

She and Tyler were whisked away from the barn and into the back of a limo that would take them to the community center for a continuation of the celebration.

She stared down at her ring, a simple diamond solitaire and matching band that now bound them together through thick and thin.

"Happy?" he asked.

"Delirious," she replied.

"Me, too."

Those were the only words spoken, the only words needed between them. When they reached the community center, Abra's work was once again on display. Each round table sported a white tablecloth and lovely pink-and-white floral centerpieces.

Only Tyler and Greta and Big J and Abra shared the head table, and Greta's brain once again fogged over as she greeted guests, ate a chicken dinner and drank toast after toast to herself and Tyler.

When the dinner was finished, the DJ cranked up the volume, and after Tyler and Greta shared the first dance together, the real party began.

Greta danced with each of her brothers and even had a spin with Seth, who showed her all of his five-year-old smooth dance moves. She finally collapsed in a chair against one wall and looked around the room.

Daniel and Megan were dancing to a slow tune. They had announced a week ago that they were happily expecting a baby in the spring.

Jack and Tracy had learned that her unborn baby was a little girl and Seth was determined to be the best big brother in the whole wide world.

Eric trailed behind Kara as she appeared and disappeared into the kitchen area of the community center. She had catered the dinner, and not only did she glow from all the compliments she'd received about the meal, but Eric was also obviously proud of his wife's success.

Brett and Hannah were seated at one of the tables, laughing as baby Alex in a bouncy seat worked his little arms and legs as if dancing to the music.

Ryan and Susie had returned from their belated honeymoon three days earlier, and by the way they clung to each other on the dance floor, they hadn't quite got honeymoon fever out of their veins yet.

Finally, there was Big J and Abra. They had surprised

Greta by seeing to it that Alice had been transferred to a private facility where she would still be locked up but would be treated better than where she had been, at Golden Oaks. They intended to pay the expenses for as long as Alice remained there. Their generosity had brought Greta to tears.

Abra had become strong and Greta knew her mother would be at her father's side if and when he needed her. Her family had weathered a storm and come out stronger on the other side.

"What is my bride doing sitting here all alone like a little wallflower?" Tyler's voice shot a thrill through her as she looked up at him.

"I was just sitting here and feeling the love and counting my blessings."

"I'm the one counting my blessings," he replied. He gave her a look filled with nothing but pure love. "How soon do you think we can blow off this celebration?" His eyes now held a wicked little glint.

"Why, Mr. Stanton, what could possibly be your hurry?" she asked.

"We have a luxury hotel room booked and I confess I'm eager to be alone with the woman of my dreams." He leaned down to whisper in her ear. "And inside my suitcase I packed a chess game. I demand a replay."

She grinned. "It depends on what the stakes are."

He pretended to think. "I've got it. If I win, then I get to spend the night making love with you."

"And if I win?" she asked teasingly.

"Then you get to spend the whole night making love with me."

"So it's a win-win situation for you," she said.

"And for you."

A thrill fluttered through her. She turned her head to gaze around the room one last time and then stood. "I think we can blow this celebration right now," she said and raced for the exit door.

His deep laughter sounded as he ran after her. This was just the beginning, Greta thought. There would be love and more laughter to come. There would be family gatherings and new babies born and the tomboy horse trainer had finally found her happily-ever-after.

* * * * *

YOU HAVE
JUST READ A
HARLEQUIN®
INTRIGUE®
BOOK

If you were **captivated** by the **gripping, page-turning romantic suspense,** be sure to look for all six Harlequin® Intrigue® books every month.

HALOHIINCI012R

The moment Fiona found the letter in the bottom of Chase's sock drawer, she knew it was bad news. Fear squeezed the breath from her as her heart beat so hard against her rib cage that she thought she would pass out. Grabbing the bureau for support, she told herself it might not be what she thought it was.

But the envelope was a pale lavender, and the handwriting was distinctly female. Worse, Chase had kept the letter a secret. Why else would it be hidden under his socks? He hadn't wanted her to see it because it was from that other woman.

Now she wished she hadn't been snooping around. She'd let herself into his house with the extra key she'd had made. She'd felt him pulling away from her the past few weeks. Having been here so many times before, she was determined that this one wasn't going to break her heart. Nor was she going to let another woman take him from her. That's why she had to find out why he hadn't called, why he wasn't returning her messages, why he was avoiding her.

They'd had fun the night they were together. She'd felt as if they had something special, although she knew the next morning that he was feeling guilty. He'd said he didn't want to lead her on. He'd told her that there was some woman back home he was still in love with. He'd said their night together was a mistake. But he was wrong, and she was determined to convince him of it.

What made it so hard was that Chase was a genuinely nice guy. You didn't let a man like that get away. The other woman had. Fiona wasn't going to make that mistake, even though he'd been trying to push her away since that night. But he had no idea how determined she could be, determined enough for both of them that this wasn't over by a long shot.

It wasn't the first time she'd let herself into his apartment when he was at work. The other time, he'd caught her and she'd had to make up some story about the building manager letting her in so she could look for her lost earring.

She'd snooped around his house the first night they'd met—the same night she'd found his extra apartment key and had taken it to have her own key made in case she ever needed to come back when Chase wasn't home.

The letter hadn't been in his sock drawer that time.

That meant he'd received it since then. Hadn't she known he was hiding something from her? Why else would he put this letter in a drawer instead of leaving it out along with the bills he'd casually dropped on the table by the front door?

Because the letter was important to him, which meant that she had no choice but to read it.

Don't miss
Steel Resolve *by B.J. Daniels,*
available July 2019 wherever
Harlequin® Intrigue books and ebooks are sold.

www.Harlequin.com

Need an adrenaline rush from nail-biting tales
(and irresistible males)?

Check out **Harlequin Intrigue®**,
Harlequin® Romantic Suspense and
Love Inspired® Suspense books!

New books available every month!

CONNECT WITH US AT:

Facebook.com/groups/HarlequinConnection

Facebook.com/HarlequinBooks

Twitter.com/HarlequinBooks

Instagram.com/HarlequinBooks

Pinterest.com/HarlequinBooks

ReaderService.com

**ROMANCE WHEN
YOU NEED IT**

SGENRE2018R

Reward the book lover in you!

Earn points on your purchase of new Harlequin books from participating retailers.

Turn your points into **FREE BOOKS** of your choice!

Join for FREE today at
www.HarlequinMyRewards.com.

Harlequin My Rewards is a free program (no fees) without any commitments or obligations.

MYR18